D0935013

Where the River Narrows

WHERE
THE RIVER
NARROWS

Aimée Laberge

Harper*Flamingo*Canada

A PHYLLIS BRUCE BOOK

Where the River Narrows

Copyright © 2003 by Marie Andrée Laberge.

All rights reserved. No part of this book may be used or reproduced in any manner whatsoever without prior written permission except in the case of brief quotations embodied in reviews. For information address: HarperCollins Publishers Ltd.

2 Bloor Street East, 20th Floor

Toronto, Ontario, M4W 1A8, Canada

www.harpercanada.com

HarperCollins books may be purchased for educational, business, or sales promotional use. For information please write:

Special Markets Department

HarperCollins Canada

2 Bloor Street East, 20th Floor

Toronto, Ontario, M4W 1A8, Canada

First edition

National Library of Canada Cataloguing in Publication

Laberge, Aimée

Where the river narrows / Aimée Laberge.

ISBN 0-00-225495-6

I. Title.

PS8573.A1675W4 2003   C813'.6   C2002-904699-8
PR9199.4.L333W4 2003

HC 9 8 7 6 5 4 3 2 1

Printed and bound in the United States

Set in Monotype Van Dijck

Québec: "Where the river narrows" in Mi'kmaq

À ma mère, Jacqueline,
qui aimait tant lire

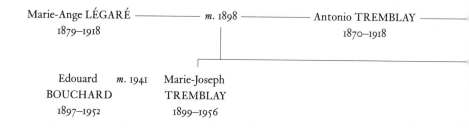

Marie-Ange LÉGARÉ ——— *m.* 1898 ——— Antonio TREMBLAY ———
1879–1918   1870–1918

Edouard   *m.* 1941   Marie-Joseph
BOUCHARD   TREMBLAY
1897–1952   1899–1956

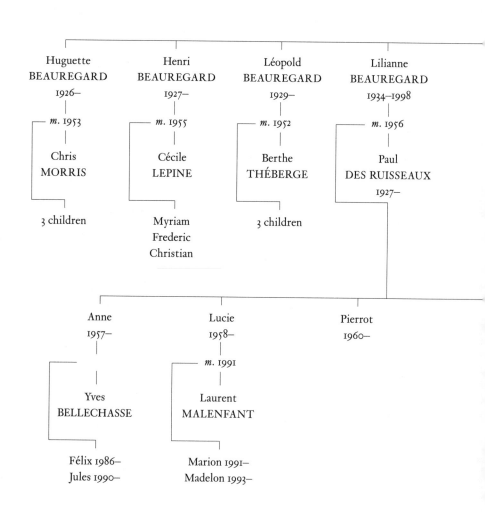

Huguette   Henri   Léopold   Lilianne
BEAUREGARD   BEAUREGARD   BEAUREGARD   BEAUREGARD
1926–   1927–   1929–   1934–1998

— *m.* 1953   — *m.* 1955   — *m.* 1952   — *m.* 1956

Chris   Cécile   Berthe   Paul
MORRIS   LEPINE   THÉBERGE   DES RUISSEAUX
                                                                1927–

3 children   Myriam   3 children
                      Frederic
                      Christian

Anne   Lucie   Pierrot
1957–   1958–   1960–

                      — *m.* 1991

Yves   Laurent
BELLECHASSE   MALENFANT

Félix 1986–   Marion 1991–
Jules 1990–   Madelon 1993–

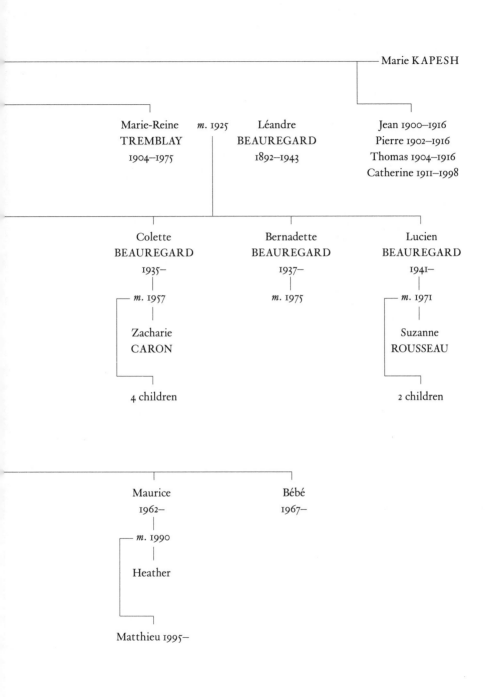

Marie KAPESH

Marie-Reine   *m.* 1925   Léandre   Jean 1900–1916
TREMBLAY   BEAUREGARD   Pierre 1902–1916
1904–1975   1892–1943   Thomas 1904–1916
                                            Catherine 1911–1998

Colette   Bernadette   Lucien
BEAUREGARD   BEAUREGARD   BEAUREGARD
1935–   1937–   1941–

— *m.* 1957   *m.* 1975   — *m.* 1971

Zacharie   Suzanne
CARON   ROUSSEAU

4 children   2 children

Maurice   Bébé
1962–   1967–

— *m.* 1990

Heather

Matthieu 1995–

Where the River Narrows

After the Deed,
November 1918

Everything is still and wet in the clearing. Last night's snow has melted in the unsteady morning sun, a light fog rising from the dead leaves. A hay cart pulled by one skinny horse threads slowly along the forest track leading upcountry from Laterrière. The new parish is ten miles south of the town of Chicoutimi and the river Saguenay, in the province of Québec. The man holding the reins whistles and cries out to his struggling horse, his shouts muffled by a piece of fabric tied around his face. The cart is already heavily loaded with two layers of corpses, hastily wrapped in dirty sheets or torn rags, and the track's two deep ruts are full of mud. The rough ride has rattled the cart's load, baring a dozen white and stiff feet, frozen at unnatural angles.

Beside the man holding the reins is a priest in a black cassock. On his chest hangs a crucifix on a string of wooden beads, and a pouch of camphor. His face is also hidden behind a mask. The man brings his horse to a halt beside a weathered cross erected by the road, the sodden wood almost black, a clump of dried-out scrub limp at its base.

Not only is the clearing dead quiet, so is the Tremblay house. No smoke rises from the chimney, the curtains are pulled, the kettle is still upside down on its post. An axe leans by the shut door. The gravedigger gets off the cart first and ties his horse to the cross before helping Father Théophile Pouliot down. The priest lifts his skirt to walk from the road to the door. He signs himself before knocking, expecting the worst. Three more corpses: Antonio, the father, Marie-Ange, the mother, and their oldest daughter, the devoted Marie-Joseph.

"Mademoiselle Tremblay! Êtes-vous là?"

Not a sound, except for the horse pulling and chewing on the scrub. The priest knocks again, louder, and waits a moment before pushing the door open. As soon as his eyes get used to the dim light in the one-room shanty, Father Pouliot sees Marie-Joseph kneeling by one of the two beds with her back to the door. Her head rests by her mother's hands, where a rosary has been woven between rigid fingers in one everlasting prayer. Two dull copper coins weigh the eyelids down. Marie-Ange Tremblay, née Légaré, has been washed, dressed, and combed. She has stockings and shoes on. It's Marie-Joseph who is barefoot, her soles crusted with dirt, the hem of her skirt caked with dry mud.

"Mademoiselle Tremblay!" Father Théophile Pouliot calls again, softly.

Marie-Joseph doesn't move or answer.

Alarmed, the priest hurries to touch her shoulder. The young woman screams and jumps to her feet, scaring them both. Her face is drained of colour except for the deep blue circles under her pale eyes.

"N'ayez point peur, Mademoiselle Tremblay. It's me, Father Pouliot."

"Ah, c'est vous, Père Pouliot," Marie-Joseph repeats, searching the room. When she sees her mother's darkened face, Marie-Joseph crosses herself and slumps back down on her knees, broken.

The priest looks at the bed pushed against the opposite wall. It is made up tight with a homespun blanket. "Where is your father, Mademoiselle Tremblay?"

"My father?" says Marie-Joseph, looking over her shoulder with unseeing eyes.

Ma reine, mon ange, Marie Kapesh, Catherine . . . He called their names in his fever, but never hers, Marie-Joseph. He never looked at her. Remember me, forget him; these were her mother's last orders. Marie-Joseph had rolled her father's sick body out of the house and through the mud to his dogsled. She had lifted his axe to sever the lead tied to a tree and brought it down with all her might to excise his memory, setting his starved dogs free. They were as wild as wolves, smelling blood on the fresh snow. This would be his last ride into the forest that stretches from the edge of the clearing to the outermost posts of the Kingdom of Saguenay, the smudged red patch of the sled but a faint throb soon smothered by darkness.

"What is wrong, Mademoiselle Tremblay?"

"The deed is done. He's gone." Marie-Joseph's voice is toneless.

xiv

Father Pouliot shrugs. "*Then let him be. Your father turned his back on God a long time ago. All we can do is pray for his soul to find a place to rest.* I believe in God, the Father Almighty, Creator of heaven and earth . . ."

"*Do you want to keep the shoes, Mam'selle Tremblay?*" *asks the gravedigger after the last prayers.*

PART ONE

J'estime mieulx que aultrement que c'est la terre que Dieu donna à Cayn.
Première Relation de Jacques Cartier, 1534
[on discovering the coast of Labrador]

I am rather inclined to believe that this is the land God gave to Cain.

Première Relation:
Hats

Hats. As simple as that, my country's raison d'être.

To tell the truth, the hat is not where it's at, not at first. Commerce and greed were the much less intriguing motives setting the Age of Exploration in motion. Europe's kings and queens were hungry for cinnamon on their buns, salt and pepper on their meat, and gold, always more gold, to bankroll the costly internecine wars tearing the old continent apart. This is why they equipped rakish caravels and hired skilled navigators in a race across the seas. Cristoforo Colombo went west for Spain's monarchs until he tripped over the Caribbean islands and the coast of Mexico. Vasco da Gama went east for the king of Portugal until he also fell upon Mexico, by way of the Pacific coast. Magellan sailed so far westward he died along the way, but his ship came back to where she'd left from, namely Seville, thus proving the world was round. But between the Orient and the Occident was the New World, an unforeseen obstacle the explorers hacked and chipped at to get a sense of its size and shape, pushing their way up wide rivers to get through. They reported what they saw to their kings and queens: a mystery of unbelievable proportions and endless promises.

But isn't a country popping out of a hat a much more attractive proposition than one founded by greed?

*　　*　　*

3

London, November 1997. The Old World. Time to get off the bus in front of the National Gallery. I stumble down from the top deck on the coiled stairs as the bus jerks forward, a telescopic umbrella in my hand and a pile of newspapers under my arm. That's me, Lucie Des Ruisseaux, a clumsy person with newsprint on her fingers and across her forehead: thirty-nine years old, married mother of two, Québécoise in London and part-time librarian at Canada House. The rest of my work day is spent doing research for graduate students and university teachers at the British Library. The latest request I received is from a master's student doing his thesis on the early economics of Nouvelle-France, namely, the fur trade.

The green man lights up, and the crowd pulls me across the road. A wave of traffic hurtles clockwise around Trafalgar Square through the November rain, past the remnants of the once glorious British Empire and the imposing facades of the old colony houses: South Africa, Rhodesia, now Zimbabwe, Australia. Across the street from Canada House is a dilapidated building wrapped in green netting and scaffolding. A carved stone plaque protrudes near the roof with fading words, The Canadian Pacific Railway, while at street level a bright sign announces the opening of an American hotel next summer. To the right, the shabby Admiralty Gate frames the entrance to the Mall, the traditional parade route to Buckingham Palace. On Sundays it is open to pedestrians only, a wide and even space where children can learn to ride a bike safely. On the opposite corner of the square stands the ancient, ill-named church of St. Martin-in-the-Fields, surrounded by concrete and pavement. A side door leads into its cool Crypt Café, where I like to go for lunch: jacket potato with cheese and a salad, the soles of my shoes rubbing against the worn stone slabs of the long dead. I find their silent company comforting.

A man jogs by, brushing against my coat sleeve. The pounding beat spilling from his earphones paces his stride as he runs, light on his feet, a focused expression on his face, oblivious to the school children's squeals as the pigeons perch along their outstretched arms. A seagull sails above the square and barks at the bright baseball caps of the tourists. I look up, trying to find a piece of immobile sky, but between shifting layers of clouds at least three airplanes move past Lord Nelson's head as he stands tall on his column, at the epicentre of Great Britain. The empire's fleet revolves once more around the British admiral before being slung to the four corners of London: south to Elephant and Castle, east to Broadgate and the City, north to King's Cross and Camden Town, and west where I came from.

I stand still, turning my face towards the light rain. I close my eyes, trying not to hear a helicopter staccato, an ambulance siren, the sputter of the buses' diesel engines, and the blare of black cabs' horns. The city's frantic flux soon recedes, one thousand feet shuffling towards as many destinations, while the slate blue shade of the St. Lawrence at high tide floods my mind, clouds casting fleeting purple bruises on its water.

Home.

The dome of the British Library is the second largest in the world after the Vatican's. Under this imposing roof, Karl Marx once sat in a turquoise leather chair and Sigmund Freud rested his illustrious elbows on the matching mat. Along the round walls run three tiers of uninterrupted shelves filled with books, seven million and counting. It's all here, in the books, and this is my world. My mother wanted me to become an artist, a wish she was not allowed to fulfill. Instead, she became a whirling dervish with five children, a two-storey house, one husband, and a hundred dreams to nurture. But at the end of the day she stopped and sat down in a good chair, tucked her legs under herself, and propped her elbow on the arm. Her hand turned the pages of a novel, one by one, her gaze caressing the words, sentence after sentence, as if under a spell, transfigured. Then, I could see her at last. That's when I decided to spend my life surrounded by books.

But in this particular institution that is the British Library, to get to the books one has to go through a process that can be described as mind-boggling or charmingly idiosyncratic; it is, simply, English. First, a transparent plastic bag is provided at the coat check (no purse or briefcase allowed) to carry valuables (wallet) and essentials (keys, Tampax, lipstick, newspaper). The on-line catalogue consulted at the bank of computers will search by title, author, or key word, and surrender the appropriate shelf mark. The pre-technology generation still looks for this information on lecterns where heavy binders lie open, revealing pasted-up rectangles of paper, scrapbook style.

I fill in the order slip. PLEASE WRITE FIRMLY IN BLACK INK. A blue ballpoint or a felt tip won't do. The appropriate pen is sold at the photocopying counter. I walk to and fro and spend ninety pence before facing the slip again. Six pieces of information need to be provided. I start with what I know.

Surname: Des Ruisseaux. From the butcher to the market researcher, they all ask me what my French name means in English. Lucy of the Streams, or of the Brooks, I answer. If I'm in a gregarious mood, I will go on to explain that, unlike the French from France who have names devoid of narrative, we in Québec often carry part of the landscape with us. The Wood (Dubois), the Stone (Lapierre), the Shore (Laberge), the Mountain (Lamontagne). Other names are more romantic, as in Pretty Heart (Jolicoeur), Bit of Love (Brindamour), Beautiful Gaze (Beauregard), or have a religious overtone, as in Godgiven (Dieudonné), the Charitable (Lacharité), or the Distraught (Légaré). Malenfant, my husband's name, could mean either a wounded child or a naughty one. But I do not feel sociable today. Des Ruisseaux, L., desk no. 287.

I walk towards the "Applications for Books" window with my five request forms, valuables and essentials still in tow: *Histoire du Canada et voyages*, Baron de Lahontan. *Relations*, Jacques Cartier. *Fur Trade Canoe Routes of Canada*. *La vie traditionnelle du coureur de bois au XIX et XX siècles*. *La flore Laurentienne*, Frère Marie-Victorin. Each slip's three copies are set on course: one copy for the reader, one copy left on the shelf the book is taken from, and the last one filed in a battered wooden tray. The library clerks are fond of a textured rubber fingertip that looks like a louche medical device or a straightforward sexual aid. With this stray thought I retreat to my seat to read the *Obtaining Books* leaflet. "Books are normally delivered to your seat within an hour and a half." In reality half the collection is "out-housed" for lack of storing space, and it can take up to three days to get the book delivered. Shelf marks starting with D indicate books destroyed during the Second World War. "However, not all destroyed books have been marked in the catalogue," the leaflet kindly informs us. Naturally, this being the Humanities Reading Room, mislaid, missing, and unsolved cases abound.

Keyword: Exploration, Canada.

Sponsored by François I to look for gold and a passage to Cathay, Jacques Cartier launches west from Saint-Malo on April 20, 1534. On the first of his three journeys, with two ships and sixty-one men, Cartier touches land at Cape Bonavista, the easternmost point of the New Found Lands, after a short three-week crossing. From there he sails north towards a small island covered with birds and on to the coast of Labrador near Blanc-Sablon, where he notes a hostile landscape of rocky shores and stunted trees. Facing stormy waters as he heads south across the Gulf of St. Lawrence, he misses the entrance to the great river entirely.

Cartier is one of the most knowledgeable mariners of his time, having mastered astronomy, cartography, and mathematics to become a royal navigator. From the moment he leaves port he records the details of his journey in a document he entitles "Relation." The first printed version of this text, a brief account and succinct narration of his voyage to Canada, will be sold by the second pillar of the Grande Salle du Palais, in Paris. There will be three *Relations* in all, in which Cartier describes and names the places he discovers, the characteristics of the shores he visits, and the depths of the water he sails through. He lists the flora and fauna familiar to him and describes the strange creatures he encounters: large swimming bears as white as snow, hunchbacked and bearded horses with wooden wings growing out of their heads, half-fish and half-dog whales, and a people painted red and dressed in leather and fur with feathers stuck in their hair.

The virgin forest skin, the desolate heart of solid rock, the blue veins of running water: Cartier's meticulous quill and meandering sentences not only capture the body of the land but also reveal his own character. The slender cursive f instead of S suggests to me how he might have fpoken then: flightly lifping all the way to the New World, chewing on soggy sea biscuits and guzzling goblet after goblet of sharp claret since fresh water was scarce and meat preserved in brine. I can see Jacques Cartier calculating he is in the middle of nowhere: water, water, and more water all around. I imagine him waking up the ship's boy, asleep by the precious hourglass, with the tip of his boot. The hourglass, suspended from a beam to isolate it from the ship's roll, needs to be turned every half-hour, day and night, to keep the exact time. This information is essential to read the ship's position by instruments, and to calculate its speed and the distance covered. This is also why Cartier takes the polar star's coordinates with his astrolabe under a clear night sky, and looks at the sun, ever so briefly so as not to be blinded. Time and latitude, no longitude yet. When the map of the sky is hidden behind clouds, a magnetized needle floating in water keeps pointing north from inside a portable wooden box.

Cartier's first exploration is deemed a success by the king of France, even if his royal navigator returns without gold or evidence of a passage to Cathay, and on May 19, 1535, the explorer leaves Saint-Malo again with three ships and 110 men. The crossing is stormy. After almost two months at sea, Cartier's ship arrives at Blanc-Sablon on July 8. Pushing farther inland, past the gulf and Anticosti Island into the Grande Rivière de Canada (the St. Lawrence River) to Stadaconé (Québec) and Hochelaga (Montréal), Cartier meets uneasily with the Iroquois tribe. He and his men experience their first bitterly cold winter in a makeshift fort where they fight off the ravages of "mal de jambes"—scurvy. The Iroquois give the Frenchmen a lesson in survival, including the secret of a remedy for scurvy called annedda. But Cartier still has not found any gold when it comes time to go home so, shrewdly, he kidnaps the native chief Donnacona and his two sons to show his king.

The original version of Cartier's third *Relation* is regrettably lost, and Richard Hakluyt's English translation, *The third voyage of discovery made by Jacques Cartier unto the Countreys of Canada, Hochelaga, and Saguenay,* closes on these words: "The rest is wanting." What we know is that things go awry even before departure, when the Sieur de Roberval, a poseur with no navigational skills whatsoever, usurps the leadership of the mission on the strength of his family's relationship to the king's mistress. After the worst crossing ever, thirty-five men are killed by Iroquois, and more fall victim to scurvy during the winter of 1542. On the way back, Cartier encounters Roberval in Newfoundland. The leader of the mission is arriving one year late, having had problems raising funds for his expedition. He orders Cartier to turn around and follow him back to Stadaconé. Instead, the contemptuous navigator hurries to France, only to find out that the gold and diamonds he brought back from Canada are only pyrites and quartz. Roberval also returns home a year later with only failure to report, his efforts to start a colony in Nouvelle-France thwarted by the harsh climate and a hostile native population. But the king of France is too busy with his wars to notice, and no one else is sent to the New World until the beginning of the seventeenth century.

So closes the first chapter of Québec's history, and no hat yet.

Or couvre-chef, as it is called a century later during the reign of Louis XIII and Louis XIV: cover-the-chief. The tricorne is a piece of felt shaped into a cocked hat, its brim turned up on three sides. Top-quality felt is made of a mix of beaver and cat or rabbit hair mashed together. The beaver barbs—not the long, glossy, and coarse top layers of the pelt but the wool, or duvet, hiding underneath—make the best bond for millinery felt. The hat brings status to those who wish to intrigue at the king's court, and every status-enhancing detail is worth its weight in gold. Who takes it off in front of whom, who leaves it on—this is the sort of gossip that keeps the nobility abuzz. The tricorne virtually bankrolls the trade between the Northern Amerindian hunters and the

French coureurs de bois. A coureur de bois, or wood runner, is the middleman who moves the beaver pelts by canoe through hundreds of miles of untouched forest from the natives' hunting grounds to the merchants' trading posts. Between 1660 and 1760, an estimated twenty-five million beaver pelts are exported from the New World. Six beavers buy one musket, or one barrel of corn, or one white Normandy blanket. One beaver buys two pounds of powder, or four pounds of lead, or eight knives with wooden handles. The commercial rivalry between English and French brings on a pricing war: a musket is worth two beavers in Albany, five in Montréal. The easiest way to get rich is to trade beaver pelts for firewater. One barrel of rum bought for two hundred livres, the French currency, can be traded for fifteen thousand livres worth of furs. That's a profit of 7,500 per cent. The king gives exclusive rights to the fur trade to a small group of privileged courtiers, the Cent-Associés, while the people of Paris go without bread. By the time the French Revolution lets the heads roll, starting with those of Louis XVI and his scandalous queen, Marie-Antoinette, the days of the fur trade and the great beaver massacre are almost over.

No head, no hat.

Pelts and quills, dreams and deceits, facts and fiction: these are some of the things my country is made of. But what brings me to the library is not only my research of the early history of Quebec. Because it's not all there, is it? The past is not contained within the library's subterranean stacks, frozen in an immovable alphabetical order. History is rewritten every day, and the more I read, the more voices I hear whispering between the lines.

Inside Cartier's *Relations* I saw two kings, one Iroquois, one French, face to face, and a spy listening to the tale. Within Samuel de Champlain's biography I found two women, the founder of Québec's wife and a native princess, observing each other. There was a dead convent girl in one of Marie de l'Incarnation's twelve thousand letters home, and only one God, the Christian one, according to the Jesuits' catechism translated into Huron and Montagnais. The Amerindians didn't leave any books, letters, or maps behind. They didn't need them. They were trained to memorize the course of the rivers they had travelled since childhood and could call up this image when needed, with a stick on wet sand or fresh snow, or with charcoal on bark or deer hide. They carried the land in their blood.

The British Library is where I come to summon the unremembered and the unwritten. My great-grandfather Antonio Tremblay was a trapper and a lumberjack, one of the last coureurs de bois. He disappeared without a trace into the forest surrounding Chicoutimi during the 1918 Spanish flu pandemic, his daughters the only thing he left behind: Marie-Reine, my grandmother, the orphan and the widow, and her sister Marie-Joseph, the perpetual virgin. All I have to do is close the books, scatter the words like small bones, and wait for them to get up and walk. Wait and listen.

At first my pulse is faint, just a detail among the other noises; the irregular tap of fingertips on plastic keys, the ruffle of pages, the muffled thump of leather bindings put up in a pile, the swish of fabric against fabric. But all these sounds soon disappear as my heartbeat grows stronger and my breathing slows like waves rolling in and out along the shore. As my gaze turns inwards I catch a glimpse of a man on a dogsled painted red, riding at the speed of light from the dark, endless forests of Québec to the hustle and bustle of Trafalgar Square on a rainy day. This is the man whose own daughter had vowed to forget, the man I, his great-granddaughter, will remember.

Saguenay/Lac Saint-Jean,
1898–1918

T HE pots have been scrubbed and the wood stove is stocked for the
night. The table is clean, the four chairs pushed in. Marie-Joseph
sweeps the floor around her mother. This is Marie-Ange's favourite
place, the polished floorboard where she kneels for hours, arms widespread in front of the man she loves. "Mon doux Jésus," she murmurs.
He is half-naked, not even a foot long, his broken body nailed to a cross.
Droplets of blood are painted on the palms of his hands, on his crossed
feet, his side, and his forehead, where a crown of thorns digs into his
skin. Marie-Ange's grey eyes darken with fervour, her buckteeth
pressing against her parted lips. She prays for the victims of the flu
until Marie-Joseph stops sweeping and asks, "Can you hear, Mother?"

Marie-Ange can hear. Barks and jingles and the rattle of a sleigh still
set with wooden wheels, the runners unusable on the dirt road. She
signs herself and gets up.

"What is he coming here for? As if there isn't enough going wrong,"
Marie-Joseph whispers.

They wait for him side by side, silently.

Marie-Joseph Tremblay is nineteen in the fall of 1918, when the Spanish
flu enters the country through the port of Québec. Many will die across
the province, but it is here, in the impoverished Saguenay area, that
the toll will be highest. Before the hard-working people of the

Chicoutimi diocese know what is happening, half the population is sick with la Grippe. Just about every family of isolated settlers living along the Chicoutimi River, more than an hour away from the closest village, is afflicted and needs help. On the boarded doors of the school and the church in Notre-Dame de Laterrière is plastered a desperate plea: *Do your duty to your citizen neighbour in distress. Your turn to die may be next. Die like a man fighting the battle of the sick!*

Marie-Joseph, who was already a plain girl, has grown into an even plainer young woman. Sallow skin, straight and thin hair. There is a spark in her quick, darting eyes, but no flesh on her bones, no grace in her limbs. Like her mother, she has always preferred to pray than to play, and now devotes herself to the sick and the dying. Her younger sister, Marie-Reine, fourteen, has been sent to her uncle Rodolphe's house in nearby Chicoutimi.

La Grippe starts like an ordinary cold, with a stuffy nose and sore throat, but a fever as high as 105°F quickly follows, bringing delirium and a paralyzing ache to muscles and joints. Unlike most other contagious diseases, this one spares the elderly and the children. It takes the most able, the mothers, the working fathers, and whatever young men the war has left behind to work the land. Mustard and turpentine poultices, sucking cups, purgative water and gargling salts, camphor, creosote, eucalyptus—nothing works, not even the crazy cures. Marie-Joseph witnesses a desperate woman drinking skunk oil. All it does is make her waste a good bowl of soup.

Some just bleed to death from a nosebleed. Mattresses turn into sponges, white sheets to scarlet. Most of the ones who bleed are saved, but when the lips turn blue and the face purple from a lack of oxygen in infected lungs, Marie-Joseph packs the children's belongings and tries to find some relatives. She follows the instructions. Always wash your hands before you eat, and eat nutritious food, easy to digest. Breathe through the nose, not the mouth. Seek the sun, which kills germs, sleep with your window open. And above all do not fear the disease. Easier said than done, when the wheezing gets worse as the lungs fill with liquid. It is like looking at someone drowning very slowly.

And she prays, along with her mother. She speaks the sacred words over and over until they feel like pebbles in her dry mouth. Over and over, another rosary, like a knotted rope hauling her through the sleepless nights, Father Pouliot's white silk stole the only morning light among the misery of the shanties and log houses.

A sour whiff drifts in as the door opens. Sweat, unwashed skin, and clothes. Alcohol. Something else too, something worse. A man is leaning by the door, trying to catch his breath. He gives in to the weight of his ripped buffalo coat and the rifle strapped to his back. Marie-Joseph quickly ties on the muslin mask she keeps around her neck.

"Marie-Ange!" the man calls. "Tu viens pas embrasser ton homme?"

Marie-Ange doesn't open her arms to the husband she has not seen in more than a year. She covers her mouth and her nose with her hands.

"You're sick too, Antonio!"

Marie-Joseph takes one step closer to her father, her hand open. The wages she earns as a washerwoman are not enough. She would do better as a maid, but who would take care of the house? Not her mother, absorbed in prayers, nor Marie-Reine, who is out in the woods from morning to night. Money had to be borrowed from Antonio's brother, Rodolphe Tremblay.

Antonio fumbles in his pocket. His fingers seem numb, useless. Finally, he puts a single silver dollar in his daughter's hard hand. That's when she sees he has lost his thumb. So it is true. Antonio Tremblay has been fired from his own brother's mill in Chicoutimi after showing up drunk for his shift and losing his thumb to the barking machine. Marie-Joseph slips the coin into her apron pocket. Only then does her mother open her arms. Antonio takes one step across the threshold and collapses, half in and half out of the house he built with his own hands twenty years ago. His coon hat rolls off, his forehead shining with sweat under the matted white hair. "Why is it so hot in here?" he asks, tugging at his heavy coat.

Marie-Joseph runs into her mother's arms, crying out, "Non! Laisse-le pas rentrer icitte." She lowers her voice to finish. "We're going to die if you let him in. He's going to kill us."

But people talk. They can't let him die on the front steps of his own house.

Three days later the night is slick with freezing rain, sealing the house in the clearing in a thick coat of ice. The flames hiss in the wood stove, seizing a wet log. At one end of the house's north wall, where there are no windows, is the bed Marie-Joseph has shared with Marie-Reine since her sister outgrew her crib. The bed is empty. Marie-Joseph hasn't slept since her father's return. At the other end of the wall two candles seem to float on a chair set by Marie-Ange's bed. They are tacked in cold wax on the flat edge of the chair's back. They have run out of oil for the lamps. Sitting on the chair is an enamel basin of fresh water Marie-Joseph drew from the river before nightfall. She dips, then wrings out a cloth and bathes her mother's face. Marie-Ange is calm now, but Marie-Joseph doesn't expect her mother to live to see another dawn. Her lips are blue and her breath laboured.

"Marie-Reine . . ." The whispered call for her younger sister comes from the floor, where Antonio lies wrapped in his coat, a tin cup beside him, the water spilled. "Where are you, Marie-Reine? Are you hiding again? Papa can't play today, Marie-Reine . . . I am so cold." The man on the floor has been riding one wave of fever after another but has always come back. He calls the names of people Marie-Joseph has never heard of. Jean, Pierre, Thomas, and other words in the language of the First People of God. Kapesh, Kushipigan, Ashuapmushuan. He calls for Marie-Reine, who is probably being served a potage and fresh bread with butter and meat every night at Rodolphe Tremblay's big house in Chicoutimi. The only thing Marie-Joseph has had since Antonio Tremblay came back were two pieces of stale bread and a dozen apples.

"No, no! I don't want to go, I don't want to see them, no!" Marie-Ange screams, pulling Marie-Joseph away from her bitter thoughts. She digs her nails into her daughter's arms, her eyes fixed on the ceiling. "Ayez pitié de moi, doux Jésus!" she cries out. "They were my sacrifice, my offering, I gave them to you." Blood starts to gush again from her nose as her hands claw furiously at the empty space in front of her face. "They would have killed me, I know it, that's why, that's why. Lord, have mercy, get them off me, please!"

Marie-Joseph stuffs her mother's nose with small pellets of cotton, trying to avoid the windmill of her arms and the kicking feet. When Marie-Ange quiets down again, Marie-Joseph props her mother up so she won't choke on the increasing amount of fluid filling her lungs. The fits are getting shorter as her strength drains away, but the words are always the same. The never-born children have come back to haunt the shanty.

"Marie, ma reine, Catherine, où êtes-vous?" the man on the floor asks. This lawless and faithless man, this blasphemy of a father.

Later in the night, when the candles have burnt down and the stove fire has turned to crackling coals, before silence drowns her forever, Marie-Ange pulls her daughter close to her. "Forget about him, and remember me," she murmurs. "He made me sin, he gave me death, and now I'm damned forever . . . I curse the day he laid eyes on me!" she screams, starting to thrash again.

"Maman, don't!"

"Make Marie-Reine forget about him too. You're all she has left."

"Don't worry, Maman. I'll take care of everything. Prions le Seigneur."

It doesn't take long after this. Marie-Ange, née Légaré, dies, while Antonio sleeps like a child, curled up on the floor.

Love in the House of God

The day Antonio Tremblay laid eyes on Marie-Ange Légaré was a sunny Sunday in May 1898.

The new church, the pride of the St-François Xavier parish of Chicoutimi, is as big as the Gare du Palais in Québec, and all the pews are packed tight for the ten-o'clock mass. La grand' messe. The church has cost forty thousand dollars to build, creating a debt of eighteen thousand dollars. Once this amount is paid in full, the new church will be consecrated as the cathedral of the Chicoutimi diocese, a large territory extending along the shore of the St. Lawrence River from Cap-Tourmente, thirty miles outside Quebec City, to Tadoussac, and along the Saguenay River to Lac Saint-Jean. There are more eagles than roosters, more moose than horses, and more trees than souls in this land opened for settlement only fifty years ago, each of its lots sold for four dollars apiece, but the people of Chicoutimi are good Christians—they pay the tithe, come to church fasting, and go to confession once a week. They work the land from dawn to dusk and have big families. The farm follows the rhythm of the seasons, and the farmer's family the rites of the Roman Catholic Church: baptism at birth, first communion at seven, confirmation at thirteen, marriage as soon as possible, and, God willing, funerals coming after many more baptisms.

Nostre domini Patre. In the name of the Father, the Son, and the Holy Spirit . . . The bishop of Chicoutimi's voice is a modulated lament rising through fragrant clouds of incense to the blue nave painted with gold stars. The choir starts on the first hymn, a cappella. *The grace of our Lord Jesus Christ and the love of God and the fellowship of the Holy Spirit be with all of you.* One thousand voices answer as one, *And also with you.*

Antonio Tremblay had three eggs and back bacon at nine in the morning to chase his hangover away. He has just arrived from Nicabau Lake, up the Chamouchouane River, where he spent the winter hunting and trapping with a nomad band from the Montagnais tribe. Next week he will leave Chicoutimi again, this time for the Price Company log run. The English merchants have exclusive rights to exploit all the forests of the Saguenay and Lac Saint-Jean. They sell the wood to independent mill owners like Antonio's oldest brother, Rodolphe, who has inherited part of the Compagnie des Pâtes et Papiers de Chicoutimi from their father and his associates. Rodolphe has asked his brother to come and sit in the Tremblay family pew at the front of the church. Antonio is twenty-nine and it's time to settle down. This is why he is attending the ten-o'clock mass, coming in late and standing at the back of the church, a much better place than the family pew to eye the local beauties of marrying age.

As we prepare to celebrate the mystery of Christ's love, let us acknowledge our failures and ask the Lord for pardon and strength.

The farmers look uneasy in Sunday suits either too small or too big. Their faces are ruddy, tanned by the sun and the wind. Their boots have been carefully shined but still carry the stubborn stench of manure. They mumble the prayers humbly. The ceremony is sumptuous. Monseigneur Racine's chasuble and the altar cloth are richly embroidered, the choirboys' surplices bordered with the finest lace. The chalice, the ciborium, the censer are of silver and gold. The local trees have been hacked and sculpted into saints with serene faces, draped in clothes with deep folds, their fingers long and gracious. These are not the hands of the people who work the land, and this place has nothing to do with the houses where most parishioners live. Sunday mass is the most awaited moment of the week, when, taking a day off from the backbreaking chores of the farm, having fasted since midnight and confessed their sins, the celebrants receive the body of Christ in a state of grace.

I confess to Almighty God that I have sinned through my own fault . . . Mea culpa, mea culpa, mea maxima culpa. The Latin words flow effortlessly from Marie-Ange Légaré's long lips, baring her slightly prominent teeth. Her mouth is like a rabbit's, constantly aflutter with whispers, and her hands, tangled in a long rosary of jet beads, are restless. Her skin is so pale and thin, the faint shadow surrounding her grey eyes seems pale blue. Her lashes and brows are gold filament, and her hair, braided in a crown is a strange shade between white and light brown. She is thin under her frayed woollen coat, long and willowy in a black dress and a corset. A crimson relic is pinned to her undershirt of rough wool. Marie-Ange Légaré should look dull, and she does on most occasions. But prayer brushes a serene sheen upon her face, illuminating her from within, darkening her eyes and stretching her mouth in an adoring smile. The only one Marie-Ange wants to marry is God himself. She loves him with all her might.

In my thoughts and in my words, in what I have done and in what I have failed to do . . . One thousand fists beat against one thousand chests. The hollow sound of these imperfect souls, like a barefoot army running along a tall ship's deck, reverberates under the church's high nave. Marie-Ange Légaré strikes her breast harder than anybody else, punishing this disobedient body she doesn't care for. Marie-Ange's older sister married the neighbour's son last year and died giving birth to her first child nine months later. She was eighteen. The neighbour's son is not even twenty himself and already a father and a widower. He is eyeing Hector Légaré's second daughter.

The new priest, fresh from the Séminaire de Québec, is a good speaker. Père Théophile Pouliot stands above the crowd, pointing to a faraway field, somewhere above their heads.

"Do you see these gold and green fields under the sun, this beautiful land stretching ahead of us? This, brothers and sisters, is all we have. We are now a people at peace, living side by side with the English. Our conquerors have respected our churches and our will to celebrate the Roman Catholic faith from the start. But let's not forget that they took away from us the right to the more lucrative trades of this country: fur and fisheries, and now the forest. I know, brothers, that you don't even have the right to sell the extra wood from your cleared land to the mills. Only the English can sell our forest. So this government has decided, and all we can do is to pray that one day God might give us back our full rights."

The priest bows his head, pausing for reflection. Monseigneur Racine joins his hands at the fingertips and taps them lightly against his nose, a sign of displeasure. He will have to warn Father Théophile Pouliot that this is not the way it's done: there will be no meddling with politics from the pulpit on Sunday morning. A discreet chat, letters going back and forth between the Québec bishop and the Compagnie Price—that's how it's done. The new priest needs to be broken in, if possible in a smaller community upcountry.

"But the Conquest of 1760, when we lost to the English, might have been God's way of telling us to repent of our sins, because we have sinned. Mostly you, brothers, and your fathers before you. The first men to come from France neglected to build houses and work the land. They refused to marry and have children, to attend mass and respect the sacraments of the Church. The coureurs de bois lived a pagan and lewd life, turning their back on their own. What kind of country can God build on the shoulders of such men, I ask you?"

The priest's gaze sweeps over his captive audience. Coureurs de bois still thrive in the diocese of Chicoutimi, living in and from the forest.

"The family is God's divine institution. Where there is no family, there is nothing. And to feed these children who are our future, God wants all available men to reclaim this land from the forest. Yes, the cold season is long. Yes, the frost often comes too early. Yes, we have to fight many plagues and woes to grow our first harvest of wheat or corn. And that is why some of you, brothers, don't have the choice but to leave your families on their own and hire yourselves in forest camps for the winter. Thanks be to the Lord, that's all that can be done for now. But what God also sees is too many men coming back from the bush having spent the winter away from him and his Church."

Father Théophile Pouliot's voice rises a notch.

"Not all logging camps are the same, but we know the name of God is taken in vain, temperance is not respected, and unchristian habits are formed in some of these places. And too many men, my brothers, having worked long and hard in the cold and the dark of winter, spend their wages on alcohol and gambling, rather than bringing them back home. And that, my brothers, is not God's will!"

The new priest's voice now thunders over the parishioners' heads. A child starts to cry.

"This land is not paradise, but it is our lot. Let us pray to the Lord to give us the strength and courage to turn more and more acres of forests into more and more golden fields, waving in the summer breeze."

Father Pouliot raises his hands, palms turned towards the nave's gold stars, and all rise. *We believe in one God, the Father, the Almighty, maker of heaven and earth, of all that is seen and unseen.*

The bread of life and the spirit of wine are blessed, a choirboy shakes a bell, and the faithful kneel and bow as the Host and chalice are raised in turn. *This is the Lamb of God who takes away the sins of the world* . . .

Marie-Ange's nostrils flare and two crimson circles spread on her pale cheeks. Her body tenses under her coat and her face turns towards the Host. She whispers, *Lord, I am not worthy to receive you, but only say the word and I shall be healed.*

Antonio is two pews behind her. He keeps trying to catch another glimpse of her radiant profile in the throes of passion. When Marie-Ange joins the line of communicants, Antonio makes his way through the crowd to be right behind her. He can see the top of her head. He can smell the fresh soap on her warm neck. He can touch the thin rabbit fur of her collar. Marie-Ange turns around suddenly, having lost her concentration. Who is this bearded man towering behind her? She shrugs him off and walks to the long table. Her mouth opens and her eyes close as the priest approaches, proceeding swiftly down the transept with the body of Christ. Marie-Ange Légaré brings the Lord inside, pressing him against the roof her mouth.

Le Corps du Christ . . . The priest has to repeat his offer three times to get Antonio Tremblay's attention. The sinner has seen the light, and he wants to hold this light in his hands.

Joy Ride

The sled flies through the powdery snow, the deep end of the day turning blue. The painted houses with covered verandahs grow smaller, and sparser, as they hurry away from Chicoutimi. The open fields vanish. Groves of naked maple trees give way to banks of aspen until the thick spruce forest blots out the sky, standing like a wall on both side of the narrow track. Marie-Ange is scared. She is alone with her new husband, Antonio Tremblay.

Tssk, tssk, tssk! the man urges his dogs on, faster and faster.

After the wedding, Antonio asked Marie-Ange to change from her pretty but modest wedding dress into strange clothes. Fur-lined moccasins and mitts, a pair of jambières, and a long skirt of soft butter-coloured leather. He has given her a hooded robe made of rabbit fur strips, twisted and woven, to wear on top of this. He said these would be warmer than her wool clothes. Marie-Ange sits covered in a large bearskin in the box of the sleigh. Antonio stands behind her, his feet apart on the runners. He has put a fresh coat of red on the wooden box, and painted a pattern of heart-shaped flowers on the side in honour of his bride.

The silence around them is complete except for the dogs' panting, the bells' rattle on their leather harness, and the soft hiss of the waxed runners on the crisp snow. There isn't a wisp of wind, and they are the only two souls in this blue and black world. Marie-Ange prays. Her face shines like a fresh drop of milk in the winter night. She had even chosen her convent name: Soeur Marie Gabrielle de Saint-Ange. Instead, she is now married against her will.

Marie-Ange has heard of this man's reputation with women, cards, and alcohol. But this is not what scares her the most. The Tremblays are half-heathen, half-Christian, however they try to pretend other-wise. Scorched Wood. Their mother was a Montagnaise and had three sons. Rodolphe is the eldest. Rosaire, the second, is "not all there" and lives with Rodolphe. Antonio, the youngest, left town at fifteen to live in the woods with his mother's band, far up the Chamouchouane River.

Marie-Ange holds back a moan. How could her father give her away after what happened to her sister? How could she marry her to this six-foot-three half-breed trapper and lumberjack? It is not Antonio Trem-blay Hector Légaré has given his daughter to. It is to the family who owns the mill.

"Allez, allez! *Tssk-tssk!*"

Hurry, hurry. Hurry away from the church bells, the benediction of the priests, the wedding feast set on tables in the church basement. Hurry through the ten miles of country between Chicoutimi and the area called Grand-Brûlé de Laterrière, then veer east at the fork for the four extra miles to the new house Antonio Tremblay has built for his bride.

Antonio didn't join the log run last spring. Instead, he bought a plot backing on the Chicoutimi River and worked all summer and fall to set up house. First he had to clear the way to the land with the new landowners before getting to his own patch of forest. Four months of swinging his axe all day long, his hands sticky with sap, a cloud of blackflies trying to eat him alive as the sun bit his neck and shoulders. No wonder logging is a winter job.

Then Antonio squared the biggest and straightest trees on two sides and dovetailed the corners. He chopped the rest down for firewood and lit a great bonfire to burn down the roots and the stumps, leaving only the roasted rocks and the rich scorched earth. It was October by the time the house's four thick walls were up, and November before the roof was finished. The wood stove and the few pieces of furniture they needed were brought in just before the snow blocked the road for the winter. The land was half-cleared, the house built. Antonio Tremblay could marry Marie-Ange Légaré before spending the winter in a forest camp to earn the cash he would need for his first crop. Marie-Ange would go back to her family until spring.

"Heeyah! Yah!"

Hurry, hurry, they're almost there. The trail takes a sharp curve to run parallel to the river, sloping towards its bank. That's when one of the runners hits a stump, tipping the sleigh over and tumbling the newlyweds head over heels into the snowbank.

"Marie-Ange!"

She doesn't move. Her eyes are wide open and darting left and right through a mask of snow.

"Marie-Ange?"

Antonio takes his mitts off to wipe her face, pushing back stray strands of hair into the fur robe's hood. A sharp surge passes through him. This is the first time he has touched her. She has escaped the wedding ceremonial kiss, pulling down her veil to hide her tears.

She closes her eyes, still refusing to look at him.

"Regarde ton homme, Marie-Ange," he tells her. He is not sure if it is the restless dogs that moan, or her. She is shivering. Antonio picks her up and rights the sled with one kick of his boot. He lays her down on the bear blanket. He climbs in and kneels, her thin body between his legs. He grabs her small head between his hands.

"Look at me, Marie-Ange, I'm telling you it's not anything like they told you."

Marie-Ange gasps, her eyes wide open again, as Antonio's bare hands feel their way inside her clothes. He slips his tongue in her mouth. She bites him.

"Ouch! What is the matter with you?"

She tries to make him roll off, hitting him with her fists. It only makes him laugh.

"Think of someone else then, like the one you were thinking about in church," he cries before burying his head in her neck, licking and biting at her bare skin, pinning her down with his legs and his arms, tighter and tighter.

"You evil man, how dare you!" she screams. These are the first words she has spoken to him. She wouldn't even say "I do" in front of the priest. Quickly out of breath under his weight, she goes limp. "Please, spare me . . . Please, Antonio." She has said his name, finally. He wrestles with the heavy skirt, trussing it up to feel the soft skin of her inner thighs. Her flesh fills the palm of his hand, his fingers busy finding a way in. At last. He stands up to ease himself out of his pants, his knees still holding her tight. He doesn't smile anymore. She whips her head from side to side, crying, "Have pity on me! I will die if you do this to me, Antonio, I will die like my sister if you make me pregnant. I beg you, no!" Antonio holds on just long enough to reassure her: "You will have a hundred children, Marie-Ange, and I'll never let you die." Marie-Ange clenches her teeth and prays, trying to pretend she is not there. "Dieu le père qui êtes aux cieux , ayez pitié de moi. . ." Antonio looks at her face as he enters her slowly, trying to spare her the pain. Soon her prayer slows down, uttered in short spurts. Her heaving throat is pale blue under the slight moonlight. "Dieu le père . . . et le fils et le saint . . . et le saint . . . et le saint . . ." Her body arcs and her arms stretch out high above her head, grabbing on to the back of the sleigh. She can't pretend anymore this is not happening to her. Antonio brings her to the edge of pleasure, rocking her deeper and deeper until a succession of short spasms ripples across her body, leaving her silent. Marie-Ange might not have known the love of a man, but the love of God has guided her hands to pleasure before. Antonio whispers in his bride's ear, for nobody, not even God, to hear: "You're built for sin, Marie-Ange, not sainthood."

When they get to the house, Antonio carries his new bride, her long pale lips split in a lazy smile, across the threshold of the log cabin.

Life on the Land

Marie-Ange Tremblay, née Légaré, might have what it takes, against her own will, to enjoy her conjugal duties, but it quickly becomes apparent she is much less gifted when it comes to the house chores of a settler's wife. She has the wood stove, the treadle machine, the iron pots, but no strength for hard labour, no will to win over the land, no know-how for making bread or starting a fire. In Antonio Tremblay's house, it is all glory to God and daily misery. If Antonio doesn't bring game and fish to their table, she lets herself go hungry, and if he doesn't take care of the wood supply, she lets herself freeze. And when it comes time to deliver their first child from a difficult birth, the overlong labour impeded by her narrow haunches, Marie-Ange refuses to push, calling on the Saviour to come and take her now, like her sister. Antonio has saved more than one cow and her calf from agony, so he knows when it's time to pull the baby out. He slaps the precious bundle to life without ceremony, and the newborn girl spits mucus back in his face. Antonio laughs, blood up to his elbows: he knows this one will be able to take care of herself. They name her Marie-Joseph.

Marie-Ange has a slow recovery, spending more time thanking God for saving her life than caring for her new child. Antonio is never far, keeping an eye on his daughter. No more babies are born in the next few years. Notre-Dame de Laterrière is now a proper village of four hundred souls rather than a patchwork of burnt lots, and its parish priest, Father Théophile Pouliot, pays a visit and inquires. Marie-Ange Tremblay cries as she explains in hushed tones that something inside her must have gone wrong after the difficult labour. She keeps losing them. She also complains how hard life is on the land and how their log cabin is too far for her to attend church on a regular basis. They pray together for her fertility to be restored and for God to hear her. He does. Five years after Marie-Joseph is born, a small, screaming miracle arrives on St. Valentine's Day: Marie-Reine Tremblay. Even the foul-smelling potion Marie-Ange took to purify her body after each inter-course with her husband couldn't get rid of this one.

"Where did you go, Papa?"

"I went to the end of the world, ma reine, where the trees are no big-ger than matchsticks and the bear are white, the birds wear feather shoes and the people live in houses of snow."

"Where is this place, Papa, where?" says Marie-Reine, jumping around him, delighted.

"Up the Chamouchouane to Mistassini Lake and Némiscau, then down to the land of the Englishmen on Rupert River, to James Bay. That's how far you have to go nowadays to trap decent-sized fur-bear-ing animals."

"Can I go too? Can I go with you next time?"

In this house of silence only Marie-Reine asks questions.

"And how do you know where to go, Papa?"

"I just know, petite chouette. It's all in here." Antonio puts his large splayed hand against his chest where Marie-Reine can hear his heart beat, strong and slow.

"What if you get lost one day and never come back?"

Antonio laughs. "Me, lost? Never! Your sister would be too happy."

He winks at Marie-Joseph, who is banging pots and pans and peeling potatoes at the counter. She is thirteen, Marie-Reine eight.

"Give me an axe, a rifle, and a knife, and I can survive anywhere!" Antonio brags in a booming voice. "I can cut my way through the thickest forest, build a shelter, hunt for food, light up a fire with my bare hands to keep me warm. All I need is the sky to find my way back, ma douce, the sun and the stars and also a little voice in my house that keeps on calling me home. So just keep calling, and I will come back, always. Now, do you remember the best place to catch a beaver, Marie-Reine?"

"In his dam!"

"What kind of trap for the mink and the marten?"

"A small wooden house with a door that slams to break their back!"

"The wolverine?"

"Bend a young tree and tie a snare so the black cat will fly up in the air and not be able to eat his leg off!"

"Very good, Marie-Reine. Have you practised the knots for your snares?"

"Yes, I have!"

"And what did you catch this winter, ma reine?"

"I put some sunflower seeds by the house and I caught five squirrels this fall."

"That's all, squirrels?"

"They're fun to play with."

"What else?"

"I put a snare with bits of fresh fish by the river this winter and I caught an otter! I brought it back but"—Marie-Reine lowers her voice—"Maman and Marie-Joseph didn't know how to prepare it. They said we couldn't eat it and they threw it away!" Marie-Reine looks furious for one second before asking again, "Papa, how many moose have you caught?"

"Twelve!"

"How many caribou?"

"Tons!"

"How many bears?"

"None. I leave these to the young ones who need to prove they're men. I got something for you, ma reine."

Necklaces of feathers, quills, and shells. A flat bone with a rough texture, a caribou's shoulder blade, to find good hunting grounds. A small hat with a bushy tail made from an Arctic fox, all of this for her. Marie-Reine runs wild through the house covered in necklaces, her hat on her head, jumping on and off the beds and running around the stove.

"Marie-Joseph!"

Marie-Joseph knows better than to listen to this man spinning magic tales with his golden voice. She looks at him from the safe distance of the kitchen counter where she busies herself. Antonio throws two fresh rabbits on the table. "Bring these to your sister, Marie-Reine, so she can cook us dinner."

Marie-Reine pretends to be dancing with the rabbits, holding their front legs and swinging them around until Marie-Joseph snatches them away from her.

"Don't, Marie-Reine. They're dirty."

"Marie-Ange?" Antonio calls. His wife stands in her favourite spot, by the crucifix hung on the north wall behind the wood stove. "This is for you." He throws a half-full pouch of silver dollars on the table. "Come, come, Marie-Ange, come see your husband."

But it's Marie-Reine who climbs back on her father's knee, putting her small arms around his neck. She asks him in a low voice, "What kind of house do you live in out there, Papa?"

"I live in a house of wood and hide, with beds made of fur and spruce boughs."

"Who with?" Marie-Reine whispers, even lower.

"With a little girl, much smaller than you," Antonio teases her, although it is also true.

Marie-Reine frowns and jumps off his knee, running to her bed to hide her tears. Antonio laughs and turns to his wife: "You cry too much, woman. Look at the example you give around here. Marie-Joseph! When will dinner be ready?"

Marie-Joseph's face is roasting as she stocks the wood stove to cook the rabbit. "Not for at least an hour," she tells her father.

"Plenty of time for a walk," Antonio says, taking his wife by the waist and leading her out the door. "How are the fields, Marie-Ange? Have you learned to grow carrots yet?"

Marie-Reine cries harder. She is never allowed to go for a walk with them.

Once her parents have left, Marie-Joseph mutters, "Not again. Why can't he leave her alone? As if we need more blood and misery. Why doesn't he go back where he belongs, with his own kind?" Marie-Joseph has heard the rumours, and she has told her little sister to stop adoring a father who spends more than half the year in the wood with his Indian wife and children.

White Water, Black Ice

When Antonio appears at the door of his Laterrière house in May 1916, his hair has gone grey. His beard is stained yellow around his mouth, his buffalo coat and his coon hat dirty. He has no gifts to offer, only a handful of dollars. He sits down at the pine table, heavy with silence, and he drinks. As steady as a clock, the glass bottle taps against his teeth, tick, and down against the table, tock. Marie-Joseph can tell that all the water of all the rivers of the New World, from the Mistassini to the Mississippi, will never quench this man's thirst. Eau-de-vie, eau-de-feu: the evil spirit has taken over. Antonio Tremblay drinks until alcohol dulls his senses, and then he spends the night outside chopping wood while his wife weeps and his daughters hold onto each other in the other bed, full of fear.

He comes back even less after this, and a good thing too. His visits only make matters worse. Something is missing from him, but he never bothers telling them what. Not for the women in the farmhouse, Antonio's secrets from the forest. It happened a month ago, by the Chamouchouane River.

* * *

"Let's go catch white fish!"

The sun radiates on the mottled snow, scattered with rough crystals from the unexpected touch of thaw. Antonio calls his daughter and three sons, the ones from his wood wife. She has kept her Montagnais name, Kapesh, but has also chosen the Christian name of Marie.

They all walk down the packed snow path leading from their camp to the river, screaming and laughing, the dogs barking and dancing around them. When they get to the edge, Antonio stops the children and ventures out, cautiously at first, tapping the ice surface with a stick where the river flattens in a wide gap between two narrows. The ice doesn't protest under his weight, so he allows the four of them to come and find their holes. Jean, Pierre, Thomas, and Catherine Kapesh. All they have to do is break the thin seal that has formed overnight and throw their baited lines in. Four holes, but only three lines.

"Where is my line? I want to catch a fish too!" cries the little one, Catherine, who is five. Antonio can't bear to hear his daughter cry. So fragile, her light bones like a bird's, her hair like partridge feathers, blonde and brown and red, her voice a melody tickling his pride.

"You stay here with your brothers and I'll run back up to get you a line," Antonio says.

Catherine pushes the youngest of her brothers, Thomas, off his log and sits down, sulking, while Antonio strides up the steep path.

The sun on the snow has blinded him. He stops on the threshold of his caribou hide teepee, waiting for his eyes to see again. Light pours down from the open hole at the top of the tent, while smoke from the fire streams out. He likes what he sees, maybe more so because he will have to leave again soon. Marie Kapesh's skin is like wood polished to a high shine, its grain lustrous under the water she pours over her head to wash her long hair. She is strong, her firm muscles shaped by the hard work that is life in the woods: lugging their belongings from winter to summer camp, splitting wood, carrying water from the river, paddling for miles on strings of lakes and rivers, preparing Antonio's pelts and hides for their clothes and their shoes. Fighting the cold throughout the long winter. Not eating every day. Antonio loves every well-defined curve of Marie Kapesh's taut body. He pulls her down on the blankets, kicking the dogs out. Soon she is sweating as they wrestle for pleasure.

"Hush!" Marie Kapesh gasps, suddenly dead still.

An insistent, nasal call . . . But it isn't spring yet, it can't be. Marie Kapesh leaps to her feet and rushes out of the teepee. The birds from the south are calling too early, the bark of the snow geese filling the sky. A child's shrill cry. "No!" Marie Kapesh wails, running as fast as she can. Antonio catches up with her on the way down to the river.

"Papa!" Catherine screams, frozen in her tracks in the middle of the path, her eyes on the river. Antonio plucks her out of his way, throws her into her mother's arms, and keeps on going. Behind the call of the birds is another sound, gaining, crashing, coming closer and closer. The white thunder. La débâcle. When Antonio gets to the water's edge, the river has already ripped open. No more fishing holes, no more lines, no more logs.

He crawls to the edge of the broken ice slowly, carefully, his shirt ready to be thrown to a small white hand, surging. The ice burns his bare chest as he stretches his arms out, but he can't even reach the water where no wet head, no hand, comes to the surface. The angry river, a wide black mouth, has eaten up his three sons. The cries of the snow geese grow louder, louder than the barking of the dogs, Marie Kapesh's low groan, and Antonio's voice calling his sons' names.

The small bay is framed by tall pines with red bark and soft tufts of dark green needles. This is where the white water comes to rest after a quick and skittish run between narrow rock walls. This is where Antonio

Tremblay knows he will find them. A sheet of ice covers the still water.

The shadows are already losing their sharp edge, and the melted snow is turning to dirty ashes in the gunmetal light. Antonio Tremblay kneels down. He crouches until his whole body covers the cold surface, his hands wiping it as clear as a window until what lies underneath is revealed. Long black ribbons of hair and the fringe of a buckskin coat flow lazily in the swirling undertow, the water tainted red. Three bodies, all face down, their soft skin waterlogged, their limbs broken by the rocks, the small white hands and bare feet pressed against the ice.

Entre chien et loup.

This is what the moment riding the hinge between day and night is called, when dogs prick their ears to the call of the wild, tempted to run back and join the wolf pack. Antonio Tremblay lays his lips, then his cheek, against the frozen river. He howls and hits the ice, hits it with his big head and his bare fists, hits it again and again until it breaks, until he can touch his three lost sons.

When the snow was gone and the ground had thawed out, Antonio took his sons down from their resting place up in the trees. He buried them and raised three wooden crosses carved with their names. Jean, 1900–1916, Pierre, 1902–1916, Thomas, 1904–1916. Marie and Catherine Kapesh planted a bush of wild roses, a clump of freckled lilies, and another of the forest orchid called virgin's clog at the foot of the pine crosses. They never spoke the boys' names again.

Couvent des Ursulines de Québec,
1918–1925

Mon père?

As strong as Victor de Lamarre, from Kénogami, who can twist silver dollars and lift a horse up a pole.

As smart as a fox, as cruel as a wolverine.

As almighty as God himself.

Marie-Reine longs for a father, but not any kind of father. A giant of a father. If there isn't one available, she will make one up out of bits and pieces stolen here and there, like a thieving magpie putting together her own scarecrow.

Recollections, hearsay, stories, slander. This is all that is left. There isn't even a photograph. You need to sit still for a precious moment to let light trace your face, but Marie-Reine Tremblay's father, the coureur de bois, never stopped running away.

When the Ursuline nuns open the gates of their Québec convent to welcome their new pupil on a grey December morning in 1918, they wonder if there's been a mistake. A young lady would sit with a straight back beside the coachman, wearing a coat and a hat, or at least having braided hair. Instead, the wild-haired girl from Chicoutimi is wrapped in a Hudson's Bay blanket, crouching on top of the first load of firewood from the Saguenay that will pay for her education. The mare's coat, steaming from the steep climb up Côte de la Montagne from the port to the convent, is of the same rusty red colour as the girl's hair.

The nuns cross themselves at the sorry sight before questioning the coachman: "What on earth is the matter with her?"

"You tell me," answers the harassed man, throwing a cover over his horse. "The wood is green and the girl is wild. She bit me and tried to run away as soon as we took her off the boat. I'm sorry, but I had to tie her up."

Mère Supérieure frowns at this and walks towards the shivering shape, calling: "Mademoiselle Tremblay? Marie-Reine Tremblay?"

The only answer she gets is a quiver.

Patience is not one of Mère Supérieure's qualities. She grabs the blanket and pulls. "Oh, mon Dieu!" The girl is covered with flecks of bark and white worms from the green wood. Her skinny face is dirty and her round blue eyes stare, frozen by fear. "Come and help me, Soeur Sainte-Rose, quick. You," Mère Supérieure orders the delivery man, "untie the poor thing and help her off, would you? Then you can unload the wood near the back wall, in the courtyard."

The fourteen-year-old orphan from Chicoutimi screams all the way into the convent.

This is how Marie-Reine Tremblay enters what will be her only home for the next seven years. Rodolphe Tremblay, her legal guardian, has struck a deal with the nuns: they'll get fifty cords of quality firewood a year in exchange for Marie-Reine's education and upkeep. With many fireplaces and wood stoves to stoke throughout the winter in the large convent, the dry wood is essential. The nuns can get rid of the bad batch, but not the girl.

The first thing they do is to pick the worms off Marie-Reine's head. Then they give her a hot bath and a good scrubbing, which brings colour back to her cheeks and stops the clatter of her teeth. She doesn't move when they lay a clean uniform in front of her, so they have to dress her like a child. She remains unresponsive in front of the hot meal they give her. They lead her to her room and make her kneel with them. They offer a prayer to their founding Mother, Marie de l'Incarnation, to whose spirit they always turn when confronted with a difficult situation, and send a letter of complaint to the girl's uncle. Rodolphe Tremblay apologizes by return post for the shipment's poor quality. He didn't check it himself in his haste to see it go before the cold season. He mentions that a foreman has been fired for his negligence, and that an extra twenty-five per cent will be added to this year's shipment, to be sent off in the spring.

Marie-Reine Tremblay remains prostrated past Christmas and into the new year. Alarmed by the girl's melancholia, the nuns write a second letter to Rodolphe Tremblay. This affliction bears many similarities to one Mère Marie de l'Incarnation described in her letters dating from the foundation of the convent, when native girls with souls made of a greener wood than this one came to learn about the glory of God. Their saint mother's missionary zeal was first met with an enthusiastic response by the sauvagesses of Stadaconé, but as soon as the good mother tried to fence them in for cloistered life, they fell into a deep melancholia that killed some of them within a month. The nuns thus enquire tactfully about Mademoiselle Tremblay's blood stock, but Rodolphe Tremblay doesn't deem it necessary to let them know his own mother was one of the First People of God. He reminds the nuns kindly of the child's double loss and decides to send Marie-Reine's older sister, his new housekeeper, for a brief visit. To Monsieur Tremblay's surprise, Marie-Joseph says she can't leave her new duties because the cleaning of all drapes and carpets in the house is urgent. She says she will write to her sister. The nuns approve. Wasn't this how Marie de l'Incarnation herself kept her beloved son back in France informed of her mission in Canada?

Marie-Joseph's letters to her little sister are dictated to Rodolphe Tremblay's wife, Jeanne. Marie-Joseph didn't get an education. Her mother taught her to read only one book, a catechism including a selection of psalms and a calendar of the saints. The letters always start the same way: "Marie-Joseph fait dire que . . ." Then Marie-Joseph inquires about Marie-Reine's well-being before describing the various minor ailments afflicting her. She also informs her little sister of the good ladies of Chicoutimi's latest charitable drive or repeats the curé's Sunday admonitions. She closes with "Que la paix de Dieu soit avec toi, Marie-Reine" or something of the sort.

Québec, le 27 janvier 1919
Fête des Quarante Martyrs de Sébaste

Chère Marie-Joseph,

Merci pour ta lettre. Tell ma tante Jeanne she has lovely handwriting. Could you please ask mon oncle Rodolphe to bring me back home? I don't like it here at all. It makes me sick because I can't breathe and I can't move. I spend the whole day sitting and silent, and there are so many rules I'm sure I'm breaking one right now.

We get up before the sun at 6:00. I am one of the lucky ones. I have my own room because I am a senior girl and a full-time boarder. But like all the others, the first thing I see in the morning is Soeur Sainte-Rose de Mai, standing still by my open door. She watches me when I change from a white flannel nightdress to a black wool uniform with a small lace collar. I have to do this with modesty. It's not easy. When this is done I slip on my sleeve-covers to protect the white cuffs.

At 6:30 we're in the chapel praying to the saint of the day. I do like the martyrs. The story is different every day. Today we were told that the forty martyrs of Sébaste spent the night naked on a frozen pond as commanded by the Roman emperor Licinius because they had refused to make sacrifices to pagan gods. In the middle of the night one of them got weak and threw himself in a tub of lukewarm water. He died immediately from the change of temperature, losing both his life on earth and all hope of eternal life. But as soon as he died, a blinding light appeared and angels came down from the sky carrying not thirty-nine but forty

crowns in their hands. That's when one of the Roman guards
threw his clothes off and shouted, "This one will be for me!" The
next morning, since the martyrs were still alive, the emperor
ordered that their legs be broken, but the nuns didn't say how,
and then they were all thrown in a fire to die.

The chapel is the prettiest place in the convent, all white and
gold with pieces of coloured light. But it is cold, and our bare
wooden prie-dieux are not padded like Mère Supérieure's. Mass
starts at 6:45, and at 7:15, when I am ready to faint, we head to
the réfectoire for breakfast. The food is boring and always the
same. Milk and tea, eggs, bread for breakfast. Milk, cabbage
soup or pea soup, cheese and bread for lunch. Milk, boiled meat,
cabbage, potatoes for dinner. Milk and tea and molasses galettes
for snacks, pie or cake, butter and jam only on Sundays and feast
days. I know you will say I shouldn't complain since I get three
meals a day. We didn't even always get that at home, but at
least we had candies. Please, please send me some of your red
and green barley bonbons, Marie-Joseph!

We go back from the réfectoire to our classrooms, where the
nuns teach us three types of lessons. First is the academic work,
with writing, reading, counting, history, and geography. Then,
on to manual work, such as knitting, sewing, embroidery,
weaving. And last, singing, piano, drawing, and all lessons having to do with deportment, protocol, politeness, and other
niceties I have no use for. But the most important subject is the
Science of Salvation. What the nuns are doing is preparing us to
marry God. Mon oncle Rodolphe should tell them not to waste
their time with me, or to send you here instead.

We have lunch at 11:45, in silence again. Once we've cleared
the réfectoire tables we are allowed our promenade, which
means a *slow* walk outside, no running. It breaks the day in two
and never comes quickly enough. The only other moment I like
is chores time, when I am assigned to split wood for kindling.
Papa would be proud if he saw me swinging that axe high above

my head, my feet wide apart, and slam! Just the way he did. I've never lost my balance once. The only problem is the early darkness. I had to ask for a storm lamp so I wouldn't lose any fingers or toes. The nuns are so happy with my work they said when summer comes they will give me gardening duties. I told them I would be in Chicoutimi. I really can't wait to go home! Why am I here, and you up there? It strikes me as so unfair, Marie-Joseph. You say I am lucky, but I can't see that, however hard I try.

But my dear sister, my one and only sister, my hand is tired, my fingers stained with ink, and Mère Sainte-Rose de Mai is at the door, calling for me to blow the candle out. I don't like it in the dark. It's so cold without you beside me, and that's when I think about Maman and Papa the most and can't stop crying. Bonne nuit, Marie-Joseph.

Ta soeur qui t'aime,
Marie-Reine

The convent's walls are grey, the stones silent. It smells too clean, a mix of wood polish and incense. There is a potted fern in the parlour, bouquets of dried flowers here and there, gathering dust. Six squat apple trees half-buried in a snowbank are the only reminder of the forest. Marie-Reine's beloved forest. Wave after rippling wave of shades of green—cedars, aspens, pine, poplars—deeper, darker, until there are only black spruces on a bed of moss, and no more light. Trees die too. Before they do, they shed all their cones, like tears. Marie-Reine will never climb to the top of the big white pine, the only one her father spared when he built the house. From there she could see the Chemin St-Paul, a thin brown line running along the Chicoutimi River, forking off to a handful of unpainted houses built around the church of Notre-Dame de Laterrière. Green and gold fields, ringed by dark peat bogs, surrounded the village. On the other side of the river ran the Chemin St-Pierre, ending at Lac Kénogami, where barges ferried goods and travellers to Lac Saint-Jean. Marie-Reine will never go again to the river to fetch water, or pick berries in the summer. No more mush-rooms, hazelnuts, wild onions and garlic, chives and parsley, for Marie-Joseph to cook. No more yellow bouquets of mustard flower, goldenrod, buttercups, and camomile, armfuls of white trilliums, lily of the valley, immortelles and daisies, or bunches of wild roses, violets, and forget-me-nots. "Leave them outside at the foot of the cross, to praise the Lord our Father." No more Marie-Joseph, bossing her around. A red fox, an owl, a chipmunk, and a black squirrel stare back at Marie-Reine from the display case in the back of the natural sciences class. Their lifeless glass eyes are enough to make her cry. Here, the gate cracks open only once a week.

Every Saturday afternoon a flock of couventines in black dresses and pèlerines run out of the convent, skates slung over their shoulders. The rue du Parloir is narrow, a wedge of powder blue sky stretched thin between high walls. As soon as the girls pass the first sharp corner into rue des Jardins, they start to run as fast as they can, the hoods of their capes slipping to reveal mismatched muffs, and bright bonnets that they snatch off each other's heads and throw up and away.

Their weekly three hours of freedom is supervised by a "dizainière," someone worthy of the nuns' trust and intensely disliked by the other girls. Last time the snitch told on them, they shoved her head down a fresh snowbank long enough to make her smarten up. This week she will let them talk to the boys. The girls weave through the carrioles, box carts, and horses, skip to avoid steaming manure, keeping a sure foot on patches of sand and treading more daintily on ice. They make their way through the crowded streets surrounding the Château Fron-tenac hotel, heading for the terrace and the skating rink. The boys from the Séminaire steal appreciative glances at the narrow ankles and thick legs in striped wool socks as the girls hike up their skirts to lace up their black leather skates. Soon the couventines step out to dance two by two to the upbeat tempo of a Viennese waltz, even daring a pirou-ette here and there. The boys zoom past them low and fast, one arm behind the back, then flip around just in time to flash a smile, crossing one blade over the other to manage the curve. It is when both boys and girls stop to catch their breath, leaning with a studied nonchalance against the boards, that contact is made. The snitch watches sourly, but the boys have their own snitch too, and once these two start to exchange views on the finer points of the catechism, the young people are free to enjoy each other's company.

The first thing Marie-Reine Tremblay does on reaching the open vista by the rink, high above the St. Lawrence River, is to run off the path climbing towards the heights of the Citadel. Once she is far enough, she lets out a big cry, Ho! Ho! Ho! A call for a moose, or a father.

Un bon à rien. Always these words, held tightly between Marie-Joseph's thin lips. Ne'er-do-well.

Marie-Reine digs herself a hiding place in the snow. When she lies down flat on her back, her heart pounds against her rib cage. Her face turns towards the infinity of the sky and her senses tune in to the life around her. Snow crystals melting one by one from her body heat. The capricious wind swirling on the snowbank. The faint music arising from the skating rink in the distance, the ferry's horn, the church bells, the horses' hooves, soft on the snow, harsh on the dirt. A shovel scraping the ground. The girls calling her name: "Marie-Reine! Où est-ce que t'es, Marie-Reine?"

She pretends to be dead. Her freckled face is serene. Her eyelids look like the inside of an oyster, iridescent mother-of-pearl. Her bare hands rest beside the never-to-be-lost mittens on a string, on her dark immobile chest.

"Marie-Reine?"

A frozen martyr whose bones will never yellow, whose body will be kept intact in a casket of ice.

"Marie-Reine! Stop this right now!"

Not for her, martyrdom. Marie-Reine rises, cleansed of the convent smells of disinfectant and boiled meat, ready to indulge in bad behaviour with the boys at the rink.

"Let's go, Marie-Reine, let's go!"

But after skating in circles for half an hour with the boys, Marie-Reine is bored. She walks on her skates towards the terrace's railings, looking over the steep edge of Cap-Diamant. From here she watches the ferry go back and forth across the St. Lawrence between Québec and Lévis on the opposite shore, drifting downstream with the ice floes on the swift current. She spies on lovers kissing under the white and green roof of one of the gazebos dotting the terrace. She looks at the sky above Île d'Orléans, mauve already running over blue, and she knows that's where he will come from. Not God, with his cohort of crowned angels—her father, in his flying dogsled. Her father the skinner.

He loved beautiful things, Rodolphe Tremblay said of his brother. Too bad he turned his back on us.

Québec, le 22 septembre 1920
Fête de Saint-Maurice

Chère Marie-Joseph,

Merci beaucoup pour la nouvelle hache et le pot de confiture de bleuets. The new axe is much more suitable than the half-sized one I have used all these years, and although heavier, it is more efficient. It takes just one swing to chop even the biggest log. As for the blueberry jam, my mouth waters just to think of it! How I would have liked to go with you to do the picking. I am much quicker at it than you are, remember?

The other girls came back from the summer holidays full of stories about the things they have done and the places they have seen and the cousins they have kissed (if we are to believe a word of what Françoise Chassé has to say). They don't ask me or Laura Beaulieu, the snitch, what kind of summer we had at the nuns' farm in St-Joachim, by Cap-Tourmente. We were kept busy pulling weeds from the potato fields and spraying camphor on the cabbages before picking off the worms. This is the one job I cannot do, Marie-Joseph. The mere sight of a white worm makes me retch. But I was the best at climbing up the apple trees to get the biggest fruit. We did all this in our long-sleeved cotton dresses, so once or twice, when it got really hot, we were allowed to go for a dip in the rivière Jean-Larose by St-Ferréol-les-Neiges in our undergarments. We were also allowed to fish for trout on Fridays.

But now it's back to the routine and the wool dresses, even though the weather is still hot for September. Back to catechism, read to us over and over again at mealtimes three times a day, mass and communion every morning, confession and choir once a week, praying for this, praying for that, and falling on our knees at the drop of a hat—and you complain that your kneecaps hurt from waxing the floor, très chère Marie-Joseph?

It's also back to the réfectoire for the same meals as when I first wrote to you, except September's fare is better. We have corn on the cob and apple pie every day because of the abundant harvest, rendons grâce à Dieu, and down on our knees we fall again. And back out in the yard with the two-by-three apple trees and thirty strides in between for a total of 90 steps from east to west and 120 from north to south, rain or shine. This is the size of my world, Marie-Joseph: 10,800 square strides. I have outgrown it now, just like last year's uniform. When will I be allowed to go home? I know I am lucky to get such an education, but my luck sometimes feels like a punishment, and a punishment for what, I wonder? I will be sixteen years old shortly, Marie-Joseph. I am not a child anymore but a well-educated young woman. I beg you to ask mon oncle Rodolphe to let me come home this summer. It would be much easier to wait for Father to come back if I were in Chicoutimi.

Ta soeur qui t'aime,
Marie-Reine

But Marie-Reine does wrong. Again and again and as often as she can and sometimes she gets away with it and sometimes she gets caught and beaten or locked up. She tries everything she can think of to get the good mothers to send her packing. But all they do is inform Marie-Reine Tremblay's uncle of her latest escapade, and Rodolphe Tremblay thinks the wild streak runs as deep in his niece as it ran in her father. Maybe a few more years at the convent will dull the edge enough to turn her into bride material.

Québec, le 14 février 1922
Fête de Saint-Valentin

Très chère Marie-Joseph,

Merci pour le gâteau aux fruits, le bonnet, et l'écharpe rouge. The red is perfect with the black uniform, and warms my heart as it should, since this is my birthday and Saint-Valentin's day. As for the fruitcake, a leftover from Christmas no doubt, it does preserve well, doesn't it? I can eat a slice a week until the summer! Please thank mon oncle et ma tante as well for the beautiful gold chain and cross. It also looks good on the black uniform, but our Bonnes Mères promptly asked me to wear it inside.

I just thought I would ask you who to thank for the fur coat I received in a brown paper parcel. It didn't bear a postmark or the sender's name, but was still found in the mail bag. It is a beautiful thing, a brown shorn beaver of the lightest and warmest fur. I do seem to remember that you received a fur coat from our father on your eighteenth birthday. Wasn't it a grey fur of some sort, fox or wolf? Do you still wear it?

Well, Mère Sainte-Rose de Mai has just called for all devils to scram and for God to stretch his almighty arm over our pretty heads for the night, so I find myself having to sign off.

Ta soeur qui t'aime,
Marie-Reine

P.S. You forgot to send my monthly bag of toffee!

In November 1918, Marie-Joseph had told Marie-Reine her father was dead. She had let the young girl attend their mother's unceremonious funeral, standing in the crowd by the common grave where she had to be buried quickly, but not her father's. Marie-Joseph had said their father didn't live like a Christian and was buried the First Peoples' way: up a tree. This much she told her sister, every word an effort between her clenched teeth. It was clear she didn't wish to speak of him anymore. Marie-Reine looked at every treetop around the cemetery and around Rodolphe's house in Chicoutimi, but she didn't see anything up there but crows. She stopped asking. As the years passed, the confines of convent life made her memories of him fade. Until last month, when the mysterious package arrived.

Her father had given a fur coat to Marie-Joseph on her eighteenth birthday, five years ago, a silver wolf that made her skin look grey. This coat's pockets were full of pine cones and rocks, the grey and pink quartz of the Saguenay. Who else but him?

A letter from Marie-Joseph comes by return post. For the first time in four years this one is not dictated to their aunt Jeanne. The letter is short; the handwriting is not fancy or fluid, but slow and clear. The lines are not linked but separated from each other. Marie-Joseph's signature is the most assured part of the letter, with the elaborate flourish of the M, J, and T.

Chère Marie-Reine,

The coat is a gift from your uncle Rodolphe.
It was not ready on time.
We couldn't send it with the other gifts.
I gave my wolf coat to the poor.
They need it more than I do.
I don't like fur.
I don't remember who gave it to me.
Mon oncle Rodolphe asks you not to mention the gift anymore.
Your cousins Prudence and Constance have only fox jackets.
Joyeux anniversaire.
Que Dieu le Père soit avec toi, aujourd'hui et pour toujours.

Marie-Joseph Tremblay

Québec, le 8 mars 1922

Stop lying to me, Marie-Joseph.
I know he is not dead, as you have wished for all these years.
You can't even bring yourself to say his name, can you? And
don't talk to me about mon oncle Rodolphe, who has forgotten
me in this convent. He's not the one who sent me the fur coat.
My father will come and save me, in spite of your treachery. He
will get me out of here.

Marie-Reine Tremblay

Marie-Reine crumples the short letter in anger. She gets up and
pushes her chair against the wall to look out the high window. *Angelus
Domini* . . . The sound of evensong streams across the inner courtyard of
the convent, where dry snow powder spirals up in a sudden squall

before drifting back down, a shimmer across the chapel's gold light. Her mind drifts away with the snow while she hums a Gloria.

He will come for her and they will ride away past the convent's gates in triumph, careening through Québec. First around the corners of rue du Parloir, des Jardins, and Saint-Louis, then past the Château Frontenac and up the Cap-Diamant to the Citadel. They will speed up and down the rolling hills of the Plains of Abraham, and from there take a straight line down to the Lower Town and across the frozen ribbon of the rivière St-Charles. They will ride hard in the bright red sleigh, the dogs puffing and huffing, a smear of wet fur against the moonlight. They will follow the polar star, shining at the head of the Big Bear constellation, travelling farther north through the Laurentian Mountains, past Chicoutimi and along the Chamouchouane River all the way to her father's house in the forest. This is where his other family sleeps with dogs on beds of fir branches, in the country where bears are white, birds wear feather shoes, and houses are made of snow.

Marie-Reine's room is cold, drafty from the open window. The oil lamp flickers while the good mothers call on the angel of the Lord for protection. A crumpled ball of paper rolls onto the floor. Marie-Reine has wrapped herself in her fur coat and her head lies on her writing desk, her pride broken. There has been less and less to say, but from now on, rather than calling her sister a liar, Marie-Reine has vowed to remain silent. Nobody will come. No saviour, no angel, no father. Every night when Marie-Reine falls asleep, he runs away. At the threshold of her dreams he vanishes from the hollow chambers of her heart.

The evensong service is over and the clear spark of Venus rises in the cold sky. Marie-Reine cries until a tall shape fills the open door, calling for lights off. "May God be with us through this night, keeping all evil at bay." Marie-Reine jerks her shoulders and pushes herself up. As quick as a wildcat, she's on Mère Sainte-Rose de Mai, pummelling her with both fists. Mère Sainte-Rose de Mai's name doesn't suit her. She is as thick and square as a brick house and has the same complexion: red and grainy. The name must have been chosen for her inner qualities, the kindness hidden under a stern disposition. She grabs Marie-Reine's fists easily and holds tight until the girl starts to lose her strength. Slowly, trying to appease her with a soft voice, she encloses Marie-Reine Tremblay in her wide sleeves and lets the curly copper head weigh down on her shoulder until the tears run dry. It takes a while, long enough for the snitch to peek out of her room and for Mère Supérieure to stand still, watching from the end of the corridor. The next day, after four years of night porter duty to the senior girls' dorms, Mère Sainte-Rose de Mai is reassigned to the laundry room.

From then on and for three more years there are no more tears and no more letters from Marie-Reine Tremblay, only the cold bite of frozen time.

Première Relation:
Canada

WHAT is it, Canada? A country as big as a continent stretching from the Atlantic Ocean to the Pacific, divided into ten provinces and three territories, inhabited by more than thirty million Canadians, six million of whom speak French.

It's also just a word, six letters trying to hold all the granite, the grain, the timber, the fish scales, and the fur together. A word with a shifty meaning, a name for a shifting place.

First, it was the place where the sixteenth-century navigators from France and England didn't find what they were looking for: a passage to Cathay. Spaniards and Basques had visited Terra Nova's inauspicious coast before them. *Hay nada*, they had declared, spitting against the nor'wester into the choppy ocean of grey slush.

They didn't find gold mines: *Aca nada*.

They didn't find anything: *Nada*.

But once their blinding disappointment subsided, they realized the sea held a riotous abundance of cod in the Grand Banks, offshore from Newfoundland. In all of Europe's Catholic countries, the Church forbade meat 153 days per year, so salted cod, a great source of protein, was much in demand.

But long before the Spaniards came prowling about *Hay nada*, the Land of Nothing, the Iroquois already roamed the great river in their birchbark canoes. In their language a village was *kanata*.

48

Cartier's first mention of the name Canada, although not indicated on the maps of his time, points to the site of Stadaconé itself, now the city of Québec. An addendum inserted in the Presses de l'Université de Montréal edition of his *Relations* encloses Canada between two dotted arcs, circumscribing Stadaconé and its immediate surroundings: from the southern tip of the Isle of Bacchus, now Île d'Orléans, to the fort Sieur de Roberval built on the king's orders, in hopes of starting a colony at Cap-Rouge, a little farther upriver from the Huron settlement.

That was Canada. Forty-seven and a third degrees from the North Pole, not much more than twenty-five square miles, on both sides of "where the river narrows," or *guébeg*, in Mi'kmaq.

The city of Québec is now the oldest continually inhabited European settlement in North America. Founded in 1608 by Samuel de Champlain, the colony still had only a hundred inhabitants twenty years later. This modest population grew into a ten-million-strong group of people with French names three centuries later, scattered around Québec, Ontario, Manitoba, New Brunswick, New England, and along the Mississippi as far south as Louisiana.

Once the colonies of New France finally started to flourish after some two hundred years of fighting the climate, the Iroquois, and diseases, France lost everything to England in a fifteen-minute battle. On September 13, 1759, on the Plains of Abraham, outside the tiny fortified town of Québec, the vainglorious Marquis de Montcalm was defeated by Wolfe, the sickly English major-general, in the defining episode of the Conquest. The scars from this defeat can still be felt today: Québec still fights to remain French, within Canada and in the midst of a vast English-speaking continent. Where the river narrows, the troubled waters of dangerous emotions stir.

Heathrow Airport, September 1995. The rugged shore of rock and sand along the Gulf of St. Lawrence is not the land God gave to Cain, as Jacques Cartier wrote in his first *Relation*. Cain's land is this place at six in the morning after a seven-hour-long overnight flight with two children aged two and four, all our belongings in six suitcases and the skin of our faces ready to fall off.

The engines roar, reversing power. It's grey and dull outside, the only flash of light the fluorescent yellow vests of the airport staff on the tarmac. With one child asleep in Laurent's arms, another one barely walking at the end of my hand, we are corralled in a gigantic room with a maze of fences, the passport checkpoint. We haven't had a breath of fresh air for twelve hours. Our passports get stamped by a churlish clerk. Nobody is waiting for us but a few locals in red caps, standing by the carousel. They want seven pounds to help us with the luggage. There is a lineup for the black cabs under the low concrete ceiling of the underground garage. The non-stop sound of the diesel taxis coming and going is amplified and echoes, and although we are technically outdoors, there still is no fresh air. We wait, standing up but barely, the girls sprawling on top of the suitcases.

"To Hammersmith," Laurent says.

On a rainy morning at rush hour on the M4 between Heathrow and London, all we see are endless traffic jams and dingy houses. In Hammersmith a two-bedroom first-floor no-yard flat with moderately modern conveniences is awaiting us, around nine o'clock. It costs £325 a week, or $3,000 a month. After paying the hefty council tax and the utilities, we find there is no money left to afford the monthly fee for the communal garden key. What are we doing here?

Holes in hearts—babies' hearts, to be precise. That's why we're here. Because of Laurent Malenfant, my husband. We were still recovering from the joy and fatigue of having two children one after the other when Laurent was asked to join a team of cardiac surgeons doing open-heart surgery on newborn babies in London, England. Laurent, an industrial designer, had already specialized in the design of spare parts for the body before working with Gore-Tex fabric to patch up holes in babies' hearts. The old murmur. Very common. My mother developed one after suffering from rheumatic fever when she was a child. Gore-Tex is resistant and stretches as the heart grows.

I first met Laurent at the college library where I worked part-time in 1975. I was seventeen, he was eighteen. I had just filed a racy book back on the shelves when I saw him reach for it. I looked on, curious. He was not the type. Nothing evasive or sly about him, no hard shell. An open face where emotions flared up, right under the skin. He blushed, and walked away quickly. I searched for his details on the library's register. Laurent Declan Malenfant, born 12/12/1957, art student. Soon he started to show up regularly on my shift. He would sit at one of the desks close to where I filed the returns on my cart, cracking open the spine of *Histoire d'O*. Then he would search for my eyes. After three weeks of this ploy he finally had the courage to come up and ask me for coffee on my break, the book still under his arm.

"You know this book is late, don't you?" The borrower's fine was twenty cents a day after the fourteen-day limit, I told him. "And someone else requested it a week ago." It was a popular book, nowhere to be found in Sainte-Foy high school's library, or even the city library. But in college, Sexuality was an optional class in Social Studies, and this kind of literature was available for reference. We sat on a square patch of grass surrounded by concrete walls with our two Styrofoam cups of black coffee, the noon sun warming the top of our heads.

"Do you like it?" I asked him, pointing at the book. I had read my own share of this genre myself, gathering as much information as I could about sex. I didn't want to look like an idiot when the time came.

"Oh." His eyebrows arched over suddenly downcast eyes, his fat lower lip curled around the sound. He had straight dark hair in a pony tail, but his front bangs, parted in the middle, were not long enough and fell in his face. His obvious shyness, as he sat on the grass with sexually explicit material between his hands, turned me on. "Yes. I do like it. But what I would like even more"—he took a sharp breath in, shifted, then smiled, looking straight at me—"would be to read it to you."

It was my turn to blush. By the time we returned inside, we had littered the grass with white specks of torn Styrofoam and agreed on a date.

* * *

We spent long hours on the brown leather couch of his parents' living room. Laurent's father was a successful architect, his mother an Anglophone with Irish roots. They had a busy social life and Laurent was an only child, so we often had the place to ourselves. Their house was clean, light, and airy, built on a prime piece of land with a long glass wall overlooking the old and the new bridges spanning the St. Lawrence River. But before lying down together on the couch we sat apart and Laurent read to me. We went through the erotic classics, like *Venus in Furs* by Leopold von Sacher-Masoch, and *Justine* by the Marquis de Sade, but quickly moved on to more subtle and textual desire from authors around the world. Harold Brodkey, Yasunari Kawabata, Milan Kundera, D.H. Lawrence, Alberto Moravia, Henri de Montherlant, Vladimir Nabokov, Anaïs Nin, their stories unravelling under evocative headings such as *Innocence, The House of Sleeping Beauties, Lady Chatterley's Lover, Les Jeunes Filles, Lolita, Delta of Venus . . .*

Whichever the book, the ritual was the same. I looked out the window into the night, trying to remain composed as Laurent's voice slowly took hold of me. I focused on the closest bridge, the old Pont de Québec, drowned in darkness. I recreated its massive presence by joining the dots of lights, the first large lozenge, the small arc of the central span and the second lozenge, the distinctive cantilever structure soon shaping in my mind. Past the old bridge was a second layer of quick lights leaving broken streaks, yellow and red, across the six-lane span of the suspension bridge—le pont Pierre-Laporte, named after a murdered politician. But soon both bridges dissolved and so did the rest, the window, the walls, the room, as Laurent's voice came through, the fleshy sentences rousing me out of the armchair. I would walk over to him, snatch the book from his hands, and suck the words out of his mouth.

We went out together for three years, but as Laurent wanted more and more of me, I wanted more and more of the rest of the world. Laurent said, Let's see the world together. It wasn't easy to explain why I wanted to see it with my own eyes first. Why should love mean no more me, but always us? Was this really the only way to make a relationship work? I was twenty years old and I valued my freedom more than this.

The entrance hall of Canada House in London is wide and impressive, with dark wood-panelled walls, and floors covered with thick Aubusson carpets. The library is set back in a narrow green room lit badly by an oversized crystal chandelier. It's a token library, really—the main body of its hundred thousand books were loaned to University College of London when Canada House had to close for renovation. Four full-time positions have been cut back to one part-time librarian. In the basement are the forty boxes loaned by the Délégation du Québec in London, which lacks space and resources to offer this service from its Pall Mall office. With the Canadian Tourist Information Office also closing across the street, I know what's in store for me. More maps, travel itineraries, coffee-table books of photographs from Cape Breton, Nova Scotia, to Long Beach, British Columbia; more queries for a mythical Canada of igloos and moose and sauvages, as the French explorers called the natives, that live as one with wolves in the virgin forest; plus a steady flow of requests for maple syrup recipes or fireside and paddling songs for the homesick giving theme parties. Never mind. This is a nice environment, the extra income is welcomed, and my research work compensates for the less challenging aspect of the job. I was lucky enough to get it as soon as Marion started school full-time last year, the British school system a year ahead of America, with Madelon in pre-kindergarten for half-days.

We've been living here for two years now and every time I leave the house I brace myself for the worst. A young man, angry at the odds stacked against him, wrestling me to the ground to steal my purse. An exasperated driver making a bold move that will kill my two daughters as they cross the street. The loudspeaker's fuzzy warning of a delay on the over-stressed, aging underground system. Dead leaves on the track, or so they bark at us, as the density of the commuter crowd increases along the platform. Another bomb scare, another suicide, more likely, something terrible always about to happen. Just moving around is a source of tension, the snarl of traffic backed up for miles because of the anti-terrorist police checkpoints at the City's gates, not to mention being a working mother married to an increasingly absent husband. Laurent leaves at dawn and comes back at night, spending more and more time in the operating room or his lab. There have been problems with the team of surgeons, or is it with the Gore-Tex patch? An unusually high rate of failure. They are losing many of their infant patients, and more are damaged than saved by the operation.

We used to go for weekend walks along the riverbanks from the Hammersmith Bridge to Chiswick and across to Richmond. We'd stop for a ploughman's lunch in pubs with worn wooden floors where liver-coloured dogs slept by fireplaces. Laurent built flower boxes for the windows and planted bright geraniums, a touch of colour throughout the one long grey season that is London weather—cool summers, damp winters, no snow. When was the last time he brought me something? The bonsai, sometime last spring. He knows I miss trees and there are none on our street. The girls have put Polly Pocket dolls and miniature tanks around it, transforming the dwarf Japanese pine into a giant. Now the only thing Laurent brings home are forms to fill in. Like last week.

He didn't even say hello. I was reading the newspaper, the dinner ready, while Marion and Madelon were drawing wriggly rainbows and girls with curly hair, six fingers, and big smiles.

"Could you fill these in, Lucie?"

There were four forms, permission to give organs in case of death.

"But Laurent," I said, not wanting to speak my mind in front of the girls.

"All of us," he said, frowning.

My silence was a protest.

"It would be such a waste," he said, his voice softer. "You have to understand, Lucie, these babies are even smaller and more vulnerable than Madelon, their hearts the size of a crabapple. I can't understand what we're doing wrong."

Two weeks before it had been life insurance policies, for him and for me. And the month before, the will. If something should happen to either or both of us while in England, Laurent said, the will we left with the solicitor in Québec might not be valid, or the fact that it is from a different country might slow down the process. So we did it again and got back to the same delicate juncture. Should both of us die, who would become our daughters' legal guardians? There is no obvious choice.

My parents, Paul and Lilianne Des Ruisseaux, still live in the house where I grew up in Sainte-Foy, a suburb of Québec. They love our two girls as dearly as Laurent's parents do, but like his parents they're too old to be given this responsibility permanently. Since Laurent has no siblings, we had to consider my brothers and sisters.

The youngest is Bébé, a physiotherapist. She met her Spanish husband on a beach in the Dominican Republic. He came to Québec for a year to study French, and then they rushed into a quick marriage, partly out of obligation. He works as a cook on cruise ships in the Caribbean and is away from home for months on end. Their marriage is on the rocks.

My brother Maurice is six feet two, so we don't call him Ti-Mo anymore. He met his wife, Heather, while doing his post-graduate degree in forestry at the University of British Columbia. They have a little boy, Matt, and live the life of bohemians in a beat-up Westfalia, loaded with high-tech gadgets to hook Maurice's personal computer to the rest of the world. He brings his family along wherever a sick patch of the virgin forest needs preservation. What is also called old growth is quickly becoming a myth rather than a reality; it makes for less than ten per cent of Canada's forested land. On the roof of the van are Maurice's toys: the hang-glider, the mountain bikes, the skis. I don't know where they'd put two extra kids, honestly.

Pierrot has not only not married, he's missed half our weddings, arriving late but with a triumphant smile below his dark shades. Some people might be offended by this sort of behaviour, but we're just happy to see him alive. A trail of smashed cars, broken relationships, as well as the ups and downs of his bank account attest to his dedication to living dangerously. But he always lands on his feet and even sells a house once in a while. He is a real estate agent in Montréal and no candidate for fatherhood by his own admission.

That leaves Anne, the oldest. I was born a mere thirteen months after her. She never married her boyfriend, Yves Bellechasse, but they have been together for more than twenty years. She's a sociologist and works at the Conseil du Statut de la Femme, where they draft laws to protect and promote women's rights. He's a historian and also works for the Québec government. They have two big bouncy boys, Jules and Félix, and they live one parish away from where we grew up in Saint-Jean de Brébeuf.

Home. Does it still have the same meaning for Anne and me?

Chicoutimi,
1925

Le lac Saint-Jean: a near-perfect navy blue circle rimmed by thin yellow sandbanks. This is what the pilot of a string and canvas biplane sees from his open cockpit as he hovers above the lake on a reconnaissance mission.

Where is she?

Through his goggles he soon spots a short white scratch on the lake's surface and plunges from the top of the sky towards the water. It is the foamy trail of a lone swimmer, training for the annual thirty-five-kilometre Lac Saint-Jean crossing. The broad-shouldered figure, slick with lard to fight off hypothermia, seems intent on bisecting the lake stroke by stroke, kick by kick, arms and legs like scissor blades. In the swimmer's wake threads a quicksilver school of trout, perch, and bass, led by the mighty pike and the ouananiche, a freshwater salmon with a white underbelly. Léandre Beauregard skims past the man's bobbing cap before letting out a sigh. This is not who he is looking for. He pulls hard on the stick and the plane veers inland, over flat fields and black peat bogs where the blueberries grow.

Who is she?

A pale moving shape catches his eye, crouched amid the reddish bushes. The net around the fruit picker's straw hat is speckled with furry deer flies. The shirt covering her dress is carefully buttoned all the way from the neck to the cuffs, but the loose tail flaps in the hot wind. Her busy white-cotton fingers fill bucket after bucket with the violet harvest.

Could it be her?

Just an inch of her skin would be enough for him to know, thinks Léandre Beauregard. That's when the woman lifts her veil to squint at the plane crossing the sunset on the far horizon. Her face bears the trace of many seasons of fruit picking and canning.

The forlorn pilot speeds up and away towards the deepening fjords of the Saguenay River, hovering above a large expanse of thick forest. As far as he can see, as hard as he can look, with the well-trained eye of a Royal Air Force pilot, the forest remains impenetrable. So he wings it past Alma, Kénogami, Shipshaw, until a line of steel, the Chicoutimi bridge, surprises him. He slows down to hedge-hop through the small city.

How will he find her, the one he knows is meant for him? So many houses where she might live, so many windows she might cloud with her milky maiden breath, so many chairs on so many porches where she might rock at the end of the day. So many bedrooms where she might rest her dewy cheek against crisp sheets. Maybe he was wrong to think there was a special someone waiting for him, somewhere.

The light is low, the sky bleeding, making his search more difficult. He heads for the highest building, a square pile of granite built on a hilltop. La Banque de Montréal. There is someone on the bank's roof. She wears a long black school uniform with torn sleeves and waves her slender arms, as white and light as moonbeams. Attached to each wrist is a scarf, a vibrant swatch of luscious flowers billowing. He steers the capricious plane as close as he can to the rooftop, drowning her silhouette in his wings' swift shadow. He is so close, there is a real danger the silver threads of her streaming hair might get caught in the propeller, but he can't help himself. He wants to see all of her, all the details: the small round face, the short neck and wide shoulders, the swelling bosom ready to burst out of the midnight dress. Léandre Beauregard makes the plane swoop and dive again and again, but the woman doesn't budge, her arms stretched out, her rosebud mouth open.

What is she saying?

He can't hear her for the rotor blades, slicing up the sounds. If he could see the shape of just one of her words, he would know. It would be like a familiar object, a bent fork, or a chipped china cup with a lonely rose, brave and faded, each brown crack of its glazing embedded in his dreams.

The woman jumps up and down now, betraying her youth, revealing pretty shoes under her dress. They are a shocking shade of pink, like twin tongues wagging signals at him: come on, come on, come and get me!

Now she reaches for her purse, like a lady. Ladies never leave home without their nifty little nothings: a powder compact, coins, candies, rosaries. But what she gets is a silver spoon she dips in a purse full of sugar, and she throws the sugar at him in long sparkling arcs, one after the other, spun by the plane's rotary engine into candy floss stars. She streaks the night alight, catching the buzzing plane in a net of gossamer.

Then the woman on the roof digs out a deck of cards from the mysterious depths of her corsage and throws all caution to the wind. The cards flash and flip in the plane's trail, and she grins, her loose hair and dark dress rippling like a wild river. Between her blueberry-stained teeth she has clenched the flying king of hearts.

Partie Carrée

They actually meet across a table covered with green felt, playing bridge in the salon of one of the good ladies of Chicoutimi. The double room's two valanced and draped front windows overlook a quiet street; the back windows, a garden. At the front of the room is the dining table where the game takes place, beside an upright piano above which hangs a hand-coloured photo of Pope Pius XI. The other room is appointed with a sofa and matching twin set of armchairs, each coupled with a side table. It is too early in the season for flowers to show much more than a tight pea-sized bud or a high green shoot, so the few vases display dried-out immortelles. The seasons arrive late in the Saguenay, three hours straight north from Québec by train. The lilac blossoms at least a month later than in Montréal, and the new fashion styles a good year after, if ever.

The hostess, Madame Jolicoeur, is a churchgoer and her husband is a law-abiding clerk at the Banque de Montréal, one of the best employers in town. Madame Jolicoeur has invited another of the parish's good ladies, Marie-Joseph Tremblay, still a mademoiselle at twenty-six. Mademoiselle Tremblay has neither good looks nor much wit, but her passion for cleanliness has made her the perfect maid for Rodolphe Tremblay, her uncle and Chicoutimi's mayor, ever since both her parents died during the Spanish flu pandemic of 1918. Madame Jolicoeur does recall that the father's death was somewhat mysterious. There was talk in town, and his body was never found. Mademoiselle Tremblay has brought along her younger sister, Marie-Reine Tremblay, to complete the foursome, since Madame Jolicoeur feels slightly indisposed tonight. Marie-Reine is back from seven years spent at the Ursuline convent in Québec, on her way to spinsterhood too at twenty-one. Too much of an education, whisper the ladies of Chicoutimi. Who would want a wife who knows more than her husband? And what about the impish streak that seven years spent in the company of nuns has not tamed? Marie-Joseph Tremblay has confided to Madame Jolicoeur that she is more worried about Marie-Reine's future than her own. It just so happens that Monsieur Jolicoeur has a colleague, an accountant named Léandre Beauregard, who is a bachelor with a university degree.

"Mesdemoiselles Tremblay, let me introduce you to our guest tonight, Monsieur Léandre Beauregard, a colleague of Jean-Charles. He will replace me at the table since I am feeling rather poorly."

"Oh no . . ."

"Tut-tut-tut! You shall not miss me a minute since Monsieur Beauregard is a very adroit bridge player."

"Indeed!" flourishes Monsieur Jolicoeur, smiling.

"Monsieur Beauregard was also a pilot with the Royal Air Force in 1918," Madame Jolicoeur adds, taking hold of Léandre's arm.

"Enough, Madame Jolicoeur! These poor ladies do not need to know my shoe size as well!" Léandre laughs, embarrassed. "You make me sound like a hero when the truth is I was assigned my first flying mission the day the armistice was signed."

"Lucky chap," booms Monsieur Jolicoeur, "on top of everything else! Well, shall we?"

Léandre Beauregard is in his thirties. Marie-Joseph has asked Madame Jolicoeur if the reasons for this prolonged celibacy might make him, perhaps, a flawed suitor. For all Madame Jolicoeur knows, many years in the army during and after the war have fed a taste for freedom in the man, but a taste that could be curbed, her husband thinks, by the right woman. Marie-Joseph just hopes he likes to eat raw fruit with bread and butter as much as he enjoys a game of bridge, and that he has learned about laundry in the army. The domestic arts are not Marie-Reine's forte. She never had to cook a meal, wash her clothes, or clean a house the whole time she spent at the convent in Québec.

But it is late, and the crystal glasses have been refilled with port wine, bringing blotchy patches to the young Mademoiselle Tremblay's cheeks and sweaty beads to Léandre Beauregard's brow. As a rule, no food is served after dinner by Madame Jolicoeur, but she makes an exception on bridge nights. Slices of fruitcake are displayed in a perfect swirl alongside a small dish of hard candies. That's when Léandre suggests a hand of poker, certain to impress Mademoiselle Tremblay with a savoir faire acquired during his air force days. Marie-Reine eagerly accepts the challenge, smiling brightly with just a shade of daring. Marie-Joseph leaves the table to keep Madame Jolicoeur company, all stiff wrists and jerky elbows in her silent disapproval. Monsieur Jolicoeur holds back a yawn, discreetly stealing a look at his pocket watch. It is late. The clerk knows he has to be back at his desk, never-ending columns of numbers spreading in front of him, at eight o'clock sharp in the morning. He doesn't even like card games. Too much uncertainty. He is doing this for his wife, who is remarkably alert for someone indisposed.

Across the green felt square of the table, Léandre Beauregard stares at Marie-Reine Tremblay, politely, but with great curiosity. She wears a navy blue wool dress with a modest neckline and a white lace collar. Nevertheless, a tight row of round glass buttons catches the light, emphasizing the triumphant curve of her bosom. She is pretty enough, if not a classic beauty, tall with broad shoulders and slim hips.

"What does it look like from above, Monsieur Beauregard?"

"What do you mean, Mademoiselle Tremblay?"

"The river, the lake, the forest, when you fly."

"It looks like a map. The water is blue, the land is green, the roads are brown. And in winter—in winter it's easy to get lost because everything is white."

"And what does it feel like?"

"Dangerous. Exhilarating. Just like the pleasure of your company, Mademoiselle Tremblay," Léandre says, half in jest, half affably.

"Oh." Marie-Reine frowns, taking a good look at him. "Is this why I'm here tonight?" she asks. "Marie-Joseph has never asked me to come before."

"I'm afraid so," Léandre answers with amusement. "Should we just . . . play along?" he adds, throwing two more matchsticks to see Marie-Reine's hand. She has three queens and two kings.

"This is unbelievable!" Léandre Beauregard doesn't feel affable anymore. "How can you be so lucky so often?"

Marie-Reine bursts out laughing, showing her pink gums above an irregular row of small teeth. Léandre feels topsy-turvy all over again, just like on a night flight. All hands and blinded eyes, and his heart in his mouth.

The shouts and laughter bring Madame Jolicoeur back to the table, the elder Mademoiselle Tremblay in tow.

"Well, well, well, having jolly good fun, are we?" asks Madame Jolicoeur.

Touché, thinks Marie-Joseph, her own pleasure always kept in check.

Second Partie Carrée

It's past midnight when Léandre Beauregard reaches for Marie-Reine Tremblay's foot under the card table. Three weeks ago Thursday her shoes were dove grey; today they're as green as frog skin. She doesn't even blush. She grins and spreads her straight flush as if nothing happened, although he feels the tip of her shoe tapping his toes. Like a knock at the door. Tonight she wears a burgundy silk dress, not a colour Léandre would recommend for a rusty head. But as his eyes again follow the pronounced curve of the black piping along the front of the collarless dress, his mind wanders past the colour and the fabric of the garment. Her high forehead, her round cheeks, her sturdy neck, her slender wrists below the three-quarter-length sleeves: that's all that's offered, naked and golden in the oil lamp light, of Marie-Reine's skin.

Marie-Joseph also observes her sister, disconcerted. Where has Marie-Reine learned to bluff? In the convent, with the nuns? Or, more likely, with the boys from the Séminaire? Oh my God. Marie-Joseph freezes at the thought. What has her little sister really been doing in Québec, from the age of fourteen to twenty-one? What has she spent her time learning, if not the finer points of les arts domestiques? How to write and read, how to think? What use are words and sophistries in a decent household? Courtship goes with court bouillon, and Marie-Reine might have learned Greek and algebra but she still can't make decent meringues. What is she going to do when the time comes for Christmas cake, tourtière, angel cake, or crabapple jelly?

And there is worse. Marie-Joseph has heard her sister speak the name of God in vain as she struggled with a whisk and a bowl of egg whites and sugar. She spied as Marie-Reine dropped six messy blobs on an ungreased baking sheet, slid the sheet in the oven, and opened up a book—without even setting the timer! When Marie-Joseph came back from hanging out the clothes to dry, the kitchen was filled with smoke and the meringues were burnt to a crisp. She ran in screaming, but Marie-Reine, still reading, biting her nails as she tortured a wisp of twisted hair, didn't even notice. Her face looked as empty and distant as the moon. Marie-Joseph pinched her with a clothespin, trying to bring her back to earth.

But it's no use. Marie-Reine just doesn't care for brooms and mops, washboards, dusters, rags or brushes of any sort. She doesn't even care for eating; she wilts away on a diet of bread, butter, and corn syrup in winter, and raw fruit during the short summer. When she's not reading she traipses for hours through the woods, wearing an old skirt, a pair of riding boots, and a man's shirt two sizes too big for her. She brings back pieces of grass, moss, smelly leaves, tiny insignificant flowers, all dirty roots dangling, for her herbarium. She comes back sun-baked with yet another sprinkling of freckles on her nose. No wonder. She doesn't even wear a hat on her elf-locks, doesn't even watch for mud on her skirt. Her bare skin is covered with mosquito bites. While she uses the Bible carelessly to press her wild harvest down between silk paper, beside her bed sits *La flore Laurentienne*, a book describing and classifying all that grows in Canada. Well, at least it is written by a priest, the distinguished Frère Marie-Victorin, but Marie-Joseph can't help but disapprove. Again and again. Marie-Reine goes to church the same way she bakes, absentmindedly, and otherwise doesn't seem to pay attention, or respect, to her Creator.

When Marie-Joseph asks, this is what her sister answers: "I have calluses from all those years spent on my knees praying for the dead and the living to Notre Seigneur. I have walked down enough corridors, followed enough schedules, and eaten enough slop for a hundred years. Now I want to live my way."

This utter lack of modesty, this unyielding disposition . . . Marie-Joseph has no choice but to cook, clean, and pray for two, and wait for a miracle to happen: a man willing to take Marie-Reine off her hands.

Third *Partie Carrée*

Emboldened by another three-week wait, the young Mademoiselle Tremblay and Monsieur Beauregard play poker for money.

Marie-Joseph's increasing disapproval is like a noose, tight around her neck. She clears her throat repeatedly but still feels about to choke. She has to excuse herself to go breathe some fresh air next to one of the windows. It is stuffy in the salon and even the night outside is heavy with heat, like a velvet tea cozy over Chicoutimi. Stars abound in the deep indigo of the July sky, and the winter bouquets have been replaced by the creamy froth of peony petals and spiky foliage. Monsieur Jolicoeur excuses himself to have a smoke at the other window, by the upright piano, on which sits a bowl of green apples. He just wishes his colleague would get on with it. He is getting very tired of these late nights, of the fever he feels but cannot share. The novelty of the situation is wearing off even for Madame Jolicoeur; she looks genuinely indisposed tonight, but perhaps it is only the unfortunate combination of oppressive heat and a tight corset. She retires to the sitting area, in a cool draft, to finish one more crocheted doily.

Mademoiselle Tremblay has red shoes on tonight and a pale blue cotton dress with short sleeves. A light shawl covers her arms, but it slips down repeatedly, and Marie-Reine soon lets it fall onto the back of her chair. The humidity makes her frizzy hairline look like moss, and wet stains spread a darker shade of blue under her arms. As soon as the other two players leave the table, Léandre Beauregard lifts the floor-length tablecloth and stares at her slim ankles, her bony knees. She has hiked up her skirts for more comfort, it is so hot. She seems so artless in her provocations, just this smile with sharp teeth bringing her face to a full bloom. When Marie-Joseph and the clerk return, Marie-Reine is busy shuffling the cards with a confident brio, holding Léandre's attention in the palm of her hands, her shoe tip slipped under the cuff of his light wool pants.

Léandre wants to call her bluff. She might be the mayor's niece, she might be well educated, but she doesn't have a gold coin to her name. When all pretenses come down, she will be revealed for what she is. But what is she? He likes not being able to tell.

After the game they share a small supper. Strawberry and rhubarb pudding, lemonade for the ladies and a finger of cognac for the two men. For Marie-Reine, a rather large porcelain bowl full of blueberries. She throws a teaspoon of sugar on top. Marie-Joseph scolds, "Tssk-tssk, quel gaspillage! Le bon Dieu les a faites sucrés," but Marie-Reine already has her mouth full. She eats with neither grace nor restraint, but with mechanical precision. She brings the silver spoon to her lips and fills her mouth with the violet fruit. Her hand clenches the white bowl as if someone might steal it away from her. Monsieur Jolicoeur is shocked. Léandre is transfixed by this display of raw hunger. When she smiles again, Marie-Reine's teeth are stained blue. Not a penny to her name, he reminds himself, fighting the urge to pick a handful of ripe berries and bring them to her mouth, not one cent, his fingertips sliding between the dark wet lips, except the two silver dollars she won at poker tonight, his fingernails grazing her teeth's stained enamel, feeling the muscular flesh of her tongue, the ribs and grooves in the roof of her mouth, the lining of her cheeks. He doesn't want to be left out of her pleasure ever again, he wants to enter this house of soft skin and cotton stockings, he wants home. A strangled sob stops him short.

Marie-Reine is standing up, the glow gone from her face, the backlight setting the contour of her russet hair on fire. She throws the spoon down, and the berries roll onto the white tablecloth like black pearls from a broken necklace. Her mouth is aghast, her eyes enlarged, her forehead crumpled up.

"What is it? What is it, Mademoiselle Tremblay?" asks Léandre Beauregard, his chair tipping over as he tries to reach for her from across the table.

"Ma foi du bon Dieu, Marie-Reine, un peu de sang-froid," commands Marie-Joseph.

But Marie-Reine runs out of the room, both hands pressed to her blue lips, trying to hold back her heaving stomach.

Marie-Joseph's first inquiring glance is for Monsieur Beauregard's trousers. Could it be? No. They were not left alone once. Not even for an instant, she has made sure of this. That's when Marie-Joseph looks down at the table where, in the yellow light, a small white worm dangles from the edge of the spoon. She sighs and signs herself quickly. How could Léandre Beauregard know about the worms weighing down Marie-Reine's memories? Marie-Joseph runs after her sister. He will find out soon enough.

Léandre shakes with silent laughter. He understood the old girl's puzzled glance, before she discovered the worm. How he wishes, oh how he wishes Mademoiselle Tremblay's discomfort were the result of such an intimate encounter.

"What is the matter?" asks Monsieur Jolicoeur, confused.

Marie-Reine Tremblay is the mayor's niece, and the mayor is a man of influence. She is worth marrying, money or not. With this final and hopeful argument, the part of Léandre Beauregard's mind that demands straight accounting is put to rest, although the emotions stirring his body are not. Not yet. He picks up the small worm with infinite care before sending it flying out the window.

"Women!" he says with a gay lightness. "Shall we call it a night, Monsieur Jolicoeur?"

The Last Partie Carrée

The fourth partie carrée is the last. The air is already cooling off at the edge of the shortening days, August all but gone. The faintest smell of rot rises from the garden where the late-summer flowering is rampant. A bowl of pears, peaches, and plums has replaced the frugal green apples on top of the piano; a bouquet of dahlias and sweet peas, the peonies. Léandre Beauregard can't avert his eyes and Marie-Reine finally blushes. She is wearing the burgundy silk dress again, and it is as if he is peeping right through her petticoat's buttonholes.

"Game over, Mademoiselle Tremblay. Tonight I'm calling your bluff," he whispers in her ear.

No poker this time. Instead, they play bridge badly. After a warm apple pie is eaten without any incident, a ring is produced and accepted. It is not a diamond but a lovely tear-shaped ruby, one size too big for

Mademoiselle Tremblay's thin finger. The Jolicoeurs and Marie-Joseph applaud and cheer, although Marie-Joseph would disapprove of this man's taste in a bride, were Marie-Reine not her own sister. At least she won't have to worry about the girl's future now. Yes, this family is getting sorted out, thanks to nobody else but herself. Marie-Reine needed a husband and she's got one. Faut ce qui faut. Marie-Joseph shivers in her black dress, always the same, its colour faded to grey from too many washes. The betrothed will marry before the first frost sweetens the crisp yellow flesh of the late apples.

Chicoutimi,
1937–1942

THE bank manager's wife, yes, she is very elegant, if slightly odd. Look at her vermilion shoes. A touch of je ne sais quoi, something sauvage. Madame Beauregard has a full head of rusty curls, a mop of unruly red and gold slipping from the combs, the pins, the hats, a sprinkling of freckles she likes to powder down, and forget-me-not eyes. And she detests black, an aversion developed during her convent days. She owns shoes every shade of the rainbow, for every day of the week. She asks the cobbler to dye the fabric or the leather.

Cabbage green? It must be Tuesday.

Marie-Reine Tremblay has certainly changed in many ways. She is happily married to Léandre Beauregard, manager of the Banque de Montréal, one of the only two banks in Chicoutimi. These are the highlands, the back country of Québec, an area so remote that it was opened for settlement not even a hundred years ago. Much has changed since and Chicoutimi can now be accessed by boat, train, and road. There are more souls and fewer trees—the pulp and paper industry has taken a big swipe at the local forests—but it doesn't matter because the American companies are now after electricity and cheap labour. They get both at the aluminum works in Arvida and the Company Price mill in Alma, since a new hydro station has been built on the Grande Décharge River between the Saguenay and Lac Saint-Jean. You can run out of beaver and cod and trees, but never of white water.

Much has changed, but some things remain the same. This is still the

Kingdom of Saguenay, and Marie-Reine Tremblay acts as if she were its reigning queen, wearing gold shoes to church on Sundays. Everybody remembers she is Rodolphe Tremblay's niece, now that she is Léandre Beauregard's wife, but they haven't forgotten that she is also the daughter of a coureur de bois and the granddaughter of a Montagnaise. Forget about the education, the silk and leather shoes, and even the bank manager. People talk, and what they say is that, given the choice, Marie-Reine Tremblay would have followed her father into the forest rather than be fenced in a convent.

The Beauregard family lives, for free, on the top two floors of the Banque de Montréal, an imposing three-storey building made of cut granite. In the back is a large garden with fruit trees, a vegetable patch, and flowers everywhere. No more traipsing about the woods for Marie-Reine Tremblay, mud on her skirt and dirt under her nails. Motherhood has grounded her, but since she cannot go to the flowers, she has brought them back, roots, clumps of soil, and all. Where the land drops and becomes spongy, bulrushes grow, and in the shady spots ferns uncurl from late May on. Fiddleheads, they're called. The Beauregards have them for dinner in season.

Madame Beauregard bears her husband a new child every two or three years. Most Catholic wives, on the Church's exhortations, do better than that and have them one year apart. But Madame Beauregard does suffer from morning sickness. It makes her spoil a great deal of good food, and soil many a pair of fancy shoes.

Marie-Reine Tremblay was married in an off-white silk dress and caramel mink stole under the starry vaults of Chicoutimi's cathedral. It was the fall of 1925 and the maple trees were on fire against the cool stone of the church's portal. The bride was twenty-one and the groom didn't look twelve years her senior. The soon-to-be Madame Beauregard actually appeared slightly taller than her husband due to the height of her burgundy high-heeled shoes. A large matching mink toque gave her another few inches. A first daughter, Huguette, was born one year later, then two sons in a row: Henri and Léopold. It is now 1937 and the family counts six children, with three more daughters: Lilianne, coming five whole years after Léopold, then Colette a year and a half later, and just this year, baby Bernadette. But not to worry, Madame Beauregard is only thirty-three. She still has time to be blessed with many more children.

All of Léandre Beauregard's offspring were baptized the day after their birth in the Chicoutimi cathedral. Their cries, protesting the cold water, rose from the church's alcove to join the belfry's carillon, sending the good news of a newborn soul, cleansed from original sin, to the four corners of the kingdom. Madame Beauregard rejoiced at the sound of the bells from her birthing bed at home, the long labour leaving her too weak to attend.

Marriage has not only tamed but completely transformed Marie-Reine Tremblay. Indeed, she has finally learned to cook. The wood stove is at the centre of the kitchen and the kitchen is the warm, fragrant heart of her house. A long parade of muffins, scones, and hot cross buns, pound cakes, angel cakes and gâteaux renversés stream off the greased and floured baking sheets and tins. She has even mastered the art of the lightest delights, meringues, cream puffs, and soufflés. As for her Christmas fruitcake, it has a perfect balance of fruit and nuts, hard and soft, with just the right measure of brandy.

Vanilla shoes. There is no need for six or seven pairs of these, is there? After Madame Léandre Beauregard spoiled the lavender ones during her last bout of morning sickness, she went back to the black leather bottines from her convent days until Bernadette was born. Leather is much easier to brush off than silk. Such a waste. Marie-Joseph Tremblay would know. She's the one cleaning up after Madame Beauregard.

Yes, Marie-Joseph Tremblay has answered the call of duty once again. When her sister asked if she could help with the newborn baby and the household in exchange for room and board, Marie-Joseph said, "But what will Monsieur and Madame Rodolphe Tremblay do without me?" He'd manage, was his answer. His daughters, Constance and Prudence were both married by then. Still, Marie-Joseph was a little hurt when she heard her uncle had replaced her. A young girl.

People talk. They say the new maid appeared at Rodolphe Tremblay's doorstep the day Marie-Joseph left. Nobody knew where she came from, although they suspected it was from the woods since she spoke Montagnais and a little French. The sun raised blisters on her fair skin and blackfly bites gave her a fever, which is unusual for her kind, and she had a good fur coat on her back for someone who travelled so light. This one smelled like scorched wood, they said. Bois-brûlé. No manners whatsoever in her moccasins, she chewed tobacco like a man, and veins of copper and gold ran through her slick black hair. She had eyes that changed colour: sometimes green, sometimes blue, sometimes the colour of the Saguenay's deep brown water. Her name was Catherine Dubois.

People don't have enough to do, thinks Marie-Joseph. That's why they talk. They say Rodolphe Tremblay tried to find out where the girl came from, to make sure there would be no trouble. If he did find out he never told anybody, but he introduced the girl to one of his foremen as soon as she came of marrying age. Now Marie-Joseph sees Madame George-Albert Lévesque, née Catherine Dubois, at the grocery store. It took her a while but she's learned to behave like proper townsfolk. She wears boots and a hat. But she still chews tobacco.

People talk but Marie-Joseph doesn't have time to listen. There is too much to do in her sister's house. Marie-Joseph makes Madame Beauregard's bed every morning, after she's made the children's. Madame Beauregard has her sheets washed often. "Marie-Joseph, tu changerais-tu les draps?" It's nine o'clock and she still isn't dressed, lingering in front of her vanity, brushing her hair, her peignoir slipping off her shoulder, her movements so slow it is as if she is swimming. The sorry sight of the bedding, the disarray, the musky smell . . . Marie-Joseph rips both sheets off the bed in one sweeping gesture, rolls them in a ball, throws them in the laundry basket. It is hard work, washing the sheets. In Rodolphe Tremblay's household they were washed every two weeks. Marie-Joseph truly believes it is almost a sin, the way Madame Beauregard smiles at her husband in the morning, the way she laughs with him in the candlelight over dinner, throwing her head back to display her throat.

Marie-Joseph is Madame Léandre Beauregard's maid, nanny, and housekeeper. The children call her Fifine, and no two sisters could be so unlike each other. While Marie-Joseph is as thin as a rail, her voice dry and her manner brisk, Marie-Reine is in full bloom, like a yeasty dough left to rise on the open oven door. When she wears her yellow shoes, like two canaries, you'd think her toes might start to sing.

The elder Mademoiselle Tremblay is happy too, if in a smaller way. All she asks for is to be made part of Madame Léandre Beauregard's good fortune. After all, she is the one who did what was needed to make this good fortune possible; otherwise Antonio Tremblay's two daughters could still be living in a miserable shanty, upcountry from Chicoutimi.

Five O'Clock on the Dot

"Time to eat. Henri! Léo!"

The six Beauregard children have dinner in the kitchen at five o'clock on the dot. La grande Huguette, the oldest, sits at one end of the table. On her right are the two big boys, Henri and Léo, and on her left side is the high chair where Bernadette is strapped. Colette and Lilianne, an inch apart in height, their hair tightly plaited, sit beyond the baby chair. The table is wide and thick, sturdy, and the china is chipped. It's hot and steamy in the kitchen, hot and noisy. The baby is tired. When Bernadette doesn't whine, she wails. She must be teething. Henri and Léo fight for a piece of stray string, a stick of wood, anything. Marie-Joseph is no fancy cook: mashed potatoes, turnips, second-best cuts of meat boiled all afternoon to get the toughness out of them. Huguette helps her relay the plates from the stove to the table. Coco and Lili clap hands and sing: "Am-stram-gram, pique-et-pique-et-colé-gram, bourre-et-bourre-et-ratatam . . ." This is the worst time of the day.

"Start preparing to say grace when you get your plate. Can't get ready for grace while singing, whining, crying, or fighting. Henri, Léo!"

She doesn't want to but she always does end up screaming louder than they do. A small frame but a big voice, that's Marie-Joseph. She doesn't even sit down. She eats standing by the kitchen counter, keeping an eye on the milk glasses, always too close to the edge, helping cut the meat into small pieces for the small mouths, watching so Dette won't choke. Knocking elbows off the table. She eats quickly, to be done with it.

"You are lucky children to have meat every day," she tells them. "Keeps you in good health. You are lucky children to be in good health. Lucky children, you are." She would know. Marie-Joseph visits the parish's poorest once a week with a basket full of fresh bread and chunks of cheese. The economy has started to pick up again after the Great Depression, but there are still many destitute people. Lucky and always hungry, the Beauregard children are. Just like their mother.

"Henri, Léo, your empty plates by the sink, please," Huguette reminds her brothers. She washes the dishes, Colette wipes, and Lilianne puts the china back on the shelves while Marie-Joseph goes upstairs to bathe Bernadette. Then it's Henri and Léo's turn to get locked in the bathroom with a pot of hot water and a washcloth. Marie-Joseph can hear shuffles, splashes, choked-up laughter, but they are too old to be washed like babies. One day they will all be too old. What are they doing in there? Idleness doesn't suit Marie-Joseph. As soon as she stops moving, thoughts bubble up like gravy in a stew pot. She bangs on the door. "Ça fait dix minutes, là, les garçons. Open the door, time for a checkup! Léo, ears! Mmm . . . Done a little quickly, I'm afraid. Face? Hands? All right, you can go. Henri! You are wet but you don't smell like soap. What have you been doing in there? Show me your nails. Back in there for five more minutes."

"Mais-mais-mais, Fifine!"

Soon he will be stronger than I am, Marie-Joseph thinks, and I won't be able to shove him back in and lock the door. Maybe Huguette will ask me to take care of her house when she marries.

A song rises from the kitchen.

Madame Beauregard has come back downstairs to cook dinner for her husband. Two dinners, two wash-ups, twice the work. Eating all together with the children and keeping a plate warm for him would be easy enough, wouldn't it?

"Bonsoir, tout le monde!"

Monsieur Beauregard is Chicoutimi's gold keeper, and the Beauregards live on top of a pile of gold, not of bones and skulls left over from the Spanish flu, as Fifine insists.

Even if he only has to go out the front door of the bank and walk a few steps around the corner of the building to the side entrance and staircase, Monsieur Beauregard is dressed as if going to church. When he gets home, first he takes his gloves off, then his hat. He puts the gloves in the hat and gives the hat to his wife. He takes his coat off, gives it to Marie-Joseph, sits on the chair by the door and takes off his overshoes and then his shoes. Marie-Reine brings him his slippers. Fifine takes the overshoes and the shoes to the kitchen to be cleaned and shined later on.

"Good evening, Madame Beauregard. How are you?"

He kisses his wife while she still fiddles with the pins in her hair, one loose strand across her smiling face. And then, only then, does he face the stairs where his children wait for his greeting before going to bed.

Sometimes Monsieur Beauregard comes home early, a song on his lips. As soon as they hear his slow steps on the staircase, the children run from the kitchen where they are having tapioca pudding or bread dipped in molasses for dessert. They shove each other and shout, knowing what their father has brought back from the bank.

"Look at this, children, I brought you gold. Real gold!" He bites into a coin and shows them the dents. "Coins are mixed with other metals to make them hard, but pure gold is as soft as toffee." But the children know better. This is trick gold. You rip the gold paper off and there is chocolate inside.

"When will you bring me with you, when can I see it?"

"See what, Lili?"

"The gold! The real gold in the bank, all the gold of Chicoutimi and Lac Saint-Jean!"

"Ah yes, the gold! Ma pauvre Lili, you'd be disappointed. There are more trees growing in the forest and fish jumping in the lake than gold in my vaults," her father says with a laugh. "This is not a rich country, not yet, but there is enough gold to make a living being the gold keeper." Still. The chocolate coins are worth much more to the children than the money Monsieur Beauregard gives Madame Beauregard every other Friday. Five flimsy pieces of paper.

Once a month Monsieur Beauregard comes home angry with Madame Beauregard. It is the only time he does, and it has to do with the five flimsy pieces of paper. This is the day the grocery bill arrears land on the desk of the Banque de Montréal's manager. That day Monsieur Beauregard comes home frowning, and continues to do so as he dismisses the children en masse: "Bonne nuit-là, les enfants, allez." Then he turns around to face his wife, who pretends it's just another day, humming while fixing her hair in front of the gilt mirror. Everybody can hear his thunder even if he shuts the door behind them after inviting her to join him in the dining room. "Really, Reine, I give you money for food. Why do you need to run a bill? I told you it doesn't look good, a bank manager whose wife can't stick to the budget. What is it this month?" Marie-Reine puts on an offended air before offering the usual reasons: children growing too fast, shoes, coats, fabric, wool, wood, charities. The truth is, although Monsieur Beauregard enjoys his special meal, there just isn't enough money for two dinners a day. This monthly storm brings a smile to Marie-Joseph's otherwise stern face.

But no storm tonight. Though looking tired and drawn, Monsieur Beauregard greets his children one by one. Baby Bernadette first, in Huguette's arms. Then Colette. Lilianne's anxiety almost makes her gasp for air. She stretches her neck, backs up one step to be higher than Coco, her whole body pleading, My turn, my turn!

"Lili, have you got worms? Stand still for a second, would you?"

A kiss on top of her head, like the other ones. Just like the other ones. "Bonne nuit, Papa."

But he has already moved on. "Henri and Léo, up you go, up the stairs, straight to bed. No side-step, no slowpokes. Fifine is watching."

Itch from God

Marie-Joseph visits the parish's destitute with a food basket every Wednesday morning. But this week they give her something back, and now the entire household is infested.

"Ouch! You hurt me, Fifine," Lili screeches.

Newspaper is spread on the kitchen floor to catch layer after feathery layer of blond, red, and brown wisps.

"Faut ce qui faut." The voice is stern, the touch harder than usual. Three heads down and two more to go, no time for tears. Huguette has run to hide in her bedroom. From the top of the house everybody can hear her laments. "I am not coming out of here until it has grown back!" Léo and Henri are sitting in a corner, sniffling and stuffing themselves with sucre à la crème. Marie-Joseph has whipped up a big batch to bribe them. Lili and Coco are standing in the kitchen's farthest corner, flattened against the wall. Bernadette, now two years old, is upstairs with their mother, who is inspecting the toddler's head.

"Lili!"

"I don't want to."

"Come on. You won't remember it on your wedding day."

But all Lili can see are the big kitchen scissors in her aunt's angry hands.

"And what if I don't get married, huh? I will remember this until the day I die!"

"Sit still."

Clip-clip. The two braids fall to the ground, intact. Three or four more clips take off most of it, then Marie-Joseph reaches for the clippers. She squashes the lice one by one on Lili's shaved head. "You can go have your sucre à la crème now. Colette, come here."

Colette wails at the top of her lungs as Fifine screams, "Henri, Léo, come and give me a hand! Why do I have to do everything by myself here, all the dirty jobs?"

At six-thirty Monsieur Beauregard can be heard walking up the stairs, as usual. He opens the door to an unusual scene. The children are lined up on the stairs for their good night kiss, but Huguette is not there and neither is Madame Beauregard. Little Bernadette can be heard crying upstairs. Fifine is still busy in the kitchen.

"What's going on here?" asks Monsieur Beauregard. He sniffs the air and smells camphor and bleach instead of roasted pork with herbs and beer. And the children . . . The hat, the gloves, the coat, the shoes. Monsieur Beauregard slows down the ritual while he tries to keep his composure. When he finally pauses to look at his sorry brood, it starts as a trickle and ends up a storm.

"Lé-andre!" Madame Beauregard calls him to order from upstairs, a shade of reproach in her voice.

Monsieur Beauregard laughs. His paunch bounces about, his watch shakes. He laughs until the children start to laugh too. There have been enough tears today. That's when Monsieur Beauregard realizes that there is nobody to put them to bed, and that dinner will probably be omelettes and toast. He shakes his head and has one last snort of laughter. Women! He walks the boys to their bedroom first, Colette under one arm, Lili holding his hand. When he gets to the girls' room, he sees two beds. He puts Colette down on the first one.

"Papa!" Lili shouts, insulted. "That's not hers, it's mine!" He knows how much gold there is in Chicoutimi, but he doesn't even know where she sleeps.

After he's kissed them good night he walks along the corridor, slow and heavy, and knocks at Huguette's door.

"Bonne nuit, ma belle Huguette."

A renewed wave of sobs greets him, and a cry from the heart: "I am not coming out of here until she shaves her head too, do you hear me?"

Everybody has heard. Monsieur Beauregard sighs again before going back downstairs. The next morning Fifine wears a long face and a scarf on her shaved head. Lili think she looks like a stewed prune.

*　　*　　*

"I don't care about my hair. What I care about is the destitute!" Marie-Joseph blurts out in confession to Father Théophile Pouliot, who was called back to Chicoutimi in 1919 after eleven years spent shaping the rough souls of Notre-Dame de Laterrière. "What will become of them? So much misery. My sister has a cold heart, forbidding me to go out and do good!"

"It is not right to speak wrong of your sister."

But Marie-Joseph cannot stop. "I am not speaking wrong, I am telling the truth. All the food they eat, all the red meat, the cream, the sugar, the butter . . ."

Father Théophile smiles behind the gold screen. Sloth, yes. Madame Beauregard has confessed sloth. On the other hand, Monsieur Beauregard doesn't consider a good meal a sin. A good man he is, Monsieur Beauregard, a man of duty—no qualms about that. He shelters his wife's older sister and he pays his dues to the Church. He is always ready to give his time to knock on doors and raise whatever monies are needed: the church roof, the hospital's new wing, the special fund after last spring's flood.

"They certainly could let the poor have some! And did you know they dance, Monsieur le curé? Every Saturday night! And with a war going on!"

The conflict raging in Europe doesn't seem to have put a dent in the Beauregards' life. Monsieur Beauregard did his round of duty in the Royal Air Force in World War One, and his sons, Henri and Léopold, are too young to volunteer. As it happens, bank managers also manage food vouchers, so the Beauregards do not seem to go hungry. As for the people of the Saguenay and Lac Saint-Jean, they might eat less butter, bacon, and sugar, but mainly the war has made their sons disappear into the forest to log wood. Conscription is not a popular issue in Québec, unlike the rest of Canada. Who wants to fight for the English? And Nazi Germany might not be such an evil nation if Catholic France has surrendered and even set up a government in Vichy that is not at odds with the invaders. The pope has remained neutral, but isn't Rome in Fascist Italy? This war is a much trickier moral issue than dancing. Father Théophile grunts to show disapproval, but this is an edict from Québec's bishop, not Chicoutimi's. As long as his parishioners do not dance in public, he will turn a blind eye.

"And only six children in fifteen years of marriage, and it's not for lack of—" Marie-Joseph stops, her voice now barely audible, her forehead on fire. "You don't know how often I've had to change their sheets, you don't know what it's like, to have to look at her in the morning, to look at them at night, to . . . I found . . ."

Marie-Joseph's head bobs up and down as she frets with her gloves. Father Théophile holds his breath. This is what he has suspected all along.

"What did you find, Mademoiselle Tremblay?"

"Numbers, on a piece of paper, in the drawer of her night table. And a thermometer, but not the kind for fever. Doesn't go higher than 101 degrees."

Only six children in fifteen years, deliberately obstructing the ways of God, and Madame Beauregard has never confessed! She might have had an education in Québec, but nobody is above a few spiritual tips, not even the bank manager's wife. "I love my husband. How can it be a sin?" That is all she had ever confessed to him, complaining her sister, Marie-Joseph, saw evil everywhere.

"Love is never a sin, Madame Beauregard, but love can make one sin."

Father Théophile had waited. The perfunctory pause usually bore fruit. But this time the silence was stubborn. He had to ask: "Is there something else weighing on your conscience?"

He almost heard Madame Beauregard's heart clap shut, like his parishioners' purses after their offerings clanked into the tin box. When she spoke again, her voice was light and clear, truly innocent.

"Non, mon père. J'pense que j'ai finis le grand ménage."

"God is the one, lest we forget. God is the one we should cherish, above everything else."

"She should know better!" Mademoiselle Tremblay barks.

Father Pouliot sighs. "Let your sister come and confess her own sins,

Mademoiselle Tremblay. You cannot do everything for her, can you? She's lucky to have you." And he is lucky to have Marie-Joseph Tremblay, to keep a record of Madame Beauregard's faith and failings. "We will miss your good work, but there are other ways you can help. Wool socks and mitts are most needed for the Canadian Army."

She Doesn't Eat Fish, He Doesn't Play Cards

"Ben dis donc, Fifine, aren't you a sly one. Nine years! This has been going on for nine years and you didn't tell us! I can't believe it, really, Fifine!" Monsieur Beauregard laughs, happy for his wife's sister.

"What, Fifine is getting married?"

"Who is Fifine going to marry?"

"Fifine, Fifine!"

The children fill the dining room, the Sunday meal almost over. Marie-Joseph has waited for the right time and the right place to break the news. Now they are prancing around her, threatening to tumble the wineglasses and smash the plates. But today Marie-Joseph is not the one to calm them down. Today she doesn't care. The children grab her navy skirt, pull on her arms as if she were a bell, down one side, then the other side, now-now-now. The big boys whip their Fifine around in a crazy jig, Huguette throws her arms around her aunt's neck. She is already fifteen, hard to believe. She was only six when the old mailman died and the new mailman started his rounds.

"Qui? Qui? Qui?" they all chant.

Le facteur.

"Oh Fifine, I am so happy, are we going to be invited to the wedding?" Huguette cries. "Will I be allowed a pretty dress, not buttoned up to my neck for once? Are we going to dance, can I invite someone, a boy?"

"Huguette!"

Monsieur Beauregard frowns, but Fifine catches him winking sideways at Marie-Reine. And then he winks at Marie-Joseph too and all of a sudden she feels dizzy.

"Stop it, stop it, I am going to fall! Stop it right now!"

She pulls herself away from the boys and Marie-Reine comes to her, making her way through the children, her hands ruffling their hair. She takes Marie-Joseph's face in her soft palms, tears swelling in her forget-me-not eyes. She can't say a word but whispers Marie-Joseph, Marie-Joseph . . . Fifine tears away from her to hide her face, to hide her own tears, her budding smile.

He was the only man in her life, besides Monsieur Beauregard and her spiritual director, bien entendu. She saw him every day of the week for nine years without noticing so much as the colour of his eyes, or the way he combed his hair. Brown, plastered on top to hide the bald spot. Every day he rang the door to hand over the paper harvest. The bills, the letters from Marie-Reine's old school friends, Mademoiselle Laura Beaulieu, Madame Gustave Tachereau, née Françoise Chassé. The pink and blue birth announcements, the wedding invitations, the thank yous, the black-edged cards. Nine years and nothing for Marie-Joseph, until one morning: "Mademoiselle Marie-Joseph Tremblay." Not Fifine. Not Madame Tremblay's housekeeper, not Marie-Reine's sister. Just her own name spelled out carefully. No stamp, no post-mark. Fifine frowned and looked at him, the mailman. He smiled. "C'est pour vous, Mademoiselle Tremblay."

"Goodness gracious me, you're right, Monsieur Bouchard. It's for me. Merci!"

But he just stayed there, a smile glued to his face and his foot stuck in the door. It was cold. A draft climbed up Fifine's legs under her skirt. She practically had to shut the door on him and after the door was shut, she started to shake.

But not to worry. The letter was not from the man Marie-Joseph still feared would come back. It was only from Edouard Bouchard.

They walked across the Saguenay on the Sainte-Anne bridge the next Sunday. Marie-Joseph went to church earlier than the Beauregard family, after setting out the children's clothes, clean and stiff with starch, for the grand' messe at ten o'clock. She didn't look her best beside them—that's why she went earlier. She also liked to hear herself praying, which was impossible when she had to keep an eye out for dropped gloves, stray missals, runny noses, and the like.

Marie-Joseph had never crossed the Saguenay River before. She had never had business calling her across, and didn't have a curious nature. A fine day it was, couldn't be better. He had his fishing gear with him. He was not much of a talker, Edouard, but on the way back he made Fifine stop by the shore. The river was brown and strong, wide and deep set. When he took her hand, a musty wet smell rose from the basket slung over his shoulder. The catch of the day was one big ouananiche and two medium-sized trout. He told her how empty the house he had shared with his mother felt since her death two months ago. And who was going to eat the fish?

"I don't like fish, Monsieur Bouchard, but Madame Beauregard is very fond of it. She cooks it with butter and wine. Do you play cards?"

"Cards?"

He asked her to marry him.

Spring 1941: a wartime wedding, and a middle-aged bride and groom. A small affair. As for children, Marie-Joseph doesn't need any. She already has her sister's, and that's enough. Marie-Joseph has not forgotten all the blood her mother shed with each miscarriage. And six times, soon seven, Marie-Joseph has held her sister's hand, wiped her brow, brought hot water and ice for this messy business. So much pain and soiled linen. The truth is, nobody needs to know. This is between them only. There will never be children. Marie-Joseph gave Edouard her hand, he is the companion of her days, but she can't let him in when night comes. The ghosts of the past are her only companions. If Edouard minds, he doesn't let on. He likes fishing anyway, and he seems to like Marie-Joseph's company the way it is offered. He is also welcomed at the Beauregards' table for Sunday dinner, which is generous; they don't have to. But now that the two married orphans make a foursome, Marie-Joseph thought they would be invited to the other table, the small one covered with green felt. Marie-Joseph tried to show the mailman how to play bridge, but his mind strays quickly back to the river, as his eyes look out the window. So Monsieur and Madame Beauregard keep their old habits and play bridge with the Joli-coeurs on Saturday nights, and this is how life goes on until everything changes.

Marie-Reine will never learn. The only immortal love is the love of Our Father.

Falling Stars

Why can't Lili remember the night of the shooting stars? Everybody else does.

The Banque de Montréal is on top of the hill, the house on top of the bank, the roof on top of the house, and Lili is on top of the world. They had to climb up a ladder through a trap in the bathroom ceiling, one by one, to reach the roof.

Colette and Bernadette sit with Lili on the Hudson's Bay blanket, white with red and green stripes, the low clouds racing right by their head. They clap hands and suck on barley bonbons as they wait: "Un-deux-trois, nous irons au bois, quatre-cinq-six, pour cueillir des cerises . . ." Lucien, now a year old, sleeps right beside them, bundled up in his basket. Such a good baby. "Sept-huit-neuf, dans mon panier neuf, dix-onze-douze, mes pommes sont toutes rouges!" Huguette is sixteen and sits on the edge of a folding chair, set right beside her date's chair, attentive to the presence of the boy's hand in hers. This is her first date, and her carefully curled hair is messed up by the wind. Huguette has to keep an eye on her two brothers, Henri and Léo, who both lean dangerously over the ledge. They're supposed to be playing cards as they wait but they prefer to throw them off the roof.

Marie-Joseph is not here and neither is her husband. "This is the end," she has warned them, "this is it." They have tried to reason with her, but Fifine is convinced the rain of meteorites is going to hit Chicoutimi and the rest of the world full blast. She is in bed with her head under the pillow and she will not see what happens once a final gust of wind rips the last layer of clouds. The sky suddenly opens above Chicoutimi, alive with a crazed scatter of skipping stars. Huguette, her date, the two big boys and the three little girls all jump to their feet to point north and south, east and west.

"Regarde, regarde celle-là!"

"Make a wish, make a wish!"

"Ici, là-bas!"

"Another one!" The kiss falls on Huguette's lips, so light, so quick, the trace of a kiss brushing her lips. "Oh."

Beside the girls, Henri and Léo's heads spin this way and that, like two weather cocks. If only their arms were long enough they could catch the stars like fireflies in their cupped hands and put them in a glass jar with a pierced lid.

By then Lili is not looking at the sky. As the first handful of stars shoot over Lucien's quivering eyelids, Lili walks away from the cosmic fireworks and towards the faint shadow of the chimney, black on dark grey, where two shapes are wrapped in one cloak. Two heads and only one patch of light, her mother's red hair, pulled up, her bare neck, so white. Lili moves closer, slowly, until she sees her father's face nestled in her mother's neck, the wool cloak draped around his shaking shoulders, his eyes criss-crossed with tears.

All Lili remembers is her father's tears, falling, falling.

Hôtel-Dieu de Québec, 1943

QUEBEC City has been frozen solid since the beginning of February. The thermometer's red line wakes up every morning, stubbornly, around twenty degrees below zero. By midday it might rise to minus fifteen, but the sun, such a pale yellow, is barely able to break through the window panes' frost flowers or spill on the hardened snow peaks. A little after four o'clock, the pale pastel tones start to recede in the steely grip of dusk's icy mist. It is so cold, the older houses of Québec burn down one after the other from overheating or furnace malfunctions. Madame Beauregard takes the streetcar every day from her house in Saint-Sacrement, a new parish set past the beaux-quartiers bordering the Plains of Abraham, to the Carré d'Youville terminus by the city's old walls. The Beauregards left Chicoutimi in the hope that Léandre could be cured in Québec, at the famous Hôtel-Dieu hospital. Madame Beauregard walks through the Porte Saint-Jean and on to the Côte du Palais, oblivious, her fur toque pushed down low over her ears and forehead, holding a corner of the shawl to her mouth and nose, her hand as thick as a bear paw in the layers of gloves and mitts. She can't feel her fingertips, or her toes in her boots. Her tears freeze before they have time to drop.

When Madame Beauregard gets to the hospital room, she puts her shawl and mitts out to dry on the clicking radiator. The room fills with the smell of wet wool, a smell so strong and vivid, so startling and so real among the man-made hospital whiffs of bleach, camphor, menthol, iodine, it is as if a sheep and its water-logged fleece were present, grazing peacefully on the green linoleum floor. But there is no sheep. There is a man under the crisp bedsheet, a sick man dying of cancer.

Marie-Reine has to watch as death marches on relentlessly. This is not the same man she bluffed with shamelessly in her twenties, the man who yelled at her once a month for eighteen years, the man with whom she had dinner each night and made love to with such abandon—the man who fathered the seven anxious children awaiting his return. Léandre's life has drained away a little more every day since he has been hospitalized, a slow but steady stream of planes, decks of cards, and gold coins as the winter wind pounds the northeast window of his room. The stubborn northeaster. Le Nordais.

For a while Léandre could still be propped up on his pillow, he could still look out and see. First the harbour's rectangle, the Bassin Louise, sealed in ice. Even the to and fro of supply-boat convoys and submarines across the minefield of the Atlantic has almost come to a halt. The allies' activity in the Québec harbour and the Gulf of St. Lawrence has slowed to a trickle during the cold spell. The dry docks are crowded with boats leaning on each other, their hulls black on one side, white from the snowdrift on the other, like a pile of dominoes ready to topple. Behind the bassin rises the Abitibi-Price paper mill's smokestacks and mountains of pulp, and farther past the mill's Victorian bricks the bruised tip of Île d'Orléans at Ste-Pétronille, the island plowing through the river like an icebreaker. The blue-brown wave of the tired mountains of the Canadian Shield runs along the top of the window, just below a narrow strip of pale cold sky.

But now Léandre is in a morphine dream, senseless. His limp hand in hers is heavy, the skin dry and yellow. Sometimes she can't hang on to him anymore. She drifts away. She is sitting by a round lake, holding a warm pebble in her hand. Eating sweet, juicy blueberries, shooing flies away. A sudden jolt of cold metal, the wedding band on her husband's finger, pulls her back into the room. The flying man will be grounded forever, too soon, and Marie-Reine doesn't want to remember, not now, their night flights: all hands and blinded eyes, their hearts in their mouths. Not with him like this.

"What colour are your shoes today, Marie-Reine?" Léandre whispers, his fleeting smile stolen from pain.

She has taken her own wedding ring, the ruby tear, off her finger. She will pass it through the buttonhole on Léandre's lapel when, dressed in his best suit, he will be boxed in forever. The red teardrop, born from the earth, will survive even his bones. He might not be the man she has known anymore, but he is still the man she loves.

"Couleur de loup-marin, Léandre. It is very soft, seal fur. Do you want to touch it?" She helps him find her ankles.

Every day from December to March, Madame Beauregard, née Marie-Reine Tremblay, walks to her dying husband's bedside through the frozen city. Her russet hair turns grey, she almost loses her mind. She grabs the spoon of medication from the nurse's hand, imagining white worms curling up in the transparent syrup. The Augustine nuns have been here, healing the good and the bad, the rich and the poor, the English and the French, from the beginning of the colony, just as the Ursulines have educated the settlers' and the natives' daughters. At least these sisters do not adore only the Sacred Heart of Jesus, like Mère Marie de l'Incarnation's disciples. They extend their charity to every part of the human body. But the nuns' compassion and selflessness, their adoration of the dying and their sufferings, are just as revolting to Marie-Reine. The swish of their robes along the hospital's corridor brings back the long days of desperation spent in the convent, in a city of stone and ice.

It is so plain to see.

The priests can spin fairy tales from the safety of their confessionals, they can point the way to redemption's high road all they want from their pulpits, but death still is death. Forget about trumpets—death is silent. Forget about swans' feathers and celestial robes—death is naked. Forget about holy ghosts and angels, forget about spirit—death is decaying flesh. As to the soul, the only purpose of this fiction is to soothe the raw grief of the living.

It is so dry and stuffy in this room, Marie-Reine's thoughts stir such sorrow within her body, that her nose starts to bleed and big tears roll down her chapped cheeks. She can't place her heart on the radiator to thaw, not now. It's better buried safe in permafrost: the heat would bring out an unbearable pain.

*   *   *

Chicoutimi, le 23 mars 1943

Très chère Madame Beauregard,

I have been reviewing the state of affairs of your deceased husband, Léandre Beauregard, since the last time we met.

The good news first: the house at 1502 Louis-Fréchette, Saint-Sacrement, Québec, is all yours. It has been paid in full by your husband, with his life savings and stocks. Your husband has also left a special amount of money to ensure at least your eldest children will have the opportunity to finish their Cours Classique.

The bad news is that there is not much else by way of regular income. I understand there will be a small monthly annuity from the government since Monsieur Beauregard was a war veteran. But together with your family allowance, your total intake will barely suffice to feed and dress seven growing children, let alone pay for the utilities and taxes on the property. I am afraid this means you will have to find an extra source of income. The exact numbers are listed in the adjoining papers.

Should you require any help to get a head start through these difficult changes, please do not hesitate to contact me.

As the new manager at the Chicoutimi branch of the Banque de Montréal, it would be my pleasure to assist you in getting a loan at preferential rates. Another solution might be to get a mortgage on the house, which can be easily arranged as well.

Your husband is dearly missed by all of us at the bank, and we hope that life in Québec will be good to you.

Bien à vous,
Votre dévoué,
Jean-Charles Jolicoeur

PART TWO

*Il y a des gens à ladite terre qui sont assez de belle corpulance mais ilz sont gens effarables
et sauvaiges. Ilz ont leurs cheveulx liez sur leur testes en faczon d'une pongnye de fain
teurczé et ung clou passé par my ou aultre chosse et y lient aulcunes plumes de ouiaseaulx.
Ilz se voistent de peaulx de bestes tant hommes que femmes mais les femmes sont plus closes
et sçaintes par le corps. Ilz se paingnent de certaines couleurs tannées.*
Première Relation de Jacques Cartier, 1534
[on his first sighting of natives at Blanc-Sablon]

*There are people on this coast whose bodies are fairly well-formed, but they are wild and
savage folk. They wear their hair tied up on the top of their heads like a handful of twisted
hay, with a nail or something of the sort passed through the middle, and into it they weave
a few bird's feathers. They clothe themselves with the skins of animals, both men as well as
women; but the women are wrapped up more closely and snuggly in their skins; and have a
belt at their waists. They [all] paint themselves with certain tan colours.*

Deuxième Relation:
Sagana

THE door to the Kingdom of Sagana, as it was called on Cartier's map, is where the ocean ends and the fresh water begins, at the mouth of the Saguenay River by the old trading post of Tadoussac. *Saga-nah*, an expression common to both Algonquins and Iroquois, means to recount a voyage taken to the land of spirits.

The time is between Cartier's second and third navigations, the place is the royal palace. Present at the scene is François Premier himself, spitting cherry pits through the open window, his fingertips stained violet. On his left is Lagaro the Portuguese, his confidant, and on his right is Jacques Cartier, his royal navigator, and Donnacona, the king of Canada. Donnacona is blinded by the crystal chandelier's shimmer and the mirrored wall, reflecting two, four, six Iroquois kings like him. Marble floors make the sound of his voice reverberate as if he was on a lake surrounded by rock walls. Draped in pelts and feathers, covered in shell necklaces, the native chief hides his fear and awe from the Pale Faces before describing all the riches of his kingdom.

Funny king he is, thinks François Premier, wiping his fingers on the front of his stiff brocade doublet. But of the two kings, the French one is the bigger fool, because Lagaro the confidant is also a spy on the payroll of his brother-in-law, Jean III, the king of Portugal. The race for the ownership of the new countries has been heating up ever since the treasures of Mexico empowered the king of Spain and his formidable Armada. In a secret letter to the king of Portugal, Lagaro questions the veracity of Donnacona's testimony. Obviously, the man wants to go back home; what better way than to make his kingdom sound attractive to his captors?

Donnacona, like the rest of his people, is well versed in the art of the tall tale. He's been asked the same questions many times before, by different waves of greedy pale faces washing up on his land's shores. Shiny metals and stones, the not-so-magic powders they sprinkle on their food, the light and useless fabric of their shirts, too fine for the harsh winter: this is their idea of riches. Donnacona and his people value bravery, a gift of meat, and a good story above all. When it comes to goods, the wampum shells they use as coins, a beaver robe, and a canoe are their most prized possessions. Donnacona even had to tell these white men about the annedda root last winter; otherwise, they would have all died of the disease they called mal de jambes, scurvy. It darkens the legs first before rotting its way through the rest of the body. Napu toudaman asustat: the king of Canada and his people have welcomed the foreigners as friends, but what kind of friends are these?

So Donnacona tells his captors that the Kingdom of Sagana is a land of gold and silver and spices. This kingdom is on an immense land-locked sea that takes two days to cross in a canoe, at the end of a deep river cutting through bare-faced stone walls. Donnacona tells the French king, his confidant, and his navigator that the people of Sagana are as white as they are and dress in cloth as well. For good measure he tells them there are flying men in the kingdom.

"Des hommes volants?" says François Premier, raising one eyebrow.

After this last fantastic tidbit the king of Canada, happy with his story, stuffs a pipe and tries to do tabagie with the two men, but they don't know about tobacco either. The dirty-fingered roi de France chokes, coughs, and turns green.

In the end, Donnacona was never allowed to return to Canada. His body is buried in France, under the name he was given at baptism: François. The other king's name.

*   *   *

Is it the dust from the books, eating away at the sheen, or is it only the start of the ineluctable process of adaptation? The pepper moth's wings turned from mottled white and grey to black within twenty to thirty years, to blend in with the soot saturating the skies and chimneys of Victorian London. It took even less time for the sedentary French peasants arriving in Nouvelle-France to become nomadic coureurs de bois living in the forest.

This is how I look on the photo ID from my library pass: dull and grey, except for a stubborn red dab of lipstick. The freckles have faded from my face, my skin is thinner and needs cosmetic assistance to glow, my hair is mousy except for the highlights. My eyes do not look as blue as they really are behind the permanently smudged glasses. Long hours spent processing data from computer screens and studying footnotes have burnt and dried my corneas to the point where, after one too many bouts of conjunctivitis, I had to shelve my contact lenses and return to the nerdy glasses of my youth. The first thing I do when I wake is reach for the twin pieces of plastic that give a distinct shape back to my hands, forcing me out of the amorphous world of dreams. Where have I been, other than here?

It was so bright, so clear. The water under the bridge was a deep green, heavy with slush. On each side of the thin free-flowing channel, chunks of ice kept breaking loose from the snowfield stretching from the riverbanks. The floes ground against each other before slowly drifting away. Sharp hillsides rose from the expanse of snow covering both banks, their mauve underlay covered with a lace of thin grey trees. In front of us, the landscape opened up to accommodate the bulk of Île d'Orléans, the sky eating up its low-lying fields. A square-fronted icebreaker worked to keep the seaway clear, its red hull and white cabin bright in the oblique rays of the sun. I could see all this from the passenger seat of the car, where I had scraped a small patch clear on the window. We were driving across the Pont de Québec. The narrow road was sleek with ice and the car defroster was broken. The windows were covered with sprawling frost flowers, the same pattern as on the wallpaper in my grandmother's house. Laurent drove crouched over the steering wheel. "Did you sign the forms, all the forms?" he shouted as we skidded off the road, out of control.

I woke curled up tight on the sagging mattress, shivering, my tongue salt-tinged and Laurent long gone. It's as if our love has lost its moorings since we left home.

Quebec City, 1990. Rosy-cheeked and dishevelled revellers spilling from a nineteenth-century country inn at dawn. The great river of Canada frozen into a plain where sleighs race each other on ice about to crack open. Women holding happy children and men smoking pipes as they play cards in dark kitchens, always a crucifix on the wall; these were the images awaiting me on my return from Toronto. I was going to be the archivist in charge of the glamorous Cornelius Krieghoff corpus of paintings at the Musée de Québec, thanks to my master's degree in library science and my four years of experience as a visual researcher for television. I had applied for the position on an impulse, knowing I didn't have much chance of landing such a great job. I didn't even think through what it would mean to leave Toronto. Everything happened so fast. But immediately after the celebration surrounding my return home, I had to face my mother's worries about my prolonged celibacy.

"Is there something wrong, Lucie? You can tell me, you know."

It was like being a teenager all over again. "Just because I'm thirty-something and single doesn't mean there is something wrong, Maman." I didn't tell her I was still reeling from a severe case of broken heart contracted in Toronto.

"I know having children is not the only option for a modern woman, but if you want children, Lucie, it's time to stop playing the field and start thinking about who you're going to have them with!"

I got angry to hide my pain. Not only was the relationship in Toronto terminated abruptly, so was my pregnancy. My mother had never had to face this kind of decision.

"And where am I going to find this perfect man? Playing tennis, like you did? And nobody marries their high-school or college sweetheart anymore, before you mention Laurent Malenfant again."

"Lucie?"

"Laurent?"

Twelve years since I had heard his voice.

"I ran into your sister at the hospital cafeteria and she told me about your new job at the Musée de Quebec. Congratulations."

"What about you, what are you up to?"

Laurent was working for a team of surgeons at the Université Laval teaching hospital, developing artificial heart valves and ducts. I knew he had gone to Montréal to do his design B.A., and to Rhode Island for his master's in medical design, but I didn't know he had come back home until Bébé told me.

"I'm looking for a date to go to a wedding."

"Whose?"

"My father's."

"Your father? What happened?"

"Nothing really dramatic, just a slow drift towards divorce."

All I could hear was the rhythm of the voice that could move me across a room, his tongue hitting the roof of his mouth, curling around *dramatic* and *drift*. "My father has fallen in love again," unrolling into the softer sound like a lull, *love* . . . "What can I say?"

"I wish."

Laurent sighed, "Same here."

There was a small, stunned silence.

When he spoke again, after clearing his throat nervously, his voice was altered, the rhythm of arousal gone and the shyness back. "I just thought you'd be the perfect date."

Laurent lived in Lévis, on the road bordering the south shore of the St. Lawrence River. I had an apartment in l'Anse-aux-Foulons, on the north shore, halfway between the ferry landing and the Pont de Québec.

By the time the wedding was over, his voice had taken hold of me again. It was an odd feeling, the unlikely mix of the comfort provided by an old friend and the excitement of sleeping with a new lover. Was this why I let my guard down and got pregnant? I felt so safe with him.

Safe and happy, everything finally falling into place. Our parents were thrilled, particularly my mother; another of her children settling down, and one more joy about to be delivered. Laurent gave me a beautiful diamond on a gold chain. We married in a short civil ceremony in 1991, with our newborn daughter, Marion Malenfant-Des Ruisseaux, screaming herself hoarse in my arms. Madelon Malenfant-Des Ruisseaux arrived less than two years later. That's when I decided to give all of us a break from the insane lives we were leading. My professional ambition was getting in the way of motherhood, and motherhood was an impediment to my career. I was doing a half-assed job of both. What I had refused to accept at twenty became my reality. I had been overruled by us.

Keyword: Sagana.

"Why on earth would you want to go to Chicoutimi in April? I bet there's still snow out there," says my father.

"I've been invited to a librarians' conference in Montréal and I have personal research to do in Chicoutimi. I'd like to see where Maman grew up."

"Can't you just phone, or write a letter? Isn't it all on computers nowadays?"

"You really don't want to go, do you?"

"I just don't know if your mother will be up to it. She's been down with the flu all winter and she still doesn't feel great."

I tell him it would be only two nights: one day to get to Chicoutimi, where we would sleep at the hotel, look around, and then one night in Péribonka, at Bernadette's cottage, before coming back to Québec.

My mother calls back the next day to ask me why I've become so obsessed with the past since I've lived in London. "It's my job," I tell her.

She also says she hasn't seen her sister Bernadette since Christmas and that she would love to go back to Chicoutimi.

I cook and freeze meals for the ten days I will be away. Ozlem, the young Turkish woman who is my "mother's helper," assures me everything will be fine, as the girls dance wildly around her.

"Aren't you going to miss me at all?" I ask Marion. She's seven, in grade three, and looking very grown-up in her British school uniform. She is already fighting every inch of the way for her independence.

"Non, non, non!" she chimes, trying to climb on Ozlem's back. She stops abruptly to ask, "Did you leave enough money for Ozlem to take us to the movies? And buy popcorn? And candies?"

"Yes, I did."

She runs to me, gives me a fierce hug, and says, smiling, two teeth missing, all freckles and blue eyes, "Goodbye!"

Now it's Madelon's turn to cuddle. "Moi, je t'aime, et moi, je vais pleurer. It's so unfair, why can't I go see Grand-Maman too?" Caramel curls, baby-fat cheeks, hazelnut eyes from Laurent's side, she dries her tears quickly enough to remind me to bring her back a big gift.

I kiss her all over and then I kiss a worried-looking Laurent quickly, shoving a piece of paper in his hands listing things to do for a single father on a rainy weekend in London.

"I'll miss you," he whispers, folding the list into his pocket.

"I bet you will!" I tell him, only half-joking. I am not sure Laurent realizes how much of our children's care he has surrendered to me since things have started to go wrong in the operating room. Maybe it's time he does. I give a last round of hugs before leaving, alone for the first time since the births of our daughters. I keep feeling I've forgotten something important all the way to Montréal.

It rains on the road to the Saguenay, it snows in Chicoutimi, and there is a windstorm in Péribonka. "Si l'hiver peut finir qu'à finir," my mother says, "maybe I'll finally get better." Her face looks thinner, her skin paler, but then everybody is pale after the never-ending Québec winter. She still coughs, and I notice her neck seems stiff when she turns around.

"We're almost there," she says when we see the sign for the Laterrière exit. "This is where my mother was born. It used to be called Grand-Brûlé de Laterrière because of the scorched earth the settlers left behind. They even burnt the country down once, from Saint-Félicien, on the Chamouchouane River in Lac Saint-Jean, to the Baie des Ha! Ha! on the Saguenay."

The great fire of 1870 burnt for six hours, racing along a one-hundred-mile-long strip. Chicoutimi was spared, but everything else was destroyed: churches, houses, cattle, and the spring sowing, in Pointe-Bleue, Roberval, Chambord, Métabetchouane, Jonquière. The mills, all the bridges. People had to jump into the rivers and the lakes, throwing water on each other to survive. As soon as the diocese of Chicoutimi had finally finished rebuilding its churches, the Spanish flu closed them down again, decimating the most able part of the population. Then came the Crash and the Depression. Not that anybody was rich in the Kingdom of Sagana, but there's always a way to get poorer, according to my mother. By the time she has finished talking about how tough the old times were, we're driving by the main street of downtown Chicoutimi. Her mood changes quickly when we get to the intersection of Racine and Sainte-Anne streets.

"There's the bank!" she cries out, excited. "The top of the world. That's how high it felt, from the roof." The Banque de Montréal still stands tall and square at the top of a steep hill climbing from the old bridge. "That's where we went to see the shooting stars, the night Chicoutimi went through the tail of the comet. Just before we moved to Québec, in 1942."

"Ben voyons donc, Lilianne, in 1942? It was not a comet at all, it was a meteorite shower. Shooting stars, all over the sky. I was out with my friend Rodrigue that night, with our dates."

He sneaks a wink at my mother, who just snorts back, "Tu parles de la belle Hortense, j'imagine? She looked like a horse."

My father goes on, speaking to me. "Your mother was only a girl, but I was already a man. We couldn't believe our luck that night, so many wishes we could make as the stars rained all around us! God knows, young men have many longings, but I had only one true wish." He reaches for my mother's hand. "And my one and only wish was granted to me." My father has always been romantic enough for two.

"Did you make a wish too?" I ask my mother.

"Oh yes."

"What was it?"

"I wished for that night never to end."

"Why waste a wish on something you knew was impossible?" I ask.

"I was young."

"We still are!" my father claims, parking the car.

We get out of the car to use the automated teller machine in the bank's lobby. It's seniors' day, and coffee and face-to-face service is available to the sixty-plus. On our way out we stare at the upper-floor windows where the Beauregards used to live. It is now a clinic specializing in sports injuries. There is a supermarket at the next main intersection, up on rue Price, but the small grocery store owned by Lévesque et Fils is still there, to my mother's delight. Everything is so quiet here. There are few people on the street, unhurried, and the traffic is light and lazy compared to London. It's snowing when we park the car again by the Chicoutimi cathedral, but before going into the church, we head for the diocese office. I want to request copies of the birth and death certificates of my grandmother Marie-Reine Tremblay, her sister, Marie-Joseph Tremblay, and their parents and grandparents on the Tremblay side.

"And what about my side? Don't you want my side of the family too?" my father asks.

I laugh. "Your side is too boring. It took three generations of Des Ruisseaux to move around three city blocks and your grandfather was a clerk, not one of the last coureurs de bois!"

A middle-aged woman is counting money in the overheated office. It takes about fifteen minutes to explain the request and ask for the documents to be sent to London. I write a cheque while the clerk explains it will take between three and six months to get the copies. "But if you're in a hurry, you can check some dates in the cemetery. There are many Tremblays there."

"We will, merci beaucoup."

The cathedral of Chicoutimi is huge and cold, gold and blue inside. As soon as my father dips his finger in the holy water and signs himself, he slips back in time with the ease of a traitor. The altar boy returns, drinking from the sacred claret behind the priest's black robe, while the Parti Québécois member who traded his faith in God for faith in a new country, is gone. He walks straight to the front of the church while I follow my mother along the Way of the Cross, reading aloud from information sheets I took by the entrance.

"This is the third cathedral of Chicoutimi. The first one was built in 1878 and burnt in 1912. It was rebuilt and inaugurated in 1915, but burnt again in 1919. The present cathedral was finished in 1921 and consecrated in 1972, by the time it was finally paid for in full." The gold chalice, the fine laces and silk stoles, the sculpted wood, the wine, the bread; all paid in full with the farmers' sweat as they harvested their golden fields in August, and with their wives' tears of pain as they laboured through one more childbirth. They bowed and they knelt and they atoned for their sin, one thousand voices speaking as one. But there is no more sin now, nothing to confess anymore. No traces of calluses or stretch marks on these stone walls weeping dampness, or the immaculate cloth of the long table, and the polished grain of the wooden prie-dieux. *"The cathedral is built in the shape of a cross, like most of the Catholic churches. The nave, from the Latin 'navis,' or 'ship,' is where the faithful sit."* It is so vast in here, so vast and so still, the cold smell of spent incense hovering under the vaulted roof.

My mother points to the third pew on the left. "Right behind the mayor and the doctor, that's where we sat. This is where my mother was married, and where all my brothers and sisters were baptized. Look how empty and dull it is now," she says, disappointed. "They have all fled the ship."

We have caught up with my father, by the altar, where the relics are kept.

"Where did they all go?" I ask.

"Home. To watch TV and feel lonely," my father answers, an unusual streak of bitterness in his voice. It must be harder to peel the believer skin off than to put it on. "I heard on the news some churches have to sell their bells to fix up their roofs."

A door opens at the side of the church, a furtive flash of light letting a woman in. She's dressed in black, with hat and gloves, sensible shoes. She walks slowly to the nearest pew, where she kneels and signs herself. This place feels hollow once you've become a spiritual tourist leering at the real thing: the ones who still hear and speak to God.

A draft makes the flames flicker in the votive candle rack. "I wouldn't want this heating bill," says my father, folding a ten-dollar bill into the Offrandes tin box. I slip some quarters in to light a candle for all the babies born with holes in their hearts too big to be patched. Then I light another one for Antonio Tremblay, my great-grandfather, almost as a taunt. It's hard to honour the memory of someone so elusive.

Outside, the sun shines through a few last dizzy snowflakes, and the Saguenay River, behind four tall maple trees, is not dark blue as before but brown, streaked with veins of gold.

"Anything else?" I ask my mother, shading my eyes from the brutal light.

"There's Marie-Joseph's house, on the north side of the river."

We drive through Chicoutimi-Nord slowly, windows lowered. We go around in circles for a while, until the name of a street triggers my mother's memory. We turn and drive by monster homes in pale brick with ten different styles of windows hiding behind triple-car garages.

"Wouldn't want these heating bills either. Look at the size of those windows."

"Is that all you can think about, Paul?" says my mother, slightly irritated. As she says this a dog leaps to the side of the car, a husky or a German shepherd, snarling at us. An automatic garage door opens. There is no car inside, just a cord of tightly packed firewood. An old woman walks out, a long white braid on each side of her face. She whistles, and when the dog comes back to her, whimpering, shaking its tail, she bends down and lets it lick her face.

"I wonder if this could be her," says my mother.

"Who?" asks my father.

"Marie-Joseph's housekeeper, the one who got her house."

"Her housekeeper?" my father says.

"Catherine Dubois," my mother whispers, inspecting the old woman in her lumber jacket and long skirt. "Marie-Joseph got fancy after her husband's death. Or lonely. Bought herself some company. People said she was her half-sister."

"And where would the half-sister come from?" I ask, vaguely remembering my grandmother rattling on about this housekeeper who played poker.

"From the same place Antonio Tremblay spent most of his life, the woods. Which is not so surprising. His own mother was a full-blooded Montagnaise from Lake Nicabau, up the Chamouchouane River. That's why I doubt you'll get her birth certificate, by the way."

"What?" says my father, as surprised as I am. "You have native blood in your family, Lili, and you never told me?"

"You never asked," my mother says, unruffled.

My father stares at her.

"Oh come on, Paul, what do you think? Everybody has some sort of mixed blood in Québec. There were no women on the boats coming from France in the early days. You think the men kept their tackle tucked in their trousers for one hundred years? Nobody talked about it, that's all. You were looked down on if you had Indian blood."

"If Antonio Tremblay was half and half," I wonder aloud, with a certain amount of pride, "that makes Grand-Maman one quarter native, you and your brothers and sisters one eighth, and it means that one sixteenth of my blood is native!"

"I'm afraid that's not much to brag about," my father says. "What else have you never told me, Lili?"

But she is not listening. The old woman stares at us from the garage, her dog prancing around. "Monsieur Jolicoeur and his wife used to come and play bridge every Saturday night at our house, and when it was Madame Jolicoeur's turn to be the dummy, she'd come in the kitchen and play the tattle-tale instead. She said Catherine Dubois was Antonio's Métis child. His bois-brûlé."

"How old would she be?" my father says.

"Voyons voir . . ." My mother does the calculation. "Marie-Reine was born in 1904 and she married at twenty-one, in 1925. Marie-Joseph left Rodolphe's house shortly after Huguette's birth, about a year later, in 1926. The new maid was young, let's say about sixteen years old, born around 1910. So she'd be almost ninety."

"She's probably dead," says my father.

"Well, at least that puts her birthdate about eight years before Antonio's death," my mother replies.

The woman we're all watching starts to walk towards our car, holding her dog by the collar. I smile at her and lower my window, the fraction of native blood rushing in my veins. She leans down to me, smiling too. She has a pale face, no red skin, but singed eyes, rusty brown with veins of gold and deep blue water, just like the Saguenay River.

"Bonjour, Madame! We're looking for Marie-Joseph Tremblay's old house," I tell her. "Do you know where it is?"

The woman smiles but doesn't speak, holding the dog with a steady hand.

"Marie-Joseph Tremblay?" I ask her, louder. *"Tremblay?"*

She looks at all of us, studying our faces. Finally she points to her ear and starts to back off, the dog straining to get at us, panting.

"She's stone deaf," says my father.

I let myself fall back on my seat in frustration. If this is Catherine Dubois, she is the only one to know, and I'm not about to let her go. "Who are you?" I shout, my head out of the window. "Êtes-vous Catherine Dubois, la fille d'Antonio Tremblay?"

She grins. A wide, cheek to cheek, toothless, devil-may-care grin. Then she puffs up her chest and jerks her head back, a sudden fit of laughter swelling up and spilling out of her throat, rising to the sky, Ho-ho-ho! And again, Ho-ho-ho! Back and forth, her braids swinging, her dog howling along. Ho-ho-ho!

"She's insane!" my father mutters. "Let's go!"

"Wait!"

The old woman's laugh has shrunk back to a gummy grin and she digs in her pocket, shaking her head. She grabs my hand. Her joints are swollen but I can feel her strength when she makes me close my fingers on her gift. A piece of bone. Picked clean and very white, as smooth as a pebble. When I look up again she's waving at us from inside the garage while the white door whirs down, erasing her eyes first, then her grin, her jacket, the skirt, until there is only her snowmobile boots and her dog's dainty paws.

"Must be one of her dog's old bones, Lucie, you should throw it out," says my father, already driving away.

"Slow down, would you?" I hurry to note the street and address, 149 Jean De Quen. Maybe the old woman can write, if she can't hear.

"Let's go, Paul. Bernadette expects us by six for dinner in Péribonka and when Dette says six, she means six," says my mother, her voice tired.

"Are you all right, Maman? I'm sorry, maybe this is too much for you . . ."

"No, I'm glad we came, Lucie," she says. "I was very happy here."

I spin around to take a last look at the street. All the garage doors are closed. There is no more sign of life anywhere, not even a brave tulip or a new leaf yet, but the bone feels good in the cup of my hand.

Chicoutimi, Shipshaw, Péribonka.

No man running between the trees, no flash of fur and skin, no red dogsled. Antonio Tremblay was not hunting the incandescent fox we glimpsed in the red blueberry bushes by Bernadette's cottage. The coureur de bois was not on the sandy shore of the Péribonka River, shooting at the flocks of geese heading north for the summer. I didn't see him by the aluminum bridge in Arvida, in the pine grove at the Shipshaw dam, or on the long road circling Lac Saint-Jean. I didn't feel his presence either under the cream and gold vaults of Chicoutimi's grand cathedral. He was not walking on the main street, rue Racine, or chatting on the threshold of the Banque de Montréal before going in to withdraw money at the wicket. His name was not engraved beside those of his brothers, Rodolphe and Rosaire, in the cemetery, where I wandered while my parents were having a nap in the car.

Mistassini, Chamouchouane, Métabetchouane: Antonio Tremblay was nowhere to be seen. The only ones of his kind were the truck drivers drinking bad coffee at the stopover, halfway between Québec and Chicoutimi. They wore Kodiak boots and lumberjack coats, their netted baseball caps pushed back for comfort. The highways are not rivers anymore but grey ribbons of pavement, cutting through mountains and forests, riding high across streams and torrents, and the dogs have been harnessed into horsepower.

I take back to London souvenirs from the Kingdom of Sagana—two small raccoon hats from the Pointe-Bleue souvenir shop for the girls and a baseball cap from Tremblay et Fils timber yard for Laurent—but I keep my sauvage blood to myself.

Saint-Sacrement,
1943–1948

Lilianne doesn't like it here. Québec. There is no gold here, there are no singing names. Chamouchouane, Mistassini, Péribonka, Kénogami. No gold, and too many saints. Saint-Sacrement, Sainte-Foy, Saint-Cyrille. No more gold, not even the watch. They moved into a new house, but her father moved into the hospital. He never came home. He's dead. And now her mother cries all day long. She doesn't even comb her hair anymore, doesn't even dress up. Doesn't cook. The gold watch is gone and what's left is tears. The last time Lili saw her father, he was resting in a box. Fifine pushed her forward to kiss him but Lili wouldn't. His face was too thin, the skin too tight, the pink on his cheeks too bright. He had his three-piece suit on, a white starched shirt. But no watch. Where was the watch, what would he do without his watch? How would he know when it was time to go to work, or come back home? Lili looks everywhere but she can't find the watch. She asks her mother, but her mother starts to cry even harder and runs away. Huguette takes Lili on her knees.

"Fais la grande fille, Lili. Papa won't need his watch because he doesn't need to work where he is. Don't you worry. He will be happy. He already is."

"How can he be happy when Maman cries so much? How can he be happy without us? Without me?" Lili looks at Huguette, her eyes wild with indignation.

"He will miss us as much as we miss him. But he knows, and we

108

know, we will be together again one day. If we are really good."

But Huguette's voice is too soft. What Lili needs is Fifine's marching orders. What the whole tear-filled house needs is Fifine to keep everything together. Fifine will find the watch. She always finds everything. Fifine will punish Lili if she finds out she's been bad, that Lili has played all afternoon in the melting snow, big rivers flowing down the street, without a coat on or a hat, and her shoes got wet and her feet got cold, so cold. And now Lili feels hot, so hot, and her mother hasn't even noticed. Lili's body aches and her bed is soaked but there isn't anything to drink. Her lips are dry, so dry that not a word passes through her throat. Her mother wouldn't hear anyway. She is crying in her bedroom, doesn't even bother with powder on her nose. She walks barefoot, the soles of her feet crusted with dirt, her hands without rings. She doesn't know the boys are running wild, the baby needs to be changed. Or that Huguette falls asleep beside her bowl of soup at night.

"Fais la grande fille, Lili."

Lili hates it here. Saint-Sacrement. And what is this loud buzz, this vibration in her ears, up in the sky? Could it be . . . ?

A plane.

Hates it here, 1502 Louis-Fréchette, hates it in this bed where she's burning and freezing, and those maggots. Lili knows. Lili's heard enough of Fifine's stories to know. The maggots are eating her heart out, making holes like worms in an apple core. Her mother won't come, but the plane is getting closer. Let's throw the letter to the wind in small pieces like snowflakes, the letter that made her mother cry. After the letter, the gold watch disappeared. Her mother never liked this Monsieur Jolicoeur. Doesn't like Québec either, her mother said it too, I hate it here, what are we going to do? Where is Marie-Joseph? Marie-Joseph!

Lili feels lighter now that she has thrown the letter away. The bed has stopped sticking to her like glue, keeping her down. There is just this extra weight behind her eyes, making her head heavy, all the tears she hasn't shed. She was too angry to cry, but it won't stop her now, won't stop her.

Papa! Come and get me, don't forget me! Papa!

Lili rises above the sheets. She floats through the room, just a feather of a girl, but the window is closed and locked. The high light of the moon gleams on the wet street, but there it is! Lili sees the plane crossing her windowpane, still so far away. Why have you locked me in? I know I have been bad, but I've asked for forgiveness, I have said at least five paternosters, Fifine! Lili can hear Fifine's steps on the staircase, Fifine is telling stories, worms and skeletons under the bank and the end of the world. Let me out, please, Fifine, my father is looking for me. I promise I will be good.

The first time Lili leaves her room after her sickness, everything has changed. It smells good. It smells like roasted meat. Lili's mother smiles. She has powder on her nose and wears a pretty dress, although it hangs on her like a rag. Her red and gold hair is pulled back tight, streaked with silver threads, and she has blue rings under her eyes. Lili looks at her mother's brown shoes. Huguette smiles too. And Henri and Léo bring her daisies and dandelion chains. And Colette, always followed by Bernadette, shows her drawings they have made together. Lucien climbs on the bed to give her a wet kiss, his small arms tied around her neck, but they shoo him away.

"Leave your big sister alone! She needs to rest."

Everything has changed. They all look bigger, older. And there are all these people she's never seen before, going up and down the stairs with books under their arms.

"Who are all these people, Huguette?" Lili's voice has shrunk, reduced to a murmur.

"I'll tell you later, Lili. Don't talk. Don't make yourself tired. I have a surprise for you. Look who's here!"

Lili's hope stirs so hard it wakes the pain. She remembers the plane crossing her dreams.

"Lili, ma belle Lili. I am so happy to see you."

Even Fifine's voice is softer than it used to be.

"Fifine! You're back!"

"What can I say? I missed you all so much I came back to say hello."

"Are you going to stay?"

"For a little while. Until you get better, all right?"

There is another question on Lili's lips, but she knows better than to ask. Her mother is smiling, Fifine is here, why mention it? Everything has changed. It is four o'clock, and outside the closed window the spring light already thins. Under the trees the shadows dance in silence; pollen swirls in the air like gold dust.

Merci, Papa, merci.

Solitaire

Marie-Reine is playing solitaire in the dim dining room where a small red lamp is on all day long. It's raining, one of those short, tight, light spring showers, just enough water for the pale green tendrils and shoots. Marie-Reine puts the queens on kings, spade with spade, cleans up and reorders the pack of cards systematically, heart with heart. She wears a shirt, white, its starched collar closed with a tie pin, mother-of-pearl cufflinks at her thin wrists. Her husband's.

Marie-Joseph barges into the room and switches the ceiling light on. "Marie-Reine, what are you doing in the dark?" She is back with the groceries, Henri and Léo helping her with their wagons. They haul the boxes into the kitchen. No money for taxis anymore, or fancy dinners.

Marie-Reine's eyes flicker in the sudden brightness, two blinded blue moths. Her cheeks are wet, her eyes rimmed red.

"Marie-Reine?" asks Marie-Joseph, alarmed. She comes to her grieving sister and takes her by the shoulders, forcing her to look up. "Come on, Marie-Reine, get a grip on yourself. You have to fight back, you have responsibilities, and not only to his memory."

Marie-Reine refuses to lift her face; her fingers fiddle with the cards.

"May he rest in peace," Marie-Joseph mumbles, crossing herself. "But don't you think a picture of him might help? I like the one where he is in uniform, standing in front of his plane, don't you?"

"Not now. I just can't." Marie-Reine finally turns her face towards her older sister, pleading. "I can't talk either, Marie-Joseph, please."

Marie-Joseph braces herself. "Then let's play a hand of bridge, shall we?"

A shadow passes over Marie-Reine's face.

"Oh, I'm sorry, Marie-Reine. We don't have to."

Marie-Reine takes a deep breath and relaxes her shoulders. "Yes, let's! Huguette, Henri, let's play bridge!" Her enthusiasm sounds hollow.

"But what about dinner?" says Huguette from the kitchen, where she is sorting the groceries.

"Later, later!" Marie-Joseph calls.

Grilled cheese and tea were served for dinner that evening at Madame Beauregard's boarding house.

Through the Hole in Her Heart

A polar bear, a lady in a white feather hat, a snowy tree.

Lili sits still. When she lifts her head, the sky makes her dizzy. The fluffy clouds change with every gust of wind. The leaves flutter and whisper softly, a choppy sea of green mermaids with silver backs. The apple tree sheds its blooms, a rain of soft pink petals, on Lili's dress and the book left open on her knees. Lili's fingers hold on to the Sacré-Coeur de Jésus, an illustrated bookmark given to her by Fifine. The Sacred Heart is on fire, belted by thorns, and it bleeds big fat red drops. It's Fifine's way to remind her niece not to run or talk too much, to eat well, red meat, and pray for recovery. Lili sits like a princess in her Sunday dress even though it is Monday. She never gets dirty. They carry her around from one chair to another. Her feet never even touch the ground.

Lili shuts her eyes.

Lilac, apple blossoms, fresh-cut grass. The sweet smells close in on her, pushing the sounds away. Bees, flies, her brothers' screams, a ball bouncing off a wall. The kitchen window is open, the radio on: *doo-daaah, doo-daaah, wabadabadoo*. Huguette sings along, always one step behind, a clatter of pots and pans marking the beat. The musical program gives way to the five-o'clock news. June 1943, warm in the sun, cooler in the green tinted shade. The war rages on in Europe, reaching all the way to them here at home. Madame Beauregard calls, her voice clear and sharp: "Dépêche-toi, Huguette! We're late, the boarders will start to come back soon."

Lili stands still, watching the merry-go-round gallop full throttle. Her fingers loosen their grip, the Sacré-Coeur slips. The grey underwear, the tea towels, and the faded tablecloths flap on the clothesline. Colette's skipping rope scrapes the pavement with fury, Bernadette jumps in and bobs up and down, her pink cheeks quavering, a vein throbbing at the base of her neck. Colette's blonde plaits shine so fiercely in the sunlight that tears swell in Lili's eyes. Her brothers dart in and out of the cedar hedge, their legs a blur like the wings of hummingbirds, as they play tag with the neighbours. From the maple trees lining the street a thousand propellers twirl, slashing through the slower fall of petals and the low flight of the dandelion's fuzzy parachutes. The details are so sharp, the colours so intense, the fragrance so heady that Lili would rather go back to her bedroom. Instead, she closes her eyes and whispers. "God, I give you my heart. Take it, if you please, make it yours, mon doux Jésus, and may nobody ever take it away from you."

Marie-Joseph prays for two again. She doesn't pray for Marie-Reine this time, but for Lilianne to get better. She travels from Chicoutimi to Québec once a month, now that her sister answers the call of duty. She brings Lilianne, still weak from the rheumatic fever, relics, and religious medals. Marie-Joseph's husband, Edouard Bouchard, doesn't come with her to Québec. He doesn't want to sleep in any other bed than the one where he was born. He is happy like this. He is not a curious man, Edouard. Marie-Joseph has discovered that she likes to take the train and cross the Parc des Laurentides. She even talks to strangers.

"Tu vois, comme ça. You pin the relic to your undershirt, right there. That's good."

The relic is a small square of plain fabric whose virtue comes from having touched the bones of a saint. This one is from Saint-Attale's hands, kept in a shrine in Europe.

"C'est lequel, Saint-Attale, Fifine?"

Fifine never travels without her book of the saints. *"We remember Saint-Attale on the second of June, the anniversary of his death in Lyon, in the year 177,"* she reads. *"Saint-Attale was one of the disciples of Saint-Pothin, first bishop of Lyon. They were all arrested and tortured by Marc-Aurèle, the Roman emperor. Saint-Attale, while he was sizzling on a hot iron chair, defended the Christians from some odious accusations. He shouted, 'It is not us Christians who eat other men, it is you.' His tormentors also asked him what his God's name was and he answered, 'We have names because we are mere mortals. God has no need for a name.'"*

"How come there are no saints from Québec in your book, Fifine?" On every street corner and none in the book.

"Did you know," Fifine answers, "that Jean de Brébeuf, the saintliest of the Canadian martyrs, fell on his knees when he saw his torture post, and kissed it? And that the Iroquois also cut the skin off his scalp in the shape of a crown and put burning embers on his exposed brain? Saint-Jean de Brébeuf was the bravest they had known, and that's why they honoured him by eating his heart."

"I think he suffered much more than Saint-Attale, don't you think, Fifine?"

"I think so too, but to make room for Saint-Jean de Brébeuf, we would have to kick another saint out. We are a young country, but our day will come. Next time I'll try to bring you a relic from Mère Marie de l'Incarnation. She is not a saint yet, but they're talking about her beatification in Rome. You can go and kneel right where her bones are, in the chapel of the Ursuline convent where your mother went to school. And when you're stronger, we'll make a pilgrimage to Ste-Anne-de-Beaupré to see the crutches and the canes hooked on the walls by all the people who were cured, healed by their faith. That's why you have to believe, Lili."

"Oh, I do, I do, Fifine. "

"Then let's pray for our beloved deceased, let's pray for your father."

"I am sure he is all right now, Fifine. Should we pray for another father, one who needs it more?" Lili asks, her big eyes as innocent as a swatch of clear sky. "What about yours, Fifine?"

The girl looks just like her mother. Marie-Joseph signs herself and waits a little before saying in a kind voice, "There's always been only one father for me, Lili, and you know where he is." She points upwards with her bony chin. "I never needed any other. Notre Père, qui êtes aux Cieux."

Two Sisters, She Knows Better

Madame Beauregard est une femme d'un certain âge. Yes, a woman of a certain age. At forty she is a widow, a mother of seven, and a boarding-house lady to four. So much to do, so little time. She wears brown shoes, scuffed, with curling toes, thinning soles, and broken eyelets. Nobody calls Madame Beauregard Marie-Reine anymore but her sister.

As for Madame Édouard Bouchard, or Mademoiselle Tremblay as many people still call her in Chicoutimi, for the first time in her life she has nobody to take care of. Monsieur Bouchard is out all day doing his mail round and he spends the summer evenings fishing. Marie-Joseph is as stiff as a two-by-four. It's as if inactivity has taken a bigger toll on her than washing clothes in cold water, scrubbing floors bent in two, and praying on her knees. Her knuckles have swollen and her joints ache. She still bends at the knees, even though they hurt, but not at the waist. She tries to help in Marie-Reine's house when she visits, but nowadays all she does is get in the way. Even Huguette gets impatient when her aunt insists on slowly pushing crumbs into the dustpan in the middle of the crowded kitchen.

The two sisters sit together at night in the dining room where nobody ever dines. The big table is pushed against the wall, littered with books, food vouchers, newspapers, wool spools, patterns, and fabric remnants. It is really a sitting room, with rocking chairs scattered around the big radio. Madame Beauregard is swift and sharp, with no more time for solitaire. She cooks and cleans and sews and knits for everybody, and she makes do. Everybody does. This is 1944 and the war keeps on spreading from the Atlantic to the Pacific, sparing nobody. Prime Minister Mackenzie King has promised not to conscript in Canada, but there is increasing pressure to do so. The Allies are running out of men along a front line stretching across Europe and the Pacific. Boys as young as fourteen can become part of the reserve army with a signature from their parents. In Québec there have been demonstrations in the streets, riots, and burnt Union Jacks. Why should French Canadians enrol in English regiments where they feel they don't get a fair chance to become officers and will be used as cannon fodder on the front line? Why should they give their lives to defend the British, the very people who tried over and over again to defeat them and cut off their French roots?

"Don't forget, housekeepers, your war effort! Do not waste any bacon or frying fat. Strain it and pour it in a can, and bring it to the closest butcher every time you have a pound. He will pay you the fixed rate, and don't forget, mesdames . . ."

Madame Beauregard is working on a sweater, twin flying ducks. She's out of brown and green so they spread their wings in orange and blue. The two older boys grow so fast: Henri is nearly seventeen, Léo fifteen. They have their father's nose, long and thin, the same droopy eyelids on steel grey eyes.

Marie-Joseph looks sideways at her sister, slumped in her chair. No more loose strands or unruly curls; the silver and gold are pulled right back in a tight bun. Forty and a woman of a certain age, her beauty not what it used to be, her charming wit sharpened into caustic humour. Marie-Reine's je ne sais quoi, the beacon of light she has cast for so long, has faded. The lines in her face have set, more frowns than smiles, deepest between the brows. She's gained back some weight, her flesh obvious and loose under her dress.

"Dis-moi donc, Marie-Reine . . . Don't you wear a corset anymore?"

"My old ones were too tight, I couldn't breathe. I gave them to Huguette."

Marie-Joseph's sharp eyes slip down to her sister's thin legs, crossed at the ankles. The white skin is firm, just a few blue veins running under the surface.

"No stockings either?"

"No. No stockings."

"Really, Marie-Reine! You're letting yourself go."

"Think of it as my own war effort, if it bothers you," answers Marie-Reine, her old indolence gone. "Once you don't care to please men anymore, comfort becomes more important than elegance. And I have other things on my mind."

"Ten pounds of fat equals explosive for forty-nine air bombs! Straight from the frying pan to the line of fire, oui, mesdames!"

"You won't marry again, then?"

"Why bother?" is Marie-Reine's answer, her voice weary. "There are no men left anyway with this war going on."

"Just like after the first one." Marie-Joseph sighs. "I would know, wouldn't I?" Her inquisitive eyes search past the living room's sliding doors where the piano, inherited after Rodolphe Tremblay's death, gathers dust. "You don't play piano either, do you?" she asks again, pretending to work on a pair of socks.

"Can't keep a boarding house, feed a family, *and* play piano, can I?"

"What about the girls?"

"No money for the lessons, no time to teach them. I'm thinking of selling it."

"That would be a shame."

There are only two or three books on the table, but Lili has told Fifine about many others in her mother's bedroom cupboard. "I hear you read a lot."

"I read at night, when I can't sleep."

"What sort of books are they?"

"French books, novels."

"Not everything that comes from Europe is commendable, I heard the curé tell us."

"I heard it too, Marie-Joseph," Marie-Reine snaps. "I go to church every Sunday with the children and I even wear stockings and a hat, if you must know."

Saturday night, seven o'clock: it's time for "Jean-Baptiste s'en va-t-en guerre," recorded in London. All of Québec listens to the broadcast of messages sent in by their boys stationed overseas, hoping to hear the voice of a son, a fiancé. The young soldiers speak up in turn: *"Your last letter made me so happy, I have already read it a dozen times! If you only knew how ready I am, how ready to fight for you."*

"They should know better," says Marie-Reine with a grunt. Fools for love. Marie-Reine has seen the women to whom these letters are sent. They hang on the arms of any English sailors or soldiers stationed in the port of Québec before their departure overseas, their pockets full of money from their factory jobs, living for today. Love isn't forever.

"Each one of your letters brings me the courage to 'carry on,' as the English say. The victory is at our door and soon we will be reunited again, as before."

"I am almost happy I don't have children, with all this going on. Although if I had a son, I would be proud of whatever he could do against the forces of evil," says Marie-Joseph.

"How would you know, Marie-Joseph? And what would you do if your eighteen-year-old son, far from being the hero you wanted him to be, married the girl next door in a hurry or begged you to cut his finger off with an axe because he didn't want to be blown to pieces on a beach in Normandy?"

Marie-Joseph looks down, abruptly.

"Everything is always black and white with you. Why should I send my sons to fight for England? We already give them all our bacon, our eggs, our butter, all for the British. Enough is enough. My sons are going to university, not to war. I'll scrimp and take more lodgers if I have to."

Marie-Joseph doesn't answer. The radio breaks the silence: *"Jerry is right above us, the sirens can be heard for miles, everybody is nervous. But I am in my room, writing to you. If you receive this letter, and it isn't finished, you will know that Jerry caught me . . ."*

On the wall above the table where nobody dines, there's a map of Europe showing the Allies' progress. Every day it is updated religiously by Henri and Léo. They spend long hours with a pair of binoculars on the Plains of Abraham, trying to spot the enemy's submarines in the St. Lawrence, their slingshots stuck in their waistbands. They dream of glory while their mother can think only of death. She just hopes she never has to wield an axe on her own children.

"Jean-Baptiste s'en va-t-en guerre" is over and Marie-Joseph is asleep in her chair. The Saturday-night hockey game from Montréal is on the radio, the only program that makes Marie-Reine stop knitting.

"Envoye, vas-y, Rocket, vas-y, Maurice!"

Les Anglais say the Montréal Canadiens are winning because all the best English players have volunteered for war. Maurice Rocket Richard has tried to enrol but they turned him down. Hockey injuries. More useful here, supporting the morale of the population. War cannot be all there is. There's already no tea or coffee, so little sugar, stretching the butter with milk and gelatin. "Envoye, Maurice!"

"He shoots, he scores! And it's a hat trick for Maurice Richard and the Canadiens tonight!"

"Quoi? Quoi?"

Marie-Reine's cheers wake up Marie-Joseph.

Her Mother's Shoes

Six heures du matin. Get out of bed and get going, Huguette. The floor is cold and it's dark in the early morning, all the bulbs forty watts instead of one hundred. Save the heat, they say, save the light. Save electricity for the army plants, save on everything. But what about life? Huguette is eighteen.

She throws water on her face; the white towel is grey and rough from second-rate soap and cold-water washings. Then Huguette grabs her clothes from the chair, by the wobbly desk where she left them last night. She puts her ill-fitting corset on, her mother's hand-me-down. She has to stuff the cups with thin Victory toilet paper, so scratchy on her breasts. Got to make do. She is going to itch all day.

They now have eight lodgers, two per room on the third floor. Henri, Léo, and Lucien have to sleep together in a double bed, Lili with Huguette, Bernadette, and Colette in the small room by the front door. The children are growing. They eat so much and food is scarce, inflation is soaring. She throws her mother's old navy blue dress on, the one with chains of daisies. The fabric is now worn, the colour faded, the dainty flowers exhausted. A narrow strip of fabric was left after Huguette took it in. She ties it around her neck when she goes to church on Sunday. She wishes the scarf would billow behind her in a romantic way, but the fabric is too heavy. It dangles along her back, above the seams of her fake silk stockings. They lied on the bottle: *doesn't stain, easy to rub off, won't run in the rain.* Huguette applies the lotion on her stringy legs every Sunday morning and asks Lili to draw the black line with a pencil. Even the curé is fooled, and thank God he is. What would he think, bare legs in church! She wishes she didn't care, like her mother. This is no time for vanity, but Huguette is still young.

Her dress doesn't smell fresh. Huguette's own laundry comes last, after the lodgers' sheets and Lucien's and Bernadette's soiled clothes. Huguette ties a big brown leather belt around her waist to hold the corset and the floppy dress in place. Her father's belt. Huguette had to hammer extra holes in with a sharp nail, but it does the job. She hurries and stuffs her feet in the scarlet shoes, the extravagant silk shoes with a little heel that she stole from her mother's cupboard. They might be dirty, but they are still like a flash of hope in the grey wartime days. They are also a little tight. Huguette has bigger feet than her mother.

She heads downstairs, her hand on the banister, careful not to tap her noisy heels on the bare steps. The first thing she does is turn the radio on in the sitting room. Then she boils water, a big batch with the cover on the pot and only one light on. On the back porch is a pile of newspapers, another one of bones, an old tobacco can filled with grease, filtered and clean. Dirty rags in a heap. Salvaging is Henri and Léo's job, but the porch is overflowing. Won't they stop the news and put some music on? It helps Huguette, the music, gives her an upbeat rhythm. And singing cleans the algebra away, the numbers still crowding her head from last night. Hot water but no coffee, no tea. Just hot water and toast, no butter, and the thinnest coating of tart marmalade. Coffee and oatmeal on Saturdays and Sundays only. Bitter black tea after dinner. That's all. Huguette has caught her mother with her finger in the precious butter. Here she comes. Huguette hears her steps, slow, heavy, steady. She never stops working. After Huguette has dished out breakfast to her brothers and sisters and the lodgers, when she leaves for school, her mother cleans and dries the dishes, her mother sweeps, her mother shops, chops, and peels, her mother stirs the pots, cooks, and serves the food with an even hand, and then her mother knits— socks and mitts and scarves, sweaters—while she listens to the radio. And then her mother goes to bed, but she doesn't sleep; the light under her door burns as late as Huguette's. Her mother reads.

Why does it need to be like this? The lodgers have all day and all night to study, and Henri and Léo too. When Huguette comes back from school, she helps her three younger sisters with their homework.

"Des voyou*s* . . . Des chou*x* . . . It's an exception, Coco, remember? Bijou-caillou-chou-genou-hibou, plural in *x* instead of *s*. Dette, le verbe être, à l'indicatif présent."

"Je suis, tu es, il est, nous sommes, vous êtes, ils sont."

Dinner, dishes, sponge baths in lukewarm water, a real bath and hair washed only once a week. Huguette makes the girls kneel for their prayers, repeat the catechism, sing a hymn or two, and then she tells them a story. They ask for princesses and charming princes. Huguette doesn't have the courage to tell them the truth. How they might have to make do without love if this war goes on killing the young men.

Huit heures du soir. Huguette has no time to smile, although when she does she is pretty. A pretty brunette with sparkling eyes, the thin mouth forgotten. Most of the girls her age have a soldier on their mind and spend the war waiting for the mailman. Not Huguette. When everything else has been dealt with, when the double feature starts at the local cinema, Huguette walks up to her room and shuts the door. She sits at her desk where math books are piled high beside bitten pencils and a chewed-up eraser. She is so tired, but this is the only time left to study. The numbers lose their sharp familiar edges, the algebra formulas melt away, the already dim light fades out. Huguette dreams of the charming prince, and her charming prince is a serious young man with books under his arm. Not a soldier. He comes walking through her dreams, but she can't follow him. She can't open her eyes, can't lift an arm, or wave, or call. Her head is so heavy, a paperweight on the unfinished homework.

Huguette is so tired, all she wants to do is cry. Her mother wants her to stop going to school to get a job at the factory. Sticking her hand inside the shells with sandpaper, stitching miles of parachutes, putting wires and screws in radio boxes. All day long, the same one gesture. You don't even need a brain to do this, but the pay is good, thirty dollars a month. They need the money for Henri's university. Huguette knows that's not what her father had in mind for her. She wants to be an accountant, just like him. She lifts her head, rubs her eyes, and goes on with the numbers. When the line of light under her door goes off, it's past midnight. Huguette has shed the paper stuffing, her father's belt. She is just a slender girl, tired to the bone but dead certain no charming prince is going to sweep her off her feet, out of her dirty scarlet shoes, until her arithmetic dreams come true.

Grand Séminaire de Québec, le 2 juin 1945

Madame Beauregard,

I felt the need to send a letter with the school examination results of your two sons, Henri and Léopold.
First to Henri's performance. It is exceptional. I want to underline the need for your son to go on with his studies, and I

think a university degree in engineering is what he should be aiming for. I also realize that to go on studying costs money, and I understand your financial circumstances have been reduced since your husband's departure for a better world, que Dieu ait son âme. I just thought I would let you know that the Grand Séminaire is always ready to support exceptional students with an interest in the vocation. Henri is a very good boy, studious and perceptive. A mother certainly would be the best person to sound a son's soul. Henri was so absorbed in his studies last year, he never had the time to do so himself. University or a vocation within the Church would also prevent, as you are probably aware, any imminent departure. I don't need to remind you how long and devastating this terrible war has been, and although it is over in Europe, our neighbours in the United States are still fighting Japan in the Pacific. God only knows when and how this conflict will end. We would never want or wish to force anybody's hand or heart, but I just want to remind you of the options available for a boy as promising as Henri.

But now to a less brilliant performance, that is, Léopold's results. Two brothers couldn't possibly be so unlike one other.

Léopold's marks have been going from low to below average, and it is not for a lack of intelligence. But Léopold's attitude, his unacceptable behaviour, his weakness in front of every evil and temptation, be it alcohol, gambling, frolicking, swearing (and the list goes on), make it impossible for me to recommend him for any further education within our Cours Classique. I tried as hard as I could to be the father figure he seems to need desperately, but to no avail. I think it is time to find an education better suited to his present state of mind. Thus I would recommend a switch to Collège Technique: nuts and bolts and electricity might hold his attention better than algebra and physics. And within a year he could start earning wages.

If you wish to discuss these two matters any further, please do not hesitate to meet with me. It is always a pleasure to keep the dialogue alive between parents, teachers, and students, under God's attentive ears.

Yours truly,

Père Maurice Rodrigue
Directeur du Cours Classique
Séminaire de Québec

Forbidden Words

The Abbé Audette's name is posted outside the confessional in Saint-Sacrement's church, but the sinner is anonymous behind the red velvet curtains. Confidentiality is guaranteed by a golden lattice separating the confessor from the confessed. Madame Beauregard steps in and sneezes before she kneels. Every time. It must be the dust. Click. The red light outside switches on. "Occupé."

"Mon père, je m'accuse . . ."

The Abbé Audette and Madame Beauregard have a good working relationship. He has seen her through the loss of her husband, her grieving. He has come to her house often, throwing the word of God as a buoy to a woman sunk deep in depression. With moderate success. He came back again to administer the last rites to Madame Beauregard's daughter Lilianne, when they thought she wouldn't make it. A tough breed, these Beauregards, their roots somewhere in the thick woods of the Saguenay.

"Father, I have sinned. I have read *L'Assomoir*, by Emile Zola, without knowing it was one of the forbidden books from the Index list."

"Did you like it?"

The books Madame Beauregard reads can't be found in the libraries or the bookstores. Seuil, Gallimard, the pages come uncut, their edges rough, the paper unbleached. One of Madame Beauregard's old friends from the Ursuline convent, who now lives in France, sends them to her. She reads them at night, propped up on two pillows, butter knife in hand. The children might come in and out of her bed, trailing various ailments and nightmares, the boarders might tiptoe up or down the stairs, shoes in hand, but nothing stops her. She rips the pages open, one after the other, and devours the words.

"Yes, I did. I have never read anything like it before, all the laundry, all the misery! It was hard work even to read, it wrenched my guts, it's like my life. It's almost life itself, isn't it?"

"An interesting work, for sure."

"I must confess, Father, that I don't understand why it is deemed unchristian to read Emile Zola's books."

"Well, it is not this book in particular, it's Monsieur Zola's oeuvre in general that is condemned. No redemption, no hope. His later work has attacked the Church in a particularly virulent fashion, and although I know you are a discerning reader, most people aren't. I will have to ask you not to waste any more of your time in the company of the black-listed books. The absence of faith, the emptiness at the core of some of these works, is chilling. Others are pure and simple trash, atheist anthems or communist tracts, like this Charles Baudelaire. Avez-vous lu le dernier de Gabrielle Roy? *The Tin Flute*, now that's a good book!"

"You mean another story of giving in to duty? Non, merci!"

All Madame Beauregard can think about is the next shipment from France. Another Zola, *Nana*, and a certain Gustave Flaubert's *Madame Bovary*, still a succès de scandale more than fifty years later. She can't wait.

"If you want absolution, Madame Beauregard, you will have to promise not to read one more forbidden word."

As usual, there is a price to pay for the pleasure: Index librorum prohibitorum. Madame Beauregard has had her doubts for a long time, but this is the last straw. It must be a fragile God to be so afraid of thin fonts on flimsy sheets of paper, pigment and pulp, and it must be a servile Church to listen to this fragile God's instructions to expurgate or burn the books. It would be easy to go on reading at night and still show up on Sundays for mass with her children, in the sweet comfort of this crimson and gold world.

"Lying is a sin, Father."

"It is indeed, Madame Beauregard."

"I can't make that promise. I can't see anything wrong with these books."

"It is not for you to decide, Madame Beauregard."

"I am forty-two years old, Father. If I am old enough to work myself raw bringing up seven children in a decent manner, I think I am old enough to decide what is good for me and what isn't. You don't understand, Father. Those words make me feel alive!"

"What about the words of God, Madame Beauregard, what about the Bible, the daily prayers? Don't they make you feel alive?"

"To be honest, Father, they're starting to feel as tired as my bones. God's words speak of death much more than life. They threaten rather than inspire too much for my taste. Merci quand même, mon Père, merci pour tout."

Madame Beauregard gets up slowly with a sigh and a huff. She has gained even more weight. The flowers on her dress have expanded as well.

"Madame Beauregard!"

Click. The red light switches off.

Madame Beauregard pushes the curtain away. The air feels fresh and cool, free-flowing under the high stone nave. She takes out a kerchief to sponge her sweaty forehead under the hat band. She pulls her dress down, smooths the wrinkles, pushes the kerchief up her sleeve, readjusts the angle of her hat, then lights a candle in memory of her beloved husband, Léandre. She would like to hear him laugh with her, discussing the finer points and absurdities of the Church's politics. Instead, she drops a dime in the near-empty tin box, and the small clang clamours in the expanse of the church. Madame Beauregard's loneliness is just as vast, and full of the lingering echoes of her married life. But she knows better than to start feeling sorry for herself again. She is also lucky. Only one candle to light up, only one clang in the tin box.

She genuflects to the Virgin. Mary doesn't look like someone who would care about a forbidden book or two. She is a woman, after all.

Madame Beauregard walks down the aisle, nodding to her neighbour, Germaine Lasalle, on her way out. She already knows what the likes of Madame Lasalle will say. When the Church told the Lasalles of this province to vote for the Union Nationale and its leader, Maurice Duplessis, they did. They are in cahoots, the clergy helping the politicians to get elected, the politicians staying out of the clergy's territory, and both keeping the dreaded Liberals and their new ideas at bay. So if the Abbé Audette, the parish priest, says to stay away from the books listed on the Index, why doesn't Madame Beauregard go and enjoy an evening playing bingo instead? Or bridge, if she likes it. Whatever. There are other books. There are enough books. Madame Beauregard takes her summer gloves off, dips a chapped hand in the holy water, lightly sketches God's sign upon her face, her chest, and her shoulders. Then she walks out for good, chin up into the blinding sunlight.

The next day she gives her rainbow of old shoes to the Salvation Army. She needs more room for the forbidden novels.

Henri

It's Monday night, seven o'clock. Madame Beauregard waits by the phone. He phones on Mondays, Wednesdays, and Fridays. She visits him on Sundays. Her son, Henri. In the sanatorium.

What was she to do?

Madame Beauregard sits by the phone at the bottom of the stairs with the lights turned off. In the bright kitchen Lilianne and Colette are doing the dishes with the radio on. They swing to the jazz line, tea towels flung over their shoulders, wet hands in wet hands. The mood is light, the war behind them. Huguette is in the sitting room holding hands with Chris Morris, an engineer from Ontario doing his apprenticeship at the Dominion Textile plant. The first of her children's romances is taking place in English . . . Madame Beauregard would laugh if she could. Léandre had courted her in a conversation sprinkled with British expressions. Chris Morris tries his best to win them over, his French laborious and slow. But this is just a stray thought. All stray thoughts race away. Henri. Who wants to live in a house with tuberculosis? If she'd kept him home, the lodgers would have left. And what about her other children? She had to send him to the sanatorium, in St-Adolphe de Stoneham, and she got the telephone installed.

"Maman! Téléphone! Ben réponds, voyons!" Colette's face in the doorframe is puzzled. "Réponds!"

They haven't found a cure yet for tuberculosis.

"Maman?"

That's where they put them to die.

"Henri? C'est toi, Henri?"

Every time, she's scared.

"Oui, Maman. C'est moi."

"How are you today, Henri?"

"Not so great, Maman." Henri's voice is no more than a whisper. "When you come next Sunday, Docteur Pratte will show you the X-rays. I have been here three months and in spite of the fresh air, good food, and bed rest, it is worse. This operation is my only chance, Maman. Docteur Pratte is a specialist. He thinks my chances are really good because I'm young, and still strong. Please, Maman. Sign the form."

"I can't. I can't do this to you, Henri. It was hard enough to send you to the sanatorium, but this, I can't! It's not surgery, it's slaughter, pure and simple."

"But if I stay here . . . You've heard the wheezing, the hacking, during the day, but you don't know what it's like to listen to this night after night after night!"

Madame Beauregard has locked herself in the living room. She opens the piano lid. Her hands span the width and breadth of the keyboard, her fingers travel along its surface without playing. Charting the territory. Her knuckles are stiff from all the dishes, the potato peeling, the knitting. The white ivory is smooth and familiar, the black keys just slightly rougher. Tentative at first, she lets the sound rise, an incomplete scale here and there, major, minor, feeling for the tension of the cords, the pressure of the hammers. The sound is loose, out of tune. Madame Beauregard doesn't even like music anymore. She plays so they won't hear her cry. Her daughters, her lodgers. Léandre.

On the first X-rays, it was no bigger than a nickel. An opaque area on the translucent shape of the lung. A small shadow, tuberculosis. Henri's chest so white. He has turned twenty in the sanatorium.

Presto, prestissimo. Con brio.

What the doctors want to do is cut through the white skin of his chest and saw the ribs, taking three or more out. Thoracoplasty. Then sew him back up and wait. The soft tissue falls in, collapsing the diseased lung, setting the scene for the next operation. The pneumonectomy. When the pain subsides, when the wounds heal, when the patient has regained some sort of strength, if the patient has survived, they will go at it all over again.

Forte, fortissimo, mezzo-forte.

Slashing through Henri's skin and muscles with knives, tearing out his empty lung.

Furioso.

Maybe that's why nature has given us two of almost everything, she thinks. So that we have a spare. Maybe there are two Gods too, a spare one for those who don't believe.

Appassionato, ostinato.

Once the lung is out, the disease should stop spreading, but the pain after the operation is terrible. Morphine, oxygen masks, catheters, enemas, the hose draining the side. The cough, making the shoulder slip out of place, the slow uphill battle to sit on the edge of the bed, to walk. The ones who have had the operation are easy to spot. Marie-Reine has seen them creep along the corridors with their backs bent, protecting their damaged chest from anybody, anything, who could touch it, hurt it some more, holding their temporarily paralyzed arm. Henri's posture would be changed forever, one shoulder down, the chest's volume flattened, its symmetry altered. A stray knife could also mean a useless arm and hand for life. Who do they think they are? Docteur Pratte is ambitious, and he says it is a revolutionary operation. The survivors have a good chance of recovery.

Strings and hammers and ivories, black and white, a solid bronze table inside. Upright piano.

Spirituoso.

She thought she would have forgotten the music lessons from the convent. Grief has claws, long and tough. The first war, the flu, her mother's death, and what happened to her father? Marie-Joseph said he was dead, but Madame Jolicoeur told her nobody had seen the body. She waited and waited for him to come back for so long.

Chamouchouane, Mistassini, Péribonka, Chicoutimi.

Madame Beauregard's mind sinks into the past, and the past spills from her fingers, the notes rushing down, a wild scramble of arpeggio and counterpoint, strange melodies. Her foot on the forte pedal, calling for her father's strength, her husband's wisdom. Good thing her fingers remember because she can't see for all the tears, can't think straight for the sorrow.

Métabetchouane, Shipshaw, Piékouagami, Sagana.

She will have to start believing again, for her son's sake. She won't allow them to rip through the flesh of her flesh like butchers carving through a quarter of meat. Henri didn't escape the horrors of war to finish like this. He will have to start believing too.

The door opens. "C'est donc ben beau ce que tu joues-là, Maman." Léo can barely stand, a smile plastered on his face. He reeks of beer and smoke, and his shirt-tail hangs out.

Marie-Reine's anger pulls her up, and she shoves her other son against the wall as hard as she can, punching, kicking, with her fists, her feet, again and again. Again.

Deuxième Relation:
The Brides

IT's early summer in London, the cool winter grey flecked first with bright yellow daffodils and orange tulips, then with mauve and magenta rhododendrons while the trees push electric green leaves and the merry-go-round of buses goes on in red. On a sunny day, it almost looks garish; garish and allergenic, the air thick with pollen and pollution. Too many male trees in London, claim the newspapers, blaming their more potent pollen for the abnormal number of respiratory tract ailments afflicting the urban population. A shot of nasal spray to coat the soft tissue with steroids or a puff from an inhaler alleviates the symptoms temporarily, but I hate to use the drugs on my children. Both Marion and Madelon cough at night, their noses raw from blowing, their eyes as red and tearful as mine. A permanent drip at the back of my throat tastes metallic. The only thing that keeps me going right now is the promise of a month in a rented cottage by the St. Lawrence. I don't know what keeps Laurent going anymore. He usually joins us for two weeks, but not this year.

"A week? Maybe?" I cry out to him.

Laurent throws his hands up and shrugs, heading for the door. "Can we talk about this later?" I know we won't talk about this or anything else, now or later. Laurent's silence is like silt, stubborn and slow, building up into a rock. His rounded shoulders, the slow shuffle of his feet when he walks into the apartment after work, the big set of keys, a sharp jangle he throws on the table. The briefcase he drops. The way he lets himself collapse on the couch, the sky a paperweight pushing him down a little more every day. "What is happening at the hospital is tragic, but what about us?" Us, again. An empty shell filled with the echo of the past.

I grab Laurent's arm and yank him away from the door. "Look at me, would you? Not only sick infants can die, Laurent." Anger hisses through my clenched teeth, my nose sealed solid and my eyes unbearably itchy. "And do you know what's next?" I let go of his arm. "I won't care anymore either."

It's as if I've just beaten him up. "How can you think I don't care? I do care, I care so much. I know you're unhappy here, and I just can't bear to be the reason why. But what do you want me to do? How can I go for Sunday walks by the Thames while parents are crying for the child they have lost in our care? Give me some time, and I promise I'll get us out of here as soon as I've done my report. We'll go back home, if this is what you want, and I'll stay away from vital organ design, okay? Look at me, I promise. Artificial hips, glass eyes, cyber hands. Brain chips for rodents . . ."

I laugh. My hands reach for the sudden smile that floods his face with light. When he smiles, he is the young man with a racy book in his hands again. He takes me by the waist and brings me close to him, my silk shirt against his wool sweater sending static sparks flying.

"I love you, Lucie," he says. "Please help me get through this."

London wouldn't be so grey if there were more moments like this. I have a hard time keeping track of what I read at the library as I gather information for a gender studies professor from McGill University. Her thesis tries to define the politics of reproduction in Nouvelle-France but all I can see is couples walking hand in hand or kissing on the wide marble steps leading to the sunny courtyard.

*　*　*

Keyword: Hélène de Champlain.

The sixteenth-century physicians of the Old World believe a woman is made of cold and wet humours, and a man of hot and dry ones. The woman's character is described as changeable and deceptive. Her womb is a hungry animal, which must be fed by sexual intercourse and kept busy with reproduction; otherwise, the unruly beast might overtake the woman's senses. Champlain notes that among the tribes of the New World are found powerful women of extraordinary stature. He adds, admiringly, that their breasts hang down very little except when they are old.

In between Roberval's failed attempt at settlement in 1543 and the revival of the colony a century later, very few women crossed the Atlantic Ocean to Nouvelle-France. The first one to settle in Québec, in 1617, is Marie Rollet, the wife of Louis Hébert. In 1620, another woman gets off the ship. She is the wife of Samuel de Champlain, the royal navigator who founded Québec City in 1608.

Hélène de Champlain walks down the precarious gangway, having no choice but to lean on her husband. Her sea legs refuse to acknowledge solid ground. The crossing was very long, two months spent battling the rough seas of the northern Atlantic.

The woman standing in front of Madame de Champlain is as tall as a man. She is dressed in soft skins almost the colour of her own, ornate with scarlet porcupine quills. Her long black hair is tied with bones and feathers, her inquisitive hands are large and square, the palms thick and hard. *Canisa!* she says. Snow. She touches Hélène de Champlain's skin, as pale as a moon. Not that there's much of it showing: only the pinched-up face, both hands, and a little strip around the neck.

Hélène de Champlain is well trained in the art of composure. She withstands the scrutiny with her chin up, her mouth shut and her back straight, sweating in her heavy dress. Past the small crowd gathered on the muddy landing, all she can see of the habitation her husband showed her on his drawing board is a dirty courtyard littered with debris. No curl of smoke peeling from the chimney. No flying colours in the wind. And where are the pretty gardens, Versailles-style? The habitations' planks have shrunk, leaving big gaps for the wind to blow through, and the roofs let water in where the buildings are still standing. A half-collapsed wall gives the settlement an air of abandon, and the white faces dotting the small crowd of natives are still taut from the punishing winter and the grieving of many deaths.

The leather-clad giantess now touches the flounces of Madame de Champlain's dress, *cabata*, an ample and sad-looking expanse of dark wool fabric. Then she reaches for the lace of the scarf crossed on the white woman's breast and tugs at the calico bonnet. The bonnet falls in the mud and the long golden fleece of Madame de Champlain's hair spills on her shoulders.

Isnay! The sun!

Madame de Champlain's eyes dart up and down and all around, betraying a mix of guarded distaste and curiosity. At least the air is uncorrupted, the St. Lawrence River still ten times wider than the Seine where it narrows. She has spent the whole voyage locked up in a small, fetid room, enduring the sounds of wave after wave of broken china while cursing her husband between retches.

The tall woman now marvels at the white woman's blue eyes. *Queneya*, the sky. She reaches for the necklace, the earrings. She approves. She would like to explore the white woman's body to make sure they are the same, but it is hidden like a precious thing behind layer upon layer of fabric. Emboldened, she lifts the pale face's long skirt and again coos at the sight: first the red stockings, her favourite colour, and then the size of the *atha*. The shoes. This is the whitest, stiffest, smallest person she has ever seen, her wrist bones no bigger than a large bird's skeleton. Hélène de Champlain pushes her skirt down with one swift hand, her fingers reaching for the cross at her neck. From her lips silent words of prayer are born. She traces the sign of the cross upon the First Woman of God, the tall tanned woman with a generous mouth full of very white teeth. There is no sugar here, no salt.

The native woman takes Hélène de Champlain's hand, as fragile as birchbark, a hand that has never gathered wood and rocks, never prepared skins or kneaded sagamité. What could such hands have done for a living?

These hands have turned the pages of immaculate books, written with the lightest goose quill, grazed the ivory of a clavichord, plucked the strings of a harp. These hands have lain like shot doves on the sheets as Monsieur de Champlain, twenty-eight years older than his child bride, has claimed his conjugal rights.

But the copper-toned woman cannot read this story in the small, reluctant hand. She encourages the white woman to reciprocate and touch her own clothing, the quills, the beads. Then she takes her wampum necklace, made of shells that are her people's most precious possession, and offers it to the white woman, a smile rippling on her lips. If Hélène de Champlain knew that the natives submerged a corpse, slashed open at the thighs, buttocks, arms, and shoulders, in the river and brought it back up after half a day to harvest the shells, she might have backed off in horror. But she doesn't know. Hélène de Champlain thinks it looks like a paternoster, a rosary, and on a sudden impulse she unties the black grosgrain ribbon from her neck and offers her silver filigree cross to the other woman.

Ho! Ho! Ho! says the woman, in hearty cheer. And the native part of the crowd assembled on the shore joins in and repeats, in one big booming voice, lifting the last syllable up to the sky, Ho! Ho! Ho!

Oui, oui, oui. Wild and free.

Hélène de Champlain will soon learn how these women live. How they can stare for hours at their reflection in mirrors, having only known the still water of the lakes before. How easily they rejoice at the mere sight of brightly coloured ribbons or treasures of trinkets and glass beads. How they dress in skins and Normandy blankets, and can walk through snow almost naked. How they paddle in bark boats, and how these boats become the roof they sleep under in the summer. How they sleep inside hide tents in winter, with bear blankets and spruce boughs thrown on the snow for bedding. How everything belongs to everybody, how the mothers never scold the children, and husbands and wives never need to quarrel because they can part if they wish to. How the women work as hard as men and the men live within the women's families and have no authority over them. How they suffer from hunger and cold in winter, and from mosquitoes and flea bites in the summer. How they never save for tomorrow and live for today. How they think this is the best life because it is the only life they know and how they are still innocent of their sins. Hélène de Champlain will pity them, but she will envy them too. She will give the Huron and the Montagnais women mirrors, beads, and ribbons, along with the word of God, but still they will be free. Free to dance all night and strip down by the feast's fire, and free to lie down with the man they choose for the night.

Hélène Boullé was bought by Champlain when she was still a twelve-year-old child. Champlain was wealthy but he needed political clout at the court of the newly appointed king. Louis XIII had succeeded his murdered father, Henri de Navarre. He was controlled by his powerful mother, Maria de Medici, who was advised by the ambitious Cardinal Richelieu. Champlain was looking for an insider to lobby for him and help fund his grand obsession, the exploration of Canada and the establishment of its first colony, Québec. So he married Hélène, daughter of Marguerite and Nicolas Boullé, secretary of the King's Chamber.

The wedding contract dealt in matters financial, spiritual, and sexual, allowing for two years before the consummation of the union, because of the bride's tender age. When she turned fourteen, Madame de Champlain lay down with this man who was older than her own father. She was sixteen when she ran away and went into hiding, bringing dishonour to her parents. In the face of her unmentionable actions, they had no choice but to disinherit her publicly before returning her to her husband.

But she learned.

Now she is twenty-two and her husband trains her to take care of his interests while he travels far away, and this trip is part of learning about the business of discovery. She doesn't know it yet as she stands in front of Québec in the year 1620, but destiny will grant her her dearest wish. Once she becomes a widow, in 1635, she will be allowed to take the veil. Headstrong to the end, she will ask to found her own nunnery, and only amid women like her will she find a degree of freedom.

But nothing like the First Women of God, in their harsh land of innocence.

Canada House, July 28. "Madame Des Ruisseaux?"

Not now, go away, Roy. I recognize the suave voice of our communications officer, my eyes glued to the incomprehensible windows and prompts on the computer screen. The technical department has installed the new high-speed cable and changed the connecting software without warning. Part of Roy's job is to give tours of the renovated splendours of Canada House to a never-ending flux of visitors and officials. He has acquired the habit of dumping them in the library if he has an emergency to deal with, counting on me to take over.

"Yes, Roy, what can I do for you?"

"Stephen Young is visiting from Brazil to attend the telecommunications conference sponsored by Nortel . . ."

I almost fold in two, the name like a punch in the pit of my stomach.

"Lucie? What are you doing here?"

Before I can brace myself, Stephen has crossed the room and is standing in front of me. This is the man who hit me with his car at the corner of Avenue and Bloor in Toronto. The man who left me. Roy's mouth opens and shuts in the background, but I can't hear him. I can't hear the traffic around Trafalgar Square either, or the hum of the computer. Stephen's eyes close in on me, small motions, left and right, up and down, scanning my face to glean information. What does he see? My hands slide down my hips along my stretch pants from Marks *&* Spencer, checking for unsightly panty lines. Which underwear am I wearing, did I put lipstick on this morning, are my grey roots showing, oh my God, it must be more than two months since I had my highlights done, oh just stop this now. I straighten up, toss my hair back, push my glasses away to put him out of focus, and offer a professional hand to shake. "Stephen, so nice to see you again. How have you been?"

Instead, he reaches for my hands, looking down a fraction of a second for the glint of a ring. But there is no ring, and he misses the meaning of the diamond on a chain around my neck. "How are you? You look great."

The cocky tone of his voice makes me furious, and now that I am furious I can hear the traffic, the computer, and Roy distinctly: "I see you two know each other."

"Yes," says Stephen, finally letting go of me. "We met in Toronto."

"Just before you left for Singapore, wasn't it?" I hope he thinks it's all long forgotten, and forgiven. The truth is, his touch awakens the old wound.

"So, Madame Des Ruisseaux, I don't need to worry about leaving Mr. Young in your company for ten minutes then?"

Roy, you idiot.

"Absolutely not!" Stephen answers for me. "We have a lot of catching up to do."

My mind flip-flops between the desire to be truthful and tell him I am married and the temptation to be deceitful. But I don't even get a chance to test myself. As soon as Roy is out of the way, Stephen says, looking at his watch: "I've got to go, Lucie, a meeting I must attend. I was trying to cut the tour short without being rude."

I'm stunned. "Yes. You'd better go. You're good at that."

He stops, then leans closer, his lips brushing against my cheek, touching my earlobe. "Let's have dinner. I've missed you so much but I never had the courage . . ."

You coward, you don't even have the courage to finish a sentence let alone—but I knew this man could make me slick with desire before he even laid his hands on me. Maybe it will all go away if I stop breathing.

"No dinner? What about lunch then?" He sounds more tentative now. "I have to attend the conference tomorrow, but I think it wraps up around noon on Friday morning. So Friday lunch? Should I pick you up here, around one?"

I put my glasses back on to see what I'm getting myself into. His dark eyes are puffy, and not as magnetic as I remembered. I start breathing more easily. Glossy black hair, very short. His smile a little too muscular—too much time spent using his charm to close deals. Bright tie, stripes, yellow, green, and pink. Pale blue shirt, dark suit. Still tall, if a little fuller. Same skin.

"Yes, why not? Let's do lunch on Friday."

"Here's my card." He flips it over and writes something. "And this is where you can find me." His hotel's phone and room number.

He backs out of the library, his thumb already on the call button of his cellphone, flashing one last smile. "I can't wait!"

The green room feels lifeless as soon he's gone, the chandelier's crystal tears still shivering in his wake. I look at the shelves covering the walls. Books? Why should I settle for dry paper when there is Stephen's soft saffron skin? Why should I have to stare at the cold light of a computer screen when there are his eyes like black ink ready to pour over me? It's only in the ladies' room as I glance into the mirror, trying to study my face with Stephen's eyes, that I remember. My plane leaves on Friday at one-thirty. I take his business card out of my pocket, tear it into small pieces, and flush it down the toilet before I have time to memorize it. Then I touch my face and smell my hands, trying to bring him back.

He almost killed me, the day we met.

I was in a hurry. I didn't look before crossing the intersection; he was making a right turn on a red light. By the time I heard the tires screech, his car bumper had hit my thigh, hard enough to knock me off my feet. I got back up immediately, my folders, my gym bag, and my purse strewn around the pavement. I hit the hood with my fist so hard, I put a dent in it and split my knuckles. This injury would end up hurting more than the bruise on my leg. "I'm so sorry, I never saw you, you came out of nowhere. Are you all right?" he asked, getting out of the car, checking the dent with a worried look. I went on gathering my scattered belongings, ignoring him. Three cars were honking behind him but he would not budge. "You're limping." He took hold of my elbow as I tried to walk away. "Listen, just in case, here's my business card. Call me." That's when his eyes closed in on me, and I was forced to see him. There was no looking back. I wanted him right there, right then, and I wanted him forever after, over and over again.

He hit me and I fell for him. He was a man in an even greater hurry than I was. He proposed but left town without waiting for an answer, or the good news. I was pregnant. All of this in six months, a modern love story. I have never talked to him since.

Keyword: filles du roi.

If Nouvelle-France quickly became a commercial success, thanks to the fur trade's profits, Samuel de Champlain's colony at Québec was left struggling. There were too many coureurs de bois and not enough settlers. While the wood runners made quick money, took a liking to the free ways of the forest, and forged tender, if fleeting, ties with the Huron and Montagnais women, the settlers faced constant attacks from the Iroquois, a short growing season in summer, and a long, harsh winter spent in primitive accommodations. Without a woman to help out and provide children, the settlers saw no point to this life.

To remedy the situation, eight hundred filles du roi, the "daughters of the king," were sent to the colony between 1663 and 1673. Acting as a symbolic father, Louis XIV provided the orphaned or destitute young women with the dowry essential to marriage. The king also signed an edict forcing Nouvelle-France's bachelors to marry and settle down within fifteen days of the women's arrival, or have their rights to trade, fish, and hunt withdrawn. Each one of the king's wards received ten livres for transportation from their country home to the departure port of La Rochelle, thirty livres for clothing, and sixty livres for surviving the crossing to Québec. Each brought along a trunk containing one taffeta handkerchief, one bonnet, one comb, one spool of white thread, one pair of shoe ribbons, stockings, gloves and scissors, two knives, one hundred sewing needles, four lace braids, and a small box with two livres in coins. On signing their marriage contract, the brides-to-be were promised between thirty to two hundred livres, but only 250 of the 606 marriage contracts mention this sum. All the newly married did get cows, pigs, chickens, and two barrels of salted meat. Later on, to encourage the colony's natural growth, every family with more than nine children received a one-time allowance of two hundred livres, and every man married before the age of twenty-one received ninety livres.

The filles du roi were either "filles"—women of modest origin destined for the habitants—or "demoiselles" from the small nobility who would marry officers from the Carignan-Salières regiment. For a long time there were rumours questioning the virtue of the king's pupils. Mère Marie de l'Incarnation herself wrote that since the young women came from all walks of life, some were very unrefined and hard to discipline, while others were more honest and gave Madame Bourdon, their chaperone for the crossing, more co-operation. Poverty was widespread in seventeenth-century France, particularly in and around the capital. Many of the Parisian filles du roi came from La Salpêtrière and La Santé, both shelters for orphans, beggars, prostitutes, the mentally ill, and the homeless.

Françoise is one of ninety filles du roi arriving in Canada in the summer of 1669, one of the "dainty young ladies, getting off their wood jail." This is how the Jesuit priests describe the triumphant arrival of the wards of Louis XIV in the port of Québec. The Jesuits also describe Canada as the last border before hell, a place of horror. Only forests line the shores of the great river up to Québec, but here on the headland that is Cap-Diamant, tall buildings with towers fly colourful flags and spires show off large gold crosses. Françoise thinks this is a very pretty sight after the dire crossing: five hundred grams of hardtack biscuits a day, cheese and smoke-cured meat with ale or claret since fresh water is scarce, and no fruit or vegetables whatsoever for almost two months. Mass was celebrated on deck once a day, weather permitting, but all the prayers did not prevent most of the sick ones from dying. Their corpses were sewn up in sailcloth and weighted with a cannonball before being thrown overboard to rest for eternity as far from heaven as can be: at the bottom of the cold, grey sea.

The crowd on the docks cheers, cannons are fired, and the bells from the cathedral's carillon peal out. The young women are herded up the Côte de la Montagne to the Ursuline convent, where they will be housed until they get married. The procession is led by Madame Bourdon, the Québec widow in charge of the shipment. She walks beside a couple of good mothers from the convent, in white wimples and black veils, and the ship's captain, wearing a very large felt hat with feathers. Behind the ninety young women come the sailors in red wool hats, pushing carts loaded with the filles' chests, and supplies for the convent. Behind the carts come the cattle, the sheep, the pigs, and the horses. On each side of the road are soldiers from the Carignan-Salières regiment, holding back a raucous crowd.

Jean is one of the young men pushing against the soldiers' chain of arms. We'll get the best, you'll get the rest, the officers in blue uniforms and cocked hats whisper to the coureurs de bois, feeding the young men's frenzy. Within two days, Françoise and Jean will have met each other. Within a month they will be married, and within a year there should be a new soul, born where the river narrows.

It took a few years and a steady flow of correspondence to get the formula right. Mère Marie de l'Incarnation asked for more girls from the country and fewer from Paris. The parisiennes were not tough enough to work like men on the land. The intendant, Jean Talon, for his part, told the king there were not enough filles and too many demoiselles. He had received fifteen of these rather than the four he had asked for. The operation was deemed a success by all involved from Louis XIV and Jean Baptiste Colbert, his minister for the colonies, to Governor Frontenac and Jean Talon. Ten years after the last filles du roi had arrived, the population of Québec had tripled through natural growth.

Marriage in the New World, this place of horrors, turned out to be a better choice than starving to death in the Old World. Statistics show that the French women lived almost twice as long in the harsh climate of Québec as they would have had they remained in the abject misery of France.

Saint-Sacrement,
1950–1956

"Mais pour qui qu'a se prend, celle-là, avec ses grands airs?" Madame Lasalle asks her husband, George-Albert. Germaine Lasalle is watching Madame Beauregard, her next-door neighbour, walk down the street in a bright blue and green dress with a red cloche hat on. She takes small steps in her brown shoes, pulling her empty shopping trolley behind her. "One day she says her uncle was Chicoutimi's mayor, the next that her father was a coureur de bois. She also says she was an orphan and went to the Ursuline convent until she was twenty and that her husband was a bank manager! Then how come all she has is too many kids and a dirty boarding house?"

"Her children are getting a good education, maybe that's where the money went, Germaine," says George-Albert, balancing his own bank account. God blessed them with only three children, but when George-Albert sees how much it costs to raise his family, he doesn't envy Madame Beauregard's brood.

"Well, if she thinks a good education for the girls will help them marry well and better their lot, fine. But if I see her trying to hitch any of them to Louis-Philippe . . ."

Louis-Philippe is the Lasalles' pride and joy, their only son. He will go all the way to university to become a lawyer. Madame Lasalle believes in common sense. No higher education for her daughters, Mariette and Raymonde. They will do a three-year domestic arts course at the Bon-Pasteur Family Institute, as will most of their friends. Why send them to the Cours Classique for five long years, make them go through the ordeal of Greek and Latin, poetry, literature, and the art of the speech, when the girls will spend the rest of their lives at home? Maybe their elder daughter, Mariette, who's a better student than Raymonde, will take her supplementary course to become a teacher. But there is a danger. If Mariette likes teaching, she might not want to get married. Once married, her one and only job is to have children and keep house. And the Lasalles' greatest wish is to have many, many grandchildren, just what the Abbé Audette and Maurice Duplessis, the premier of Québec, both call for.

"What kind of example is this woman to her daughters, I ask you, George-Albert? She'd rather read immoral books than go to church!"

Madame Beauregard is disappearing around the corner, whistling after the birds.

"Calm down, Germaine, calm down. You know what the doctor said about your nerves."

"On sait ben, George-Albert. She comes from the Kingdom of Saguenay, land of the tall tales. She even told me her husband used to fly!"

Saint-Onge

"What am I going to do with this?" Madame Beauregard says with a laugh, holding the portrait of a woman with a green face at arm's length. "Let me put it in the sitting room and look at it some more." And she dishes out a second helping of pâté chinois—one layer of ground beef fried with onions, one layer of canned corn, and the last layer a blanket of mashed potatoes—for Saint-Onge. Nobody knows his first name. Léo's new friend swaps his art for food or booze.

"This is so good, Madame Beauregard," says Saint-Onge between two mouthfuls. "Could I paint your wall? The kitchen wall?"

Madame Beauregard looks at the yellowed wall. It could do with a good lick of paint.

*　　*　　*

Saint-Onge shows up the next day at four in the afternoon. Dinner is served at six. He said he'd come in the morning, but he doesn't look worried about his lateness. His hair sticks up, his clothes are crusted with oil paint, his fingernails permanently dirty. He smells of tobacco and turpentine. Lili cannot keep her eyes off him. Saint-Onge goes to l'École des Beaux-Arts.

She holds and cleans his brushes while he paints the wall. He doesn't plan, he doesn't draw, he doesn't wait. He grabs the lid of a dirty pot in lieu of a palette and dips a wide brush into the paint. Big dollops of cerulean blue, magenta red, acra violet, cadmium yellow. Lili reads the labels on the colour tubes he has brought along. Saint-Onge paints with his whole body, starting from the bottom left of the wall and finishing at the top right corner. A tilted tree with twisted branches, a long sky, violet with pale blue clouds. A slab of water. A flock of snow geese, barking through. Lifting off. So light. His hand with a smaller brush dancing, quick strokes, slight dabs of grey-white paint. Saint-Onge stops only to drink from a bottle of red wine hidden in a paper bag. He offers some to Lili.

"Non merci, Monsieur Saint-Onge."

"Why don't you call me Saint-Onge, like everybody else?"

He takes a good look at his silent helper. Smiles. Brown teeth, a couple of them gone missing. "Would you like to visit my studio?" he asks Lili point-blank. "I could paint you."

He looks at her so hard, Lili blushes and twitches. She shrinks in the refrigerator's shadow.

"Are you finished with the pot lid, Saint-Onge? I need it to boil the potatoes," Madame Beauregard calls from the sink.

"All done, all done, Madame Beauregard. Let me just wipe it off . . . There. So, do you like it?"

Everybody stops to look at Madame Beauregard. She is crying, the pot lid in her hand.

"You don't like it?" Saint-Onge asks, defeated.

"Oh no. No. It's beautiful, look how large the kitchen is now. It's the smell. Turpentine. It always makes me cry."

"Why?" asks Saint-Onge.

"My father," says Marie-Reine. "That's the smell of him, giving a new coat of paint to his sled. Before leaving for this place." She points to the slick wall, the sky and the water, the geese.

Lilianne takes the lid from her mother's hand and goes to rinse it off with soapy water, chasing her mother's tears away. She doesn't want to hear about missing fathers.

"There is cabbage beef stew for dinner, Saint-Onge, and you're not leaving until it's ready, hear me?" says Madame Beauregard, getting a grip on herself.

"How did you know, Madame Beauregard? My favourite!"

Lilianne cuts out her initials, L.B., from the black cover of her school notebook and fills in the two letters with a green ballpoint, over and over, until the paper blisters from the friction. There. This is hers.

She gets reprimanded on the first day of school for the wasted page. And she gets reprimanded again for the uneven red silk stitches of her name, embroidered painstakingly on every item of her school uniform: the shirts, the smocks, the bloomers, the pinafore. Her hands are not steady enough to thread through the pinpoint eye of the needle, and each stitch is like an axe's slash. The pressure to fit in goes from bad to worse until she can't stand it anymore.

"J'veux faire mes Beaux-Arts, Maman."

Lili has been trying to say it for the last month, but couldn't force the words through her throat, her teeth.

Her mother goes on knitting, as usual.

"Maman? Did you hear me?"

"Yes."

"So? What do you think?"

"Not much." Clickety-clack, clickety-clack. "You really want to go around in dirty clothes looking filthy, swapping paintings for food? Like Saint-Onge?"

"Yes. I want to do what Saint-Onge does. I want to paint." The gold watch, a small plane over the red brush, a couple of playing cards.

Clickety-clack, clickety-clack. Her mother won't look up. She rocks her chair, back and forth, back and forth. It squeaks.

Lili puts her hand down to stop it. "Maman . . ."

"We'll see, Lili, after you finish Rhétorique. By then I hope there will be a little more common sense between your ears."

"Here is the subject of today's essay: of the advantage of Modesty against Vanity. We are going to treat this subject as a metaphor, using a cricket and a butterfly. Don't forget to draw up an outline beforehand, and respect the rules of a well-balanced composition. Mademoiselle Desrosiers, can you remind us what these rules are?"

Beauregard. Yes. This is what she is going to call herself when she finally becomes an artist. She likes the sound of her family name, stark naked. No Mademoiselle, no Madame, no Lilianne or Lili. Or maybe, La Beauregard.

"Oui, ma mère. They are the introduction, the exposition, and the conclusion."

Lili doodles in the margin of her composition book. She can't help herself; the impulse is like the twitch in her hands, her legs. She knows the drawings will make her lose points for cleanliness, but she doesn't care. When it's not one thing, it's another. *Half the subject missed, the other half completely illogical. I thought you were intelligent, Mademoiselle Beauregard, but I'd rather warn you now . . . Next time I see a drawing, I refuse to read your composition. This means ZERO.*

Lili dips the pen in the ink pot. Introduction, exposition, conclusion. Subject, verb, object. Can't help herself, has to draw. One sentence, one idea. This butterfly, this flutter of bright yellow wings, just behind her eyelids. This brilliance, this flash of light . . . Snap!

The wooden ruler, hidden inside Mère Saint-Louis de Mon Fort's wide sleeves, comes down hard on Lili's knuckles, splitting the skin open. Lili screams, in surprise as much as pain.

"Mademoiselle Beauregard!"

Lili grabs her ink eraser to rub off the butterfly. She keeps her eyes down, bites her lips hard, forgets to cry. But she tries too hard and almost rips the soiled page. A few drops of blood mix with the spilled blue ink on the half-written page. All this would not be happening if her father were still around. He would make everything right. And Henri would too. He used to help her with her homework the year she spent sick at home. Henri and Huguette. But Henri is still in the sanatorium, even though he is getting better, and Huguette has a boyfriend, and her father is dead. Big sloppy sobs fill Lili's throat.

"You may be excused, Mademoiselle Beauregard," says Mère Saint-Louis de Mon Fort. Her face is very red against the immaculate collar and wimple. "I want a *clean* notebook on my desk tomorrow morning, and then you will join Mère Saint-Stanislas's sewing class. A little needlework might help you *focus* on your work, and learn to *control* yourself."

Zigzag, over stitch, buttonholes. Lili licks the split end of the thread. Her hand shakes. Again and again she aims and misses the eye of the needle. She is the laughingstock of the sewing class. She cannot put one stitch in front of the other.

"Avez-vous la danse de Saint-Guy, Mademoiselle Beauregard?" asks Mère Saint-Stanislas, her old eyes pale behind the glasses.

The laughs again, loud and forced.

"Silence, children. And a little charity. This is no laughing matter. Weren't you sick as a child?"

"Oui, ma mère. I had rheumatic fever."

"Maybe you should see a doctor. This nervous agitation is a common result of cardiac diseases. I'll have a word with your mother."

This is just a phase, all this shaking. Lili is simply trying to get out of the straitjacket, the tight cocoon wrapped around her. It is just a pause before the final metamorphosis when Lili will become Beauregard, the artist, and fly.

Up, up, up and away.

*   *   *

"Lilianne?"

"Oui, Maman?"

"Could you come downstairs for a second."

"Oui, Maman."

Her mother doesn't sound too angry as she slowly removes the long pin from her straw hat, the one with paper pansies.

"You know where I have just been, don't you, Lilianne? I guess you didn't think it important enough to tell me what you've been up to at school, did you?"

"Mère Saint-Louis de Mon Fort hit me. She made me cry in front of everybody else."

"And are you the only one she hits, Lili?"

"No."

"And does everyone she hits put dog dirt on her chair?" Madame Beauregard snaps back.

"No. But I'm not like everybody else. I'm an artist. "

Her mother carefully puts the pin back on her hat. "If your father were here, he'd give you the belt. But he's not here."

Lili's defiance fades immediately. She can count on one hand the number of times her mother has mentioned his name in the last seven years. Madame Beauregard walks towards her daughter. Lili stands very straight on the last step of the staircase. Not a twitch, not a shake, just a shiver giving her goosebumps. Her hand grips the banister, swollen knuckles tight.

"Les Beaux-Arts, Lilianne?"

"Les Beaux-Arts, Maman."

Her mouth starts to tremble as she repeats the hopeful words.

"Come with me into the living room for a second, Lilianne." Her mother lets her go first across the hall and shuts the doors behind them. "Les Beaux-Arts!" she cries out in anger. "Over my dead body! Do you hear me?"

Everybody else does, upstairs and in the kitchen. Someone cranks the radio up. The hand comes down so hard on Lilianne's cheek, her head jerks.

"Go pack up. You're leaving tomorrow morning." Madame Beauregard throws her hat on top of the piano and the music sheets. "You're going to Toronto until Christmas, to work. The orphanage is under the supervision of Mère Marie de Sept Douleurs, Mère Saint-Louis de Mon Fort's sister. You will also learn English. English is useful. Art is not." She opens the door and shouts, "Huguette! Come and give me a hand with Lilianne! I have to get the dinner going."

Lili is so stunned she doesn't move.

"You don't give me any choice, Lilianne. I don't have time for this kind of trouble."

The First Wedding, April 1952

"So sad," whispers Marie-Joseph, dabbing a tear, "to see our Léo getting married. He is still only a child, Marie-Reine, isn't he?"

Marie-Joseph has cried easily since she lost her husband of eleven years, Edouard Bouchard, in January. He died suddenly in the bed where he was born. A stroke, the doctor said. But Marie-Joseph's old housekeeping habits took over her grief, and within a week of his funeral, she had given away all of her husband's clothes and shoes. No point letting them collect dust while other people went without. Then she cleaned the cupboards and the drawers and hired someone to repaint the inside of the house.

The church is gloomy on the sunless April day. The groom isn't exactly beaming and the bride, Berthe Théberge, is very pale. She doesn't look well. Even the Abbé Audette's face is pinched. He doesn't like rushed ceremonies like this one. The couple had only one "Initiation au Sacrement du Mariage" session instead of the usual five.

"Yes, it is a shame, isn't it?" Marie-Reine whispers back. "She's even younger than he is. Eighteen years old. Not much education either, really."

"What does she have then?"

The soon-to-be Madame Léopold Beauregard is quite homely. Marie-Reine sighs. "A bun in the oven."

Marie-Joseph chokes. The delicate handkerchief she has dug out of her black purse to dab a tear now stifles a dry cough. The abbé gives the two sisters a sharp look before continuing with the wedding vows. The guests have been hastily invited, so there aren't as many as both families would have liked. But after discussing the situation, they all agreed to go on with the marriage as quickly as possible. Marie-Joseph didn't even have time to buy a new dress, let alone matching accessories. When she got off the Chicoutimi–Québec express, Henri picked her up and drove her to the Saint-Sacrement church where she met her sister in the front pew. Everything so quick, the young ones in such a hurry to live.

"That's how it is now, Marie-Joseph, and I have to marry these girls of mine before the same thing happens to them."

"Not *your* daughters," an indignant Marie-Joseph whispers in her handkerchief, throwing a furtive look over her shoulder to the pew where Lilianne, Colette, and Bernadette are seated. Behind them are Huguette and her fiancé, Chris Morris, Henri, and a young woman Marie-Joseph has never seen before. Lucien slouches at the end of the pew.

The je ne sais quoi. Marie-Joseph has tried her best to break the rebel streak in her nieces and nephews. "Is there something wrong with Lilianne, Marie-Reine?"

"Lilianne? No. Mind you, she got proposed to by the Italian janitor while she was at the orphanage in Toronto."

"Proposed to? Last year? But she was only sixteen!"

"Seventeen."

Now it's Léo's new mother-in-law's turn to glare at them. Madame Beauregard nods back and smiles graciously while whispering, "I'll be polite, but I won't be quiet about this shrew's loose daughter forcing my son to marry her! Anyway, Lili did the right thing. She turned the janitor down. She told the nuns. She came back home, but she has changed. Now it's the neighbour's son who can't take his eyes off her, and she enjoys every minute of it!"

"And who's this with Henri?"

"His fiancée. He met her at the sanatorium. Cécile Lépine."

"And?"

"Very pretty if a little . . . dramatic."

"And what about Huguette?"

"I'm not worried about Huguette. She's as good as married, but they're waiting to finish university."

"She has a solid head on her shoulders, doesn't she?"

"Yes," sighs Marie-Reine, "she's got her father's head. I don't know what I would have done without her."

Marie-Joseph keeps silent, savouring the moment. Marie-Reine finally acknowledges where the wild streak comes from, and it is not from Léandre Beauregard. It is not from their mother either, God bless Marie-Ange Légaré's soul. It comes straight down the line from Antonio Tremblay.

When Huguette catches up with them as the two sisters follow the newlyweds out of the church, she reprimands them. "Franchement! You had a lot to say, you two. Couldn't it wait until after the wedding ceremony?"

"We haven't seen each other in a long time," her mother replies.

"Since Edouard's funeral," says Marie-Joseph, wiping a tear again. "My dear, dear, Edouard."

"Oh, Fifine, I didn't mean to . . . How are you getting along without him, are you lonely?"

"I'm doing all right, ma grande," says Marie-Joseph, latching on to her niece's elbow, "but when are you going to introduce me to your fiancé?"

Louis-Philippe Lasalle

"Enfin, les Belles-Lettres! Next year I will finally be allowed to read what I want and express my true self! I know it is going to be a disappointment for my parents, since they had hoped I would become a lawyer."

It is so much easier with Louis-Philippe Lasalle. He thinks he knows everything, his small mouth full of long words and his puffed-up chest ripe with opinions, his elocution perfect. Louis-Philippe Lasalle is a mommy's boy.

Lili draws in her sketchbook with a piece of charcoal. Her fingertips are black, the side of her cheek is smeared and so are her jeans where she wiped her hands. She wears a straw hat that she has tied up with her scarf because of the wind. The three top buttons of her red plaid shirt open generously on a skin made of cool gold and warm shadows.

"Do you have something against buttons?" her mother has asked her daughter, giving her a once-over at the door.

Madame Beauregard can say what she wants, but there isn't much she can do. Lili has given in on everything else but the dress code. She has finished her Rhétorique, just one year late, and is now taking night classes at the Sullivan School of Business to perfect her English and learn secretarial skills. What Madame Beauregard doesn't know is that her daughter often skips night class to catch an American movie at the Empire. This is where Lili learns how to say *baby* the right way, how to whisper *Come on, big guy* and *No, no, please don't*. Better than to repeat endlessly *My name is Lee-lee-ann Boowegawr and I live in Kwebek City*. Louis-Philippe Lasalle is always ready to buy her ticket. Lili can hear him beside her, swallowing hard, when Burt Lancaster and Deborah Kerr kiss on the beach.

As to les Beaux-Arts . . . Lili has decided she doesn't need to take courses to be an artist. She draws whenever she wants and whatever catches her fancy. She signs everything with a flourish, Beauregard.

"The problem is, the Church should keep out of higher education.

When the Church decides we cannot read the giants of French literature, I think they're going too far. This is where the line should be drawn."

Lili has just turned eighteen. On her birthday her mother gave her two things: a set of watercolours and a fur coat. It is Madame Beauregard's old coat, shortened and streamlined to a knee-length wrap with a bright yellow lining. But the old pelt, the brown shorn beaver, is as soft as ever.

"I agree they have to enlighten the ignorant masses but leave the elite to decide for themselves!"

Lili's laugh fizzles in the wind. She lifts her eyes from her sketchbook, where a fuzzier Louis-Philippe sits still. Behind him white triangles criss-cross the narrow water, manoeuvring to avoid the two flat-bottomed boats ferrying cars between Lévis and Québec.

"Why do you laugh?"

They have nestled in the crook of a green knoll right by the high point of the Plains of Abraham, beside the Citadel, their two bicycles lying on the ground beside them. Lili pulls on a strand of wheat and starts sucking on the tender white shoot. The sun is almost warm when the wind drops.

"Have you read *Madame Bovary*?" Lili asks. "Great book."

Louis-Philippe's mouth is agape. "What do you mean? You have read a book à l'Index?"

"My mother has them all in her bedroom cupboard. Flaubert, Zola, Balzac. I spent hours hiding in there. I'm sure you heard about my mother and her books."

The charcoal glides on the paper, and now that Lili's wrist has warmed up, her motions are fluid, the line elegant. She catches Louis-Philippe's expression. Small eyes, a few long spiky locks slipping from the tweed cap, the ribbed turtleneck under the open sports jacket.

"I am not sure it is the best choice of book for . . . for such a young person. Taken literally, it might induce the wrong ideas."

"What's all the fuss about? Wasn't it just the story of a hapless woman locked in a loveless marriage, pining for another man, having an affair, and losing everything? What was her lover's name, Rodolphe?"

"Oh, Lilianne, such ugly words in such an innocent mouth," Louis-Philippe tries to flirt.

"That's what you think," she flirts back, her laugh now just a purr rolling deep down in her throat. Her eyes cut away to spare him the embarrassment of the intense glow rising from his neck to the tip of his ears under his matching tweed cap. It is just a game, with Louis-Philippe Lasalle.

Théo Potvin

Lili throws the letter Louis-Philippe has sent from summer camp on top of the piano, with the hats and the sheet music. She and Colette have so many suitors that even Bernadette cannot keep track of who is going out with whom when she peeks through the doors of the living room. That's where the couples meet in the evening to play records, dance a little, and laugh a lot. Madame Beauregard retires early to read upstairs, leaving Henri or Huguette to play chaperone and close the house down at eleven. Henri came back from the sanatorium fragile but healthy, not a boy anymore but a man, with his fiancée in tow. Cécile Lépine is a small brunette from Sainte-Rose-du-Nord, a few miles upstream from Tadoussac on the Saguenay. Huguette is still dating Chris Morris, the quiet man who can play a mean trumpet jazz line. Just one more year and Huguette will be finished her math degree. They hide cold beers under the couch and pray that Léo and Berthe won't show up. Their marriage has been rough going ever since Berthe's miscarriage. Most evenings spent with them end up in screams and tears, with Léo drinking all their beer.

But Lilianne's only torment is deciding which invitation to accept for the famous graduation ball of the Séminaire de Québec. Bertrand Lagacé, Robert Boisvert, Théo Potvin? The ball takes place at the Château Frontenac and has a reputation for lasting all night long, finishing at dawn with breakfast at the Riviera—Chinese and Continental cuisine, open twenty-four hours, right by the ferry house. After ten days of intense negotiations Lili finally says yes to the one who asks her with confidence: "Would you honour me with your company on the evening of the Séminaire de Québec's graduation ball, Mademoiselle Beauregard?" No fumbling the words, no wet palms, no shuffle. The straight goods. "Avec plaisir, Monsieur Potvin." He is charming, if a little formal.

And everything goes according to Lilianne's idea of a romantic evening, at first anyway. Théo Potvin shows up on time for the sparkling wine and grenadine cocktails that Madame Beauregard serves in the wallpapered jungle of her living room. He helps Lili in and out of the taxicab, his conversation an easy banter, and guides her to the ballroom where he introduces her to his friends, their dates, and his teachers alike, making drinks appear as if by magic. He leads Lili through waltzes from Vienna, big band songs from New York, and rock 'n' roll from Tennessee with the same savoir faire, never leaving her behind unless another partner requests the favour of a dance with her. Lili doesn't sit down all night; she is giddy from the drinks and the non-stop spins on the dance floor, light on her sore feet, the new shoes not yet broken in. She knows she looks beautiful, the pale blue froufrou of her skirt underlining her small waist in the strapless bodice, and everything would be perfect if only Théo Potvin would hold her a little closer or brush her cheek or whisper something, anything, in her ear. If only he would make her twirl out to the Terrasse Dufferin in her bare feet before framing her with his arms, leaning against the gazebo posts to steal a slow, wet kiss in the misty mauve haze rising from the river below. That's what the other couples do.

But Théo Potvin never tries any of this. Maybe he is shy, thinks Lili. Maybe he doesn't think it proper on the first date. It is past five in the morning when the taxi stops in front of the rooming house on Louis-Fréchette. Lili loses all hope when Théo Potvin ignores her face stretching towards him like a flower to the sun and kisses her hand instead, in a gallant but distant fashion.

"Thanks for the wonderful evening," she tries.

"The pleasure was mine, Mademoiselle Beauregard. Allez, au revoir!"

His eyes still don't waver, his smile is frank and warm, but he doesn't linger. He doesn't even walk her to the front steps, waiting by the taxi until Lili disappears into the house. When she turns around to wave from behind the star-etched windowpane, he has already moved on. Lili stands there, defeated.

Lili spends the next three days by the phone at the bottom of the stairs, but the calls are not for her, not from him anyway. After three days her hope dies. She locks herself in her room and cries herself hoarse, refusing to eat. Her only joy is watching the numbers go down on the scale: 136, 134, 131, 129 pounds. When she finally emerges, seven pounds thinner, Madame Beauregard settles the issue over chopped onions: "You shouldn't raise your hopes too high when it comes to a Potvin from Des Braves Street. He just wanted a show-date. Veux-tu un morceau de sucre à la crème?"

Her mother has done it again: chucked her dreams out the window as if they were dishwater. Lili fills her mouth with sugar, hiding her humiliation under a thick coat of face cream and her puffy eyes under two cool slices of cucumber. She bangs her way back to her room against the walls, blinded. When she re-emerges, she proceeds to date as many boys as she can, with a predilection for Monsieur Potvin's friends, but only one time each. If they call back, she turns them down with transparent excuses. She doesn't gain back the seven pounds of baby fat.

The Second Wedding, November 1953

"So sad."

That's what Marie-Joseph thinks as drizzling rain beats down the windows of the Saint-Sacrement's church basement. It is grey and damp. The thirty-strong crowd huddles at the front of the large room where, under the golden light of the candles, the bride smiles in an off-white suit, nipped at the waist, and the tall, wiry groom bows his head to look with unabashed joy into the new Mrs. Chris Morris's eyes.

"What are they smiling about?" whispers Marie-Joseph to her sister.

But Marie-Reine is smiling too. She doesn't care one bit for the church's approval, only for Huguette's happiness. The Abbé Audette has refused to let her daughter get married in his church because the groom is a Protestant from Ontario. These people do not recognize the sanctity of the pope or honour the mystery of the Immaculate Conception. The heretic is only welcome in the basement, where a civil ceremony has been permitted to take place in exchange for a donation. Huguette said yes when Chris Morris asked her to marry him on the day she received her university degree. Tomorrow they are moving to Richmond, Virginia, where Chris has accepted a job offer in a cotton textile plant.

"Your first daughter married in the basement of the church!" Marie-Joseph complains.

Nothing splendid about the crowd either, Marie-Joseph thinks again. These people from Ontario sure don't know how to dress. Only the groom's parents, his sister and her husband, and a younger brother came for the wedding. They are drab and gauche in grey and navy blue, the Beauregard girls like a rainbow in contrast, standing in the second row. Lilianne wears red, Colette is in pale yellow, and Bernadette in Irish green. Marie-Reine is in purple lace, with a flat hat that looks like a blueberry crepe. Marie-Joseph is in navy blue polka dots, a brand-new dress for the occasion, but she wears her everyday black lace-up shoes. Her feet swell too much for fancier ones and nobody looks at shoes anyway.

As soon as the groom kisses the bride and the papers are signed, the wedding guests stampede across the linoleum floor to pick up their dripping umbrellas and head for Madame Beauregard's house on Louis-Fréchette, where champagne cocktails will precede a dinner buffet. The boarders have been kicked out for the weekend to accommodate the new in-laws.

* * *

"Un verre de champagne, Madame Morris?" Madame Beauregard offers from a round tray.

Mrs. Morris smiles and repeats the word: "Champagne? Qu'est-ce que c'est?" The Morrises live in a dry town, in northern Ontario.

"It's all right, dear," Mr. Morris assures her.

"Do I have to?" asks Mrs. Morris.

"C'est du vrai," Madame Beauregard tells her, "pas du mousseux. Vous serez pas malade!"

"I think you should, dear." Mr. Morris smiles back at his son's new mother-in-law, passing the glass of sparkling wine on to his wife before taking another for himself. Mrs. Morris lets out a small, surprised yelp. She's brought the glass to her nose and the sharp bubbles have startled her.

"Is she going to sniff it up?" Lilianne whispers to her mother.

"Santé!" calls Marie-Reine, trying to jab her elbow in Lili's rib in return for her disparaging comment.

Lili dodges the jab expertly. "It means *Cheers!* in English, and *Cincin!* in Italian," she says, showing off. Mr. Morris looks exactly like his son, just a little older and skinnier. He has the same kind, patient smile.

"What am I supposed to do?" Mrs. Morris asks her husband.

"Just do what they do. Sanntee! To the noovow maweahey!" Mr. Morris adds, throwing all caution to the wind and clinking glasses with Madame Beauregard and one of her many daughters.

It's still raining outside, still November, but even a battalion of Anglo abstainers and Marie-Josephs couldn't dampen the party. The rainbow of Beauregard girls shines through the day and night, well after the din of the tin cans, clanking from the bumper of Mr. and Mrs. Morris's new car, fades slowly into the wet snow. Chris Morris is a cautious driver.

Marie-Joseph doesn't like the Month of the Dead. She eats peckishly, does not indulge in more than a sip of champagne for the toast. She won't dance to the savage music of today's youth any more than she used to square dance. Instead, she prays for the newlyweds and goes to bed early.

What's the Matter with her Daughters?

École du Saint-Sacrement, le 11 mars 1954

Madame Beauregard,

I regret to have to inform you of Bernadette's repeated absences. Although these absences have been explained by notes signed in your hand, the reasons stated have appeared increasingly suspicious. The assortment of ailments has included the usual monthly cramps, the less usual head lice, poison ivy, and voice loss. Yesterday it was consumption, which prompted this note.

Please contact us to let us know what is going on. Bernadette is a hard worker, but she seems to have lost the motivation she has displayed in the past.

Bien à vous,
Mère Sainte-Thérèse de l'Enfant-Jésus

"So, playing hooky are you, Bernadette?"

Bernadette's tears explode from her large green eyes, bouncing off her plump cheeks. Finally, her mother is asking. Bernadette has her father's long, straight nose with a thin ridge. Madame Beauregard doesn't understand why her daughter pulls her hair back so tight. She doesn't know how much Bernadette hates her brown hair, how much she would like to be blonde. Like Colette.

"Come on, Bernadette, tell me. Where did you go?"

Bernadette has been waiting a long time for this moment.

"Nowhere."

"Try again, Bernadette. Nowhere doesn't exist. Smoking with the girls, necking with the boys?"

"Maman! How can you say this!"

"I can say anything if you don't tell me. I can make it up, just the way you did. Anything I want to think of. Rolling up your skirt. Shoplifting nylon stockings . . ."

"Stop! Stop it! I'm not like that."

"Where were you, then?"

"I was hiding."

"Where?"

"Behind a tree, in the park. I sat on my school bag."

"All that time? Behind a tree? That's it?"

Yes. That's what she did. No cigarettes, no boys. Just the light green shadow of the tree all around her while she wondered, over and over, why she wasn't born just a little earlier. Why did she have to work so hard on her homework to get a second-rate blue star while Colette breezed through and got a gold one? Why did the boys see only her sister's blonde angel face? Bernadette feels invisible, with her long nose, thin lips, and dark hair.

"And why were you hiding?"

Bernadette sat under the tree and plotted ways to be just like Colette. Her heroine, her sister.

"I was hiding to cry."

"You already do that here. Why did you have to miss school to cry some more?"

"I don't like school."

"I know. Were you crying because you don't like school?"

"Yes, a little bit."

"And what is the big bit?"

Silence.

And then more noisy tears, one after the other, the size of hail pellets. Madame Beauregard sighs. Maybe Bernadette should be an actress. She loves to cry.

"Parce que tu m'aimes pas! You don't love me, nobody loves me!"

Love, love, and more love. That's all they seem to think about, her crazed daughters. What about potatoes to peel, meals to cook, dishes to wash? What about cleaning the hall floor, always muddy, beating the carpets, always dusty? There has been only hard work and the burden of raising seven children on her own for her, and the loneliness papered over with books at night since Léandre died. Between the pages she stops worrying about her sick son and her drunk one, about yet another wedding coming up, and Lili and Colette staying out at night later and later. Madame Beauregard won't encourage this need for love, won't feed this foolish heart. Her daughters will be stronger than she was. Love is not forever, but living is.

"Y a pas juste l'amour dans vie, Bernadette. And I'll tell you something else. You need school more than you need love, and you also need a job more than you need love. Don't forget it or you'll end up with seven children to raise, four lodgers to feed and clean, six fish in a tank, and a bunch of books in a cupboard. That's all. Next time I get a letter telling me you are hiding behind a tree to cry because nobody loves you, I will take you out of school to help me clean up and cook."

"You won't send me to learn English, like Lili?"

"So an Italian Lothario can try to steal you away? Absolutely not!"

Madame Beauregard gives Bernadette an awkward hug, but when her daughter lifts her needy eyes full of wet hopes, she looks away.

Children are so selfish.

Voice

"Télephoniste. Puis-je vous aider? What number? One moment, please . . . Mister Robert is calling from Toronto, do you accept the charges?"

To become an operator, first you have to be a woman. *The girls and the telephone are natural friends,* says the manual distributed to them on the first day of the training. You also need to be between seventeen and twenty-five years of age. The candidates have to take a short oral test, where they are screened for clear and distinct enunciation, a hearing test to make sure their own basic equipment is in order, and a long English test, which half the hopefuls flunk. Bell Telephone is a big company, run with almost military precision and discipline, but the pay cheque is good and comes in every other week. Lili breezes through the tests; the English she learned in Toronto is paying off.

To practise and exercise your voice is as important as to practise your handwriting. Lili is better at harnessing her vocal cords than she was at writing papers. Her voice becomes a tool. *Each syllable has to be pronounced clearly and accurately, and with the rising inflection that gives a pleasant tone.* It is a studied voice, low, warm, clipped. Efficient. The important thing is to sound genteel, not too rough or too high-pitched. Ladylike. What the operators have to know about the technical system is easily mastered, and the lines they rehearse are few. What takes longer to learn is how to say the lines. When she rehearses for the teacher, Lili calls on the memory of all the American movies she has seen and heard, and she hits the right note every time. When nobody's listening, she works on her sexy voice, even though the instructions are clear. *That charming huskiness would never do in a telephone operator.*

In any case, Bell Telephone's motto is productivity. The shorter the answer, the more calls are processed. The trainees are drilled over and over again to erase any emotion from their voice except for an unwavering politeness and a welcoming manner: *The customers can't see you, so get that smile into your voice!*

But there is one thing Lili cannot flatten in her voice. The harder she tries, the worse it gets. "Un, deux, tr-rois . . ."

"Booth number four, Mademoiselle Beauregard, or should I say Mademoiselle Beaurregarrd, try not to let those *r*'s roll away, please."

"One, two, thr-ree, fourr . . ."

"Mademoiselle Beauregard, repeat after me. One, two, three . . . That's it, the tongue just behind the front teeth for the *th* sound, and no rolling *r*'s."

"One, two, fr-r-ree . . . Maudite marde!"

"Mademoiselle Beauregard! Self-control, please."

Lili wipes her brow. They don't roll their *r*'s in English. It is a flat language.

"Excusez-moi, Mademoiselle Matte, but my tongue feels like ground beef."

"It has been only an hour, Mademoiselle Beauregard. How are you going to feel after four?"

"Operator, how may I help you? Which number, sir?"

No more baby, dar-rling, or big guy, no sighs or purrs. Almost no more rolling *r*'s. No more time to fool around, this is the real thing. Lili has to keep an eye on her average, and she has a good one. She is twenty years old and a working girl now, paying room and board to her mother. Mind you, it's half price for the family, so she has enough left for fancy clothes, lunches with the other Bell girls, and the movies. Lili doesn't go out with Louis-P. anymore. She'd rather be with her new girlfriends and feel free to make all the risqué comments they hold back during the working hours. The birchbark letters from Louis-Philippe have been stowed away in an empty box of Black Magic chocolates, along with the ones from the Toronto janitor and the invitation to the Séminaire de Québec's graduation ball. A crazy American pilot Lili met at a dance a few months ago also keeps on writing to her from military bases all over the States. She hasn't sent him the bathing suit shot he keeps requesting.

"Six-cinq-tr-rois, qua-tre-cinq-huit-zer-ro . . ."

Lili has grown into her voice.

The Third Wedding, January 1955

"So sad," sighs Marie-Joseph.

"What did you say?" shouts Marie-Reine into the phone receiver. A bad ice storm hit the whole eastern part of the province the previous day and many lines have been damaged. This one crackles with static.

"So sad!" Marie-Joseph shouts back.

"You're starting to sound like a broken record, Fifine." The old name comes back when Marie-Joseph exasperates her sister. But it is not hard to exasperate Madame Beauregard today.

Marie-Joseph goes on, her voice thin under the noise. "I can't believe I won't be there for Henri's wedding. Our Henri!"

The bad weather conditions have also kept the Chicoutimi–Québec road closed. "Have the Lépines changed their mind?"

"No, Fifine, they haven't."

"So they won't be coming to their own daughter's wedding?"

"No, Fifine, they won't."

"Who do they think they are?"

"You tell me."

"Didn't you let them know that our uncle, Rodolphe Tremblay, was Chicoutimi's mayor? Cécile's father is only the mayor of Sainte-Rose-du-Nord, just another village along the Saguenay. Pretty, I hear, but not as pretty as Tadoussac, or as big as Chicoutimi."

"Keep mon oncle Rodolphe out of this, Fifine. He's long gone, may he rest in peace."

"And did you tell them your husband was the Banque de Montréal's manager? And a pilot in the Royal Air Force?"

"Let Léandre rest in peace too."

"And if they're so rich, why didn't they offer to pay for the wedding expenses, as they should if they are good Christians."

The crackling increases sharply, like a steak thrown in a red-hot pan.

"I can't hear you, Fifine!" Marie-Reine shouts again, now beyond exasperation. "I have to get dressed or I'll be late. I'll call you tomorrow to let you know how it went. We'll miss you!"

Henri's wedding to Cécile Lépine takes place in Saint-Sacrement's church because the bride's parents refused to organize their daughter's marriage ceremony in their own parish, as wedding protocol demands. They almost lost her to tuberculosis, and now they are losing her again to a man they firmly believe is not good enough for her.

The bride is ravishing, her dark hair and eyes contrasting with the white velvet dress and matching fur-trimmed stole. Her bright red lips leave a trace on her cigarette stubs, her champagne glass, and Henri's white collar. Maybe they all overdo the celebration because of the unfortunate circumstances. The groom, now a civil engineer, has pitched in to cover the ceremony's expenses. The champagne is flowing and there is enough food to feed an army, but only half the invited guests are present.

On the commemorative photographs taken outside the house on Louis-Fréchette, nobody looks stable. Faces are blurred, limbs askew, bodies slipping out of frame, presumably on the ice. The excesses of the day might also be partly responsible for the vague memories of Monsieur et Madame Henri Beauregard's wedding day. Even Lucien, now fourteen, is sick the next morning.

Paul Des Ruisseaux

The four brand-new clay courts are right on top of the hill, by the Côte Saint-Sacrement. Their white lines shine under the metallic light shades, swinging on the wire at the lightest breeze. Not only is it often windy on the edge of the Haute-Ville, it has also been raining for twenty-eight days in a row, from mid-May to mid-June. Now that the rain has stopped, everybody pretends summer has arrived, even though the nights are still cool.

Colette has a summer job at Bell Telephone, and after work both she and Lili wolf down their dinner and join the Saint-Sacrement's sporty set. They start the evening playing languid singles, yawning in between half-hearted racquet swings, showing off young lazy legs as white as their tennis shorts. A tan would look better, but they do get the attention anyway. By the end of the evening their wild screams can be heard all the way to the Basse-Ville as they finish playing doubles with two gentlemen eager to let them win. After the lights are switched off and the tennis clubhouse locked up, they linger with their partners around the Coca-Cola machine. They lean against the south wall of the building to hide from the Laurentian wind, smoke the cigarettes offered to them, and flirt. Nothing serious ever ensues: their partners are too young, too stupid, or too bold for the Beauregard sisters. They are on the lookout for more suitable beaux than these small-time Rod Lavers.

"Oui, allo? Est-ce que je pourrais parler à Mademoiselle Beauregard?"

Bernadette gets to the phone first, knowing it will enrage Lilianne and Colette.

"Which one?"

Here they are, swarming the receiver Bernadette is hanging on to. They whisper, "Come on, give me the phone, you pest! Get out of the way!"

"Which one?" repeats Bernadette to the embarrassed silence at the other end of the line. "Colette, Lilianne, or me, Bernadette?"

"The one who plays tennis," the brave voice goes on.

"Colette or Lilianne?"

"For crying out loud!" her two older sisters cry again, pinching Bernadette and pulling on her hair. But Bernadette won't budge.

"The one who wears a white and green striped shirt."

"Well, then, that's Lili," says Bernadette, passing the receiver to her sister.

Lili covers the mouthpiece with her hand. "Who is it?"

"I don't know. Why don't you ask him, stupid," says Bernadette, turning away.

"Hello?"

"Is this Lilianne Beauregard?"

"Speaking."

"This is Paul Des Ruisseaux. I don't think you know my name, but you might have seen me at the tennis court. I'm a great admirer of your style and was wondering if we could play a set or two together."

What has really made an impression on Paul is the length of Lili's limber legs and the bouncy fullness of her green striped shirt. Her statuesque volley destroys his concentration and she beats him six-three, loses five-seven, then wins seven-six. After the game, they sit on the front porch of Madame Beauregard's house where Colette is helping a new roomer, a medical student named Zacharie Caron, with his biology. He is hopeless with the studies but makes Colette laugh. Bernadette files her nails in a corner, pretending to ignore everybody. She has started attending classes at the Sullivan School of Business to become a secretary and has discovered how easy it is to be Strawberry Blonde by Clairol. She will become a professional blonde with nail polish and lipstick in vibrant shades to match her smart sweater-sets.

At eleven o'clock on the dot, Madame Beauregard turns off the radio, puts down her knitting, and gets up to feed her fish, shouting "Last call!" from the living room. When Lili walks Paul Des Ruisseaux to the door, she accepts his offer for a bicycle ride and a picnic the next Saturday. Then she wonders why she's never noticed him before. Such a nice young man, and he also works at Bell Telephone.

He has bought Kodacolor film and asks a passerby to take the snapshot.

They stand side by side, leaning on a large grey rock. The cantilever bridge recedes behind them. Their smiles are not just for the picture, skin deep, gums and teeth, but rooted deep inside. He makes her slide slightly in front of him so they can fill up the 24 × 36 millimetre rectangle of the photo with their hopes, their joy. Their cheeks do not touch yet, but his brown suede shoulder leans against her red wool sweater, the wind whipping her hair into a dark, tangled halo. It's a blustery day. One of those spring coups de vent, cleaning up everything in its wake; dead leaves, new pollen, all the sand spread on the icy winter road. The sky is bright blue, and the shadows of the white cumulus clouds race against the ruffled water. The bridge is getting a fresh coat of paint; it is half bright orange, half khaki green. Lili's mouth is cherry red, her cheeks rose in the fresh air, her eyes dark navy. Paul wants to catch and keep this moment forever with him. He is still not sure he can believe his eyes. Lilianne doesn't need any proof. After the photo they sit against the rock to have a picnic of fresh bread and cheese, and a bottle of cider. They scratch the rock's hard surface with a pocket knife: P.D.R. et L.B. juin 1955. When he cuts an apple in two, giving her half, a little of the stone residue grits between their teeth. And then they cross the bridge.

He takes the lead, breaking through the stiff wind for her, and she follows, pedalling at the same rhythm. They are so high over the river that the wake of the motorboats below looks like chalk strokes on grey slate, and she feels so lighthearted that she wonders, briefly, whether there could still be a hole inside of her, leftover from her childhood disease. But her breath is strong and steady even though she has to push hard and fast to keep her balance and stay on a straight course between the railings' narrow path.

Confiteor

"Confiteor Deo omnipotenti . . . mea culpa, mea culpa, mea maxima culpa. Father, I confess to many impure thoughts."

The heavy velvet curtain makes the confessional stuffy. Once Paul kneels, the organist's scales and the smell of hot wax recede, and behind the golden grid a profile gravely asks, "How many, son?"

Paul tries to take a deep breath, but he almost gags from the heat. He loosens his tie knot.

"Many, my father. So many it would be a waste of time to try to put a number on it. Father, I need help. Those thoughts are with me day and night. I have prayed and I have tried to blank them out, but how can I ignore this pulse, this throb, this ache, Father? I am engaged . . ."

"You told me, my son."

"I know you know, but how am I going to survive the next six months as a Christian? Where will I find the strength? Six months, Father! I see her every day, and she's the most desirable woman in the world!"

"What's her name, my son?"

"Lilianne Beauregard, Father."

"Oh. I see. It won't be easy. Has there been anything more than thoughts, my son?"

Silence.

"Did you come here to confess or not, my son? Without confession, no absolution. Has there been more than thoughts?"

"There has been more than thoughts, Father."

"What has there been, my son?"

"Troubled sleep, dreams, lust. I don't know which saints to pray to anymore!"

"I can recommend a few good ones, whose torments will make yours look like a picnic on the Plains of Abraham, my son. Remember Daniel in the lions' den, or Sainte-Mathilde, whose body was stretched until every bone broke, and closer to us, Jean de Brébeuf. Les Sauvages tortured him for three days before eating his heart."

"My fiancée is nibbling at mine every moment of the day."

"Now, has there been more than this, my son, this which is already a grave offence to our Creator and to yourself?"

"I have kissed, Father, I have kissed her until she had a red rash all around her lovely mouth, I have kissed her until my tongue went numb."

"Holding hands is Christian, touching the face of the loved one, her arms, her hair, is Christian. Kissing is allowed as long as it doesn't lead to more regrettable carnal activities. It's often downhill from there, my son, a very slippery slope. Kissing can lead to mortal sin, kissing can waste away the honour of your fiancée, kissing is Christian if the Christian who is kissing has self-control. I feel that you are not in full control of yourself. Am I right, my son?"

"I'm afraid so, Father."

"First, I would recommend mortifying the flesh. Go and run, up and down the Côte Salaberry, climb the Cap-Diamant, swim across the St. Lawrence River, whatever it takes! Exhaust this fire, alleviate the tension, my son. And I don't mean dancing till dawn close to the object of your desire. These parish dances have been getting out of hand ever since—what do they call it? Rock and roll. And what's his name? The king?"

"Elvis Presley, Father."

"Adulation of pagan gods is wrong, do not forget it. It's the beginning of the end! I will ask you to pray rather than dance, my son. Pray. You will find strength in prayer. For the sake of your bride-to-be as well as yours, pray and repent."

"Yes, Father."

"And last but not least, I would recommend that you come and confess every day instead of seeing Mademoiselle Beauregard. What you need is not more of Mademoiselle Beauregard but moral guidance and support through this difficult time. Weekends should be enough time to devote to your fiancée. Phone her every day. If she feels neglected, pay a mid-week visit to Madame Beauregard's house, which is, I'm afraid, not the most Christian in the parish. You are absolved, my son, but conditionally. You will say your mea culpa and one hundred paternosters. Do stay away from the Ave Maria. In your state of mind . . . In nomine Patris, et Filii, et Spiritus Sancti. Amen."

Trois-Rivières, le premier mars, 1956

Mon amour,

You will be happy to learn I have finally found the perfect love nest for us, after visiting at least a dozen apartments. It is in a new development on the edge of town, far enough from the paper mills to avoid the foul smell, unless the wind is blowing from the south, which doesn't happen very often. I saw many blueberry bushes growing along the railway track at the end of the backyard, so you will be able to make your favourite dessert and mine too, the famous Beauregard blueberry pie. The rent is a little more than I had budgeted for, but with all the overtime I've been putting in, we should be all right.

So many details to think about, Lili. It does keep my mind off other things, such as the day I will finally take you in my arms, the blessed moment when we will be husband and wife—when we will be as one, at last. At very, very, very long last, my love.

But thank God it is Thursday, and in another twenty-four hours you will be in my arms again, ma chérie.

Thanks for your letter, so understanding, so supportive—I know why I chose you to be my wife. Do you want to go dancing at the Hotel Victoria on Saturday? My friends Marcel and Josette will be there, and maybe Colette and Zacharie would like to join us too. Why don't you ask them? And to think I am missing all those evenings in the kitchen . . . That's enough to make me want to row a boat or ride a bicycle or, even better, fly a plane all the way back from Trois-Rivières to Québec!

I kiss you tenderly, my lovely fiancée.
Ton Grand,
Paul

This is the one, thinks Madame Beauregard, jubilant, with each new letter Lili receives from Paul Des Ruisseaux. Finally! And these are real letters. On standard pale blue writing paper with matching envelope, in French, from Trois-Rivières. Not in Italian from Toronto, or on birchbark from summer camp, or in English from some air base in the States. This one will tie her daughter's flighty heart down, and about time too. Lilianne will soon turn twenty-two; she's had her fun.

Madame Beauregard leans to pick up the scatter of mail on the mat by the front door. Another one tying the knot, another one off her hands. Why does she feel so heavy then? The doctor has told her to be careful about her weight, but she hasn't listened to him. It is the increasingly empty house that seems to weigh down on her. With

Huguette, Henri, and Léo married, Lilianne engaged and Colette about to be, only Bernadette and Lucien remain. When the children have all left, she won't need the lodgers' income either. But not to worry, not now. Lucien still has many years of school before him and Bernadette might not take the short route to marriage.

One hundred and twenty-five letters, one a day: this is a solid foundation for a marriage if there ever was one.

Marie-Joseph's Last Wedding, June 1956

They have exchanged rings and vows. They have promised they will be there for each other, rain or shine, for better or for worse. The veil has been lifted off the bride's face and the vows have been sealed with hot lipstick like red wax, for everybody to see. Then they have drunk champagne and eaten hors d'oeuvres, and they have danced to celebrate. They have cut the three-tier cake, each with one hand on the knife, smiling for posterity. The bride has thrown her bouquet, which was caught eagerly by Colette. Bernadette cried a little. It is late. The newlyweds are alone amid the crowd. The moment they have waited for so long, more than a year, is about to take place. They look at each other, their eyes blazing, their love incandescent. Madame Beauregard takes her daughter in her arms and whispers something that makes her laugh. Madame P.E. Des Ruisseaux looks at her son one more time before letting him go, tears in her eyes. Her last child, her baby boy. Six feet tall, twenty-seven years old. He was supposed to be a priest.

Monsieur et Madame Paul Des Ruisseaux are leaving, blinded by the rice grains and confetti, when Lili feels something on her arm, holding her back. Right by the front door is Marie-Joseph, as pale as if she's seen a ghost. Paul is pulling hard on his wife's hand, trying to drag her away.

"Wait, Paul, just a second. I have to go, Fifine, and so should you. You don't look well. Too much champagne maybe?" Lilianne squeezes her hand. "Go to bed. That's where I'm going too!" She winks and she is gone, carried by the crowd following them to the car. Marie-Joseph backs up from the noise, the lights. She shuts the door and lets her fingers run along the engraved starburst in the glass panel, muttering to herself, "I just did what needed to be done and I don't know if it was right or wrong anymore."

A few hours before, while the wedding reception was in full swing, Marie-Joseph's mood had been very different.

"Isn't she beautiful? Isn't he handsome? Don't they look happy?"

"Yes, they do," Marie-Reine answers, glowing with pride.

"There is nothing wrong this time, is there? Why does his mother look pained?" Marie-Joseph asks, as if something was bound to be sad.

"Madame P.E. Des Ruisseaux? She always looks like this. She thinks it's classy."

"And everybody was able to come, even Huguette! Doesn't she look lovely? Don't they all?"

Huguette is in a coral-coloured suit, maternity-style. She is about six months pregnant and her first-born daughter, Marilyn—a good name in both French and English—never leaves her father's arms. He visibly adores the imp pulling on his ears and climbing on his head, all dimples, sparkling brown eyes, and freckles. Cécile is pregnant too, although it doesn't show much yet. She looks well, smokes and drinks champagne and orange juice—no morning sickness for this one. "Solid peasant stock," sneers Marie-Joseph, remembering the pretensions of Cécile's father, the mayor of Sainte-Rose-du-Nord. Berthe, Léo's wife, also smokes and drinks champagne, no orange juice, and is also pregnant, for the third time. Lucien is supposed to be keeping an eye on her two young sons, but he is absorbed in the task of stuffing as many cocktail sausages wrapped in bacon as he can into his mouth, lining up the half-burnt toothpicks on the white damask tablecloth. He is careful not to drink champagne; the smell of it is enough to make him feel unwell. His two nephews are playing quietly beside him. One of them is taking a bite out of each strawberry he fishes out of a big glass bowl before throwing it on the floor, while his small brother is on tiptoe, dipping his hand in the whipped cream and licking each finger carefully before starting again. Colette doesn't leave Zacharie Caron's side. They are celebrating not only Lilianne and Paul's wedding but also their own engagement. They will marry next year when Zach finishes his medical training. Bernadette has a new date. They both look a little bored, waiting for the dancing to start and help them break the ice. She is now the only one of her sisters without an engagement ring.

Lilianne whirls by her mother and her aunt, her wedding dress a tight bodice with a round neckline showing her collarbone, the full double-layered skirt brushing her calves. It's the New Look style, straight from Paris and copied in Montréal. Even the Abbé Audette has admired the dress. Even he couldn't find anything wrong with this marriage, except maybe Marie-Joseph Tremblay's well-worn polka-dot dress and black shoes. The Abbé Audette knows he shouldn't be paying attention to such details, but he does. He likes nothing better than a grand wedding. He's also very happy Madame P.E. Des Ruisseaux's son is finally getting married. Paul has skipped confession for the last six months, telling his mother he found a new spiritual leader in Trois-Rivières.

Lilianne grabs Marie-Joseph's arm. "Can I borrow our Fifine, for just a second?" She finds a quiet corner in the kitchen to speak to her aunt. "Marie-Joseph, I need your help."

"Anything for you, my Lili, but what more could you possibly want?" says Marie-Joseph, holding her niece's hands to steady herself. She has let her guard down for a few glasses of champagne, the boisterous mood of the celebration infectious. She's even danced with Henri, and Léo, and Paul's older brothers, all so charming. She didn't enjoy her dance with Colette's fiancé. He swept her off her feet so hard, they almost tumbled on the sofa. With his big hands and hungry smile, Zacharie Caron looks more like a lumberjack than a doctor to her.

"I want you to talk to Paul's mother, Fifine."

"Oh, ma belle Lili," says Marie-Joseph, "you are the only one who still calls me Fifine, except for your mother when she gets impatient with me. It makes me feel almost young again!" She sketches a clumsy dance step, tripping over her own scuffed shoes.

Lili forces her aunt to look at her. "Fifine, listen! You have to talk to Paul's mother. She's more your type than Maman's. Let's just say that they don't get along so famously."

"Really?" asks Marie-Joseph, taking a sip from a leftover glass of champagne.

Lili frowns and takes the glass out of her aunt's hand, picking a broken toothpick out of it before giving it back to her. "Fifine, please, just show her there are not only sinners in this family. Let her know there's also a saint."

"A saint?"

"Yes, you. You've always been devoted to others, you've always known right from wrong, so please, just for me, Fifine."

"A saint?" Marie-Joseph repeats, stunned. "What do you know about me, Lili, to call me a saint? You don't know, Lili. Nobody knows. I don't even know myself."

"What are you talking about, Fifine," says Lilianne, looking around for Madame P.E. Des Ruisseaux. "There she is, over there. Will you? Please?"

Marie-Joseph smiles wanly at her niece. "Anything for you, Lili, anything. He is so handsome, you look so happy . . ."

Lilianne kisses her aunt on both cheeks before pushing her towards Madame P.E. Des Ruisseaux. They quickly find out they share the same devotion to Sainte-Anne.

On the way back the Québec–Chicoutimi bus breaks down in the middle of the Parc des Laurentides, where there are no villages or houses for miles. Only the road, the forest, a lake here and there with a fishing camp or two. It takes a long time for a spare bus to be sent from Québec, but it's only when the last rays of sun wash off the gravel shoulder that the elder Mademoiselle Tremblay, as many still call her, starts to feel bothered. The driver, behind whom she always sits, will tell the police later that she complained of pain in her chest, shortness of breath, and a tingle in her arm that she was trying to shake off. The passenger beside her, another lady from Chicoutimi she knew well, tried to make her unbutton her dress a little, to breathe more easily. When this didn't work, the driver suggested a few steps outside in the fresh air. The bus was quite stuffy, but the sound of wolves howling on and off in the night seemed to add to Mademoiselle Tremblay's discomfort. That's when she became agitated, talking non-stop in a low voice. The Chicoutimi lady, seeing her get worse, took her hand and prayed. When Mademoiselle Tremblay started to shiver, they tried to cover her with a blanket. This appeared to make her only worse. She thrashed about and fought to get the blanket off. By then, the lady will tell the police, she was delirious. Sleds, axes, wolves, bones. All sorts of nonsense. That was when the driver tried to restrain Mademoiselle Tremblay the best he could, shouting, "Is there a doctor here, a nurse?" But there wasn't, and she soon stopped moving. The good lady of Chicoutimi, still crying, will tell a heartbroken Marie-Reine that Madame Beauregard's sister seemed to be at peace during her last moments. She also relates dutifully the deceased's last words, including the expression of surprise.

"Oh. So this is where you are, Father."

PART THREE

Toute la terre des deulx coustez dudit fleuve . . . est aussi belle et unye que jamays
homme regarda. Il y a aucunes montaignes assez loing dudit fleuve que on veoyt par sus
lesdictes terres desquelles descend plusieurs ripvières qui entrent dedans ledict fleuve. . . .
Vous trouverez jusques audict Canada force . . . ballaines marsoings chevaulx de mer
adhothuys qui est une sorte de poisson duquel jamays n'avyons veu ny ouy parler. Ilz
sont blancs comme neige et grandz comme marsoins et ont le corps et la teste comme lep-
vryers lesquelz se tiennent entre la mer et l'eaue doulce qui commance entre la ripviere du
Saguenay et Canada.
Deuxième Relation de Jacques Cartier, 1535–1536
[on discovering the shores of the St. Lawrence River
between Québec and Montréal]

The whole country on both sides of the river [St. Lawrence] . . . is as fine a land and as
level as ever one beheld. There are some mountains visible at a considerable distance from
the river, and into it several tributaries flow down from these. . . . Up as far as Canada,
you will meet many whales, porpoises, sea-horses, walruses, and adhothuys, which is a
species of fish that we had never seen or heard of before. They are as white as snow and
have a head like a greyhound's. Their habitat is between ocean and the fresh-water that
begins between the river Saguenay and Canada.

Troisième Relation:
The Good Mother

T HE plane doesn't cut a straight line but follows an arc across the top of the globe: London, Ireland, Greenland, and back south across Labrador to the St. Lawrence's north shore around Blanc-Sablon. From above, England looks green and grey, a tamed patchwork of small square fields and shreds of clouds. Then comes the harsh deep blue of the Atlantic, scratched white here and there as giant waves crest and crash. The only other sign of life this high up is another plane, a little farther along the concave line of the horizon.

By the time the main meal is finished and the movie over, we have reached Labrador. I raise the plastic lid of the porthole to look down at a brown surface speckled all over like a Jackson Pollock painting, irregular shapes of blue and brown with traces of white along the shaded ridges. Soon the water comes into view, this time defined by two shorelines edging slowly towards each other. From now on the plane will track this fluid path, from the wide estuary of the Gulf of St. Lawrence all the way to where the river narrows.

Québec.

When I see the teardrop shape of Île d'Orléans at Quebec City, I know it's time to start looking for my shoes, pushed far under the front seat. Within fifteen minutes we have caught up with the paved and built-over Île de Montréal, its humble pod of skyscrapers nestled against the green lump of Mont-Royal. We descend on the approach past the mega parking lots of the West Island malls and the warehouse roofs of Dorval.

Madelon is seated by the window and Marion is by the aisle. My arms spring up to protect them, a familiar reaction as the plane touches down and bounces off the tarmac. The engines reverse power, thrusting our bodies forward. Pillows, blankets, discarded bottles of water, crayons, newspapers, and earphone sets scatter everywhere. I gather our belongings from the trip's debris as the plane taxis to its gate. It's the summer of 1998 and we are almost home. We have followed the same path as the explorers, but it has taken us less than eight hours, travelling in a bird with metal wings. What would Jacques Cartier have thought of this?

Keyword: Mère Marie de l'Incarnation, or Marie Guyart.

Mist, vast forests, high cliffs. The first time the venerable mother saw Canada, it was in a dream. Marie Guyart did not doubt that this vision was a call from God and she would answer it, even if it meant leaving her cloistered life in Tours, France. She remembered her dream when she read Jesuit father Le Jeune's *Relation*, calling for virtuous women to go and instruct "the savage girls." Father Le Jeune added that the recruits "would have to surmount the fear natural to their sex," something Mère Marie de l'Incarnation had no time for as she started the first of the many letters it took to convince her spiritual advisors of her calling.

In her dream she didn't walk alone to the top of the cliffs but with a companion. She recognized this companion when she met Madame de la Peltrie, a noblewoman who devoted her life and her fortune to Mère Marie de l'Incarnation's work. Once they had raised money and purchased and packed supplies, Marie de l'Incarnation set sail from Dieppe on May 4, 1639, with Madeleine de la Peltrie, Charlotte Barré, Marie de Saint-Joseph, and Cécile de Sainte-Croix. "When I put my foot on the boat," she wrote in one of the last-minute letters delivered from her ship to the fishermen they passed on their way out of the harbour, "it seemed to me I was entering Paradise, for I was taking the first step to risk my life for the love of Him who gave it to me." A storm raged for fifteen days, preventing mass from being celebrated on the bridge. Then, the boat had a close encounter with an iceberg as big as a city. On arrival at Tadoussac in August, the group of women transferred to a smaller boat to travel to Québec. There they shared a room with the drying cod stock, until the smell of the aging fish forced them out onto the bridge, where they sat in the rain for five hours. Finally, at Québec, a rowboat took them ashore, where, by the roasting fire, they dried their long black robes and veils and the stiff white wimples framing their faces. They spent their first night in Canada staring at the stars through the cracks in the roof of their humble shelter.

Only three years later, with the help of God and Madame de la Peltrie's money, Marie de l'Incarnation had built a stone convent at the top of Côte de la Montagne in the Upper Town, part of which still stands to this day.

A bonfire burns bright on the trampled snow of the convent's courtyard. Smoking cauldrons are hung over smaller fires, cooking a mix of corn, oil, dried berries, and whatever salted cod, fresh rabbit, or white fish can be added. Teepees are set up for the old and the young, the ones who cannot follow the hunt and are left behind. The sisters glide above the snow in their long black robes, giving bread to the girls they have dressed and cleansed of grease and vermin. The children play games of chance with small bones; the skinny dogs wander around the pots, their pelts stiff with frost. The St. Lawrence River has turned into an ice plain that the Indians use to cross over from Lévis. Without the to and fro of boats from France, the colony at Québec is silent except for the crackle of the burning wood, the hacking of an axe biting into a log, the dogs' howls, the bells from the sisters calling for catechism. Québec is hibernating, trying to survive until the spring.

Inside the convent a girl has been washed and dressed. This is

Madame de la Peltrie's favourite chore. The girl has then been given bread made by Marie de Saint-Joseph, and has received her first catechism lesson, conducted by Mère Marie de l'Incarnation herself. The girl now has a Christian name, Agnès, to use with her Huron name, Negaskoumat, and is assigned a bed in the dormitory. She has been pliant and docile, smiling and repeating the words after the good mother. But in the morning, the floor of the dormitory is as cold as the ice plain on the river, and a lick of snow has piled up by the open window. Agnès Negaskoumat's bed is empty, her black dress torn to pieces. She has escaped, naked. Children find her a few days later on their daily round to collect small wood, her frozen body half-buried in a snowbank. The crows have plucked out her eyes and pecked her nose and mouth off. When the children drag the body back to the convent's courtyard, the sisters make sure everybody has time to see what happened to the runaway. Agnès was not baptized, so there is no more hope for her. The Huron elders wrap her mortal remains in a beaver pelt and hang her up a tree near the convent, where her soul will sing like a crow and her body will remain until the ground thaws out. On sunny days the corpse's smell rolls into the convent's yard when the fires are out. Every morning when she gets up in her freezing room, her breath a cold cloud unable to warm her hands, Marie de l'Incarnation prays for the pagan girl's lost soul before bringing her fingers back to life by writing a letter. The First People of God are so destitute that the supplies brought from France are almost gone already.

The first boats arrive from France in June, announcing the start of the writing season. Letters have to be written and sealed before the boats leave again, having brought the precious supplies. Besides supervising the construction, keeping accounts, reaching ecstasy in long hours of prayer and feeding, cleaning, dressing, and converting the Huron girls, the good mother writes about twelve thousand letters in the course of her life. Where does she find time? She writes all night long, all through the summer, by the light of a lamp filled with porpoise oil. She writes to her loved ones, informing them of her fatigue but otherwise good health, and to her spiritual advisor about her mystical life. But most of all she writes to lobby and raise money to ensure her mission's continuity. These letters are sent to potential benefactors, including Queen Anne of Austria, Cardinal Richelieu's niece, the duchess of Aiguillon, one countess, and many mesdames as well as a Monsieur de Bernières.

The costs of the mission at Québec are exorbitant. Everything is imported, so freight doubles the price of supplies: clothes, food, livestock, housewares, building materials, paper, ink. Once these bills are settled, wages have to be paid to the carpenters and the masons. In August 1643 the boat bringing most of the perishable goods and all of the year's supplies for both the convent and the Augustines' hospital never arrives. The merchandise is worth two thousand pounds, or close to the annual budget for the Ursuline congregation before donations.

"Mon très cher et bien-aimé fils, très humble salut dans les plaies sacrées que Notre-Seigneur a voulu souffrir pour le salut des âmes!" Thus the good mother writes to the son she has abandoned not once but twice. Even then, in 1643, Claude Martin still asks his mother if they will ever see each other again in this world. "I don't know" is his mother's answer. "Let God decide, because I do not want anything but for Him and with Him."

The first time Marie Guyart abandoned her son, Claude was a young boy and she was a widow about to enter the cloister. She left him in the care of her brother's family, but Claude kept coming back to to bang at the convent doors, asking for his mother. His demands were met only with silence. Then Marie de l'Incarnation left France for Canada, and although she would write to her son constantly, supporting his decision to enter a religious order himself, they would never see each other again. After his mother's death, Dom Claude Martin devoted his life to keeping her memory alive, publishing a collection of her letters in 1681. Naturally, because these letters had been written in such a hurry, he had to improve their grammar and revise their content. He couldn't have his mother, so he rewrote her life.

* * *

Two freighters ride the tide out towards the Gulf of St. Lawrence on the shimmering water of the river. The traffic of goods on the maritime seaway never slacks off, day or night, tide in or out, between May and November. From the deck of our cottage we watch them go by. Once in a while the wet fur of a seal's head gleams above the water, bobbing with a family of ducks just off the outcrop of rocks at high tide. The sun illuminates our first blessed morning, our messy hair, our bowls of cereal. Until the phone rings. It's my father.

That's how it happens, when life is about to change. The most simple facts and words become impossible to decipher, to recognize. They are unacceptable. But before you can think, you know. I catch my breath, my guts balled up in a knot. Ten days ago my mother was still fighting off what is called walking pneumonia, not a brain tumour.

"How . . . when did you?"

"Yesterday. We left the cottage to go to l'Hôtel-Dieu hospital for a CAT scan."

"Why?"

"It started on one side of her mouth, a slight paralysis. Two weeks ago. Then her right arm became weak."

"But why didn't you say something? We could have been there, with you." I can't believe we drove by Québec yesterday, not even knowing they had left the cottage, or that my mother was so sick.

"I needed time. We needed time together. I'm sorry."

"What else are you going to tell me? Is she going to die?"

Marion and Madelon have come in from the deck. They look at me with frightened eyes, but I turn my back to them.

"It might not be as bad as it sounds, Lucie. They might be able to do something about it. Depends whether it's benign or cancerous. Whether they can operate or not."

His voice chokes. The silence hurts.

"Where is she?"

"They're keeping her in hospital for more tests."

"I want to go." The drive takes only an hour and a half.

"Come tomorrow."

Marion and Madelon run towards me as soon as I hang up the phone.

"Maman!"

"It's okay, it's okay. Grand-Maman is sick. We'll go see her in hospital tomorrow, all right?"

The sunshine is fierce all day. The boats go by, loaded with containers, paper, grain, wood, maybe even fur pelts, even though beaver hats have long been replaced by baseball caps. A great blue heron comes out at dusk to fish, flying slowly from a treetop to a rock, breaking through the water.

"Regarde, Maman. God's light!"

Sharp orange and yellow rays, like the spokes of a wheel, burst grey-mauve clouds, reminding even Madelon of the Renaissance's paintings to the glory of God we have seen at the National Gallery. Even higher above our heads, two white lines are slowly drawn across the open part of the sky by a silent plane. At the time of Michelangelo this would have been incomprehensible, thus noted as a bona fide miracle.

Marion is sitting beside me on a piece of driftwood set by the fire we have just started. We can see all the way to the south shore and Kamouraska, the metal roofs of the farm buildings reflecting the last rays of the setting sun. A cruise ship goes by swiftly, first just a dot on the purple water, then a growing shape, white and elegant, riding the tide out. Madelon runs along the shore, skipping and waving, before she starts looking for precious stones. The ship's deep wake soon comes crashing at her feet, wetting her shoes and making her scream with delight. Marion stays beside me, looking worried. Mothers are not supposed to cry, only daughters.

"Grand-Maman is very sick, is she?"

I nod. Yes.

"Is she going to die?"

"Maybe."

"But dying is not a bad thing, is it?"

I shake my head. No, just another journey. My mouth turns down, my chin quivers.

"Then why are you crying?"

I shake my head again, wiping my face on the sleeve of my sweatshirt.

"Because I would miss her."

She slips her hand in mine and asks, in the softest voice, "Would you like a candy?"

I don't need a bona fide miracle, just a sign. I close my eyes, holding on to my daughter's hand. Then I hear it. A muffled thump. Another one. Barely audible, at the threshold of perception. Is it the surf, my heartbeat? No, it's someone jumping up and down. The low rustle of a thick, heavy fabric. A long midnight skirt. There is someone projected on the flip side of my eyelids, someone with wild hair like a river, rippling in the wind, and long white arms streaking the blueberry night with sugar. Stained teeth, flame red shoes, as if her feet were on fire, someone fearless. Someone calling for her life to start, right now, and for love to come, whatever the consequences. When I open my eyes again I catch a scratch on the horizon—the first shooting star of August, like a match leaving a trail of light. I'm ready to wish for the impossible.

Neurology, Hôtel-Dieu de Québec.

As soon as the results from my mother's CAT scan and blood tests came in, an operation was scheduled. Even in that short time, she lost the use of her right arm. We wait standing up, leaning on the wall by the elevator shaft. A small room with narrow seats is available around the corner for family members, but it is crowded. We drink water from the fountain in paper cones. The metallic doors have slid open twice already, but it wasn't her. The stretchers are wheeled away swiftly to the intensive care, the surgeon saying brisk, brutal things to the family. There is no sun here, no windows. Only neon.

"She's been in for three hours and seventeen minutes now." My father can't stop looking at his watch. Dr. Lagrange said it was a routine operation, nothing complicated, and that it should last less than four hours. "Lucky the tumour is on the left side," my sister Anne says. The right side is the speech centre. The neurosurgeon wouldn't have operated there. No quality of life if you can't speak.

The elevator doors slide open once more. "It's her!" My father takes two uncertain steps towards the stretcher, touching the side guard, leaning over. "Lilianne?" My mother seems to be sleeping, her head as big as a volleyball in the white bandages.

"It went very well, Monsieur Des Ruisseaux," says Dr. Lagrange, taking his mask off. "Your wife is now going to go to the intensive care unit, where she should spend around three days. We have to monitor carefully for blood clots after an operation like this." He makes a little sign and the stretcher is wheeled off, two nurses holding drips and wires. "It went well but it is a large tumour. The operation confirmed our test results. It is a primary cancer of the brain. Like a potato, if you want," the surgeon adds. "A potato with black spots. Even if I take out some, or most of it, the black spots will grow back. In your wife's case, it grows very fast, and it is very toxic. We do not get consistent results with radiation treatments on this type of cancer. Madame Des Ruisseaux might also have to receive these treatments in another city. It's not that we don't have the equipment, but we're short of staff and the waiting lists are long. You should start thinking of what's best for her."

We huddle closer together.

"Take it a day at a time," Dr. Lagrange says, anticipating the next question and not prepared to deal with it today. "She should be waking up within an hour. One visitor at a time in IC, close family only, maximum ten minutes per visit."

The next day Dr. Lagrange says that without the operation my mother would have been gone in less than three weeks. She will be going back home in five days if everything goes well. We start making plans to prepare the house in Sainte-Foy for a sick person. We also prepare to fight for her. She said she didn't want the treatments available even before hearing Dr. Lagrange's prognosis. She was holding her bad arm as she spoke, like someone cradling a sick infant. It made her look vulnerable, but she sounded resolute. "Then it's going to be the leg, and I won't be able to walk anymore. I'm not spending the last five years of my life paralyzed like my mother."

Sainte-Foy,
1966–1968

DEUX, trois, trois, six.

The address has been scrawled in haste on a piece of cardboard and nailed to a short post stuck in the dirt by the curb. It is spring, and the land on the north side of Sainte-Foy, outside Quebec City, is torn open by an armada of digging cranes, overflowing dump trucks, and mud-splattered bulldozers. The building season is only six months long because the ground is frozen from November to April. Where there were fields last year there is now a complex maze of crescents, squares, and cul-de-sacs, still unpaved but clearly marked by the curb lines and punctuated by raised storm sewers. The electricity is all set to go to each new household, travelling from square metal boxes alive with a light hum. Visible phone lines are not desirable in this spanking new suburb, so they will be dug underground. Two bright green street signs already flash at every intersection, the white embossed letters bearing the new street names: Des Trembles, Des Pins, Des Bouleaux, Des Frênes, Des Cèdres. All the trees from the native forest have been cut down, but here they grow again, if in name only: aspen, pine, birch, ash, and cedar. From this wounded landscape, houses will soon burst out of their concrete and wood-frame cocoons and grow into bungalows and split-levels. From this chaos order will soon emerge. Marie-Rollet is such a new parish, it doesn't have a real name yet.

*   *   *

"Maman, c'est qui, Marie Rollet?" asks Lucie.

"Paul, c'est qui donc, Marie Rollet?" Lilianne asks her husband.

"I'm not sure," says Paul. "Wasn't she Louis Hébert's wife?"

"C'est qui, Louis Hébert, Papa?" Lucie asks.

"I think he was one of the first settlers to come here from France, but it doesn't really matter, Lucie. Marie-Rollet is just the name of the school. Once they build our church, the parish will get a proper name, a saint's name."

"What? There isn't even a church? But you said we were going to mass!" Anne complains.

"We will attend mass in the school's gymnasium until they build our church, that's all," says Paul.

"In the *gymnasium*?" says Lucie.

She looks at Anne, and they burst out laughing at the thought of the curé, arms open under the basketball net, the choirboys running back and forth in sneakers along the wooden floor's coloured lines: yellow for handball, blue for basketball, green for badminton.

2336 Des Trembles, Sainte-Foy, P.Q., Canada. This place might not be so bad after all.

The Des Ruisseaux have moved six times in the last ten years. They have crisscrossed the province of Québec in their weighed-down second-hand car from one rented house to another to keep up with Paul's rise within the Bell Telephone company. Each new promotion has brought a relocation. Madame Paul Des Ruisseaux, formerly Lilianne Beauregard, has been no slouch either, giving birth to four children in the same amount of time.

Anne was conceived during Paul and Lili's honeymoon, Lucie came thirteen months and two apartments later, and Pierrot arrived a year and a half and one move to Montréal after. This is when Lilianne, having spent most of the last four years fighting constant nausea, started to take her temperature every morning to try to establish the danger zone of her reproductive cycle. It worked. Maurice was born three years after Pierrot. Now the Des Ruisseaux are on the move again. They have left the quiet backwaters of Rimouski, a small town on the south shore of the St. Lawrence River, to come back to Québec. This is where Paul and his wife met on a tennis court. This is where they grew up, and where their respective families still live in Saint-Sacrement. This is where they feel they belong. This is for good.

"We will plant a silver maple in the front, a black spruce in the back, and a lilac shrub on the side, right there. What do you think, Lili?"

"What was that, Paul?"

Lilianne stumbles on the broken slate in her kitten heels, leaning heavily on her husband's arm. She can't think or walk a straight line anymore. They have lived in a cramped motel room with two double beds, a fold-out sofa, and a playpen for Maurice for a week and a half now. Her three older children have been dragged to school kicking and screaming every morning, and have come back home too quiet for their own good. Lili wraps her coat as close to her body as she can but still shivers in a gust of wind so sharp that large peels of tarpaper rise and fall angrily. The children huddle around her, hiding their dishevelled heads and watery eyes in her skirt. Lilianne's hand goes up and down, reassuring and light, grazing Anne's dark helmet, Lucie's light brown curls, Pierrot's golden mop, and Ti-Mo's chestnut down.

"No trees no birds no squirrels no chipmunks," spits Anne.

"There is nobody here," Pierrot whines. "Where are our new friends?"

There is no one but them, standing in their Sunday clothes on the idle construction site. Swirls of dust rise from the unpaved, silent road. Paul steadies his wife with one hand and picks up Ti-Mo with his other arm. "This is ours, Lili."

The house stands high in the middle of a gently graded street. Right across is 2335, a similar model at the same stage of completion. The two houses are surrounded by deep holes where square concrete roots have been laid. The rest of Des Trembles is a tangle of yellow weeds and thistle bushes, as is all the land stretching from the back of the house to the railway tracks.

"All of it—the front lawn, the backyard and the hill, the driveway. And see this house?" Paul stops abruptly in the rough driveway, Lili still leaning on his arm. "This is our house."

What Lili is staring at is a two-storey stone house with a sloping black roof and twin dormers, flanked on the right side by a carport topped by a large deck. On each side of the front door is a narrow floor-length French window. On the left and the right of the door are two bow windows. The house has harmonious proportions and symmetry, just like the Des Ruisseaux family: two girls, two boys.

"I can't believe you paid twenty-nine thousand dollars for a house, Paul," whispers Lilianne.

"This is for the rest of our lives, Lili. This has to be good."

"Look! It shines like diamonds!" calls Pierrot, touching the walls. He has already climbed the plank leading to the square slab of cement that is the front porch. Above the house's still exposed foundation, the concrete gives way to grey stone blocks of irregular sizes speckled with quartz.

"The outside work is all finished, Lili. The inside walls need to be primed and painted, and when that's done, the builders just have to nail the baselines, screw the switches and plugs on, and we will be able to move in. Just ten more days!"

"Ten more days at the motel!" Lili protests.

"Only ten more days before I can paint the front door red. I've always wanted a house with a red door."

Like a mouth.

A house with a mouth, swallowing her. Lili knows she should be happier, but she is so tired. The grey spring sky looms low behind the new house. This is how it must have looked the first time around, she thinks, when the settlers came to start anew. So much work. Clear the forests, pull the stumps out, scorch the earth clean to build a one-room cabin with a dirt floor and plant a crop before winter. The best land was by the river in the St. Lawrence valley, not here. Lili looks at the broken slate, the dry red dirt dusting the tips of her shoes. The unyielding granite of the Canadian Shield starts a little farther north, past the Laurentian Mountains.

A sudden stomach spasm folds her in two, bile burning up her throat. She just has time to hold the coat flaps close to her and grab her hat before throwing up, carefully, away from her shoes and behind a pile of clay pipes.

"Chérie?"

Paul is right behind her, his hand on her shoulder, worried.

The difference is that this house in Sainte-Foy is brand new, not a back-bush shanty, a second-floor apartment, or a boarding house. But all Lili can do is buckle under the extra weight she has already been carrying for four months and will carry for another five, and the weight of this new house.

"It's all right," Lili says, still bent. When she finally looks up at him, her sour breath hits him in the face.

"Lilianne . . ." He smiles at her, pushing back the eggshell straw hat from her brow. "Is this what I think it is?"

She pats her mouth dry with a tissue, trying not to smear the mauve lipstick that matches her dress, before producing a little smile. Her skin looks creamy in the sunless light, her eyes hollow, her face a little drawn, still not made full and soft, still not giving in to the new life. "It isn't even four months yet. Too early to tell."

"Lilianne!" Paul folds his wife in his arms. "I don't think I could be happier, I don't think it is possible. Moving back to Québec, buying our own house, and now, now this!" He takes her hand and pulls her with great care closer to the house. "Come, come with me. Come and see!"

"Will I have to share my room with Lucie again?" Anne wants to know.

"There will be enough room for everybody!" says Paul.

Lili follows him, tired but curious, disapproving but exhilarated by this folly, this brand-new but Anciens Canadiens–style family home with grey diamond walls, a floating deck, and a carport on a lot overlooking the Laurentians and the railway tracks. All theirs. The house, the twenty-five-year mortgage, and the five children.

A Thousand Yarns

The hill is so steep, ramps have been bolted onto the buildings' brick walls. The hill is so long, it goes all the way down to the Lower Town, barely broken by the intersection with the Chemin Sainte-Foy. La Basse-Ville: block after block of low, rickety houses punctured here and there by the steeple of a church, and not a tree or a park until the banks of the snaky Rivière Saint-Charles.

A gust of wind steals what's left of Lucie's breath away, fear having done the rest. "Grand-Maman! We can't go down there!" she says, trying to hold her grandmother back. Round blue eyes, tight bun stuck on the back of her head, Marie-Reine Beauregard is now as rotund as a barrel, but with legs like chopsticks. "It's too steep!"

"Don't make me regret having brought you with me, scaredy-cat," Marie-Reine says, the corners of her mouth going down under the weight of her heavy cheeks. "Let's go."

Lucie takes her grandmother's hand and wonders one more time why she is so big as they walk from the bus stop to the butcher shop down Côte Turnbull. She keeps her stash stuffed inside her dress, that's why. That's where she keeps the balls of wool, every colour of the rainbow, she needs to knit miles of stripy scarves, thousands of raglan sleeves, enough socks and gloves for all her grandchildren. She already has nineteen of them, forever growing, their sweaters shrinking wash after wash, the heels of their socks always in dire need of darning. Lucie used to think her grandmother knitted her new cousins up herself, but that was before her mother explained, on a chalkboard, how babies were born.

The Boucherie Bégin is around the corner and two blocks away, where Chemin Sainte-Foy turns into rue St-Jean. It is a very busy place, what with all the dead animals and the living people. Lucie and her grandmother pick a card with a number before going to sit with the other customers on the straight-backed chairs lining the front window. The meat men never stop moving, their white coats smeared red where they have wiped their bloody hands. They pick slabs of meat with sharp forks and lay them on pink waxed paper they tear from a heavy roll. They weigh the piece of meat, their hands suddenly idle above the scale, their eyes on the nervous arrow, before adding a little more or taking a little away. Marie-Reine has taken her knitting out, a boring brown sleeve. She frowns at it, makes all the stitches slip off the round needle, and before Lucie gets a chance to ask to do it, she pulls on the yarn until there is no more sleeve. One stitch at a time, it takes so long to knit a sweater but just one second to unravel into nothing but a tangle of yarn. As her grandmother starts a new sleeve, counting the stitches, Lucie walks over to take a closer look at the glass counter. Each type of dead animal is separated by green paper parsley on stainless steel trays. At the end of the display is the bizarre stuff: giants' tongues, tiny baby chicken called poussin, and skinned rabbits, their mauve flesh still stuffed in a thin layer of bluish fat. Anne would not like it here, not at all. She'd already be rolling on the black and white tile, sprinkled with sawdust, or throwing up in their grandmother's cart.

In Rimouski, the Des Ruisseaux used to shop at Chez Bourbeau et Fils, two blocks away from their home. The closest grocery store in Sainte-Foy is at least seven blocks away from the new house. It is called IGA. What does it mean? Nobody knows. "On va au ee-jay-ah!" It is so huge, they have to number the aisles so people won't get lost. There is one lady at each of the six checkouts with rolling counters, punching the price of each item into a cash register. The more she punches, the longer the ribbon. When there are no more groceries on the rolling counter, she punches one last button, barks the total—"Ça va faire $47.81." Lucie's mother cannot say the magic words, "Portez ça sur mon compte, Monsieur Bourbeau," like she did in Rimouski. The lady rips the paper ribbon, folds it, gives the change back with the stamps for the IGA win-a-bedroom-suite bingo book, throws the wood divider to the side and starts all over again with the next customer. The ladies at the cash don't even know the Des Ruisseaux by name, but Lucie knows theirs. They wear it pinned to their white apron. Claire. Françoise. Monique.

Even God feels different since Lucie has moved. In Rimouski, classes used to start and finish with a prayer and they studied the *Petit Catéchisme*. When Lucie thinks about God now, she sees him at a big cash register punching in all the sins and good deeds she confesses. Then God hits Total and says, "That will be ten Ave Marias, five paternosters, and five Credos." His three nametags in one are all pinned to his white robe: Dieu le Père Tout-Puissant, Jésus-Christ Notre-Seigneur, and Saint-Esprit. And when Lucie looks behind her, there is a long queue waiting. God has to take care of so many people in Sainte-Foy, Lucie is not even sure he knows her name anymore.

"Madame Beauregard! What can we do for you today?"

A rosbif, about five pounds, French cut with lard on top. They talk about the meat as if it were a person. Lucie's grandmother actually says much nicer things about the rosbif than she says about Bernadette.

"All she does is scrub and whine!" That's what Lucie's grandmother says, the folds on both sides of her puckered mouth deep. She'd rather speak to the ceiling than to Bernadette. Her favourite corner is the centre of a water stain, where paint is peeling. Lucie's aunt does spend Saturday mornings scrubbing on her knees with rollers in. Her room is the only one in the house that is bright and clean. When she's done with her floors she does her nails, same colour as her lipstick. Everything about her is sharp and neat: her hard heels on the wooden floor, her nails drumming on the kitchen table while she reads a glossy magazine, the pencilled lines of her eyebrows . . . When the nail polish is dry she lets her two nieces in and puts a record on her turntable. She snaps her fingers to the beat and shows them all the moves, moving her hips, elbows, and knees, but not her head, her hair stiff and sticky like yellow candy floss. She is almost thirty and she is not married. Lucie has also overheard her grandmother say that her aunt changes boyfriends as often as she changes underwear since she broke up with her fiancé. "I might scrub and whine but I don't know who's going to clean your pigsty for you when I'm gone," Bernadette replies.

"Might be a pigsty, but it is still my house and it doesn't look like you're going anywhere in a hurry. What have I done to deserve such a daughter? Why do I still have to carry my cross at my age?"

"It's about time you realized that you're not carrying me, I'm carrying you, Maman. It's not Lucien who brings money home, is it? But no, so proud of your boys, they're so smart! Your soon-to-be actuary, your son the engineer, and lest we forget, your son the bum! But what about me? I had to go and start working at sixteen to help pay your debts, for my dear brothers' education."

"Pauvre Bernadette. T'as la mémoire bien courte. Hiding behind the big tree so I wouldn't see you skipping class, don't you remember? All you wanted to be was a hairdresser. It's a miracle I made you finish your certificate at the Sullivan School of Business. But go on! Go on fooling yourself all you want if it makes you feel better. Go on painting your face, pretend you're blonde, go on! Scrub your floor and your skin until they fall apart, but I am not going to take the blame for your failures. It certainly isn't my fault he ran away from you."

Bernadette's face goes pale and she braces herself. If this was a hockey game between the Canadiens and the Boston Bruins, the gloves would be coming off now. Except hockey players don't cry. Lucie's aunt does.

"At least I go to the motel, unlike Lucien and his girlfriend Suzanne. Can't you hear their racket on the third floor? I know you don't care, with him it's all laissez-faire. Maman! If you touch that butter, I'll hit you with the broom! The doctor said you have to diet or you'll blow up, your blood pressure is far too high!"

*   *   *

Mille feuille, choux à la crème, éclairs au chocolat, boules au rhum, gâteaux moka: these are some of Marie-Reine's small indulgences, helping her to carry her cross.

"Are we going chez Kerhulu now, Grand-Maman?" Lucie asks as they leave the butcher shop.

"No pastries this week, Lucie. I have to watch my weight," she says, patting her blue dress where yellow flowers grow.

They walk back on rue St-Jean before facing Côte Turnbull again. Marie-Reine pushes her cart with both hands, Lucie behind her. Lucie thinks there should be railings on the sidewalk to help them climb. Her nose almost grazes the street, her shoes slip on the sand left over from the winter. Marie-Reine soon stops to take her coat off and rolls it into the cart. "Help me a little, would you, Lucie?"

So Lucie ends up pulling on the cart her grandmother is pushing up, walking backwards and facing the hill that still runs down to the bottom of the city, and now she wishes her sister Anne could be here too. What if her grandmother's legs just snap off? She will roll away, a satin barrel full of flowers and yarns, all the way down to the Basse-Ville and into the Rivière Saint-Charles in a big splash, and Lucie will have to tug at a loose bit of wool to reel her back up, but the more she will pull, the farther away her grandmother will unravel, just like the brown sleeve, her whole stash of multicoloured yarn spilling like streamers all over Quebec City.

The Broken Door

Lili is at the kitchen table, staring at the green tip of grass pushing through the topsoil. The seeding should have been done earlier in the spring, but there had been only mounds of dirt and rocks when they first moved in. The new house still feels empty. The sound carries on the sleek surfaces, vinyl, hardwood floors, and bare walls. No curtains anywhere yet, no wallpaper, no carpets. It's June and she is six months pregnant with her fifth child. Morning sickness has abated, replaced by an unrelenting fatigue. Lili feels so heavy, as if all her children were still living inside her with the unborn baby. She has been looking at the grass grow all morning, puzzled. There is a spider on the clean wall, trying to weave a web in the new house. How did this happen? It seemed only yesterday she was newly married to Paul.

The bed is narrow, the mattress and the blanket thin, and the box spring noisy in the small cabin on the shores of Lake George, in upstate New York, where Monsieur and Madame Des Ruisseaux spend their honeymoon. The wedding night has gone awry, much to the groom's chagrin. "You're too beautiful," he has told the bride. "I can't do this to you."

"But what we want to do is beautiful too, Paul." Lili has heard it is not uncommon, this kind of thing, the first time. Too much champagne maybe. Too many expectations.

The night is clear and windless, the stars still. It is early June, and a crisp cold moon lights up the cabin's interior enough for Paul to see the satin sheen of Lili's skin on the curve of her hip, her round shoulder, the soft slant of her full breasts. They are lying side by side, facing each other on propped elbows, the curtains parted on the open window. They didn't drink too much at dinner, just one glass of wine each. Lili has suggested taking it easy, getting used to each other first. There's plenty of time, Paul, she has told him. We're now husband and wife for better and for worse and forever and ever. That's when Paul sees something move above Lili's reclining body, her tilted face where a smile floats. A black spider as large as a saucer is scaling the wall above the bedstead's veneer. Paul jumps out of bed, pulling the top sheet with him, holding it to his midriff. Lilianne, still reclining, lifts her head off her hand and turns around slowly to see what Paul is looking at with wide eyes. She dips down one arm to grab Paul's shoe from the floor and springs up, stark naked, unabashed, the muscles of her arms, her upper back, her long thighs and slender legs pulled taut under the layer of soft skin. Tall and bold and unconcerned, she smacks the spider with one sharp blow. Then she bends down to make sure it didn't fall inside the bed, although she knows it is dead from the juicy smear on the wall. Paul can't take his eyes off her now, her breasts alive, her buttocks like two halves of the moon with all the night's promises held in this rapturous slit.

When Paul sees his wife's body naked but in motion, involved in something that has nothing to do with sex, when he finally sees her as men and women lived before, hunting side by side and as one with nature, the burden of his shame suddenly lifts. This is how God has meant it to be. This is not a sin. Paul goes to Lili, still nervous but more than ready, and he will never lose his nerve again. They spend the rest of their honeymoon in the cabin while the other vacationers play shuffleboard and have long dinners.

That's where Anne was conceived, in a thin-walled cabin on the shores of Lake George. She was born exactly nine months later, in early March. Lili reaches for leftover crusts from the children's toast. The butter is cold, the honey still sweet. Only Maurice was born early. So tiny, Mo. Always was. Barely five pounds at birth. He came lightly, like a visitor, but quickly crawled on all fours like the others. A white speck in the long grass, babbling his baby nonsense to the butterflies, pointing to the sun and the crabapples, smiling his two-toothed smile, happy, chewing on a buttercup. Lili had refused to come out of her bedroom after Maurice's premature birth. The doctor had prescribed a sedative, and the Pill. "Contraception," Paul had said. "Why? Isn't this what women do, have children? That's what our mothers did."

Lili had thrown a slipper at him before bursting into tears. "Duplessis is dead, Paul, the pope is a man and I am not—do you hear me?—*I am not my mother!*"

They did fight. Paul was such a meticulous man, in need of order and routines. So unlike herself. She was always ready to postpone dinner on a nice evening to go for a walk with a cohort of tricycles, or turn her bed into a ship lost at sea on rainy days, her two daughters transformed into riotous pirates, Pierrot a stumbling damsel in distress dripping with jewellery and wrapped in one of her dresses—but a new game would start as soon as their father came through the door.

"Here he is. Papa! Papa!"

"Come on, guys, hey, let me at least get my coat off!"

Thirty dirty fingers dug in his pockets, looking for small change. They clung and climbed up on his good pants like animals, their paws sticky from all the candies, until he was down on the kitchen floor.

"No, no, my shirt, my tie, let me go!"

They brought him down to the floor and crucified him with their lollipop sticks and tried to balance the black pennies on his eyelids, his nose, his mouth.

"Close your eyes, Papa, don't move, Papa!"

They struggled to set the paper crowns they had made on his head, they tried to wrap him in the white flannel sheets, freshly laundered but not yet folded.

"Hurray! We got you, Papa, we got you!"

And just when they thought he was finally down for the count, he rose again with a roar, shook them off him like fleas and tickled them until they choked with laughter.

"Dinner's ready! Leave your dad alone and stop dragging the clean sheets all over the floor, do you hear me?"

It was even harder at first, their marriage brand new, their first apartment in Trois-Rivières already crowded. Anne was only four months old and Lili was expecting again. She knew she was not as patient as she should be with her daughter, but she couldn't help it. The only time she didn't feel nauseated was when she slept, and Anne took big bites out of that time too. Sometimes Lili sat in front of the baby's high chair on the tiled floor soiled with the food Anne spat out, and she cried too.

She was so lonely. Paul came home to a dinner of chicken noodle soup and sandwiches. He read the newspaper or talked about his mother's cooking while he ate. They both missed home.

Once she had grabbed the newspaper from Paul's hand and walked out the back door to throw it down the outside staircase. The southern wind, carrying a whiff from the paper mills in Trois-Rivières, blew the paper past the blueberry bushes and the steel railway tracks. Lili had leaned over the rickety wooden railing to retch, looking out with longing at the forest's edge. All she wanted was to walk on the tracks, adjusting her stride to the irregular gaps between the ties. Only this, one tie, a flash of ballast, another tie, until there would be no more crying child, no more cabbage smell, no more sullen husband.

There is a railway here too, in Sainte-Foy. Down the hill, past the field. But Lili doesn't have the wish to run out there anymore. Her marriage has grown along with the children, and it feels much more comfortable and satisfying than it did in Trois-Rivières. She just had to learn to take her freedom when she could, in smaller chunks of time. Five minutes here, half an hour there, to sit down and read ten pages. Lili rubs her taut stomach, humming a song.

"*Au clair de la lune, mon ami Pierrot,*" she had sung to her son, his warm head tucked under her chin. Pierrot rocked hard and low from the very beginning, when he was still in her womb. Back and forth, back and forth, taking a swing for the big leap into life. The girls had come slowly, but Pierrot tore right through her, his head so big, so hard, wanting out so much. Lili had to tie his cradle and then his bed to hooks on the wall as he went on rocking furiously. In her confused half-sleep at night, always one ear cocked for the children's cries, Lili thought the ropes had come undone and Pierrot was sailing away through the sheers and out the window into the starry night all the way to the moon.

Lucie had vanished once too. Where was it, Rimouski? There were no footprints in the snow, not a trace. Anne was at school and the baby boys were asleep. Lili was peeling potatoes. She had just lifted her eyes to see the bright red blotch of Lucie's anorak, then looked down to peel one more potato. Only one potato and the little girl was gone. Lili looked from one side of the window to the other. All she could see was Lucie's little shovel, abandoned. Pulling on Paul's boots, she hurried outside, her hands still wet and dirty from the peelings, her apron whipping in the wind. "Lucie, Lucie!" There were no cars in the empty street, only the gusting wind and a few chickadees. No Lucie at the shed or at the candy store. Lili ran back to grab her daughter's shovel and stood quietly, listening carefully, trying to calm her choppy breath. A faint cry came from inside the largest snowbank, behind the shed. The fresh powder was deep and soft, but there were no footprints, only this muffled sound. Then she saw her. Lucie's face was white under the red tuque, her eyes huge and blue and wet, her small mouth calling "Maman!" like a flower in full bloom in the snow, the rest of her body buried. "I can't move, Maman, I can't move!" There were other holes all around, filled with the lightest shade of blue. She had leaped and let herself fall, far, farther, reaching for the deepest spot. Her tiny steps were imprinted beside the low shed where the shovelled snow reached the flat roof. Lili dug her out with her dirty hands.

And now there is another one growing heavy at the threshold of her heart; another stranger with silky hair and wide eyes who will entrap her. Another child Lili will have to teach how to talk and walk step by step before letting go.

Love Again

"Mon père?" Marie-Reine finally answers her granddaughter, the one who always asks questions. Not her goddaughter, Anne. The other one, Lucie. She looks like her mother, Lilianne.

Marie-Reine's house is almost empty now. Huguette, her oldest, still lives in Virginia with her husband and their three children. Two girls and a boy. They barely speak French—what a shame. Henri lives around the corner from Lilianne in Sainte-Foy, where Léo also lives with Berthe and his children in a different parish. Colette's husband, Dr. Caron, has a practice in a small village close to the New Brunswick border, a timber town called Dégelis. Her daughter doesn't like small-town life at all, even less the non-stop stream of damaged people—the burnt, the car-crashed, the sawed-off—brought to their doorstep day and night. But her husband doesn't want to leave. As for Bernadette and Lucien, they still live with her. Marie-Reine is worried about her youngest son; he is twenty-six and doesn't eat enough greens, only meat and potatoes—a sure way to catch scurvy. Lucien has moved to the top floor of the house since he has a girlfriend, a redhead named Suzanne Rousseau. He says he needs peace to study for the ten exams he has to pass to become an actuary.

"Grand-Maman?"

"Oui, Lucie?"

Marie-Reine is making Lucie a poncho, Phentex wool, washable. Her granddaughter chose the pattern herself. Two large squares stitched together with a fringe all around.

"Grand-Maman! Comment y-était, ton père?"

Clickety-clack. Lucie pulls on her grandmother's dress and repeats her question. "What was he like, your father?"

Clickety-clack. "Mon père?" Marie-Reine finally says. Her granddaughter would not understand, would she? She lives in a large and warm house with a car in the driveway and meat in the refrigerator. Paul Des Ruisseaux comes back home from work at five-thirty every day and the only running he does is around the block. He isn't a coureur de bois. He is a jogger. Lilianne doesn't spend her days on her knees in front of a cross, oblivious to her children's needs. Marie-Reine might as well tell the truth. "C'était un bon à rien."

"Oh!" How can her grandmother say such a thing about her own father?

"That's what Marie-Joseph used to call him, a good-for-nothing. The ne'er-do-well. He was never there." Clickety-clack. "Or if he was there, he was always about to leave. When the Indian summer came he sat on a log to give a fresh lick of paint to his sled for the winter, his back already turned on us. Red paint, thick and slick in the pot. It looked so good that once I dipped my finger in to taste it. My mother scrubbed my tongue with turpentine to make sure I would remember it was wrong."

Oh! How can a mother do such a thing to her own daughter?

"When the coat of red was dry, my father took a smaller brush to freshen up the bleeding heart surrounded by flowers, in white and black. I sat beside him until he let me add a few dots here and there and my initials in the corner, so he wouldn't forget me. When the first snow came, he hooked up his canoe behind the house, took the wooden wheels off his sleigh, and fitted the runners on. And off he'd go, the dogs barking like mad. Tears, oil paint, and turpentine, that's what it smelled like when he was about to leave again. Then it smelled like nothing for a long time." Clickety-click, clickety-clack.

"My father smells like aftershave. Did you know where he went, Grand-Maman?"

"To the traplines, farther north. The day my mother died, he left and never came back."

"Do you think he went to heaven that time?"

Marie-Reine laughs, her belly jiggling. "Heaven! That's the last place I'd look for Antonio Tremblay."

"Did he go to church?" Lucie has noticed nobody goes to church in her grandmother's house.

"Only to pick up girls."

Oh! How can someone go to church to do such a gross thing?

"They say that's where he met my mother, Marie-Ange Légaré."

"And where did you meet Grand-Papa?"

"I met Léandre Beauregard playing cards." Marie-Reine has a small throaty laugh, her fingers still busy. Clickety-click, clickety-clack. "I drove him crazy."

"How come?"

Marie-Reine finishes an orange stripe and sticks the knitting needle in her bun. She looks like an old Chinese queen to Lucie, in her dress covered with large, fluffy pink flowers on a pale green background. Could she really have been young once?

Marie-Reine grins. "I cheated."

Maybe. "Grand-Maman, how come you don't have a boyfriend?"

"Who says I don't?"

Neuf heures du soir. Who can this be knocking at the door? Madame Beauregard doesn't want to get up from her favourite chair, where she is knitting while watching television. Too late for Electrolux and Fuller brush salesmen, or the boy scouts' cookie drive. It's not election time either. Daniel Johnson was elected Québec premier last year and is driving Prime Minister Lester Pearson nuts in Ottawa with his new idea: equality or independence. It's simple enough. All he's saying is that the two founding peoples of Canada, the French and the English, should have an equal say in politics. Madame Beauregard finally finds politics amusing, what with the new justice minister debating the proposed divorce law, claiming that "the state has no business in the bedrooms of the nation." He can talk. Pierre Elliott Trudeau gets caught with a different woman on his arm every month. Duplessis never had sex in his life, he just drank with the boys. No wonder Québec was such a joyless place under his long premiership.

Madame Beauregard slowly pulls herself up from her seat. This had better be good. Better not be Monsieur Lasalle, the next-door neighbour, who keeps losing his senile wife, Germaine, or one of those men who come for Bernadette. Worse would be Berthe, in hysterics, coming to complain about Léo, although this has not happened much lately. It is Henri who has been showing up at her door these days with his oldest child and only daughter, the eleven-year-old Myriam, in tow. He doesn't say much, just that Cécile is "acting up" and could she take Myriam for the night. Madame Beauregard almost misses her lodgers. What they needed was simple enough: a bed, a sink, and food.

"Madame Beauregard!" The man at the door had already turned around to leave. He smiles at her with fondness. His skin has not seen much sun in his life, and the hands holding his wool cap have not done much work either. Madame Beauregard knows this short man, but who is he?

"How can you not recognize me?" he asks, enjoying her puzzlement. "We used to meet in the dark once a week." But Madame Beauregard is frozen, her hand on the doorknob, neither inviting this man in nor asking him to leave. She almost has it, his name, on the tip of her tongue.

"Mind you, you always saw me in my robes."

"Ah ben, si c'est pas l'Abbé Audette!" She smiles back at him, her face and her door open. "Come in, come in, what are you waiting for? It's getting chilly at night, isn't it?"

The Abbé Audette stands there looking at her, his mood altered now that he is recognized. "Do you know how much I have missed you all these years, Madame Beauregard?"

"Oh, Monsieur l'Abbé, don't be silly," she says, humouring him. She leads him to the kitchen.

"You can call me Herménégilde now, Madame Beauregard."

"Why on earth would I do that?" she asks lightly.

The abbé sits down slowly on the chair she has pulled out for him.

"Because I am not the Abbé Audette anymore."

"What do you mean?"

"I've lost it. I've lost my faith, and I've left the Church. I have opened the door, and I have walked out on the people I've been living with for the last forty years."

"Oh. I see. I think we will need some toast and tea."

As she fills the kettle and lights up the gas range, Madame Beauregard asks: "I can't call you Herménégilde. What's your full name?"

"Joseph Alphonse Herménégilde Audette."

"I'll call you Alphonse if you call me Marie-Reine."

"I would love that, Marie-Reine," says the abbé with a soft half smile. He has lost weight and has black circles under his eyes. Marie-Reine recognizes this mental condition. She had lost her reason for living too, years ago, and the Abbé Audette had helped her through.

Alphonse Audette comes once a day to Madame Beauregard's house to learn how to live. She shows him how to fluff and cook an omelette, how to brew coffee and peel potatoes, how to wash and dry his clothes, and how to iron. She brings him along when she shops, telling him about soaps and cuts of meat and baking needs, and how much things cost. That's when he realizes he will have to find a job and earn money, because his small savings account is melting away at an alarming rate. After a few nights of seeing her knit while she watches television, he asks her if she could teach him about this too. "It's quite useful, isn't it?" he asks her. "Oh yes," she says. "Not only can you make your own sweaters and vests but also your own socks, gloves, scarves, and tuques, even Phentex—that's the new washable wool—slippers and blankets!"

"Really?"

Alphonse Audette brings an endless curiosity to his new life, but he also tells Marie-Reine, with frustration, "I'm afraid I don't have much to give you in exchange for your kindness and patience."

They talk for long hours at the kitchen table. What could he do? Marie-Reine suggests teaching. The minister of education has now completely taken over control of the school system from the Church and the province needs teachers. Within a month Alphonse Audette finds a position teaching philosophy at the new college, and as soon as he starts to receive a regular pay cheque, he finds a studio close to his work and the Plains of Abraham, a nicer place than the room he had rented at first.

"Do you still read, Marie-Reine?" Alphonse asks.

"What do you think? Sure I still read. But since nothing is forbidden anymore, it's not so much fun!"

"You were right, you know. I read them all now."

"Have you read Simone de Beauvoir, *The Second Sex*?"

"No, I haven't. But I've read Albert Camus. It was the beginning of the end for me."

"Do you go to the movies too?" Marie-Reine hurries to steer away from the subject of forbidden books.

"No, I haven't. I have never been to the movies. So many new things I can do now."

"Should we start with a walk?"

"Yes, let's go for a walk."

This is what Bernadette sees when she gets out of her car in front of 1502 Louis-Fréchette one evening. This is what Lucien witnesses too as he walks back from the campus, holding Suzanne by the waist. They all stop to look at this woman, twice the size of the man beside her, walking away with tiny steps in the crisp fall air, the red and orange star-shaped maple leaves drifting down slowly around them, dancing back and forth before landing silently on the ground where they crunch underfoot. That's when Alphonse Audette, the short man walking with their mother, takes one longer stride and launches into a cautious leap, the soles of his shoes off the sidewalk for the briefest moment, just long enough to catch a leaf in mid-flight. But that's all it takes. He offers the leaf with its dainty edges to Marie-Reine Beauregard. She laughs and leans on his arm, and they turn the corner in the dusk, leaving their long shadows to linger behind. While Lucien and Suzanne hurry to the deserted third floor, Bernadette, a tear in her eye, runs in to phone Lilianne.

"Lilianne? Guess what?"

"What?"

"He's walking hand in hand with Maman!"

"Bernadette, what's going on? You sound half out of your mind."

"I'm telling you, our mother is dating again!"

"Really? It's been so long . . . Who's made her break her vow of solitude?"

"You will not believe this."

"Dette, that's enough, stop it."

"L'Abbé Audette!"

"What? She can't date a priest, for heaven's sake."

"The abbé isn't an abbé anymore. He has given up the robe. You should see them, they look so cute together." Bernadette sighs, sniffling a little.

"Our mother dating a defrocked priest, what next? Maybe you can find one too, Dette!"

It's Spring

Lilianne is spread out on a lounge chair on the carport deck. The winter is finally over and she can't get enough of this sudden heat pushing back the cold edge of April. The soil sweats with the last of the deep thaw under the born-again heat of the sun. After an hour spent roasting in her two-piece bathing suit, Lilianne has to bring out a bowl of cold water to dip her hands in. Her feet still hurt and her legs are sore from last night. Her cheeks ache from all the smiling, but she doesn't care. She's going to do it again tonight. She will run upstairs as soon as dinner is over to pull on the nylon stockings under the short dress, quick, slip into the medium-heeled shoes, quick-quick, crimp up her chunky white highlights, apply the orange lipstick, the green eyeshadow, quicker, run down and out of the house. She has to meet up with Francine Rinfret, a fellow volunteer, at the local Liberal Federal Party headquarters at six-thirty.

"Excuse-moi, Francine!"

However hard she tries, Lilianne is always late, and Francine on time. She has only two children.

"I've picked up the pamphlets for you," Francine says, handing over the red and white folded glossies claiming *Jean Marchand, l'homme du moment!* This is not Francine Rinfret's first electoral campaign. She is the one who carries the clipboard and ticks the appropriate box beside the names, trying to identify the voter's leaning. "Dress smart and never stop smiling, whatever the prospective Liberal voter has to say," Francine and Lilianne have been instructed.

When they come back to headquarters around nine-thirty, many ticks are lined up under the Liberal Party logo, few under the others. That's when Jean Marchand himself gives a pep talk to his supporters in front of a huge photo of Pierre Elliott Trudeau. Trudeau is running for prime minister of Canada, and he is from Québec. Lilianne's sense of purpose, of empowerment, swells above her tired legs, cramped cheeks, and blistered heels. She is convinced she is fighting for the right cause, for one country from coast to coast, Canada, and two peoples, English and French, living in harmony under the leadership of the man with a modern vision and a rose in his lapel. Lili can finally do something to show Paul he's wrong, with his separatist rant. Leaving Canada would ruin Québec and bring poverty to every household, says Jean Marchand. Why go through this again when things are finally getting better? Smaller families, better education, more food on the table, a new car every five years, a house you can own within twenty-some years, a fat pension from Bell Canada . . . Who is Paul fooling with his big ideas? Lili won't end up like her mother, breaking her back eighteen hours a day and seven days a week for years on end to feed her family. No way. Lili's children will go to university, and Lili's daughters will have jobs and financial independence. Nobody will have to sacrifice their life for the sake of their children ever again. Not in Pierre Elliott Trudeau's Canada.

Hot skin, cold fingers.

Lilianne stretches her tired limbs, staring at her almost flat stomach and touching her new-found ribs. She's lost ten pounds since Christmas. She should be getting the summer clothes out of the boxes in the basement, or finishing the curtains she is making for the girls' room. She should wake

Bébé up or she won't sleep tonight but the heat makes her feel lazy. The phone rings. Three o'clock. It's Cécile Beauregard, her brother Henri's wife. La Fatiguante. Lilianne should answer and try to extract a promise from her sister-in-law to vote for Marchand, but this would mean having to listen to her tiresome complaints about the local school for the one-hundredth time, about her daughter Myriam's problems or her eldest son Frederic's academic prowess for the one-thousandth time.

The phone rings on and on.

Lilianne flips onto her back and lets her top slip off. Who cares? Trudeau is forty-nine, still a bachelor, and the most charismatic man she has seen in a long time. Though Jean Marchand preaches with gusto, he's not the one Lilianne looks at. She looks at the larger-than-life poster of Trudeau. A high forehead and quick, intelligent eyes, a generous mouth with full, sensual lips, high cheekbones, slightly exotic—he is intoxicating.

Lilianne wants a golden skin for Trudeau's visit to Jean Marchand's riding, scheduled for next week. She'll get off her chair when the line of cold shade from the roof catches up with her feet.

When Paul comes home from work the kids have stripped to their underwear and are jumping through the sprinkler in the backyard. They have trampled the patchy grass so badly it has turned into a big mud puddle. Lili is as red as a lobster in her sundress, a strong aroma of mothballs mixed with Noxzema rising from her as Paul leans to kiss her. They're having baloney sandwiches for dinner and launch into the same argument. Again.

"You're not going to put your neat little check mark beside my name, Lilianne Beauregard."

But Lilianne knows *everybody* is a prospective Liberal voter.

"Pierre Elliott Trudeau is one of us, can't you understand? They all are—Chrétien, Pelletier, Marchand. They fought for us before, and now they'll do it from Ottawa. It's the best lineup a federal party has ever had!"

"They can keep their wise men and their French Power all they want, I'm still not giving my vote to Canada. I'm voting for Québec. And this is what all of our people should do."

"And how are you going to do this in a federal election, Paul?"

"I just want to let you know that I will." Paul crosses his arms.

"Don't you do it out of spite, because of the baloney sandwiches!"

Silence.

Lilianne has been warned that the "male" vote might be harder to sway, but that if the Liberal volunteers succeed in getting all the housewives out of their homes and into the polling stations, they will win because more than half this country is made up of women.

"What are you going to do, Paul?"

"This is between me and me, Lilianne."

"I certainly hope it is. You don't work for Hydro-Québec, you work for Bell Canada, and you are management now. You might want to keep the 'masters in our own house' talk quiet, and to tell the truth, I don't think you'd look so good if your boss learned you were voting Communist!"

"Communist! This isn't Russia."

"You're right, it's not. This is Canada. And do you know something else? I can do more than change diapers and load the washing machine and be pecked on the cheek at five o'clock. I can actually take part in the making of this country, just like you."

Lilianne grabs the car keys from the hook beside the door and leaves, slamming the car in reverse so hard the tires protest with a short, loud screech. Paul turns around to finish the dishes, thinking the women's vote will probably prevail. With a French-Canadian helmsman in Ottawa, the provincial government will have a harder time selling its vision of a more independent Québec.

The next Saturday, a flashy car is parked in front of 1502 Louis-Fréchette, right behind Bernadette's white Volkswagen Beetle. It's a violet Plymouth Duster with a black hard top, and Lucien is shining its chrome with soapy water. Lilianne's mother is out on the sidewalk in a short-sleeved dress, her restless feet shuffling back and forth in a little dance. She is all smiles in the bright day.

Lilianne isn't even out of her Impala, Anne and Lucie still in the back seat, when she starts to shout. "Maman, veux-tu ben me dire qu'essé-que c'est ça?"

"It's a car, Lili, can't you see? My car!"

"But you don't drive!"

"Not a problem, I have a chauffeur."

Lucien springs up from behind the impressive hubcaps.

"I've had enough of taking the bus. I am going to get my driving licence, and in the meantime, Lucien can use the car and drive me around."

"Nice, isn't it? Do you want to go for a ride, girls?" asks Lucien.

"Oh shut up, Lucien," says Lili, in front of her two daughters.

Bernadette bursts out from the house and skips down the front steps, careful to avoid the rotten bits here and there, her curlers bouncing on her head, her housecoat a trail of pink nylon. She runs straight to Lili, ignoring the girls.

"Pis-pis-pis? Raconte! How was Trudeau?"

"He cancelled at the last minute—"

"Oh no!"

"—but he is rescheduled for next week."

"Great!"

Lili returns to her unfinished conversation with her mother. "Get your licence? At sixty-four? What is the matter with you, Maman?"

"Now that I've raised my children, why can't I have a life of my own too?"

Lili's tone softens a little. "I'm just worried, that's all. You've been doing so much—the bridge nights, the Scrabble tournaments, the new dresses, the hats, and now driving a car! You're not twenty-five any-more. Even Lucien isn't. Have you been to the doctor for your blood pressure checkup?"

"I might not be twenty-five but I'm not dead just yet, so mind your own business and I'll mind mine. Do you see me asking where you caught leprosy?"

The Noxzema didn't help. Lili's skin has been peeling all week, on her nose, her arms, her legs, leaving bare patches of pale pink skin.

"Did you try olive oil, Lili?" asks Bernadette.

"Anne, Lucie, come on!" beams Madame Beauregard. "Allez chauffeur! Let me get my hat and off we go for a spin in town!"

Blow-Up

The August evening is as transparent as a watercolour, fed by the gracious liquid arcs of the sprinklers. The sun has blasted through the kitchen window all afternoon, and a fan whirs by the transistor radio. The heat wave smothering Québec shows no sign of relenting yet.

Coffee percolates on the stove top. Lilianne brings out four Expo 67 souvenir mugs, already worse for wear, the milk carton from the refrigerator, and a pot of ill-assorted stainless steel teaspoons from the cupboard.

"Time to go to the grocery store," she says, holding the empty Tupperware sugar container. "I'm also out of saccharine. Which do you prefer, brown sugar or honey?"

"Which one do you think has less calories? And don't make the coffee too strong or I'll be up all night," says a worried Bernadette.

"Got to be crazy to drink coffee in this heat," says Colette. She lifts the slinky fabric of her blouse off her skin and blows in. "Can I make myself a gin and tonic?"

"I didn't remember it could get so hot here. Don't you have an air conditioner?" says Huguette. She doesn't have an accent from all the years spent in the States, but sometimes the French words are slow to come. The oldest of the Beauregard sisters holds her chin up; her gaze is steady, full of poise, and her features are just a little too fine and sharp, too harsh to be beautiful. Her nose is exactly like Bernadette's.

"It's this heat that did her in," says Bernadette vindictively. Her lacquered helmet has a golden sheen, her eyebrows are plucked, eye-liner and mascara set out big green-brown eyes. Her thin-lipped mouth is like a stroke, the fold of her plump cheeks drawing its corner down. It's hard to come right after beauty, and Bernadette was born after Colette, a natural blonde with delicate bones, regular features, and a narrow waist, even after four children. Colette's beauty is heightened by an expression of helplessness, her wounded periwinkle eyes constantly on the lookout for salvation.

"You can't blame the weather, Bernadette," says Huguette. "She wasn't taking her medication, was she?"

"Made her dizzy, she said," Lili comments, distressed.

"You should have seen what she cooked for the abbé," Bernadette says. "Cream and butter all over! He needed fattening, she said." She pours skim milk up to the brim of her half-cup of coffee. "I had to get out to escape the smell. I'm on the grapefruit diet, you know? Half a grapefruit and bacon in the morning, another half with a peanut butter sandwich at lunch, and two halves with shrimps at night, and if you are really really hungry before going to bed—"

"Another half grapefruit," Huguette interrupts.

"All the food she shouldn't have been eating. The doctor warned her she had to lose weight," says Lilianne.

"I told her too but when did she ever listen to what I had to say?" Bernadette says, defeated.

Lilianne looks past Huguette's shoulder and out the window, to the children playing on the swing set in the backyard and Paul refuelling the unreliable lawn mower. Pierrot and Maurice sit on each side of the rocking horse, Pierrot pushing hard to make Maurice scream with joy. "I had never seen her happier, though," she says, getting up for more coffee as her children scatter away for a new game.

"Cré Maman!" Huguette smiles for the first time since she arrived. But her smile does not hold, her face like wax softened by the heat. Silence swells among the four sisters as they drain the last of the cold sludge and unmelted brown sugar crystals at the bottom of their mugs. They are a tough breed, having learned early that a display of emotions only made them vulnerable. A Beauregard's heart is not silent but it hides untamed deep within, braced for survival. That's how their mother brought them up. "Do you think she was in love?" asks Huguette.

"Love!" yelps Bernadette. "Look what it brought her."

"Love. Look *where* it brought me," says Colette. "The great darkness has not receded just yet in my neck of the wood. The curé still calls the tune and the tune is always the same: the sanctity of marriage!" Colette crushes the last piece of ice from her drink between her teeth. "Do you mind if I get a refill?" she asks, getting up.

Lilianne and Bernadette look at each other. Colette had a minor car accident on her way here from Dégelis. The small mill town close to the New Brunswick border was supposed to be a temporary exile, a place for Zacharie Caron to get started after his graduation from medicine at Université Laval. But four children and almost ten years later, they're still there, and Colette's sisters haven't had the courage to tell her that drinking is not going to solve her problems.

"Has the abbé gone to visit her?" Huguette asks, unaware of Colette's situation.

"He comes every day, but it's a pity to see him," answers Lilianne. "He's so upset. I can't do anything for her, he says. I can't even pray." Tonight it's their brothers' turn to go to the hospital and wait, listening to the slow rhythm of their mother's deep sleep. "Just when she was finally starting to live for herself," says Lilianne.

"Life is so unfair," sighs Bernadette.

Huguette rolls her eyes. Colette fiddles with the radio dial until she finds a rollicking tune. She hums and clicks her fingers, sketching a few steps between sips of gin and tonic before slipping outside with the music. The lawn mower now sputters up and down the steep incline, tied to a rope Paul is working from the top. He has taken off his shirt but is still wearing a pair of work gloves.

"Should you start thinking about what you will do with the house?" asks Huguette.

"That's a little fast, isn't it?" says Bernadette. "We don't know, anything is possible, she might come out of this coma and be just the way she was before."

"Stop kidding yourself," Huguette says. "This was a major stroke. She could be brain-damaged, she could be paralyzed—if she comes around at all. Well, at least there isn't a slew of children left behind to feed, not this time." After all these years, she still feels the sharp pang of loss caused by her father's death.

Bernadette shreds a Kleenex into her empty cup before starting to cry. She is the only child left behind. She is the spinster, at thirty-two. Lilianne puts an arm around her sister's shoulder and offers her another cup of coffee. "Who am I kidding anyway? As if I'm going to sleep a wink," Bernadette rallies, pouring a scoop of brown sugar in her mug. From the far end of Sainte-Foy to the west, a train's gloomy whistle tears the murmuring night.

"Oh mon Dieu, presque neuf heures! I've got to get these kids in bed!" says Lilianne, bolting out the back door.

Colette is laughing, tossing her blonde curls about as she dances barefoot in the grass with Paul, the radio set on top of the choked lawn mower. Lili turns it off. "Make yourself useful, would you, Paul? Call the kids in for their baths."

"Too bad the summer is almost over, isn't it?" says Colette, her eyes on Paul's back as he walks away, her voice lazy.

Lili glares at her sister.

"What's wrong?" Colette asks.

"You have a choice. Either you come in for a cup of coffee or I'm going to shove your head in the sprinkler to clear it up."

She Won't Need Shoes Anymore

Alphonse Audette takes off his small straw hat and holds it between his fingers as he stands in his seersucker suit, immobile. One more step and he will be in Marie-Reine's hospital room. It's a tough step to take today.

"Bonjour, Marie-Reine, comment ça va aujourd'hui?" he asks the patient in a jolly voice, testing the ground.

Madame Beauregard has awakened from the coma, but her entire right side is paralyzed. The physiotherapist's efforts to teach her how to live with half her body are not very successful. She is still a very big woman.

Madame Beauregard laughs. "Marie-Reine? Nobody's called me Marie-Reine since Marie-Joseph died. Can you pray for me, Abbé Audette?" she begs him.

Herménégilde Alphonse Audette bows his head to hide his sorrow. She always asks him this.

"I'm not an abbé anymore, Marie-Reine. Don't you remember?"

But she doesn't listen. "If you pray for me, Abbé, God will hear you, and he will give me my leg and my arm back. He will. You are such a good priest."

The Abbé Audette sits close to Madame Beauregard. Metal railings on each side of the bed make it look like a cage. It's the beginning of the fall, still unusually hot. The abbé considers the bouquet he bought for her at the Saint-Roch market, by the Bassin Louise. The heavy blooms of the dark red dahlias nod gently in the fan's stream. Alphonse Audette deposits his gift, the wet stems wrapped in newspaper, on the blanket. His head feels heavy too, and he lays his forehead against the railing's cool metal, holding Marie-Reine Beauregard's hand in silence.

He had hoped she would get better once she came out of the coma. But this is it. This is how she is going to be from now on, a woman with an insatiable desire for a miracle he can't provide. All Madame Beauregard wants is to walk back home, and she is ready to believe in God again to make her wish come true.

A few days ago he thought she was back, all there.

"It's only your faith you lost, not your legs," she had told him spitefully.

"What's the point of having two legs if I have to walk alone?" he had answered, with infinite sadness.

"I can't pray for you," he tells Madame Beauregard now, raising his head again to look at her. "Isn't it a shame? Maybe it's your turn to pray for me, Marie-Reine. Would you like a chocolate?" he asks her, offering from the box of Black Magic.

"Oh oui, un chocolat!" Her eyes like a child's. She licks her fingers, a sweetness lining her right cheek.

"I'm leaving, Marie-Reine," says the abbé.

"Already?" she asks, sucking on the thick caramel. "Could you bring me more of these tomorrow?" Ignoring the flowers, she points to the chocolate box.

"I'm sorry, Marie-Reine. I'm so sorry. I will already be far away tomorrow."

"Oh," says Marie-Reine. "Where are you going? Why?"

"If I can't pray for you, if you can't walk with me and hold my hand, there is no reason for me to stay here. I'm going to Africa. Senegal. I have joined CUSO to help build a school, and a church, with my hands. Maybe it will help me build my faith up again, brick by brick. Maybe one day we will pray together, Marie-Reine."

"You will come back, then?"

"I hope so."

The abbé gets up and sighs, leaning over the railing to kiss her forehead lightly.

"I can hear Lilianne and Bernadette coming, Marie-Reine. I'd better go."

He is at the end of the corridor when Madame Beauregard's daughters come through the door, but he is not quick enough. He hears her starting to cry.

"I want to go home, I'm all right now. Please, take me home."

Lucien gets the Plymouth and the aquarium. Bernadette gets the washer and dryer and the living-room set, which she will get reupholstered. Colette gets the dining-room suite, Lilianne, the piano. Léo buys the house, which is in poor shape. He will have to get it fixed up.

Henri takes back what he gave: the good jewellery and the Saint-Onge paintings, now worth real money. Huguette, who lives far away, doesn't want anything but a few photos. She buys her mother an electric wheelchair. Whatever small item is of value—china, silverware, and the like—is written down on a slip of paper and put in a hat. Everyone pulls something out. The garbage trucks get the rest.

Once the house is empty, the builders move in and the bugs move out. More than thirty years worth of bugs, tucked behind the walls and under the floors, hard and shiny, soft and hairy, carrying out with them the smells, the sounds, the busy heartbeat of Madame Beauregard's old rooming house.

When the workmen push the refrigerator and stove out of the dim kitchen, the long-hidden linoleum tiles flash brighter than elsewhere, while a cloud of bluebottles and green fruit flies rises from the grime coating the appliances' fuzzy underbellies.

When they peel off layer after layer of wallpaper from the ground-floor and first-floor walls, like tired petals, a mixed army of red ants and black beetles scampers away, having feasted for long enough on the dried-out paper glue.

When they rip up the carpets, worn right through on the edge of the stairs' first steps (the first steps are always worse for wear, as if the feet were heavy before they could step higher, and lighter), the builders almost choke on the dense dust mist. Black spiders with filigree legs and brown centipedes scamper away from the floorboards' rotten mush. And when they pull out the soft boards like bad teeth, they find the first of the small white worms infesting the house's weakened wooden structure.

But even before the builders move in, the exodus starts with a thick swarm of grey moths when Bernadette and Lilianne open their mother's bedroom cupboard. There, more insects have settled in fluffy cocoons, hidden in the gap at the back of the hardcovers' loose spines or the two rows of black shoes and boots. Above the books and the shoes swings the hanging garden of their mother's dresses. Violet, purple, and burgundy, fields upon fields of wildflowers spreading their green arms out: cabbage roses, tiger lilies, and pansies, lemon, orange, and grapefruit, ferns and vines and bamboo sticks, turquoise, khaki, parsley, spiralling stems on a trellis, whirls of curlicues trying to push through paisley follies. And amidst the tangle of this limp garden, the threadbare memory of a man's black wool suit and a wedding dress's silken ashes still wrapped in papier de soie.

Everything goes, even the ghosts.

The haunting shuffle of thousands of feet scraping a slush of melted snow and a thick paste of wet leaves off the front-door mat, in and out of the house, morning and night, but no noise after eleven o'clock, please. The small talk, the greetings, the recriminations, the hockey nights on TV, the 1940s crackling newscasts on the radio, the pianoforte polkas, the Stan Getz jazz as cool as cold cream. The echoes of water dripping in a tiled vault on cold mornings, the soapy smell of shaving cream, the splash of lukewarm water, the toothbrush up and down, the hair combed back and parted neatly, a hum and a bright whistle rising in the pale new day. Skinny faces, round faces, brown faces, green faces—all gone. The bouquet from all the pot-au-feu, tough beef cuts, carrots and potatoes, stewing non-stop for twenty years in an iron cauldron with a burnished bottom, onions sputtering slowly in butter until sweet as caramel, pie crust flakes spilling like snow through a sudden cold draft. Fermez la porte!

You can close the door now. Madame Beauregard is gone.

Troisième Relation:
The Bones

KEYWORD: God.

The number of entries rises on the computer screen—9 507, 21 494, 75 821—until it freezes. I hit the return key. Again. Escape. Still jammed. The screen goes blank.

October 1998 and I'm back where I was nearly a year ago, still trying to find the threads that lead to the dead: the beaver pelts and the tricornes, the coureurs de bois and the filles du roi, the pale faces, the red skins, the bois-brûlé. From keyword to keyword I have tried to unlock the past, but it doesn't seem to matter anymore. If Laurent has taken refuge away from the problems of the living heart in the operating room of a hospital, I've done the same in a world of paper and amber words, flashing like warnings in pixels of light, where I am becoming more and more insignificant. I am losing weight. I've even started to think there might be no Antonio Tremblay after all. No Catherine Dubois: the letter I sent her was returned with the word "Moved" stamped across it. No Marie-Reine or Marie-Joseph, no Paul and Lilianne. Not even Laurent. I feel utterly disembodied, just a humming brain among other humming brains, weaving an intricate narrative web across the library's dome.

But this is the only safe place. My marriage is falling apart, my mother is dying, and I need a belief system in a hurry. I reboot and log in, trying a more oblique approach. Keyword: Canada, catechism.

*   *   *

Ding-ding-a-ling!

The silver bell's clear sound chimes through the settlement at Ihonatiria, on the shore of Lake Huron by Georgian Bay. The Reverend Father Jean de Brébeuf is ready. He has put a square hat on his head and a white surplice on top of his cassock. Around him the golden cornfields rustle softly in the breeze coming from the freshwater sea. In his hands is the first book of God to come to the New World, a catechism in eighty-one questions and answers that he has translated for the natives. Jean de Brébeuf invests the moment when he calls his charges to learn to pray with the solemnity due to all matters relating to his one master, the one he is more than willing to die for. The evangelist has seen how the Huron torture and kill their war prisoners. It is a long, slow, and magnificent death, nails pulled out one by one, fingers chopped, the skin tormented with coals and hot iron, the red bleeding heart going last, pulled out still beating and eaten raw. Jean de Brébeuf has knelt and kissed the torture post. He has made a vow not to refuse the grace that could be bestowed on him through martyrdom.

The Huron call him Echon, their way of saying Jean. They sing the "pater" with him, and with him they trace the sign of the cross upon themselves. They let their children learn the answers to the questions asked by the Black Robe.

> Maître: *Qui est celuy qu'on doit appeller Chreftien?*
> Disciple: Celuy, lequel ayant efté baptizé croit, *&* fait
> profeffion de la Doctrine Chrestienne.

Echon has many magic tricks in his hat. He catches the Hurons' stories with his quill and locks their words in a paper cage, a precious book he carries along with his catechism. Echon can also capture the travel of the sun, the stars, the length of one day in a small animal with a ticking heart: a clock. And yet, for all his magic, he lives humbly. He makes his own sagamité, grinding the corn and mixing it with oil and peas, meat or fish. Although he is not as strong as the Huron are, he has taken his shoes and stockings off and trussed up his robe during the long voyage from Québec to Ihonatiria, keeping a joyous face. As recommended by his superior, he has taken care not to annoy anybody in the canoe by wearing a hat with a wide brim. "It is better to take a nightcap; there is no need for modesty amongst the sauvages." Jean de Brébeuf has also been careful not to put water or sand in the canoe, he has not complained or criticized, and has not been late for embarkation at daybreak. He has finished winning the natives' heart with his miroir ardant, or burning-glass, providing a quick flame to do tabagie at midday and start a wood fire for the night meal.

So what is this new enchantment all about?

Maître: *Qu'eſt-ce que la Doctrine Chrestienne?*
Disciple: C'eſt celle que noſtre Seigneur Ieſus Chriſt nous a
   enſeignés, lors qu'il viuoit ſur terre, & et que la faincte
   Egliſe Catholique, Apoſtolique & Romaine nous enſeigne.

It is about one God, Manitou, and one Church, a very large tribe meeting in a sacred longhouse, preaches Echon.

The Huron are suspicious. He's caught their words, the sun, and the stars—what does he want now? Their loot, their women? Echon says no. What is left, then, for this God to have but their lives? But the Black Robe says God is not after their body but their soul. The Huron don't understand. Echon promises them eternal life in heaven, but why climb a ladder to the sky when everything is fine here? And to become this God's disciples, Echon says they have to change their ways. No more shaman magic, only his. No more oki or ondaki, no more windigo. No tales of Michabou, the Great Hare who escaped the flood and created men from a dead moose and a dead bear. Or Carcajou, the Trickster, who did the same by coupling with a she-muskrat. No more bebe ataushu lullaby, no more songs for the trembling teepee, or shaking tent, where valiant warriors and agile hunters travel to the country of the dead, in a trance. No more words and melodies that reflect their lives, lives that are changing a little more with every new pale face washing up on the shore of the great lake.

The only one of their customs the Black Robe truly admires is the Feast of the Dead, when every twelve years or so the Huron walk back to the place where their loved ones were buried and dig them up to bring them home. This is what it truly means to be human, writes Jean de Brébeuf in his *Relation*. Some loved ones are now only bones and skin, as dry as parchment. Some look like cured or smoked meat, and some others, the most recent corpses, are still big and alive with maggots. But whatever these mortal remains look or smell like, the natives pick the bones clean one by one, bathe them with their tears, and adorn them with beads and shells. What's left of the dead is then packed in a beautiful beaver robe and brought back to each village, where hundreds converge with their attisken, or their loved ones' spirits, on their backs. Haéé, haé, they cry as they arrive.

But soon there won't be enough Huron left standing to carry the overwhelming weight of the bones to the next Feast of the Dead. Along with the good news, the Black Robes have brought the smallpox germs that will put an end first to Huronia, then to six million Amerindians in North America. It cannot be such a great God to let them die like this—this God with long teeth and his army of black robes, always hungry for more souls.

Ding-a-ling, ding!

Back in Ihonatiria the silver bell chimes again to signify the end of the lesson. Jean de Brébeuf hands out mirrors and beads, all the white man's cheap magic, to reward the women and children. The men get a rassade, a ladle of firewater. Echon. God's scarecrow, our first Canadian martyr. For years to come after his death his abhorred name is used among the decimated Huron to terrorize the children.

I spend two more days waiting to receive another catechism from the Rare Books department (no photocopies allowed). Stephen Young has left a short, vengeful message at the office for me: *I'll be back*. But it's not him who's on my mind as I read the horrifying details of Jean de Brébeuf's death at the hands of the Huron. It is Laurent, when we were first lovers.

We're in the living room again, it is night again. The painting hung on the wall opposite the leather couch bursts in a sultry fireworks of thick colours. Black drips and white dabs, yellow splashes and cobalt blotches, purple bruises, scarlet scars. Marcelle Ferron, 1964. Abstract expressionist with a touch of Fauve.

"You first," he says, gallantly.

I make the globe spin and close my eyes, finger ready. This is the world, and one day I will travel to . . .

"Serendip, Sri Lanka! Your turn."

Laurent closes his eyes and makes the globe spin and his finger drops down on . . .

"Québec."

I laugh. "You won't go that far."

"Unfair," he says. "Let's try again."

I spin and my finger falls in the middle of the Atlantic Ocean, the Sargasso Sea.

Laurent spins. "Again!" he protests, disappointed. Québec. But then he looks up, his eyes bright. "No, this is great, can't you see? This is fate!"

"You believe in fate?" I snigger. "Stuff written in the stars, guardian angels, and all that nonsense? Not me. I'm not going to wait for fate to take me for a ride. I'll make it happen."

"You have it all planned out, do you?" It's his turn to be snide.

"That's not what I'm saying. All I'm saying is, I'll have more control over my life than my mother had because I have more choices. I can have sex without having children, which means I can have sex without getting married, but I can also have a career and keep it even if I decide to get married and have children. I can have it all! That's why I'm not going to let life pass me by while I'm waiting for fate to fly me to Madagascar and Tasmania, all right?"

"Enough, I get the point! But take the day we met, for example. What if you had put our book back on the shelf ten minutes before, or later?"

"The moment doesn't mean anything until we choose to give it meaning. You chose to come back to the library on my shift and let me know what was on your mind by reading *Histoire d'O* in front of me."

"And did you choose me?"

"I did when I opened the file to look up your information."

"I don't care what you say, it *was* fate. And I'm not letting you go on your world travels just now," Laurent says, tackling me down to the living-room floor. Soon his fingers and his mouth are exploring my body. Borobudur, Timbuktu, Sargasso Sea, he whispers with an increasingly raspy voice. He knows exactly where Québec is, and he keeps it for last.

But in the end he got tired of waiting for me to let him in. I was allowing more and more things—skiing, friends, extra working hours to save for a trip—to come between us.

"Don't you love me?" he finally asked, exasperated by my unavailability.

"I do."

"Then what's the problem? You never want to be with me."

"I don't have a problem. Maybe you do."

Why couldn't I surrender to his love? Because I knew if I did, my fate would be sealed. Studies at Université Laval, a job in Québec, a split-level in Cap-Rouge with two kids and a dog playing on a square of green lawn. I didn't want to live my parents' life, and routine was not my idea of love. Between the time I broke up with Laurent and the time I started to pay rent in Toronto, I took off whenever I had enough money saved. I went backpacking from the outer Hebrides to Sicily, from the Canaries to Istanbul, and from Chihuahua to Lake Titicaca. I sent my mother postcards from every faraway place I went to. She pinned them with a magnet to the refrigerator and said it made the kitchen look bigger and more exotic. All these years there was nothing I liked better than to unfold the map of an unknown land or engage in conversation with a stranger.

༄

NEHIRO-IRINIUI
AIAMIHE
MASSINAHIGAN

Livre de Prières en langue montagnaise à l'usage des chrétiens de Tadoussac, de Portneuf, des Îlets-Jérémie, de Saint-Nicolas, de Mistassini, de Chicoutimi, de Sept-Îles, d'Achouabmouchouan, du Lac St-Jean et de tous ceux qui habitent le pays montagnais.

Québec, chez les Imprimeurs Brown et Gilmor,
1767

༄

The Montagnais called him Jan Batist Tsitsisahigan.

In the darkest hour of winter he crouched under the tent's low ceiling, his paper balanced on the back of a curled-up dog. His eyes cried from the acrid smoke, his fingers were stiff from the cold. He chewed on pieces of his own leather frock to try to stop the hunger churning his stomach. The light was faint and blue even at noon, coming from the shelter's wall of snow.

Come spring, he sat for days between two native oarsmen on one more journey through the quick water, protecting his paperwork from the spindrift with his wide black sleeves.

Midsummer he wrote by candlelight on a fine sand beach, the sky speckled with stars above the canopy of the overturned canoe, a waft of fish smell drifting from the drying racks, the mosquitoes zinging in his ears, his back aching from the last portage.

"Tshishi Manitu is Master of the Impossible," he used to say.

Jean-Baptiste de La Brosse lived like them and with them, constantly travelling to cover the ecclesiastical province he inherited in 1766: from the mouth of the Moisie River at Sept-Îles to the north, down the shore of the St. Lawrence River to the southern point of Île-aux-Coudres, and inland to the source of the Métabetchouane River, which flows into Lac Saint-Jean. The fourth point was undefined, the territory inland from the Moisie River and north of the Métabetchouane still uncharted. Trees, rivers, and snow, five to six thousand native Montagnais, and a handful of fur traders appointed to the Tadoussac post: that's all there was in Jean-Baptiste de La Brosse's territory, and the only tools he had to evangelize this country were his faith and one book.

Jean-Baptiste de La Brosse's *Nehiro-Iriniui* is the first Indian book printed in North America, on the press of Brown and Gilmor in Québec. The catechism includes useful prayers for the faithful about to take a long canoe journey, wishing for a good hunt, or about to be bled, and answers practical questions such as "What to do when you are in mortal danger in the forest and unable to resort to a priest?" The winters were unforgiving north of Québec. Of the 125 deaths recorded between 1759 and 1773, 50 occurred in the woods. Whole families would disappear without a trace.

No fewer than two thousand *Nehiro-Iriniui* were printed in Québec at the extraordinary cost of forty-five pounds. Even with the added income of a little fur trading on the side, Jean-Baptiste de La Brosse could never have come up with this princely sum. A Protestant merchant from Québec named William Grant did. Why would a Protestant encourage the spread of the Catholic faith? Well, money already talked louder than God. "Tourner le pays," or "to turn the country around" in fur trade jargon: that is what happened when converted natives could be counted on as allies.

"Chose étonnante!" exclaims François Pilote, a missionary sent upcountry in 1851. "After two hundred years the Saguenay's Montagnais, in spite of their nomadic and wandering lifestyle, all know how to read. Each family keeps with great care its book of prayers and hymns, and uses it on Sundays. In this regard, many of our own families are still lagging well behind. The Native learns to read as he learns to shoot his prey or steer his canoe. It is because he sees one as necessary as the other, to both his moral and physical life."

How could a single book mean so much to so many and for so long?

This notion is hard to grasp as I sit in one of the largest libraries in the world, with my own *Nehiro-Iriniui* in front of me. It's a slim volume, leather bound with yellowed pages. I touch each scratch and mark scarring the brown cover, dried out at the edges. I feel the texture of the paper, thick and rough, the black embossed ink of the front page, the fluid blue signature of the book's first owner, faded beside the bright red crown of the British Library stamp. My fingers reach for all the other fingers that have turned these pages, held this book issued from the first print shop of Québec. My eyes travel along the unintelligible sentences, following this book's journey, most probably on a canoe, from Québec to Tadoussac on the brackish course of the St. Lawrence. Here a porpoise, there an adhothuys, a great blue whale surfacing to breathe before diving back towards the deep, cold brine. As I whisper the jumble of letters under my breath in the low light of the Rare Books department, an infinitely quiet room for the number of people present, I hear other voices joining in, chanting these words on long walks through snowbanks, ice plains, and forests, in joy and in despair. This book is like a door I slip through, a little door, only eight by five inches of leather and paper, but much more than just leather and paper. When I step over its threshold, my heart opens to the other hearts, the ones turned to ice in the middle of a forest or eaten warm at a feast, still haunting this catechism.

1. Nataueritamuin. Auen'ka tfhifhihifk? Naskuhimauin. Tfifhe Manitu ni tfhifhihigu.

The only word I recognize, in what looks like a set of 149 questions and answers, is Manitu.

*　　*　　*

He is back. Stephen has kept his promise and this time there is no plane to take me away from him. We leave Canada House together and walk the short distance between Trafalgar Square and Piccadilly Circus in the rain to enter another world: a golden room with plush seats, immaculate linen, and a brisk but discreet French staff dressed in black. No stone slabs here, no long-dead as in the Crypt Café. More like the well-to-do. We order champagne and foie gras on toast, white wine, a salade de canard tiède. We talk about the places he has been and seen, which are many, his world of communications and my world of research. We even argue again about the politics of our country. Stephen could never understand Québec's aspiration to become smaller and unilingual. He was brought up in between two cultures, Chinese and Canadian, and he's an unconditional supporter of the global market economy. He had been shocked when I told him my first vote had helped put the Parti Québécois in power in 1976. I had been shocked when my Yes vote had not been enough to tilt the result of the 1980 referendum towards an independent Québec. What we don't talk about is Toronto, when I discovered I was pregnant after he left for Singapore, or how I decided to terminate the pregnancy since I did not have the financial or emotional support to raise a child. Because it had been a rational decision, the backlash caught me off guard. I felt gutted, betrayed. Empty. Maybe Laurent had been right, and life was not just a series of informed decisions. The difference was that his sense of fate had been shaped by hope, and mine now rose from a starker place.

When Stephen tries to find out about my life in London, I turn his questions around and make him talk about himself. I pretend he is a new research project and the keywords come easily. He is a successful businessman, an habitué of the first-class lounges of airports from Asia to South America who owns an interior-designed penthouse in São

Paulo. He collects Dadaist sculptures, and women. Through veiled allusions he tries to intimate he hasn't found true love. And that's what this encounter makes me think of, the dance of the seven veils in a Moorish haunt of gold silk and green palm trees. Who is going to drop one veil too many, and who will get to the other one's truth first to strike the fatal blow? After half a bottle of Veuve Clicquot and two glasses of Pouilly-Fuissé, I'm ready to dance. I'm ready to crawl on my hands and feet, to be branded and wounded again, anything to trick my mind away from the image of my mother, a floppy hat over her shaved head, waving by the red door in her bathrobe. Stephen suggests jasmine tea at his hotel, on Half Moon Street.

"Stay," he says, his hand around my arm, his thumb caressing the inside of my elbow. Grey light seeps from a crack between the heavy curtains. The quilted bed cover has rolled off, the sheets are twisted around Stephen's ankles. His face sinks in the overstuffed pillow, half a dozen beauty spots scattered across his left cheek. The bed seems too big for the room, which is not large.

"I have to go," I tell him, trying to find my clothes on the floor. I walk to the bathroom to get dressed, avoiding the mirrors. But I cannot avoid my mother anymore. She was dying on the king-size bed beside us, and she is dying here too, in this bathroom. I carry her on my back everywhere I am, everywhere I go. I wash my hands, my face, and use the mouthwash sample. I'd like to use the bidet, but what I want even more is to get away from here. I need to go home.

"What's the rush?" he asks me again, naked and relaxed, as I walk back in to the bedroom. He is unwrapping one of the mint chocolates the maids leave in the room before night.

"Can I make a call?"

"Sure."

I dial home. "Ozlem? I'm sorry I didn't phone earlier, I'll be late. Do you want to order pizza? She wants to talk to me? Tell her not now . . . Ozlem? Yes, it's me, sweetie. I know I promised, but it's raining anyway. We'll go to the park tomorrow. All right. Be a good girl. I'll see you soon, mon trésor."

I have made sure not to look at Stephen. By the time I put the receiver down he has turned his back to me and pulled the sheet up. I finish picking up my coat, my purse. My umbrella. I leave the room silently, the damage done.

Sainte-Foy,
October 1970

H E thought he could do it, kill.

Paul thought he could kill a stag. This was his second hunt and he'd never come face to face with anything bigger than a partridge, a duck, or a rabbit before. This time, he would kill. That's what Paul believed while he helped his brother-in-law, Henri Beauregard, pack up the station wagon with the gear. A wooden crate of Malpeque oysters from Prince Edward Island, two cases of Labatt Fifty, six bottles of Italian wine, one large pot of spaghetti sauce with meatballs, and one casserole of baked beans in maple syrup.

Four hundred miles later, when they arrived at Zach and Colette's cottage by the lake, they unloaded the food and the booze, unrolled their sleeping bags on hard bunk beds, stoked up the wood stove. Then they started to flip the beer caps off and pour long fingers of hard liquor into plastic glasses, and all the while Paul was still gung-ho, even though he knew he wasn't as good a shot as his brothers-in-law.

Henri hunted with the most powerful rifle, a .30-30 Winchester, which gave him first bragging rights, and he rarely missed his target. Léo was not far behind with a 308 Browning and an uncanny ability to call the moose. Paul and Lucien were amateurs and had been lent the two 7 mm Winchester Magnums Henri was saving for his sons.

Through the first skeet practice, bang-bang, flying debris breaking over the quiet lake, Paul kept thinking, Look, I can do it. When they ran out of clay pigeons, they built up a target: a pumpkin wearing

Bernadette's silk scarf set on top of a galvanized garbage can wrapped in a sleeping bag. They shot at it until the pumpkin blew up, spraying them with a mush of seeds and orange pulp.

Kill! screamed Paul amid the cheers.

By then they'd had a lot to drink, and they sent the laughing women, tam-o'-shanters askew, to fetch the camp's rickety china. Using the skeet contraption, a tireless metal arm hooked on a spring, they sent the cups and saucers and dinner plates flying through the air.

Pow-pow!

When the china was blown to smithereens, they shot at the pot lids and the beer empties, and when all these were gone too, they stood outside in the cold eating oysters and shot at the chucked-out shells. More difficult but still enjoyable were the bright copper volleys of beer bottle caps. After these, they had to dig deep in their pockets to find the small change they threw without ceremony across the sunset and down into the lake, as if for a lucky wish.

When they finally looked around and realized they had shot holes through everything they could put their hands on, they just kept shooting anyway, and as stray bullets drilled through the car doors and slashed the newspaper covering the outhouse window, Paul was adamant. It would be antlers, not feathers.

When they ran out of bullets and cheers, they dropped their rifles to the ground and went in to warm up dinner, feeling famished after the bloodless carnage.

Aux Armes, Citoyens!

Outside Henri Beauregard's house, kitty-corner from the brand-new church named after the Canadian martyr Jean de Brébeuf, cars are parked back to back in the driveway. First is Léo Beauregard's big black Buick, then Henri's sorry-looking station wagon. Paul Des Ruisseaux's burgundy Impala is by the curb along with Bernadette's Beetle, left behind five days ago. Henri Beauregard's neighbours, alerted by the car horns trumpeting the hunters' triumphant return, have stopped replacing summer screens with storm windows, and their children have dropped their ball games to go check out the kill. Tied to the station wagon's roof with ropes stained a rusty red is a big moose head with a gorgeous rack of antlers. It should be the centre of attention, but the car doors are left open to hear the special newscast on the radio.

"We repeat, the body of Deputy Minister Pierre Laporte was found in the trunk of a green Chevrolet last night, following instructions given in a new communiqué from the Front de Libération du Québec, a terrorist organization. The car, the same used in Monsieur Laporte's kidnapping, was abandoned in a suburb of Montréal's south shore. This follows the occupation of Québec by eight thousand soldiers from the Canadian Army launched last Thursday, and the decision of Parliament in Ottawa to adopt the War Measures Act in the early hours of Friday . . ."

"Tu comprends pas, Paul. Hunting is not about killing."

"What is it about then, Henri?"

"All of God's creatures hunt to survive. Why shouldn't we?"

"We don't need to anymore, that's why. We're not animals. We have grocery stores," says Paul, stating the obvious.

"If you eat meat, you're a hunter," says Léo. "Someone else is doing the dirty job for you, that's all."

"And what if we need to take up our rifles again, to protect our own?" asks Henri.

Léo and Henri Beauregard and their brother-in-law, Paul, pass a flask around to celebrate the trophy plucked from the woods by the New Brunswick border. They cock their caps off with show-off smiles and scratch their scraggly beards. Carving knives are slung from their belts and their guns are still strapped on their backs, half for show and half for safety, to make sure the kids don't get any ideas. There are enough people playing with guns in Québec right now.

"You know what I mean, Paul?" Henri says, nodding towards the radio.

"Aux armes, citoyens!" Léo Beauregard taunts his brother-in-law.

Léo has been celebrating non-stop ever since he got his moose. "Don't you believe in the same thing as the FLQ, Paul? You know, le Québec libre?"

"What are you talking about, Léo? The Parti Québécois and René Lévesque are part of the democratic process. Don't you start associating PQ members with the small-time scumbags from the FLQ, because if you do, others will too. Like in Ottawa."

"That's fine, mon Paul, but look what's happening," Henri argues. "When we left for Dégelis on Wednesday, we had a democracy, and now what have we got?"

"The War Measures Act suspends the civil rights of the citizens of Québec, giving extraordinary power to both the Sûreté du Québec and the Royal Canadian Mounted Police as well as the Canadian Army. This measure comes in the wake of the chain of events leading to Monsieur Laporte's death. On Monday, October 5, James Cross, a British diplomat, was kidnapped from his home in Westmount by the Cellule Chenier of the Front de Libération du Québec. On October 7 the FLQ manifesto was broadcast on public radio and television, one of the twelve conditions posed for Mr. Cross's release. The FLQ explained its raison d'être in its own words: 'The Front de Libération du Québec wants the total independence of all Québécois, united in a free society, purged forever of the clique of voracious sharks, the patronizing "big bosses" and their henchmen who have made Québec their hunting preserve for "cheap labour" and unscrupulous exploitation.'"

"It's war, Paul," Henri goes on, "and when there's a war, you've got to choose which side you're on. You're either on Trudeau's side or you're on their side."

At the other end of the driveway Lilianne and her sisters-in-law, Cécile and Berthe, discuss how they are going to split the moose meat.

"We'll take the heart, but you can have the liver for Henri if you want," Berthe tells Cécile. She has first pick because it's her husband's kill.

"Did you check it for parasites?"

"Would I offer you a bad piece of meat?" Berthe answers, unsmiling.

"How do we split the tenderloin?" Cécile begins to tally. "One bit each for the three of us, plus one for Bernadette and one for Lucien? That won't make much for anybody."

Berthe asks, "What about you, Lili, what do you want?"

"Something that looks like a rosbif wrapped in paper with a sticker from the grocery store, otherwise my kids won't touch it." Bébé, her youngest, clings to her leg. The children have been waiting for their parents' return since lunchtime.

"How can you ask anybody to choose between assassins on one side and a dictator sending the army against his own people on the other side?" Paul says to Henri. " 'Just watch me,' Trudeau said. 'Watch how far I can go.' Well, he's already gone too far, if you ask me. He got one of us killed by refusing to negotiate."

"Come on, you can't blame Trudeau for Laporte's death!" protests Henri.

Lili shouts from the other side of the driveway. "You can say what you want about Trudeau, Paul, but he seems to be the only one ready to make decisions and take responsibility for them. He's the only one with balls."

Paul throws a sharp look at his wife. "Don't you find it strange," he retorts, ignoring Lili's comment, "that even with the SQ, the RCMP, and the FBI on the case, with all this 'intelligence,' they still can't find Cross and they haven't even arrested one of the suspects? And now armed vehicles drive up the Trans-Canada Highway, police search honest people's houses and jail them without charges for an indefinite amount of time. Makes you wonder what they're really trying to do."

"All I know, Paul, is that from balls to bullshit to bullets there seems to be just one tiny step," says Henri. "Not good for business, all this. Better talk to my stockbroker first thing tomorrow morning."

"On Saturday, October 10, Pierre Laporte, the minister of labour and deputy minister in Premier Bourassa's cabinet, was kidnapped in front of his house in Saint-Lambert. On October 16, among rumours of popular insurrection and coup d'état, the federal government adopted the War Measures Act, suspending its citizens' civil rights. Pierre Laporte's suspicious death was reported last night, shortly after the new measures were made public."

Lilianne's eyes have drifted back to the dead moose. "Paul, nobody wants war here, nobody. Have a look around, would you?" She nods at their two sons, Pierrot and Maurice, darting back and forth between the cars with their cousins, and the three young girls, Anne, Lucie, and Cécile's daughter, Myriam, sitting on the slate steps. Bernadette and Lucien are coming out of Henri's house with cold beer for everybody. "This can't happen here."

"Pierre Laporte didn't think it could happen to him either while he threw a football to his nephew in his driveway in Saint-Lambert," says Paul. Just like here, in Sainte-Foy. Just like today, at the end of a glorious afternoon. Just like that, as if a car full of terrorists in balaclavas waving Russian machine guns could drive around the corner by the church. "And now he's dead."

"Shame on us," says Henri, his finger following a scratch on the station wagon door.

"Something is wrong. How did we bring this upon ourselves?" says one of their churchgoing neighbours, Madame Brûlé. "This is a Christian place, not one of those godless countries, you know, like Russia, Algeria, Cuba . . ." She signs herself, lowering her eyes, and they all repeat her gesture and respect the silence in homage to Pierre Laporte's memory.

"Did you know they even had the guts to stop at a gas station to ask for directions to Laporte's house?" adds Madame Brûlé's husband.

Paul isn't finished yet. "If Trudeau dares to touch René Lévesque, there will be even more trouble. I don't believe in violence, but if they use violence, are we just going to shut up? It's one thing to nip terrorism in the bud, but it's another to try to smother the whole movement for independence." His voice cracks on his final protest: "He will not break our dream!"

Bernadette, having finished distributing the beer, tightens the knot of her silk scarf against the fresh breeze.

"Qu'est-ce qui est arrivé à ton foulard, ma tante?" Lucie asks her aunt. Some of the scarf's pink roses have been torn away, leaving a hole with a lacy brown edge.

"I'll tell you one day, Lucie," says Bernadette, patting her niece's head. "The important thing is, we're still alive."

Fair Game

"First day we don't see no moose but we see the two deer, the doe and her fawn," Henri says. "We're lucky this year, we could hunt both deer and moose for a week. Deer is not so heavy to portage back, but moose tastes better, huh, Léo?"

Léo drapes a possessive arm along the station wagon's roof rail. "Nothing beats moose meat, nothing at all. Look at this, a beauty."

The moose head has been sawed off just before the back hump at the base of a neck as wide as a stump. The animal's short fur is brown except where the blood has caked in a darker shade, mostly along the ragged edge of raw flesh. The goatee hair is glued to the fur, the sur-prisingly long rabbit-like ears have gone flabby, the drooping velvet muzzle is drying out, and if a residue of fear still lurks in the wide open black eyes, a dire reminder of death, the moose antlers rise like a robust tree with a dense fine-lined bark, with many horn-tips reaching for the sky.

"But if you kill the doe, what happens to her fawn?" asks Madame Brûlé.

Henri doesn't answer. It's Berthe who says, "By fall hunting season, the fawns are old enough to survive on their own."

Madame Brûlé looks at her neighbour, distraught. Henri shrugs.

"You're not allowed to hunt fawns, surely?" says Monsieur Brûlé.

"Oh yes," says Henri. "You can. I don't. Not worth the trouble. But the docteur says baby deer meat is the best."

Leo laughs. "Have you heard how the forest rangers speak to him? Bonjour, Docteur Caron, comment ça va, Docteur Caron. Meanwhile Docteur Caron has got two dozen out-of-season trout still wriggling in the trunk!"

Berthe turns to another neighbour, Madame Paquette. "Moi, je chasse pas. I have bad legs. I wouldn't be able to take the walking." Cigarette smoke fades past Berthe's Irish green wool tam, forcing her to narrow her eyes. "Do you know how to catch lots of fish fast? Night fishing. You flash the light through the pitch black water and they come up to you, all of them. Trout, perch, carp, catfish, sunfish. Lots of trout. I still have about a dozen left in the cooler. Anybody interested? A buck a pop. We've kind of had it with fish grills for now."

"How big are they?" asks Madame Paquette, interested.

"But before we even get there," Henri goes on, "we got a transportation problem. Colette's Jeep is out of commission since she drove it into the lake the night before, on her way back from getting paper plates in the village with her sisters. Something wrong with the brakes, she said."

"Always something wrong with the car, with Colette," says Cécile, dramatically waving an arm.

"Not only with the car, if you ask me," says Berthe.

"We're not asking you," Bernadette snaps.

Henri is on the opposite side of the driveway, oblivious to the women's exchange. "Léo is still drunk so he can't drive his Buick, and Lucien can't handle his hangover so he decides to stay with Cécile and Berthe. Avec les belles-soeurs! But since the women want to come along with us we all end up in the Thunderbird with Zach driving at eighty miles an hour on the dirt road, a red-eye in the glass holder by the steering wheel. I'm sitting beside him and Bernadette is squeezed between us, and when Zach's hand leaves his drink to grab her thigh she slaps him hard. He laughs and says, 'Come on, Dette, don't play Sainte-Catherine with me! I know you're getting some even if you're not married.' While he talks, the car swerves a little and I see Paul turn green and tug at the automatic window control, but it doesn't work. 'Tabarslack Zach, how do you open the window?' Leaning on the opposite window is Léo snoring, and Zach has to fish for the window control somewhere between Dette's legs and she slaps him again and Léo shouts as his head almost drops out of the car. Lilianne is in the back between Léo and Paul with Colette on her knees, who screams, 'Leave my little sister alone, you pig!' I tell you, women. Put three sisters together and what you get is yackety-yack from dawn to dusk."

"Look who's talking!" heckles Berthe.

"He's sensitive, our Paul, very sensitive!" Henri laughs as he slaps Paul's back.

"No killer instinct. None whatsoever," Léo agrees, and he slaps Paul's back too. Paul weathers the assaults, trying not to spill his beer over Berthe, who's standing beside him.

"Hey, calm down, would you?" Berthe cautions her husband, Léo.

"So anyhow," Henri goes on, "we drop off the women as quickly as we can, a couple of miles past the gate. We tell them we'll pick them up on the way back at the end of the afternoon. As an afterthought, we drop Léo too. He actually falls out of the car flat on his back, and I think he still has a foot inside when Zach takes off in a cloud of gravel. 'Don't forget us!' they cry. How could we?"

"How could they, huh?" Bernadette throws in, a fist plunked on her hip.

"Men! I could tell you a thing or two about men!" Berthe rasps, her cigarette pushed to the corner of her mouth. "Toutes des enfants de chiennes!"

"Berthe!" says Lilianne, looking around for the girls but catching Madame Brûlé's disapproving stare instead.

"Don't worry about the girls, Lili," Berthe says. "The earlier they learn what men are all about, the better off they will be."

"We're heading for a spot Zach got a tip on," Henri continues, "half an hour in from the gates. A big boulder, a light grey quartz with dark veins, that's where we get in on a narrow track. Game only move about at dawn and dusk, and we've missed dawn so we set ourselves to wait in silence. We wait, drinking from our Thermos to keep warm. We wait and it's cold and then it gets colder until the forest starts to turn a deeper shade of grey. Can't tell the stones from the tree trunks from the sky, but still no deer. I am just about to open my mouth and suggest a move when Zach puts his hand up."

Henri takes a gulp of beer. An airplane streaks past the oblique roofline, gliding silently across the pristine sky like a water bug on a pond, white and transparent. The small crowd huddles around him in the radiant fall afternoon, the long shadows spreading, clear cut, from the driveway to the side of the cars. There are no woods around here, only skinny trees on shorn yellow lawns, no wild animals, only domestic dogs tied to the back porches, yet Henri's words reel his audience into the forest where they follow his bright orange vest. They can feel the rough surface of the rock, speckled with quartz, the mushy layer of damp leaves. They watch the trail's ragged line recede in the growing darkness, slashed here and there by the smooth grey skin of the trees, quiet.

"And then we see them, just this flicker of colour, a little yellower than grey, warmer, the white spots on the fawn like fireflies as they come to us. They come so close we can see their big, wet eyes. They graze here and there under the wind, perfect. I just can't tell when it goes wrong. All I know is that Paul—yes, our Paul—is a pretty sensitive guy!" And Henri slaps his brother-in-law's back one more time, breaking the thread. And everybody laughs one more time, and Paul has to laugh but he thinks the joke is wearing thin. "Zach goes first for the fawn and then I go for the doe, but maybe it's still the booze in our blood, or maybe it's just too dark to be really sharp . . . anyway. It's Paul's turn. 'Shoot, Paul, come on, shoot!' we urge him, even if we know they're gone. And do you know what he does?"

"Give me a break, Henri! I am not going to start shooting Bambis, that's for sure! That's not sport, it's a tragedy."

The truth is, Paul couldn't shoot. He threw his gun down and ran away from Zach and Henri and their sniggers, their loud gunfire—from the shame that would need to be burnt from his skin like a bloodsucker. He ran after the deer through the thick of the wood, the mud, the leaves, the branches whipping his face. Nothing could stop him. The more he ran, the lighter he felt. He really believed he would catch up with the frail fawn, that he would leap and throw his arms around Bambi's speckled rump—and then let him go. Fair game.

"But running, now that's sport, isn't it, mon Paul!" laughs Henri. "But it doesn't matter anyway. Léo got his moose the next day."

Bloody Murder

It's five o'clock and Monsieur Brûlé lifts his earflap to hear the news update on his small radio:

"Last night the body of Pierre Laporte was found in the trunk of a car abandoned near the Canadian Forces Base St-Hubert on Montréal's south shore. A communiqué from the FLQ claims responsibility for the murder, stating, 'Faced with the arrogance of the federal government and its lackey, Bourassa, faced with their obvious bad faith, the FLQ has therefore decided to act. Pierre Laporte, minister of unemployment and assimilation, has been executed at 6:18 tonight by the Dieppe Cell (Royal 22nd). You will find the body in the trunk of the green Chevrolet (9J-2420) at the St-Hubert base, entry No. 2. We shall overcome. FLQ. P.S. The exploiters of the Québec people had better watch out.' Witnesses to the grim discovery say it appears Monsieur Laporte's body had sustained many injuries and was wrapped in blood-soaked towels. The witnesses' report has not been confirmed by the police, no charges have been laid, and an autopsy has been ordered."

"They didn't even kill him with a gun, did they?" asks Léo, still leaning on the station wagon as close as he can to the dead head.

"A real bloody mess, sounds like," says Berthe. "A real man's job."

"How do you know there are no women involved?" says Lucien.

"Just doesn't sound like it. Sounds like a real dumb-ass half-baked plot."

Paul says, "Nobody's mentioned murder yet. It might have been an accident, there might have been a struggle, maybe Laporte was trying to escape."

"Come on, Paul," snarls Henri. "Of course, they killed him, they even said so! Are you trying to make excuses for the FLQ?"

"Was he . . . Did they . . . torture him?" asks Madame Paquette, one hand gripping her coat collar.

"High on drugs or something, I bet," says Cécile.

"What a waste," says Lili.

"Christ, the guy was not even English!" Léo says. "Why didn't they do Cross instead? Bang. Shot in the back of the head, execution style. Make your point, no mess, clean slate."

"You really are an asshole," says Berthe.

"How can you commit such an evil act while believing in the right thing?" Paul asks.

"You should watch what you believe in these days, brother," Henri answers. "The way I see it, you're talking your way straight to jail."

"A dream is just a dream . . ." sings Léo, waltzing around his brother-in-law. "Time to wakey-wakey, Paulie!"

That's when Paul throws his beer in Léo's face. Léo shoves him against the wall and the beer bottle smashes. Lucien jumps on Léo to hold him back and Henri jumps on Lucien to protect Léo, his weight making them topple over in a pile of kicking legs and swinging fists. Madame Paquette and Madame Brûlé back up, screaming. Bernadette and Lilianne push them out of the way to try to separate the men.

"You son of a bitch!"

"Stop it! Stop it!"

The children come running to see what the ruckus is all about, the young ones crying in fright and the boys cheering. "Envoye, Papa, give it to him, come on!"

Berthe has moved away only far enough not to get kicked in the shins. "Assholes, all of them. Would you look at this?" she mumbles to herself before shouting, "Aye, ça fait, là! Enough!"

Léo stops hitting first and the others follow.

"Aren't you ashamed of yourselves?"

Lilianne and Bernadette help the men to their feet, dusting their coats off and pulling their sleeves down. The driveway is littered with broken glass. When Léo finally moves, Paul lifts an arm to protect himself. But Léo's eyes are wet as his well-meaning hand lands on Paul's shoulder before they embrace. "I'm sorry, Paul, I didn't mean to hurt you. I love you like a brother. Like a brother, you know?"

"It's okay, Léo. I know."

Three Tall Women

They walk side by side on the dirt road around six or seven at night, October 1970. Three sisters, three tall women singing on a forest road, their shotguns tucked under their arms, nose down, their hands stuffed in their pockets and their feet sore in the heavy boots. Their voices trail away and die off in the dust between the two thick pads of forest on each side of the road. They have red noses from the cold, their cheeks are chafed by the stiff turned-up collars. The last traces of lipstick are long gone, but the vodka still lingers on their breath, the pick-me-up effect giving way to a bitter taste. They had only peanuts and chocolate bars to eat all day. They're hungry, filthy, and tired but they keep on walking in silence, looking down, while the indigo veil of the evening gels into the solid black pit of night.

Then it happens. Just like on the road sign, the yellow triangle with a black silhouette suspended in mid-flight. So close, the sudden rush of air makes them reel back on their heels. It takes the first deer only one leap to cross the road from side to side. The women don't even have time to scream before the second one crosses with two shorter jumps, so light, so high, the white speckles giving the fawn's rump away.

And they're gone.

But the three sisters can still guess the graceful arc traced above their heads, or so it seems, still catch a glimpse of the lustrous coats of the frightened deer, smell the musky trail and hear the dainty hooves hitting the gravel. Already gone, except for the sound of snapping twigs and rustling leaves.

"Ma foi du bon Dieu!" Lilianne whispers.

"Was that what I think it was?" asks Bernadette.

As for Colette, she just stands there, petrified. When she realizes what they've just seen, she grabs a shell from her clip belt. "No," she mutters, "that's for rabbits, ducks, small things." She picks another one, bigger, red plastic. "No, no, wrong one, why did I take these, they're for bear, where did I put the good ones?" And she discards the red bullet and stamps her foot on the ground, her fingers and her voice unsteady. Her sisters try to stop her: "Calm down, Colette, calm down. It's too late now. They're gone. You can't see a thing anyway, it's too dark!"

But Colette won't listen. She finds the right ammunition and tries to jam it in the rifle but drops it, picks another one and tries again and then, finally, she slides two shells in the chamber and bolts the gun back together with a smart snap. She takes aim, but there is nothing more to aim at, nothing but the memory of the two deer flying across the forest road. She keeps the gun on her shoulder, her finger on the trigger, pointing the barrel to the left, to the right. "I hate hunting!" she cries out. To the left. "I hate fishing!" The right. "I hate sick people!" She screams, "I hate this place, I always have, from day one!" She shoots at the wood twice, the bullets' ricochet sending pieces of bark flying. "I hate trees!" Reloads and shoots again. "I hate rivers." Loads and shoots, loads and shoots at the night. "I hate the curé, I hate the butcher, I hate the hairdresser, all talking behind my back!"

Lilianne and Bernadette crouch down and try to grab her from behind, to pry the gun away from her. "Colette, mais fais attention!"

"What if Léo is still around?"

"Get me out of here before it kills me! I hate the nurses he sleeps with, I hate his laugh, I hate him! *I hate you, Zacharie Caron!* Do you hear me? *I hate you!*"

"Colette!"

Colette slips to the ground on her knees, out of steam and bullets. "I'd do anything to get out of here." She reaches for her flask but it is empty too. She throws it away and bawls, huddled between her two sisters on the dirt road, the taste of spent gunpowder filling her mouth.

Sainte-Foy,
1971–1972

"Do you want a toke?" asks Myriam.

Lucie takes a drag and blows out the smoke as quickly as she can, relieved her cousin is not looking on. She passes the cigarette back to Myriam, who offers it to Anne.

"Yuck. Smoke." Anne fans herself with her hand, turning her head away.

Myriam, Henri and Cécile Beauregard oldest child's, is sixteen. She goes to boarding school and comes home only on weekends. Her bedroom is a mess of paperbacks stacked up against the wall and *Seventeen* magazines spread out beside her unmade bed, its frilly yellow bedspread twisted in a knot. Her night table is littered with brown apple cores, an empty bowl coated with yellowing milk, a lipstick-stained glass of water, and a green 7Up bottle. It looks so grown-up in here. Lucie thinks that maybe she shouldn't be so tidy. "Do you miss your boyfriend?"

"Yeah . . ." Myriam answers without enthusiasm.

"When are they going to let you see him again?"

"I don't know."

"Do you love him?"

Myriam doesn't miss a beat. "Oh yeah." She shivers before starting to pick at the roots of her hair over and over again, her eyes trailing off. Myriam got caught past curfew time jumping out the window of the boarding school to meet her boyfriend. She hasn't been allowed to see him since. "What about you, Lucie," Myriam eggs her younger cousin on. "You're thirteen, don't you have a boyfriend?"

"Boys are too stupid, they're all so stupid."

"I'm over boys too. I prefer men now."

"What do you mean, men?"

"Forget about sixteen-year-olds."

"I thought you said you loved your boyfriend!"

"Maybe I lied. Can you keep a secret? I don't want my mother to hear this. I broke up with him."

"Why?"

"He doesn't even drive a car. What can you do without a car? Anyway. Now he says he can't live without me. He says he's going to kill himself."

"Do you believe him?"

"His parents have phoned here to ask if there's something wrong." Myriam pulls the curtains, lights a candle and a stick of incense. Lucie hates this smell. It reminds her of the church service she is forced to attend every week.

"Have you read all this?" asks Anne, pointing to the books.

"Oh yeah," Myriam says, the sharp excitement quickly drained from her voice.

"All of them?" asks Anne with disbelief.

"I can't sleep at night, so I read."

"Until what time are you allowed?"

"Until I finish the book."

"And your mother doesn't say anything?"

Myriam's face hardens as she slips the used match into the 7Up bottle and gives it a deft swirl. "She knows better than to come in here. And anyway, she's too wasted to care. Want to hear some music?"

Wasted. Lucie and Anne look at each other. How can Myriam say this about her mother? Their cousin walks to the portable turntable and puts on the new Donovan LP. A song about witches. Anne curls up on the bed to read a book. A woman with white skin and red lips is showing as much cleavage as distress on its cover. There's something

Lucie really wants to ask Myriam. What is it the girls do in the back of the bus that ruffles their hair, makes their lips swell, and puts red blotches on their cheeks?

Myriam smiles. "You don't know what they do? Well, that means you're not ready, that's all. When you're ready, you'll know. You'll know what to do."

What is she talking about? Lucie wonders. When will I be ready? And ready for what? Myriam is wrong anyway. "I'll never be the one with a boy in the back of the bus, just look at me."

Myriam frowns, taking a good look at her cousin, willing to help. "I like your hair, but can't the glasses go? Or get cool ones, John Lennon style. Let's try some lipstick and mascara and if you see some clothes you like, just help yourself."

Anne and Lucie take the bus every morning to the high-school campus, a grand name for half a dozen brick boxes scattered on a bald patch of windswept land. It is set between the shopping centre and the express-way to the new bridge, the only bright colour being the dozens of yellow buses lining the road. The bus stop used to be at the end of Henri's driveway, but La Fatiguante complained about the cigarette butts so now it's on the other corner. The back of the bus is the Therriault sisters' territory. Sony, Josy, and Vicky never smile. Their faces hide behind two bands of straight hair parted just a crack, slicing their eyes in half. They roll up the waistbands of their A-line skirts, making them so short anybody can see the line of their pantyhose, even the cotton gusset when they bend over. They wear the matching forest green vest of the uniform open and undo the top three buttons of their white blouses, showing off the lacy edge of their bras. The rule says the skirt should not be more than four inches above the knee, but the rule doesn't say anything about how many undone buttons. Nobody cares about the rules anyway. Next year the uniform will be history and the whole campus will go co-ed.

Many things are history on the campus. Religion classes have been replaced by Morals, which is about what's right and what's wrong. It's wrong to take drugs, but it's right to go out on the street with handmade posters showing support for the public servants' strike, or the teachers' strike, or the nurses' strike. The whole campus also walks out of the classroom, everybody ending up at the shopping centre to buy records, to protest against new bills or laws. The laws have numbers, like 63; the strikers' unions have letters, like CSN. We are living our history, the teachers tell their students with pride. Paul and Lilianne Des Ruisseaux say they're missing too much school. Cécile Beauregard says it's a scandal and that's why her children will never attend public school, a hotbed for drug traffic, sexual activities, and anti-capitalist ideas.

The youngest of the Therriault sisters, Vicky, is also thirteen. She sometimes play with Lucie after school. Last year Vicky invited her to trick-or-treat with her at Halloween and Lucie thought they would be friends.

Lucie rings at the Therriaults' door at six-thirty, like Vicky said. Vicky opens the door in a bunny suit: pink fuzz and floppy ears, cherry nose and fake teeth. She has two greasy pink spots on her cheeks, and a few wisps of hair slip out from the bunny hood, catching the light. Lucie expected her to be a princess, or a dragon. Vicky disappears inside the house without a word. Lucie doesn't know what to do, but since it's Vicky who has invited her over . . . There is a roaring fire in the fireplace and two bigger bunnies, pink fuzz, floppy ears, cherry noses, and fake teeth, staring back at her from the couch.

"Salut!" she greets Josy and Sony. Maybe they didn't hear her. Lucie's voice is kind of choked up, but they have never bothered with her before anyway.

"This way, stupid!" she hears Vicky calling somewhere in the house.

She will never become Vicky's friend, Lucie can tell now. Maybe Vicky has just asked her to come because she hates her costume and doesn't want to get caught as a pink bunny by her friends. All Lucie wants now is to run back home to go trick-or-treating with Anne and her brothers, as usual. But she also wants to know more about this house and these girls, even if it means taking a risk with the unfamiliar. So Lucie leaves the stern bunnies on the couch and catches up with Vicky at the top of the stairs.

"And this is my bedroom," Vicky informs her, her fake teeth jutting out. Her bedroom is in the attic, taking up the whole top floor of the house. The roof's angle cuts short the height of the white walls, and a round window is punched out at each end of the room. The only pieces of furniture are three funny-looking beds, narrow and boxy, with high mattresses and soft duvets, like icing on cardboard cakes.

"You share your room with your sisters?" Lucie says, feeling better.

Vicky doesn't answer. Lucie notices there are no dressers. "Where do you put your clothes?"

"In the closet, stupid." She is pointing to the half-wall opposite the beds, to three low doors with white handles.

"Ah."

A light dangles from a wire above each bed's headboard, and the lampshade matches the duvet cover. Lucie has never seen a room or furniture like this before. The attic could pass for a modern illustration of a fairy tale, with danger lurking in the background. Or in the three cupboards.

Vicky doesn't bother showing Lucie the rest of the house. They go straight back to the living room. The two bunnies are gone and Vicky's mother glides in through the deep carpet and low furniture. "C'est original le déguisement, très beau, comment ça s'appelle?" she asks her daughter's new friend, touching the fake red suede of Lucie's costume with one hand, an extra-long cigarette in the other.

"Cowgewl," Lucie answers, with the accent.

And straight from the States. Their aunt Huguette sends them a box full of hand-me-downs every year. The skirt is fringed and laced up at the waist, the matching sleeveless vest comes with a gold star tacked on, and Lucie has stolen Pierrot's holster and gun to complete the kit. Her mother has insisted on the ski jacket under the vest and the wool headband underneath the already too small cowboy hat. Lucie thinks it ruins everything and now she is so hot under her many layers she sweats under Madame Therriault's stare.

"Cowgirl?" Vicky's mother looks as if she'd just walked out of a spaceship in a life-sized Barbie outfit. Her hair is a stiff black helmet, teased high on top with the ends rolled under. Her oval face is made up with pale foundation, her eyes circled with black lines, her eyelashes long and thick, the same texture as her hair, and her lips a pale frosted pink. She wears a white satin minidress with trumpet sleeves, and stockings sprinkled with a thousand little lights that turn on and off as she moves around. Lucie can't take her eyes off the finishing touch: the flat silver shoes with transparent buckles on top.

"And you must be"—she snaps her fingers, throwing a quick side-long look at Vicky, who remains silent—"Linda!" she tries, stretching her candy lips without showing her teeth. "Well," she says, walking towards a basket set by the front door, "you have deserved your first treat, unlike my daughter. She's mad at me, they're all mad at me. I had the rabbit costumes made especially for them and what do they say? Do they say, Thank you, Gina, I love you? No, they don't say that. I don't think I should repeat what they said, the naughty, naughty girls."

The apple lands with a thump in Lucie's plastic pumpkin. Maybe Vicky's mother really is from another planet, or at least another continent. "Merci beaucoup, Madame Therriault," Lucie says. An apple. Golden Delicious, mind you.

"Appelle-moi Gina! My children call me Gina, my husband calls me Gina, everybody calls me Gina!"

Appelle-Moi-Gina walks to the fireplace, her dress trapping the orange glow of the fire, her stockings making electric sounds with every step. On the mantelpiece is a long-stemmed wineglass filled with a clear liquid. She jabs the olive floating at the bottom with a plastic sword toothpick and offers it to Lucie.

"Non merci, Madame Therriault."

"What's your mother dressed as?" Lucie asks Vicky when they step out in the cold.

The big pink bunny stops to give Lucie an exasperated look. "She's going to a party, stupid. Not trick-or-treating."

"I'm not stupid, you are!" Lucie cries out as she runs away, knowing all hopes of being invited again to the Therriaults' house are now quashed. She stops only to pick the Golden Delicious apple out of her plastic pumpkin and throw it at Vicky.

"And your mother is stupid too!"

Submarines and Car Crashes

The train's whistle tears through the clear morning, just when silence has filled the house again. Paul is the first one to leave for the office, at 7:30. The girls take their school bus at 7:45 after a last-minute rush for clean knee socks and lost notebooks. The boys walk up the street at 8:05, trails of spilled milk and juice in their boisterous wake. But now they've all left except for Bébé, who is watching the children's programs. Lili is at the sink, washing the breakfast dishes. The train's cars are red, green, and brown, each one painted with the name of a place: Vermont, Alberta, Saskatchewan. All places she has never been to. The Des Ruisseaux don't leave Québec very often. Money is tight, but they are saving to go to Europe next year, or the year after, when the children can be left on their own. There is a whole world out there, isn't there? It might have happened faster if Lili had been able to keep up with her fledgling business last year.

A short French stick sliced lengthwise, with relish, mustard, and cheese on one side, and salami, ham, and shredded lettuce on the other side. The submarines were sandwiches Lili made on the ping pong table in the basement of the house, and the car crashes occurred when she delivered the submarines. Lili had two minor crashes in the first six months, but the most recent had been the worst. She was making her daily delivery to the university with four-year-old Bébé on board when she rear-ended a Brink's truck. She cried when she told Paul.

"The security guards just wouldn't get out, Paul. They thought it was a hold-up, and I couldn't get out either, I was convinced they were going to shoot at us. So I just yelled, 'It's an accident, not a hold-up, look! I have my baby with me!' And I grabbed Bébé and put her up by the windshield for them to see, but they still wouldn't get out, they just kept watching us from the side mirrors. When they finally did, it was guns first, pointed in our direction. Bébé was bawling and I was so scared, so scared."

"Don't cry, Lili, it's just a car. Nobody was hurt and that's what's important. But maybe you're taking on too much right now. Maybe you should wait until the children are a little older, a little less trouble, to get into business. We do have three teenagers in the house all of a sudden, don't we?"

Anne was fourteen, Lucie thirteen, and Pierrot acting older than eleven.

"But you know how much I want to get some of the burden of financial responsibility off you and earn extra money, by myself. You know I always wanted to have my own business, and now you're telling me maybe it's not such a great idea!"

"It's such a great idea that you will have to double your production to meet demand within a year . . . I'm just a little worried about your driving skills when you're under pressure, that's all."

"I never thought it'd be so hard, honest, and now I'm getting sued by a student who broke his tooth on a bread crust!" Lili cries.

Six dozen small-size submarines and three dozen large-size submarines a day. One hundred and eight pieces of bread to wrap, plus fifteen pounds each of salami, ham, and cheese to slice every week. Two four-gallon jars of mustard and relish to spread. A dozen heads of lettuce to shred and mix with olive oil and vinegar. Two hours a day on the road for delivery, half a day a week to get the supplies, another half day spent on accounting. That's when Lili made up her mind. One more car crash and that was it. She would go back to trading paintings made on stolen time, in the corner of the living room, in exchange for dental work and glasses for the kids, like she did before the business venture. One more car crash and she would call it quits. There was no end to her days anymore, not even time to read.

The soapy water is not hot enough in the sink and the grease of last night's dinner clings to the pots. Lili sighs. Bébé tiptoes towards her with little sticky hands, a fresh face, laughing eyes. She is in kindergarten this year, every afternoon. The phone rings. Isn't it a little early for Cécile?

"Allo?"

"May I speak to Mademoiselle Beauregard, please?"

These were the first words Paul had spoken to reach her.

Lili laughs and asks, wryly, "Which one?"

"The one I love."

Lili smiles, tickling her daughter's chin as the train's red caboose careens out of sight with a last sharp whistle.

Running on Empty

When Paul Des Ruisseaux comes home from work, he loosens his tie, unbuttons his shirt, and hangs up his suit, shedding the frustration of his management job along with his clothes. Then he gets into a pair of shapeless sweatpants and ties up his running shoes. After a numbing day spent in a small office, there's no way he's going to lock himself up in the house all evening. Off he goes. Paul runs down Des Trembles, turns left on Versant Nord, trots along the wind-whipped flat by the tracks all the way to the Toyota car dealership by the snow dump. Another left around the corner and it's five blocks uphill to Chemin Ste-Foy—and a real test of strength this stretch is—then across and down by the church, past Henri's house on Des Pins, and around the block, ignoring the stairs of the shortcut before closing the loop again at 2336 Des Trembles. Five kilometres, more or less.

Paul runs. Up and down. This is a pattern etched in his life.

When Paul's mood is up, he looks out. He checks on the state of the neighbours' properties: the size of their melting snowbanks in the spring, the thickness of their lawns in the summer, the way they wrap the bushes in the fall, the neatness of the shovelled driveways in winter. He waves graciously at Monsieur Paquette, who is going out again, what do you know, he used to be a priest, they're the worst kind. Monsieur What's-his-name, a new car, nice, life is good, interest rates are low. Far and forward, light on his feet, high on the endorphin rush, Paul sprints when he sees one of the loose dogs he fears, and his eyes reach out to the colour and texture of the sky above the mountains, looking for a clue to the weather forecast.

But when he's down, he can't keep his eyes off the tips of his running shoes. The wheeze of his laboured breath and the beat of his raging pulse overtake the outside world, shutting him in. Even the neat order he usually finds comforting becomes a threat. The houses' facades are like rows of death masks with square, empty eyes on both sides of the red door's mouth, the shrubs like teeth ready to chew him up. Paul runs as hard as he can, but he is not moving. The street is a conveyor belt, with the thin suburban decor, like cardboard cutouts, passing him by.

Up and down, looking in or looking out, Paul runs.

He runs through the maze of streets, through the dark and light hours, the heat, the cold. He runs every day, he runs for his life, he runs as if all the wild dogs have broken loose from his nightmares and are snapping at his heels. He runs to keep moving—otherwise, he knows he might just go back home and curl up in bed and never get up again.

Everything so neat and square now, that's how he likes it, the house and the yard, five healthy children, a slim-again wife taking art classes. A good job. So what is it? Why this drowning between the white sheets at night, as if his heart were nothing but a pocket full of stones, grinding down his love for his wife and his children, his pride, his faith? Lilianne tries to make him see the bright side, to unravel this inert, dense mass weighing down on him. She argues with him, one stone at a time. She says the dark mood will go away. It always does. And when this wave is over and he rolls up with the next one, she is there again, keeping him steady when he wants to do everything there is to do, a single day never long enough for his hunger. When he wants to scream how great life is.

It's a new thing, it's called jogging. It keeps Paul moving.

Room 4018

"Bonjour, Maman, comment ça va aujourd'hui?"

Lili comes to see her mother in hospital twice a week, her own woes kept in check, a piece of cake in her hands and an indomitable smile on her face. "And look who came along with me today!" Lucie is behind her mother, looking less than happy. "Can I turn the TV off, Maman?" Lili asks.

Since she half-recovered from her stroke, all Lucie's grandmother does is cry, pray, and watch TV. They lift her with a mini-crane on wheels twice a week for a bath, once for Sunday service, and once for Thursday-night bingo. She has already been here three years and her muscles have shrunk from being in bed all the time. Lucie thinks her grandmother's brain has shrunk too.

"Why turn the TV off?" asks Lucie. "There's nothing else to do here."

Lili glares at her daughter. School is out to give students time to prepare for their exams, but Lucie has spent the day in her room listening to loud music with her head against the speaker and her cheek against the record sleeve. Her mother has forced her to come. As soon as the square image has folded into a persistent white dot in the middle of the black screen, Marie-Reine starts to mumble a prayer. She still hasn't greeted either of them. She can be as sulky as a child.

"Bernadette is not here yet? I thought she said she'd come too. I'm going to get a coffee downstairs."

"I'll go with you," says Lucie.

"No you're not. Stay and talk to your grandmother. I'll bring you back a bag of chips."

Lucie hates coming here. Everybody is old or crippled and time feels

thick and slow. Her grandmother still seems to be praying, which infu-
riates Lucie.

"Do you really think God is going to make you get up and walk?"

Marie-Reine doesn't even flinch; one side of her mouth frozen
north, the other drooping south, as usual. But when she finally turns
towards Lucie, tears well from her round, pale blue eyes and roll
down her cheeks. Specialists, physiotherapy, acupuncture, many visits to Ste-Anne de Beaupré's cathedral: Lucie knows they have tried
everything they could think of to make her grandmother walk again.
She tries to backpedal but her grandmother has the upper hand now.
"You don't believe in God anymore, do you?" she asks Lucie, her
eyes shining. "I can tell. Just the way you walk, like the Queen of
England. That's it, huh? It's all sex and drugs and rock 'n' roll now,
isn't it?"

"I've better things to do with my time than do drugs. I'm an anarchist, Grand-Maman. Anarchists don't believe in God, only in free
love," Lucie says in hushed tones, leaning close enough to Marie-Reine
to slip a Marxist-Leninist pamphlet under the sheet by her good hand.
Marie-Reine doesn't reach for it. She doesn't even seem surprised by
her granddaughter's revelation. Lucie is disappointed. Being an anarchist is a big deal to her even if free love is still an undefined term in her
adolescent terminology. They both remain silent until Lilianne comes
back from the cafeteria with Bernadette.

"Did you know your daughter was an anarchist?" Marie-Reine spits
right out.

Lucie is wounded by her grandmother's betrayal, but even more by
her mother's reaction.

"An anarchist!" Lili laughs hysterically, spilling hot coffee all over
the dresser as she tries to take the plastic lid off.

"Qu'essé ça mange en hiver, ça?" yelps Bernadette, reducing everything to diet, as usual.

Lucie bites her tongue. She could tell her mother a few things she
wouldn't find so funny, like what Pierrot does when he goes to the
playground. Pierrot is not an anarchist, no, he is a capitalist. He makes

real money selling drugs and he would make even more if he didn't smoke his profit.

"I'll tell you what my daughter is. A pain in the ass, just like her father, the séparatiste." Lilianne laughs again.

"Do you want to watch TV, Maman?" chirps Bernadette. "Are you comfortable? Look at your nails! Don't they take care of you here? And your hair! When was the last time they washed it? Come on, let's make you look beau-ti-ful."

"You forgot my bag of chips."

"Oh, I'm sorry, Lucie. Here's some money, you go get it now."

Along the well-waxed floor of the corridor, the patients of the long-term-care unit shuffle back and forth quietly, one hand on the railing, or both hands on a walker. Or they just stand still, as pale as paraffin ghosts.

"Do you know where my room is?" a lady in a pink robe asks Lucie.

The Rose and the Brownies

It's seven o'clock on Saturday night and Lucie watches the sorry spectacle with resignation. All the parish's morons stand on a small stage in the church basement, the girls' dowdy A-line skirts right at the knee, the guys in short haircuts, all pimples swinging, their unplugged guitars slung on Jésus-Vous-Aime shoulder straps.

"Le Seigneu-eur est mon Pasteu-eur, Alléluuu-yah! Everybody sing! Le Seigneu-eur est mon . . ."

Frère Bob Sanschagrin, the new assistant to the curé, leads them with a tambourine, raising his arms, calling for all to join in. He says celebrating mass should be like a party, not a duty. He strides up to the pulpit in his Jesus boots, his hand-woven stole askew. "Soyez les bienvenus dans le sous-sol de Dieu, in the basement of God, where we are united tonight again to celebrate the feast of love."

"Nous rendons grace à Dieu."

The congregation's answer is scripted. Frère Bob Sanschagrin's reply is not. "Because let's not fool ourselves. Our Lord Jesus is Love, the Holy Spirit is Love, God is Love, and Love, Love is everywhere!" He raises his arms again, the sun on his tie-dye surplice rising with him, and the band launches into the Beatles' latest hit. Lucie retreats as quickly as she can from the church basement to go over an already well-rehearsed scene. The lead singer of Led Zeppelin, Robert Plant, walks into the school playground where Lucie is sitting on a swing. "How do you do, baby?" he says. "Oh Lord, shakin' all over, yes. I want to give you my love. Nice to meet you. See you later, alligator!" Lucie tries a variety of answers in her limited vocabulary.

"I really like this service, it's short and it swings," Lucie's mother comments on the way home. "On Sunday mornings Madame Brûlé thinks she is Maria Callas, the curé mumbles, and his homily doesn't make any sense. I think he's drinking. I don't know why your father insists on going to listen to him. Le Seigneu-eur est mon pasteu-eur! Alléluuu-yaah!" Lilianne snaps her fingers to the beat and swings her purse around her wrist, her skirt swirling in the spring breeze. Lucie skips a few steps ahead so she doesn't have to walk next to her mother.

"I want to talk to you about your periods. Are you regular?" Lilianne asks, louder for the growing distance between them.

"Maman!" They're walking by Uncle Henri Beauregard's place, and Lucie's face blazes at the thought of her cousin Fred hearing any of this.

"Don't get mad, you can tell me. You know you can talk to me. I am a woman too."

She's not a woman, she's my mother, and every little piece of my life she knows about is a piece stolen from me, Lucie thinks as she rushes ahead. But her mother won't let go. She forgets what she told Lucie when she gave her the rose, six months ago.

Lucie was helping her lug what seemed like one hundred grocery bags from the trunk of the car to the kitchen. She brought them to the back door where Anne took them inside and started to forage immediately for the choicest goodies. Maurice and Bébé had come to scavenge too, having caught a whiff of fresh-baked bread. As soon as the last bag was out of the car, Lucie hurried in to find the little ones attacking a golden loaf with their bare hands, tearing bits of crust off to reach the soft white centre and mop it in the jar of Cheez Whiz. She joined Anne at the kitchen table where she was wolfing down brownies straight from the package. That was when Lilianne came back from the car with one single red rose on a long stem. The only cut flowers they ever saw around the house were lilacs and iris in the spring and dahlias in the fall.

"Who's dead?" Lucie asked her, stopping to lick her fingers.

Her mother just smiled. She was wearing a white safari dress, and her big round sunglasses were pushed back on top of her brassy blonde hair.

"Nobody's dead, Lucie. This is to mark the beginning of something new and exciting."

Lucie felt a little sick. Maybe she'd been eating these brownies a little too fast. Lucie had been out of sorts for a few days anyway, since . . . her "friend" came to visit, as they said. She had to ask her mother how to stop getting her sheets and her jeans stained with blood.

"You're not a child anymore. You're a woman now," Lilianne told Lucie with pride. She gave her daughter an awkward hug, which startled both of them, and offered her the rose.

"A woman?" Anne asked in disbelief. "What are you talking about?"

Bébé and Maurice grabbed the bread and the pot of Cheez Whiz and headed for the TV room, sensing trouble ahead.

"Lucie has menstruated for the first time," Lilianne explained to Anne.

Anne got up, throwing a half-bitten slab of brownie back on the table. "What? She even has the curse before me?"

"To tell you the truth," Lucie volunteered, "I'd rather you than me. What a mess."

Anne stamped out of the kitchen, ran up the stairs, and slammed her bedroom door loud enough for everybody to cringe. Lilianne sighed.

"Don't let her ruin your day, Lucie. Her body isn't maturing at the same rate as yours, that's all."

Lucie buried her nose in the rose. It was beautiful. The velvet petals barely opened on a tight dark red bud, almost the colour of blood.

Faith Cycles

There aren't that many ways Lucie can explain to her father why she would rather play pool at her cousin's place than attend la Messe des Jeunes. Lucie said she would go to the Saturday-night service only if her mother went to the Sunday-morning one. As soon as her mother agreed, Lucie learned to play pool with her cousin Fred and his friends in Henri Beauregard's basement instead of going to church. This week her father caught her, probably on a tip from la Fatiguante, and now he is demanding an explanation.

"I can't go to mass anymore because I don't believe in the Church, Papa."

"Why couldn't you tell me, instead of lying?"

Lucie doesn't answer at first.

"Yes?"

"Because I knew you'd be mad."

"You're going to need to be braver than this. I'm mad because you deceived me, not because you don't want to go to church. But while we're at it, why don't you believe in the Church anymore?"

"I don't think I have to go to church in order to prove I believe in God. I don't think I have to honour Jésus-Christ at a given hour on Saturday night or Sunday morning. What happens between Him and me is personal, isn't it? And the Church represents the exact opposite of what I want to believe in." Lucie knows her mother and the rest of the family are standing behind the closed door of the living room, listening to every word they're saying. It makes her bold. "Look at what the Church has done! All the wars in the name of God, the blood spilled in Ireland, the torture under the Inquisition. And here in Québec, the Church again, not only forbidding Grand-Maman Beauregard to read Balzac and Zola but keeping us all in ignorance and poverty so that

Duplessis, the tyrant they told us to vote for, could keep feeding American imperialism the cheap labour it needed!" Maybe I should have become a member of the debating club after all, Lucie thinks, satisfied with herself.

"That's one way to look at it."

"How can they tell us what to read, how to vote, and even what to think? Who is God? God is everything. Where is God? God is everywhere. Questions and answers, I'm not seven years old anymore. I don't need to be told and I don't want to live with blinkers on. I want to find out for myself and make my own mistakes!"

"The Church might have put blinkers on us in the past, but don't you think there is something to be said for sitting together once a week, surrounded by the people we live with, to learn from the past and think about how to become better people?"

To be a better person doesn't appeal to Lucie right now, but she keeps quiet and nods to concede the point to her father.

"And do you still believe in God, Lucie?"

"I'm not sure. I guess I'm going through a crisis."

"And what exactly do you believe in, Lucie?"

"Nothing just now."

"Nothing? Well, that's just great, Lucie. You'll go really far with this much on your mind."

Lucie gets to her feet, sensing her father's exasperation, his disapproval. She doesn't care now, all she wants is to leave the room. But Paul pushes her back onto the sofa.

"I'm not like you, Papa!" Lucie clutches one of the sofa's blobby cushions to her chest, her voice strangled by emotion. "A, I'm not a believer and I don't need to believe because, B, I'm an anarchist!" She wants to be rational but by now both of them are screaming, and she knows she has just made a mistake.

"An anarchist?"

"Uh-huh."

"An *anarchist*?"

Why doesn't he just laugh, the way her mother and her aunt did?

"Ben oui!"

"Do you even know what it means, anarchy?"

"You should read *Free Children of Summerhill* instead of *Time* magazine, Papa."

"Don't try to change the subject, Lucie Des Ruisseaux, and listen to me. Do you know what anarchy leads to? Chaos. Social unrest." Paul is looking out the window, as if to gather strength from the power lines, the railway tracks' shiny parallel curves, the blinding squares of sunset where water has pooled on the warehouse roofs. "And terrorism. Don't you remember, Lucie? It was not much more than a year ago. Terrorism as in FLQ, as in mailbox bombs, blown-off limbs, gagged in the trunk of a car, tied to explosives—as in suspending civil liberties. Is this the kind of freedom you're looking for, Lucie? That's what was taken from us in October 1970. How can you forget? Do you know how many people still fight to have these rights everywhere in the world, and what life is like without them? Do you know how lucky we are?" He looks at his daughter. "Don't think you know everything. You obviously could still learn from going to church, but I also believe you're too old to be forced to think the way I do. Civil rights, Lucie. It's your right not to go to church if you don't want to."

Lucie's mouth opens in disbelief. She is still waiting for the clincher, as in being grounded for a week, when the door blows open and Anne barges in followed by Pierrot.

"Pis moi, pis moi, Papa? If Lucie isn't going to church, I don't want to go either!"

But their father is not listening anymore. He is looking out the window again. Lucie tugs his hand to thank him before her mother comes in.

"Paul!" she says, furious.

But Paul refuses to face her. "I'm going for a run," he says.

Troisième Relation:
Faith

Iᴛ rarely snows in London, even if the capital of the United Kingdom is situated along the same parallel as old Fort Rupert on James Bay or Blanc-Sablon on the Côte-Nord. Trafalgar Square's urban tundra takes on warm tones of grey under vaporous skies during the summer's long evenings, but it is stripped of colour altogether in the short blunt days of winter, the wet pigeons as black as crows. I hurry past St. Martin-in-the-Fields and up along Charing Cross to Tottenham Court Road and the library.

A brown envelope arrived by mail yesterday, postmarked Chicoutimi. I had forgotten all about the request for the Tremblay family's birth and death certificates made last spring. I now know where Catherine Dubois has moved: to the cemetery of the Montagnais reserve at Pointe-Bleue, where she was buried in June. Her death certificate confirmed her home address as 149 Jean De Quen, Chicoutimi-Nord.

The old woman by the electric garage door was in fact Catherine Tremblay. Rodolphe Tremblay adopted Catherine Dubois in 1926, the year she came to replace Marie-Joseph as his housekeeper. Why would he have done this unless he thought she was his kin? He probably found out she was an illegitimate child his brother Antonio had fathered with a native woman. Unfortunately, Catherine Dubois's name is not in the Diocese of Chicoutimi records, so her place and date of birth are unavailable to confirm this supposition. There is another document missing: Antonio's death certificate. Everything else is in order.

⌒ᴍᴍ๑

CATECHISME DU DIOCESE de QUEBEC
PAR MONSEIGNEUR
l'Illuftriffime & Reverendiffime
Jean de la Croix de faint Vallier,
Évêque de Québec,

En faveur des Curez & des Fideles de fon Diocefe.

A PARIS
Chez URBAIN COUSTELIER,
rue faint Jacques, au Coeur Bon

M.DCII.

1702

⌒ᴍᴍ๑

The reign of the adventurous soldiers of God in the New World is quickly coming to an end. Now come the bishops and archbishops with their purple and gold mitres, in a swirl of theological controversy and political intrigue. The time has come to set up the proper institution of the Church in the colonies.

The Illustrissime and Reverendissime Jean de La Croix de Chevrières de Saint-Vallier is well born and bred to lead. Once he is chosen to replace the first bishop of Québec, Monseigneur François de Laval, he quickly authors a catechism custom-made for his diocese. However, his oeuvre, printed in Paris in 1702, doesn't have the impact it should have. The only copies that make it across the Atlantic are the few shipped ahead of the Illustrissime himself. The bulk of the precious word of God is probably dumped unceremoniously overboard by the English buccaneers who capture a boat called *La Seine* off the coast of

Newfoundland. On board is the newly appointed bishop, en route for the colony with his entourage of twenty-six ecclesiastics and a cargo of gold and silver sacred vessels and fine silks, laces, and embroidered surplices. The pirates promptly release their prisoners and sell their loot for a profit of 1,300 livres.

After this first catechismal disaster, the responsibility for shaping the settlers' souls falls upon a certain Monseigneur Languet, archbishop of Sens in France. Languet's catechism, first published in 1765, causes a stir with its hard line in a time of religious reform. The previous catechism in circulation still presented the mystery of God in a nebulous way:

> *What is God?*
> We couldn't possibly tell in this life what is God.

Languet cuts to the quick:

> *What is God?*
> It is an infinitely perfect spirit, the absolute maker and
>   master of all things.

When Monseigneur Briand is appointed to replace Saint-Vallier in Québec, he doesn't trust another cargo to the hazard of the sea. He has Languet's catechism printed in Québec in 1765 under the title *Catéchisme du Diocèse de Sens par Monseigneur Languet*. It is still in use 125 years later, the catechism that has marked the French-Canadian mentality the most. This is the catechism that asks, What does a Christian have to do during his life? He must prepare for death.

> *155. What is a man's body?*
> Man's body is an assemblage of bone and flesh given life by its
>   soul.

157. What does our body resemble?
Our body resembles the animals'.

160. What happens when the soul leaves the body of man?
When the soul leaves the body of man, he dies.

162. What do you call a body without a soul?
A body without a soul is called a corpse.

163. What do we do with a corpse?
We bury a corpse in a grave, in the cemetery.

Le Petit Catéchisme du Diocèse de Québec, lifted almost word for word from Languet's 1765 publication, is the all-time bestseller of Québec's literature. The first council of the newly created ecclesiastic province of Québec sanctions the book in 1844. *Le Petit Catéchisme* is not only the first book put in every first-grade pupil's hand, it is also the main tool to teach children how to read. It is only with the works of Vatican II, from 1962 to 1965, that the three-hundred-year-old Q & A format is rendered obsolete.

Many of the catechism's questions are marked with a star, or an asterisk. The asterisks indicate which material is suitable for children of lesser education, or people of lesser intelligence: thick, obtuse, oafish, dense, coarse, and unrefined are some of the names used in the various editions. Education in Québec was minimal until the 1960s. For one thousand faithful souls in a church, there was one master, the parish priest. Besides a small elite of doctors and lawyers, only members of the clergy had access to higher education.

The meaning of the asterisks?

Once upon a time I was six years old. Life was simple. I believed in God, like the other thirty students in the first-grade class of Mère Marie-Thérèse. The classroom was in a convent, the convent beside the church in Rimouski. The letters were very clear, black on white on a three-foot-wide banner. The first sentence we learned was playful. René joue avec son ballon. Mère Marie-Thérèse clipped it down into words with her scissors. Numbers were small batons of bright colours, all multiples of one, a white cube. Two was red. Five, blue. Questions always came with answers. Two plus five? Green, seven. Who plays with the ball? René. This is the subject. Where is God? God is everywhere. He was at my fingertips when I held on tight to my pencil, the smell of wood and graphite grounding me as I traced the signs along the faint blue line. I chewed on the soft pink rubber at the pencil's tip when I stumbled, but the worst that could happen was to hit the metal rim with a loose tooth. God was on the tip of my tongue ready to roll off as my hand reached up for heaven, Me-me-me, Mère Marie-Thérèse! He saw everything and I had nothing to hide.

The asterisks were meant for most of us, eternal children in front of God. We were innocent, and we had faith. And it didn't matter if this faith contributed to our poverty and our ignorance, because in heaven, life would be better.

"Laurent?"

The glowing green numbers on the clock radio show 12:48. He is undressing in the dark.

"Laurent."

He stops, waits. He knows what I'm going to say.

"I'm leaving tomorrow, the one-o'clock flight to Montreal."

He doesn't come to me. He sighs.

"Anne phoned and said Maurice has to go back to British Columbia." My brother has been in Québec for ten days. He was strong enough to lift my mother by himself; they can't. Anne thinks they will have to hospitalize her. She's losing more strength every day. "They need me."

"How long will you be gone?"

"I don't know." I stop. I try to find it in me to ask, but he does first.

"Do you want me to go with you?"

If only it wasn't a question. I will go with you.

"Could you?"

"I don't know. Maybe not right away," he says. "There are three operations scheduled in the next ten days." It's already November and his report is due by January. The surgeons want more adjustments made to the procedures but the project might be put on hold indefinitely. There's talk of an internal inquiry. I know he wants out of this job but he can't now, and that's too bad. I can't wait anymore.

"I'll have to bring Madelon and Marion along. You can't take care of them by yourself, not for that long."

"What about Marion's school? And your job?"

I can't see Laurent's face but I can hear him rubbing the bristles on his chin, his cheeks. "I talked to her teacher yesterday and she will send us her homework every week until we come back. They'll hire a temporary to replace me at work." I have a master's degree and six years of experience in visual resources management. They hired a college student to replace me. But I'll miss the library, and the admiral Nelson on his column.

"I see."

Laurent unbuckles his belt, lets his pants slide to the floor. When he sits on the opposite edge of the bed, I slide towards him like a blob of Jell-O, my head rolling off the wet pillow. It's not a great mattress. It's a small room. One double bed, a chair. A globe with a light bulb inside on a shelf with a short row of books. Our books. They haven't been touched or opened for a while, although the words made flesh are still there, waiting for us. Not so long ago we still spun the globe lazily, the bedsheets and our naked limbs tangled together, still trying out different possible futures. And sometimes I would murmur in his ear the first name in the incantation, "Serendip . . ." And he would whisper back, "Sargasso . . ." And my lips would tease his, Borobudur, and his tongue, full and warm, would reach in to touch me deep where I hid, halfway across the world, and bring me back to him. Why do these moments seem as if they were from another life altogether, and not ours? Laurent doesn't try to bring me back to him anymore, and I don't know how to reverse the tide and stop drifting, farther and farther away with every new day.

His shoes tumble down, the pants come off. "I'll come when you call me, Lucie. I promise. I will. But I need to know something before you leave. What's happening to us?"

I think of Stephen. The bleak corridor, the neat row of closed doors. The unbearable pattern on the carpet.

"You know when we met again, the second time?" says Laurent. "I was there, available. You got pregnant. I think you settled for me."

"Don't, Laurent."

"You don't have to come back, Lucie. Not if you don't love me."

"Please."

"Tell me, then. Tell me what's going on."

"You know what's going on. My mother is dying."

"There's something else."

"Not now."

"When?"

I will my hand to reach out for him, but by the time I do he has walked out of the room, his bare feet silent on the carpet. I catch a glimpse of his sloping shoulders, shrugging, his long thighs outlined against the light of the corridor, just before he disappears into the bathroom. When he flicks the glaring fluorescent light on, I can almost hear him recoil from everything, the grief, the guilt, I carry with me wherever I go.

"After," I whisper to the confines of the dark room.

It was raining and cold when I ran out of the hotel on Half Moon Street. I hurried through Shepherd Market, where small groups of businessmen under black umbrellas walked the narrow streets, slowing down to congregate by red-lighted doors promising Swedish massages. I kept on walking past the dank and pungent subway under Park Lane, the rain turning to ice pellets as I entered Hyde Park and walked west along Rotten Row. The brake lights of the rush hour traffic flickered like tongues of fire through the tall, elegant trees and the lattice of the wrought-iron fence. By the time I got to Kensington Gardens I was drenched and my face, my hands, and my legs were numb. That's when my mother hovered towards me in all the seventies glory of her white safari dress and blonde hair as the snow settled on the prickly lawns of the English garden. You're a woman now, she told me with a proud smile before drifting away, weightless in her clogs. Come back! I shouted above the empty flower beds, the swell of dirt like a long shallow grave. But she was already gone. They were all gone. The coureurs de bois, the filles du roi, the good mothers, and the black robes. All dead. The sky was thick with the slow dance of snowflakes, as light as angels' hands, scouring me clean of the deed.

Later, Laurent and I lay side by side in bed like two different worlds with a vast expanse of night between us. No more friction, skin against skin, no more spark. No more bonfire. It's not his fault or mine, his sick infants with rotten luck and hearts like sieves, my mother's head where a toxic tumour grows a little more every day. But this is what makes the soft, vulnerable tissue of our love retract inside a hard shell.

Holy Night,
December 1973

THE ground was bare and brown until a week ago. Then it started to snow off and on for four days. On the morning of the fifth day the snow turned to sleet and rain, by mid-afternoon the thermometer was free-falling, and now every tree and electric wire, every telephone post, every field and lawn of Sainte-Foy is coated with candy-hard ice.

It's almost midnight on Christmas Eve. Pierrot and Lucie walk towards Henri Beauregard's house across the open space that spreads down from the back of the church. The terrain is slanted, the ice crust treacherous. When Lucie expects it the least it gives in, her foot punching right through the thin ice until she is knee deep in the softer snow underneath. It is cold, and there is a nasty wind gusting up the field from the northeastern mountain range. The old fur coat is heavy, and not so warm. The buttonholes are torn and so is the dirty yellow lining, the seams undone under the arm. The brown fur is mottled, balding right down to the leather at the elbows, around the collar and the sleeve's hem, the dried-out pelts split here and there. The shorn beaver has lost its lustre, but Lucie likes it better than her ski jacket. It is like a coat of armour, and it makes her feel inviolable.

"Christ," Pierrot swears. "What a stupid idea that was."

Pierrot doesn't punch through the crust. He's got a different problem. Their uncle Lucien has delivered the Santa Claus outfit to them in Henri's garage. Lucien has helped Lucie strap the pillow to Pierrot's stomach and put on the pants, the jacket, the belt, the beard, the hat, and the big black boots. They have filled the pillowcase with small presents. That's when Lucien saw a pair of snowshoes. "Why don't you put these on?" he said, shoving them into Pierrot's arms. Their uncle dropped them off by the school in his car and told them to walk back across the field to Henri's house in five minutes, just so he'd have enough time to bring the young children to the window. By then everybody should be back from the eleven-o'clock service.

The snowshoes are useless on the ice, and Pierrot has been falling over and over again. It doesn't help that they have smoked a joint, hiding against the wind by the school gymnasium. And, just in case, Lucie has packed a small flask of Southern Comfort in her coat pocket. With each of Pierrot's falls, more gifts have spilled out of the case. Some of the wrapping paper has started to tear.

"Just take them off!" screams Lucie.

She helps her brother undo the leather straps and stuffs the snowshoes in the pillowcase with the gifts. The soles of Santa's boots have no treads whatsoever, and Pierrot immediately slips and falls again. They both sit down for a moment, waving at the kids from the middle of the field while Lucie takes the flask out of her pocket. The golden liquor is sweet and strong, pulling tears from their eyes. Under the fur coat Lucie is wearing a powder blue nylon nightdress on top of her jeans and her white turtleneck, and a ten-cent rhinestone crown on her head. She can't feel her ears anymore and her cheeks burn from the wind bite. Her mouth is frozen, and she has a hard time shaping the words. "Let's go, Pierrot, let's just get it over with." Lucie half drags, half pushes Pierrot, blinded by the beard and impeded by his footwear, across the last part of the field. Finally they get to the lip of hard-packed snow bordering the road and tumble across the pavement, sprinkled with sand and calcium. Firm ground, at last. The kids have left the window to run to the door.

It's two minutes before twelve o'clock and Cécile, the hostess, hurries over to the stereo. She turns up the volume, letting a thundering rendition of "Minuit Chrétien" belt out from the speakers. *Peuple-à genoux! Attends-ta délivrance!* The entrance is crowded. Half a dozen children in pyjamas jump on Santa Claus and try to get to the gifts, but the Ice Maiden fends them off with the last-minute magic wand Cécile has put in her hand: a piece of cardboard cut in the shape of a star, covered in foil and taped to a broken radio antenna. The rest of the guests are coming in from the cold arm in arm, having walked back from the church singing carols. There is an ambulance in the driveway, its red flashers spinning even though there is no emergency, and Lucien helps the driver roll out his mother on a collapsible stretcher.

"Joyeux Noël!"

"Watch out, here we come, make way!"

"You're going to drop me!"

"Can someone turn down the music?"

"Where do you want her?"

"Right there, between the Christmas tree and the bar."

This is the last time the Beauregards will celebrate Christmas Eve together. The verdict will be unanimous: too many people, too many gifts, too long, too late. This will also be the last of Marie-Reine Tremblay's many Christmases. She is sixty-nine years old and by next December she will be gone. Her daughter Lilianne Des Ruisseaux is thirty-nine, and within two years she will have her first brush with cancer. Finally, this is the last winter of ignorance about sex, love, and death for Lili's daughter, Lucie, who's fifteen, but her sullen adolescent gloom is so profound she would not believe a word of this even if she was told.

"Lucie," Lilianne says, "you can't just leave Pierrot alone with all the gifts to distribute. You're the Ice Maiden!"

"I've done enough already. I got him here safe and sound, didn't I?"

"I'll do it, I'll do it!" Bernadette interposes herself between Lilianne and her daughter. "No need to fight tonight, it's Christmas, remember?"

Lucie passes along the crown and the wand, and as soon as she slips out of the blue nightdress she puts her coat back on. The padded bra her mother has forced on her is a hand-me-down that came with the box from the States. It doesn't fit and looks odd, as if she doesn't have real breasts but two irregular and dimpled growths protruding from her chest.

"Lucie, take the coat off, would you?"

"Noël!" Bernadette orders, touching their heads in turn with the wand. "Noël!"

"Go take care of your grandmother, then. Cécile needs my help in the kitchen."

Spinning Wheel

"Nobody listens to me." Marie-Reine catches herself sounding just like her sister, Marie-Joseph, even more so since God has made a comeback in her life. That's what five years of confinement have done to her, that and a steady diet of instant mashed potatoes, soft boiled meat, frozen peas, bingos, and soaps on TV. But as hard as Marie-Reine pretends to believe again in him, she still thinks the Lord has been stingy with signs of his magnanimity. A couple of prizes have been won on bingo nights, but Marie-Reine is bitter about him too.

"I'm listening, Grand-Maman," says Lucie.

"You've been drinking, haven't you? I can smell it." Marie-Reine inspects her granddaughter. "Do you have a boyfriend yet? Something wrong with you? Is it because you're not on the Pill? Just ask your mother to get it for you. She did like boys, you know, she'll understand." Marie-Reine's voice drops down. She asks her granddaughter, suddenly distressed, "Why isn't Myriam coming to see me anymore?"

But Lilianne is back with some hors d'oeuvres and throws her daughter a warning look. Myriam turned eighteen last summer and she packed up and left shortly after her birthday. Cécile wants to hush things up. She'll come back, she says. She'll need money sooner or later. "Do you want some milk?" Lilianne asks. She wears a violet and green dress she's made herself. It has a plunging V-neckline and long sleeves, and darts make the fabric cling to her body. Lilianne has pencilled a mole beside her mouth with eyeliner and has put on long silver earrings. She's not Blonde de Venise anymore but a Schéhérazade shade of brown.

"No. I want more champagne. I've always liked champagne. Makes me think of weddings. So sad, always so sad, these weddings really were. All my children going, one after the other. Who is this with Colette?"

Colette looks pale in a Peter Pan blouse, sitting very straight beside a man with a bouffant hairstyle. They chose a seat at the opposite corner of the room from where the bar is set, but to no avail. Cécile, with her scotch on the rocks and her cigarette, has draped her floor-length black velvet skirt over the arm of their sofa.

"Is this one worth mentioning?" Bernadette picks an olive from the hors d'oeuvre tray, having passed her Ice Maiden duty on to her niece, Anne.

"Dette!" warns Lilianne. "Colette is doing very well. She met Roger Carpentier at the AA meetings. I wish Cécile would have the common sense to keep away from them with her scotch." Lilianne gives a sardine on a cream cheese bed to her mother. "I told her it was Colette's first social since she started the program. It's also her first Christmas as a divorcee."

Bernadette cringes at the word and takes a big gulp of champagne. She is dating a man going through a bitter divorce. "Well, I might as well get introduced then."

"You shouldn't mix alcohol with your medicine, Maman," says Lilianne, "but since it's Christmas . . . I'll go get a cold bottle." She returns to the kitchen.

"You don't come to visit very often either, Lucie. How come?"

"You know why, Grand-Maman." Lucie has tried to get out of visiting her grandmother ever since she betrayed her trust, even though she doesn't care about anarchy anymore. She is absorbed by Marcel Proust books now, a series called *À la recherche du temps perdu*. It makes her feel as if every single moment in her own life, even the most ordinary detail, the pattern on a teaspoon, a shell, a silver curlicue, the exact shade of pink of the flower on a china cup, brave and faded, is worth noting because it might prove significant later on. So she stores the sounds, analyzes the texture of the snow, tastes the firewater, filing each snippet of information so it can remain undisturbed, and safe, in her memory.

"And what about Marie-Joseph?" Marie-Reine asks Lucie. "I haven't seen her in a while."

"She's dead, Grand-Maman. She died before I was born and I'm fifteen."

Marie-Reine stares back at Lucie with blank eyes before making a quick recovery. She can't walk but they do, all of them, in and out of her head, invited or not. Marie-Joseph is seventy-four, Marie-Ange, ninety-six. Antonio is getting old at one hundred and five but he still runs the trapline. And Léandre . . . Léandre is eighty-one. They play bridge once in a while, but it's not as much fun as it used to be. Marie-Reine can't cheat anymore, not with only one good hand.

"I asked her once if she was lonely. After Edouard passed away. In Chicoutimi."

"What is she talking about? Who's Edouard?" Lucie asks her mother as she brings back a frosted glass of champagne.

Lilianne tips a little into her mother's mouth. "The postman," she says. "Fifine's husband. Go easy on the champagne, Maman, and you," she whispers to her daughter before walking away, "keep an eye on her and try to show some respect, would you?"

As soon as she's gone Lucie takes a sip. "A little more, Grand-Maman?"

Marie-Reine smacks her lips with delight before going on. "No, I'm not lonely, Fifine told me. I go to church every day, I have my charity work, and guess what? I have a housekeeper now. A housekeeper? I said. What for? You're all alone. You know I have a bad back, Marie-Reine, she told me, and my knees and my joints and my arthritis and my heart and on and on. The usual complaints, and all this because I worked her like a dog when she was my housekeeper."

"Your housekeeper was your own sister?" Lucie says, looking in Anne's direction.

"She had nothing else to do, and she just loved these children, although she thought I was a bad influence." Marie-Reine pauses. "How many were there? Seven? And who are these people?" She looks at the hub of children crowded around the Christmas tree.

"You had seven children and they all married, except Bernadette, so that makes thirteen, plus you, fourteen. You have twenty-one grand-children, so that makes thirty-four people, but ma tante Huguette isn't here and—"

But Marie-Reine is not listening to the tally. "She even plays cards with me, Fifine told me. The only thing is, she prefers poker to bridge. She cleans me out every time." Marie-Reine lifts herself on her good elbow to grab Lucie's hand. "That's when I smelled something fishy. This was not like her at all, Lucie. My sister was a penny-pincher all her life and she never, ever gambled. Edouard had left her money, but nothing much. And where did you find this housekeeper? I asked her. Remember uncle Rodolphe's maid, she said, the one who came after me? The one who came from the bush and married Rodolphe's lumber-yard foreman? I said. Yes, that's her, she said. She got married but then she fell on hard times."

Marie-Reine stops for one more sip.

"That was even less like my sister, hanging around a fallen woman. Catherine Dubois. She had a beaver coat as beautiful as mine, made from an exceptionally large pelt. My father gave it to me when I was eighteen."

"But Grand-Maman, that can't be. Weren't you an orphan at four-teen, when they sent you to the convent in Québec?"

"Yes, that's what Marie-Joseph wanted me to believe." Marie-Reine sneers. "I haven't forgiven you yet, Marie-Joseph, do you hear me?" Marie-Reine screams, looking up, trying to throw an olive at the ceiling.

"Grand-Maman!" Lucie tries to steady the stretcher so it won't tip over. Bernadette rushes to her mother's side, shoving Lucie aside. "Enough of this," she snaps, taking the empty glass away. "She gets so excited when we take her out of hospital," she tells Lucie, as if her own mother was not there.

"Well, and guess what she said, la saprée Fifine," Marie-Reine continues. "She said, I have the fur coat. That was the only time I won something from Catherine Dubois. Ha-ha-ha! She was a sly one, our Fifine, huh, Lili?"

"Calm down, Maman," Bernadette sighs. Her mother often mistakes her for Lili these days. "Ma tante Marie-Joseph is long gone, and she was a good person, whatever horrible deed you've been trying to pin on her all these years. Let her rest in peace."

"I'm sure she's resting in peace—she thought she was so deserving—but he isn't. She didn't let him." Marie-Reine stares past Bernadette at her granddaughter, the colour draining from her face.

"Maman?" Bernadette asks, alarmed.

Who is this person in a torn fur coat drinking from a flask? Marie-Reine wonders. So familiar. The greatcoat, the long hair, the firewater. "What have you brought me this time, Papa?" Marie-Reine singsongs, jumping on her father's lap. She likes the smells he carries with him—fire smoke, sap, sweat, and wet fur—but her sister and her mother don't. As soon as he comes in the door Marie-Joseph starts to boil as much water as she can, filling the one-room house with steam. While her father washes, sitting in the tin tub, her mother scrubbing his back, Marie-Reine hums. She spells his name in the fogged-up window. Papa. "Have you brought me a sister? Maman won't give me one. Maman never gives me anything." Marie-Reine's father is beside her, wrapped in a blanket. His skin is red and shiny, and his finger traces a name. Ca-the-ri-ne.

"Get out of here," Lilianne tells her daughter in a stern voice, snatching the Southern Comfort from her hands. "Go help Pierrot and Anne get the gifts over with so we can eat soon."

Glorious Folly

At three in the morning Cécile finally flings open the French doors separating the living room from the dining room, inviting everyone to help themselves to the buffet.

The plump meat pies' crusts look positively gilded, the cheese glistens with unctuous fat, set off in a dewy casing of salad leaves, while the pâté de foie de canard gras is wrapped in a fine jellied layer. The shrimp in the shrimp boat are bright pink and the seafood cocktail is orange. Big glass bowls are filled to the brim with potato, macaroni, and green salads, and there is the usual assortment of carrot sticks, curly celery, and fleur de radish, plus the pickled onions, gherkins, and stuffed olives, displayed on the cut-glass plate. Christmas mandarins from Japan make a pyramid beside a basketful of mixed nuts. A triple sauce server filled with cranberry jelly, Dijon mustard, and homemade mayonnaise is set beside the centrepiece: a suckling pig with an apple stuck in its mouth. On the sideboard are the desserts in their glorious folly, petits fours, gingerbread men, and fruitcake. But it wouldn't be Christmas without the bûche de Noël, or Yule log, a rolled cake covered with brown icing streaked with a fork to reproduce the look of bark, marzipan holly growing where a pretend branch has been sawed off.

"So what did you get?" Fred asks his cousin Lucie.

They're sitting side by side with Anne, Pierrot, and Frederic's brother, Christian, on the wall-to-wall carpet, their plates on their laps. The adults have taken over the L-shaped sofa and the glass-top coffee table as well as the two La-Z-Boys and all the available folding chairs and TV trays. Lilianne is feeding her mother dinner with a spoon. She is wearing a pink frilly negligee, an annual gift from Paul, on top of her violet and green dress. Léo Beauregard eats with an orange hunting vest on, Lucien wears a pair of skates and a Canadiens sweater, and Lucie's father looks as if he is trying to drill a hole in a hazelnut with his new electric toy. Cécile reeks of perfume, Colette eats with glossy leather gloves on, and Bernadette has kicked her high heels off to put on her new slippers.

"C'est fini la Grande Noirceur!" says Lucien Beauregard. "We're not in the dark anymore, now we can measure everything. It is all a question of calculus." He didn't pass the ten tests to become an actuary but he made it to test seven, his love affair with numbers unfinished. "Take politics, for example, Paul."

But Paul Des Ruisseaux hasn't talked about politics since the Parti Québécois failed to win the first provincial election held since the October Crisis. He had set out on a mission for René Lévesque, the party's leader, knocking on the door of every single house and apartment in the Louis-Hébert riding, spreading the good news: yes, we can have our own country! There was something wrong with the election results because more people than ever before voted for the PQ, but this didn't translate into more seats. Something wrong with the calculations, and Paul's faith in the democratic process was shaken.

"Politics is much more about numbers than emotions," Lucien says.

"I don't think so," protests Lili. "Did you watch the election night on TV? It was really sad."

Robert Bourassa, the triumphant premier of Québec again, had his daughter riding on his shoulder. No little girl smiling in a pretty dress for René Lévesque; on his shoulder was a grown-up man, crying.

"Numbers and percentages and the right population samples, and there you go," continues Lucien. "The polls can now predict the outcome of an election before the vote even takes place. Time, light, or sound, you name it, the whole world is an equation, a stack of risks and odds."

"No room for mysteries or miracles in your world, mon Lucien, is there?" Paul says, stabbing a lettuce leaf.

"And no room for God!" Marie-Reine growls from across the room, her good hand drawing a quick sign of the cross. "How could I give life to such a pagan tribe? Seigneur, prends pitié de nous!"

"Statistically, there is room for God near the square root of pi, somewhere around the infinity loop, or a mathematical operation's infinitesimal residue, taking a life of its own, constantly in the process of redefining itself," Lucien says.

Lili shoves more cake in her mother's mouth. She has even less patience for God than for René Lévesque these days. She has no patience at all, actually. It is physically and mentally exhausting to raise three teenagers. The constant bargaining, the barrage of rebuffs, and their careless contempt drain her energy during the day and leave her awake at night. She's either up in the living room waiting for them to come back or in bed with her eyes wide open, the worries gnawing at her while Paul sleeps. She's reread the entire Agatha Christie collection waiting for them. They barely say hello when they finally come home, scurrying to their bedrooms. They never tell her where they've been or what they've done. They resent her questions. Who do they think they are?

But at least they're still hers. She can't imagine what it would be like not to be with them, like Colette. Colette probably can't imagine either. She is just starting to realize, now that she's been sober for six months.

"Only one log?" Marie-Reine asks.

"Yes, there's only one log," Lilianne says, "but there are other desserts. Would you like some fruit salad?"

"Where are the other logs?"

"What do you mean?"

"If you give me a storm light I'll go split the whole lot outside. I got a new axe for Christmas."

Lilianne drops the plate and fork in her lap. There she goes again, spinning her yarn.

"She was carrying a pile of folded sheets, a pile so high I couldn't see her face. I only wanted to give her a piece of toffee but she hurried away from me. The only love is the love of God, just like in Laterrière. But at least I could go out in Laterrière. Here I can't. I can't get out. They don't even open the gate once a week anymore. Not for me. I've been punished again, and I don't even know what for. Where am I, anyway? I'm telling you, Lilianne, this cake tastes store-bought," Marie-Reine says, opening her mouth for another bite.

"Maman!" Lilianne scolds her. "Cécile told me she made it herself."

"So, Lucie?" Fred asks again.

Lucie chews her food slowly not to have to tell him. The bra, white lace, 34A, is a new way her mother has found to torture her. "A pair of jeans," she tells her cousin. She hates anything new. She'd rather scour the Salvation Army depot behind the Bassin Louise for clothes that still carry traces of someone else's life. She's looking for clues, something that will help her find out who she is. "And the latest Bowie."

"Who's that?" Fred asks.

"Just stick with the Bee Gees, that's more your style anyway. And what did you get?"

"I got a gun. I'll go hunting with my father next fall."

Lace for her, steel and bullets for him. She can tell it makes him feel like a man. "Anyway, it's just stuff, isn't it? I should go help with the dishes."

Stinking ashtrays, lipstick-smeared crystal, puddles of meat juice with congealed fat and leftovers are processed efficiently in the crowded kitchen. Lucien's wife, Suzanne, retrieves empty dishes from the dining room and hands them over to Cécile, who transfers the food into plastic containers. Colette has swapped her leather gloves for pink rubber ones to wash the dishes, Bernadette has grabbed some tea towels to dry the good crystal stemware, and Liliannne is loading the dishwasher.

"Can I help with something?" asks Lucie.

"Only if you take your coat off," replies Lilianne.

Lucie is ready to turn around but Bernadette throws her a tea towel. "I need help here, get going. So, are you driving to Dégelis to see the children?" Bernadette asks Colette.

Colette faces the window above the sink, looking down to the soapy water. She pushes her shoulders back. "I think I'll rent a car and go for a couple of days, after New Year's Eve."

Lilianne gives her sister a quick hug. "Oh, les enfants. When they're all over you you'd kill to get away, and when they're gone . . ."

Colette reaches for a glass of ginger ale on the window ledge and clutches it so hard Lilianne is afraid it might break. But it's a china cup that falls as Colette's hand slips on the wet kitchen counter.

"I'm so sorry."

Lucie crouches to pick up the pieces. The lonely crimson rose is almost intact on one piece, its perky leaf like a waving hand, on another.

"Leave it, Lucie. You'll cut yourself," says Bernadette. "Let me get the broom."

"I'm such a klutz. I break everything I touch," says Collette.

Colette lives alone in a one-bedroom basement apartment in Sainte-Foy while Zacharie still lives in the big house by the river, right at the entrance of Dégelis, with the four children and the maids. Things had gone from bad to worse between them, with Colette ending up in the river one too many times, even though everyone knew it was not deep enough to drown in. Zach had sent her packing with a wad of cash, making her sign something she had been too drugged or drunk to read. She went on a trip as far away as she could go, Argentina, and came back with nothing. No snapshots, no money. Not even a suitcase. It didn't stop her from keeping on trying to drown in something even smaller, like a glass of vodka.

"Divorce is much more complicated when children are involved, isn't it?" Bernadette says. "My boyfriend wants sole custody of his son because his wife is completely crazy."

Léo's wife, Berthe, comes in, empty beer bottles at the end of each of her fingers. "What's the matter with you, Bernadette? You should listen to the warning signal when a man says his wife is crazy. Good chance he drove her to it and you're next in line. It takes two to tango, in case you haven't noticed. Anything else I can do for you here? I don't think so."

Bernadette's face slackens. "Maudite marde!" she says. "Why is it always so hard for me? And not only with men, at work too. You should see them coming in with their MBAs, fresh out of university, ready to manage the whole multi-million-dollar budget. They're not even twenty-five, it's their first real job, and they think they'll just sit in the big chair and ask the old bird to bring them coffee. They don't even know how to conjugate their past participles and the only tense they use is the imperative. What happened to the conditional, or the plus-que-parfait? Well, I've had enough of this. There's a new program open to everybody with more than ten years of experience in the company, and with this program, you get to be a boss too, degree or not. This is my chance and I'm taking it! The only problem is, the job is to be in charge of supplies for Northern Quebec, so you're the one in charge of nowhere. I'm telling you, Lucie, stick with school and go to university."

"Time to pack the bedpan!" calls Lucien, walking into the kitchen. "The ambulance is here!"

Nuit d'Amour

"Lili, what are you doing here? Your mother is about to leave." Lilianne has gone to hide in Henri's office, her forehead against the gun rack vitrine. "We're going home too," Paul goes on. "I've picked up most of the gifts but I can't find Pierrot."

"Five years it's been going on, Paul," Lili cries out. "How much longer will we have to go through this? My mother doesn't deserve to be this unhappy. It's so unfair. Every week, twice a week, I've been going to visit her and she has cried and she has begged me to take her home with me, every time. Five years." Lili lets her head roll on her husband's shoulder and sobs while Paul rocks her gently. "And what is it with the kids, can you tell me? The older they are, the worse it gets." Maurice and Bébé are still children, not yet tormented by hormonal changes, but since they've bought Pierrot a drum kit to keep him home, Lili and Paul can't even hear themselves over coffee after dinner. The phone rings off the hook for the girls while Pierrot's angry drumming rocks the kitchen floor. They've sent him to private school to keep him away from drugs, but Lili still find bags filled with powder and grass every time she searches the basement. They've talked to him about the danger of drugs, the school counsellor has done the same, and the police officers have warned him, but Pierrot still heads right out of the house after he's done with the drums. Meanwhile Anne refuses to come out of the bathroom where she locks herself for hour-long baths and scrubs her face raw every night to get rid of her bad skin, hoping to wake up a woman every morning. She has turned sixteen and still doesn't have her period. "I jump every time the phone rings thinking it's going to be the police station telling me to come and get Pierrot. Every morning I have to deal with Anne's disappointment, and every night it's Lucie who cries but won't tell me why."

You can tell me, Lili tries to coax her daughter. Tell you what? Lucie says. Why you are crying. I'm not crying. What more can Lili do? And every morning it starts again. Lucie wakes up complaining of head-aches and has such a hard time putting her contact lenses in she almost misses the school bus; Anne emerges from the bathroom with a long face, the new day having quashed her hopes once more; and Pierrot doesn't wake at all because he came home past midnight, three hours later than he was told.

"I know, Lili, I know."

Lili jerks away from Paul. "No, you don't! You don't know what it's like to see your own mother go, a little at a time, turning into someone you recognize less and less. And you don't know what it's like when your own children walk away from you and shut you out." Lili drives every point home with a sharp finger, stabbing her husband's chest. "You don't know and you don't care! You sleep at night while I worry and worry and worry until it's light outside again." Paul looks into his wife's face but doesn't recognize this puddle where anger is just a top layer hiding a deep sadness.

"But what is it that worries you so much, Lili?"

"I worry I've not been a good mother!" Lili cries out.

"How can you say that?" Paul holds her tighter and kisses her dark hair, turning his head to see who's at the half-open door. It's Lucie, standing still with the ten-cent crown in one hand and the wand with the dull star in the other. "I'm so tired, Paul, I don't even know what I'm saying anymore." Lili buries her head in the nook of Paul's shoulder.

"I found Pierrot," Lucie says. "He's passed out in the bedroom where the coats are."

Lilianne tenses in her husband's arms when she hears Lucie. "Come here, Lucie. Come," she calls, forcing her voice to sound calm.

But Lucie doesn't move. Before she leaves she says, "You shouldn't worry so much, Maman. We're going to be all right."

A lugubrious sound fills the deserted living room, mixing with the Christmas tenor's closing number. *O nuit d'amour, O nuit de paix . . .* Henri is in the La-Z-Boy and Léo is lying flat on his back in the middle of the carpet, even though there is a chilly draft coming from the open front door. "The thing you have to remember when you call a moose, Henri, is that you're not a man, you're a moose. You're a moose and you're in love, you understand, a horny moose." Henri nods and Léo hurls a mournful call one more time.

The ambulance is backed up by the front steps, which are crunchy with salt to melt the ice. Marie-Reine's stretcher is coming out the front door, Lilianne and Bernadette fussing by their mother's side. Bernadette tucks in the wool blankets while Lilianne wipes the tears, soothing her mother in hushed tones. "Voyons, Maman, voyons. Didn't you have a nice evening? Don't cry, now, now, we're all going to see you tomorrow but you know we can't keep you here."

"Bonne nuit-là, Maman, à demain!" calls Colette.

Lucien and Paul help the ambulance driver and the nurse lift the stretcher down the stairs to the driveway. They don't notice Marie-Reine's dizzy spell, her hand gripping the rail of the bed. The ground is giving under her and there is no more stucco ceiling, or acoustic tiles, no more light fixtures, just wide open space in front of her. The celestial vault unrolls above Marie-Reine's head, stretching as far as she can see. It is a cold and deep winter sky frosted with layer upon layer of stars arcing above. The delicate tinkle of ice-coated branches surrounds the driveway, like the sweet chimes of silver bells, filling her with wonder. "Is this the polar star, right there? Where is the north?" The end of the world, ma reine. Where the trees are no bigger than matchsticks, bears are white and birds wear feather shoes, and people live in houses of ice.

"Over there, Grand-Maman." Lucie points to the mountains and the road to Chicoutimi.

It might snow again soon, making everything white and new. "Tu changerais-tu les draps, Marie-Joseph?" Marie-Reine asks. She wants to slip into clean sheets with Léandre tonight, crisp sheets like sails full of clouds and spindrift. She wants to feel Léandre's prickly moustache against her lips again, his fingers in her hair like a river of fire on the pillow, his taut stomach against the soft skin of her belly, filled out by yet another pregnancy. How many already? It doesn't matter anymore. She is ready. Marie-Reine is ready to leave all her children behind and climb to the top of the Banque de Montréal to wave her arms like moonbeams, Come and get me! Throwing all caution to the wind again.

The red flashing light stains Colette's white lace collar. Bernadette's electric blue jumpsuit is plastered to her skin with static, and Lilianne's dress is so tight it takes an effort for her to raise her arm as they all wave bye-bye from the doorway before hurrying back in.

"We'll see you tomorrow, joyeux Noël!"

Lucie watches the ambulance leave the driveway and make a right turn. She follows the lazy red spin of the light as long as she can as the ambulance heads north towards the highway.

"Bonne nuit, Grand-Maman."

It's warmer now than it was around midnight. The deserted streets are not hard and grey with dry calcium anymore but very black, with a soft gleam. Lucie buries her face in her shoulder, her nose rubbing against the old pelt. The wind has turned. It comes from the St. Lawrence, carrying along a hint of moisture and the smell of thaw, and wet fur.

PART FOUR

Fin du descouvrement: Et despuis sçavoyr le quinziesme jour d'aoust partisme assemblement dudit hable de Blanc-Sablon et avecques bon temps vynmes jusques à la my mer d'entre Terre Neufve et Bretaigne auquel lieu eusmes troys jours continuez de grande tormente de ventz d'avaulx laquelle avec l'ayde de Dieu nous souffrimes et endurasmes. Et depuis eusmes temps à gré tellement que arrivasmes au hable de Saint Malo dont estyons partiz le Ve jour de septembre audit an.
Première Relation de Jacques Cartier, 1534
[on returning home after a voyage of discovery]

And this is so much as we have discovered. After that, we altogether departed and with a happy and prosperous weather, we came into the middle of the sea, in which place we were tossed and turmoiled three days long with great storms and windy tempests coming from the east, and upon the 5th of September, in the said year, we came to the port of S. Malo whence we departed.
translated by Richard Hakluyt, in *Principall Navigations*

Quatrième Relation:
Home

No welcoming branches like open arms. No leaves dancing, a soft rush of green silk in the wind. The family tree is not a maple, speckled with red stars, it is an evergreen, piercing the sky with its wiry spire. A forest of spruce is thick and dark and keeps its secrets. It is impenetrable.

Home. A piece of white bone in my hand.

Tomorrow morning my mother will go through the red door for the last time. She has been admitted to hospital under her maiden name, Madame Lilianne Beauregard. That's how it is in Québec now: there is only one legal name, the one given at birth, and no more mademoiselle, the old signifier for unmarried. The only correct way to address a woman is Madame. It will be difficult for people who have known my mother as Madame Paul Des Ruisseaux, but the staff at the Maison Sarrazin's switchboard will be gracious and help make the connection. On average their patients stay from three days to one month, rarely more. But these patients don't go back home. They all depart this world. This is a palliative care hospital for people in the terminal phase of cancer.

"The first thing to go in a patient entering this phase is the emotions. That's why you might find your mother remote, or uncommunicative. It's a normal reaction, a natural process. The mind starts to shut off as the body stops functioning." The palliative care specialist also tries to prepare us by explaining which functions will stop first, and which last. "Your mother has already lost the use of her right arm and her leg. As the tumour grows, the part of her brain sending signals to the vital organs will become impaired until there are no more signals. She will sleep more and more, eat and drink less and less. The actual cause of death will be either dehydration or pulmonary failure—her lungs will cease to function and she will stop breathing. There shouldn't be very much pain, only periodic headaches called encephalids, which are particular to her condition. Our job is to make sure she is as comfortable as possible throughout her stay with us, but we won't make medical interventions to extend her life. As you know, we will not feed her intravenously if she can't eat, and we won't hydrate her if she can't drink." The doctor's words are clinical, but she softens the blow with kind eyes. She takes our hands between hers in turn, and says, "We are here for her, but also for you. You can visit her any time you want, you can bring her food, you can sleep in her room if you wish, and if you have any special requests to make or any concerns, please, just come to see me."

My mother's eyes are a deeper blue now, or maybe it's just her pupils getting larger and larger. Her hair is short and barely covers the horseshoe-shaped scar on the right side of her head. Neither smiling nor crying come easily, with half her mouth paralyzed. She is propped up in her own bed on a bunch of pillows, a book abandoned by her side. She waits, immobile, at the end of her life. She tells me, out of the blue, as I paint her nails a perky shade of pink, "My mother grew up without a father. I lost mine when I was nine. You don't know what it's like, Lucie. Don't do this to your daughters."

"And what if I do?" I ask her, defiant. "I know what it is to grow up with a good mother." I uncurl her right hand to start a second coat of varnish.

"That's not enough. There will always be something missing."

They might as well learn early, I want to say. But I hold back. She looks like a child in her yellow pyjamas covered with tiny teddies, like the little girl on the roof in Chicoutimi, wishing for the impossible. For love to last forever. And she has kept on wishing all her life, with one foot in the kitchen and one in the outside world, rushing in and rushing out. My mother the whirling dervish, a cosmic streak across the bright sky of my childhood. So busy, until the end of the day.

"Do you remember what you did when the laundry was folded and ironed, the kitchen cleared, the homework done?"

"How did I ever do all this, day in, day out, year after year?" she says, looking down at her hands as if they belonged to someone else.

"Do you remember when you sat in the good chair in the living room and—"

"I read," she says with a sigh of relief coming straight from the past.

"Yes. You read." I can see the book, balanced on her curled legs, her finger, anxious to flip the page, her eyes held captive by the printed word. Pigment, iron, and wood pulp. That's what books are made of, inert matter. "You looked so peaceful, so content. You don't know how much I wished . . ." I have to stop. I ache all over with this intense longing I never knew I had. "I just wished I was that book in your hand, and that you would have time to look at me, and hold me—that I could have been a source of such happiness to you. You worried so much about us."

She stares back at me, startled. She lifts her good arm, which is not so good anymore, her nails slick with wet polish, beckoning me. I sit closer, on the edge of the bed, and put my cheek against her cheek. I close my eyes to hear past the television laughing in the living room, the loud knocks at the red door, a delivery man, my father's voice, "Encore des fleurs!" Flowers, food, cards, phone calls; the intrusion of the well-wishers never stops. My breathing soon slows and my heart beats louder, like a gong, but I hang on to her, I want to hear the broken beat better, the long string of dropped stitches—a fish hole in the ice, a red sled that never came back, a faraway plane over a round lake.

"Don't, Lucie. It's such a waste, wishing your love away. All you had to do was to come to me." After a while, when I try to break our embrace, she says, "Stay. Stay for a minute." And I stay. I stay until her cropped head rolls off my shoulder to sleep. Long after.

I'm still there.

Acknowledgments

I want to mention several of the many books that informed this novel: *Jacques Cartier: Relations*, édition critique par Michel Bideaux; *Champlain*, by Joe C.W. Armstrong; *Histoire Populaire du Québec*, by Jacques Lacoursière; "A Fille du Roi's Passage," by Adrienne Leduc in *The Beaver*, Feb–Mar 2001; *Women on the Margins*, by Natalie Zemon Davis; *Écrits Spirituels et Historiques*, by Marie de l'Incarnation; *La Production des Catéchismes en Amérique Française*, by Raymond Brodeur and Jacques Rouleau; *The Jesuit Relations*, edited by Allan Greer.

Special thanks to Martin Rochefort for historical context, to Thérèse Labelle for hunting tips, and to all my aunts, who never failed to deliver the best details.

My thanks to the Canada Council for financial support.

I am grateful to Phyllis Bruce, editor always extraordinaire, for the million yellow sticky notes bringing enlightenment to a work long in progress. I also thank my tireless agent, Denise Bukowski, navigator nonpareil when it comes to sailing the course of the publishing industry.

My thanks to all who read and commented upon this manuscript: Janice Rappoport, Aritha van Herk, Bonnie Burnard, all creative writing teachers. For early and much needed support, my thanks to Terry Riegelhof and Nikki Barrett, and also to Gaye, Anita, Trish, Simon, Ulrika, Jacqueline, René and Renée, Joanne . . . et j'en passe.

A very special thank you to the most supportive friend and reader, my fellow writer Karen McLaughlin.

Finally, I want to say that without the unconditional support of my loved ones—Marguerite, Andréas, and above all, Kevin—this story would not be.